Table of Co

Lady Warrior, Mage of Man (Lady Wa....

Author's Note ....)

In the Temple of the Seers... 9

The Bravest of All 11

Sylus.. 19

Marco of Trinik.. 41

The Master of Earth... 59

Myrth's Honor Guard 63

A True Purpose 75

Arrivals and Departures 93

Into the Mage Realm 119

Training with the Potentate... 127

From the Void... 145

The Hunt Begins... 149

The Winds of the Broodlands.. 161

Olimidia 181

The Feather on the Hill 191

Sawelt 207

Running from the Daemon 213

The Road to Sea Spray 227

Kryoso's Affinity 237

The Water Master 241

The North Road.. 259

Apprentice to Earth 269

Fallen into Shadow... 293

Daemon Hunters 315

Lady Warrior, Mage of Man 331

Returning Home... 339

About Sherrie A Bakelar 343

Connect with Sherrie A Bakelar.................................... 345

Other Titles by Sherrie A Bakelar.................................. 347

The Land-Nymph Child, the Lady Warrior Saga, Book 2................ 349

LADY WARRIOR, MAGE OF MAN

Discover other Titles by this Author
Lady Warrior Saga
Lady Warrior, Mage of Man
The Land-Nymph Child
Honor Bound

Great Danes Don't Hunt Werewolves
In My Time of Dying

For Kevin

Author's Note

In this hectic world with all its demands, I do really appreciate the time you've given to me. I began writing this novel when I was twelve years old. Life has a habit of getting in the way and as I grew and learned and experienced life, this novel changed. What began as a daydream based on a My Little Pony cartoon has become so much more. Early iterations gave way to a more critical eye as the years passed. Stories changed, characters morphed, and in 2015 it finally coalesced into the tale of a young lady who was fairly certain she was the greatest to ever live. The story, told from D'Mique's point of view with an omniscient eye that also jumps to other characters, is stilted on purpose. D'Mique believes herself to be the Bravest of All and a gift to others. Don't we all think of ourselves this way when we are young and full of spirit and life? As she journeys through life, she quickly realizes that she may not be the perfect warrior she thought she was. She can barely sit a horse and is routinely harassed by her fellow soldiers. Despite this, she perseveres through to the end. If I were to rewrite this novel, that stilting might be more deftly handled. However, I am not about to rewrite this book again. I wrote it when I was twelve, rewrote it when I was fourteen, again when I was eighteen, and again in my thirties when I finally decided that it wasn't going to get better and I couldn't be a storyteller if I spent the entirety of my life writing a single novel over and over again without publishing it and sharing it with others. There were worse writers out there...some of them published even. So, D'Mique was pushed from the nest and out into the wilds of the indie publishing world.

That was nearly ten years ago. Since then, I've awakened two hours earlier than necessary, nearly every day of the year, to hone my craft as a storyteller and grow as a writer. As the years have passed, I have grown. Through that time, D'Mique's story has become more complex, with the possibility of her actions leading to world-sweeping changes for her and her fellows. This introductory book must stand on its own for what it is. Flaws and all. I ask only that you. dear Reader, see it for what it is, a whirlwind tour of a world full of characters that grew as I did, and continue to grow to this day.

D'Mique's story continues beyond this novel in a planned quintology, and I hope you will join her on this journey.

Sherrie Anne Bakelar

May 2023

From Mistress Jay's Collection

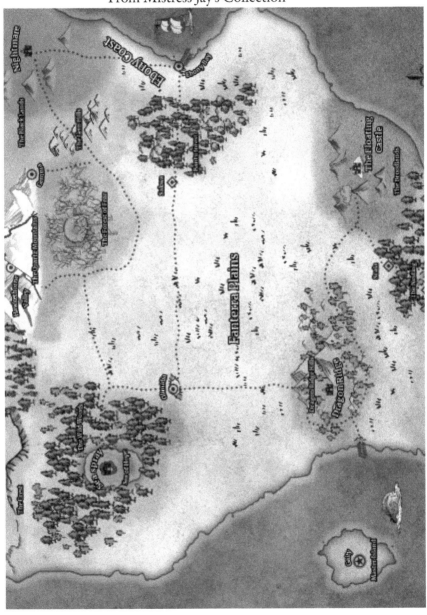

In the Temple of the Seers

Crossing the Sea of Dreams, his supple leather palace boots making soft shushing sounds as he walked, the hooded cloaked figure was nearly invisible against the black marble walls and floor. At the far end of the room with the grandiose name, a soft blue light emanated from a large circular pool in the floor, illuminating a half-dozen forms seated at its edge, their faces hidden beneath their own black hoods. The cloaked figure stopped at the edge of the glassy surface, opposite the six seated figures. As he waited, the blue light faded on the tableau, drowning them all in a tense darkness. If the cloaked figure had been versed in Time magic, as the six figures seated across from him were, rainbow-hued tendrils of light would have danced through the room, spiraling in and out of the glassy circle. Instead, to him, the room remained dark until the glass circle dissolved, its surface replaced by a lazy whirlpool of deep purple mist that burrowed into the marble floor of the Sea of Dreams. When nothing further developed, the cloaked figure cleared his throat and addressed the others, "You summoned me, and I am here," he said, his bass voice thrumming across the misty pool and echoing off the marble around them.

"We have prepared a vision for you, Master," one of the six seers intoned, her voice dry and papery, soft with age. The whirlpool grew lighter, and as the mist cleared, images playing across the glassy surface. Pictures of people emerged, some familiar to the cloaked figure others not. Their lips moved while their faces contorted with various emotions—a silent vision holding anger, sorrow, and fear.

"A Greater Daemon approaches, Master. Gather your forces," a second seer commanded. The Master glanced across the pool at the motionless figures.

"Listen well," a third voice, as deep as his and all too familiar added. The seers chanted in unison as the light faded,

Lady Warrior, Mage of Man
Earth Sons from the mountains high
And Children of the Moon Clan.
One for Shadow, Two for Light,
Five for when the lifeblood flows.
Three to taunt him,
Two to look him in the eye,
And one for the killing blow.

The Bravest of All

Sunlight gleamed off the blade as D'Mique twirled the long sword in front of her. The daemons charged across the field, a seething mass of black bodies and blade-like legs surrounding her, leaving her alone on the hilltop with no escape. Little did the daemons know that they faced the greatest swordswoman in the village! She cut into the first too-human torso, the creature's coarse black hair proving to be little protection against her flashing blade. Daemon after daemon pounced on her. Bravely, she fought her way through the horde. Blades, claws, and fangs tried for her but, miraculously, she remained unscathed through the battle. "Admit it!" she shouted as a remnant of the enemies regrouped, facing her with determined scowls firmly planted upon their goat-like features, "You are no match for my amazing skill and unwavering strength!" Screaming, she charged the daemons, slicing through them with ease. Triple suns setting behind her, the last daemon fell at her feet, its severed goat head rolling away down the hill. D'Mique stood alone on the field of battle, the daemon corpses, their blood feeding the earth lay all around her. Wind tossed her loose hair, blowing it out of her face as she turned to survey the destruction. From behind her the village cheered her name, "D'Mique! D'Mique! D'Mique!" She turned toward the grateful villagers, raising her sword in a salute to victory, acknowledging their gratitude—

A deep gong sounded signaling the end of the day's lessons. D'Mique blinked, chasing away the daydream. She stared down at the open textbook before her as her classmates shuffled papers and stuffed books back into bags before filing out of the room, the school day finally over. She closed her book, tossed her deep black braid back over her shoulder and stood, packing away the book and her notes. Sighing, she made her way out of class. *"Twenty-four days,"* she reminded herself, *"Just twenty-four days."* These last three cycles of primary school were torturous. *"How can I sit through any more classes!*" she fumed silently. Around her, children of all ages bustled past. Some, those in her same age cadre, shuffled as she did. No doubt they were counting the days as anxiously as she, though for different reasons. True, as a Child of Man, she was not expected to continue her education beyond the primary level. Of all her cadre, only one had applied to a secondary academy. Only one planned to leave the village. And for that audacity only D'Mique was gawked at, whispered about behind her back—not quite low enough for her to not know they ridiculed her. The rest of the young adults her age looked forward to signing land deeds, taking over farming and business duties from parents and even marrying! It was the simple life: A spouse, some children, and a village plot to farm. D'Mique sighed again. "*Well once Mid-Summer is over, I will be well beyond the simple life,*" she thought. By High Summer D'Mique would be in the Shining City of Olimidia, petitioning for entrance into the Academy, the first step to realizing her dream.

As she shuffled along, her friend Salva melted from the crowd, "D'Mique," she greeted, "Where are you going?"

D'Mique shrugged in response, glancing down at her friend and silently noting the marriage knot Salva wore at the nape of her neck, her hair pulled up in a bun to show off the delicately twisted leather. "I don't know," D'Mique said, "The post box and then home. I have to check again for my last form."

Salva stopped, surprised for a split-second before continuing beside her. "That's it?" she asked, "No practicing? No shopping?" D'Mique shrugged and continued walking. Despite the marriage knot, Salva enjoyed tagging along on D'Mique's practice runs, pretending she could see the animal trails D'Mique followed through the underbrush and gamely holding the shield for her while D'Mique practiced her sword techniques.

"All I need is my last paper," D'Mique explained. She could feel Salva's cool gray eyes watching her.

"There's something you're not telling me, D'Mique," her friend accused.

D'Mique stopped, shocked, "I would never!"

"You're leaving the minute you get your papers, aren't you?" Salva said, suddenly angry.

"*She can't really think that!*" D'Mique thought, studying her friend's face. "No, Salva," she answered, "No. I will stay these last three cycles, I promise. Besides, I have to finish my schooling. The Academy insists that petitioners complete at least their primary education." Salva held her tongue though her eyes did not soften. D'Mique tried on a small smile, willing her friend to believe her. "I already have two strikes against me Salva, human and female. I can't add a third by not being educated."

After a moment they walked on in silence, leaving the village schoolhouse and starting along the cobblestone road. Neat single-story farmhouses lined the road, a small garden plot surrounding each one. For most of the residents their farm-plot was everything they owned and it was enough. As the friends neared the center of the village, the farms gave way to storefronts. When they reached the well at the center of town they stopped again. D'Mique surveyed the village square. Children played in the shade of the trees while farm wives ran errands. "*It's all so...peaceful, so simple,*" she thought. She looked toward her own home, which lay north of the town center, just inside the fortified wall that kept the village safe from the outside world. Salva, the local banker's daughter, lived in a distinguished two-story home one street from her father's bank.

"I WILL stay these last three cycles Salva," she reiterated, returning her attention to her friend.

Salva looked away blinking too fast. "Oh, D'Mique," she sighed. "I know you will, but this village doesn't have anything for you. Once you leave you won't be back." Their eyes met and D'Mique fought not to flinch away from Salva's sadness. "I'll miss you," she said, fighting to hold her voice steady.

D'Mique smiled sadly and hugged her suddenly. "Oh Salva," she said against her friend's ear. "*Is she right?*" D'Mique thought, "*I was planning on coming back. But will I? My mother returned after studying with the elves. But a surgeon is always a welcome addition. Will I be as welcome? Is there room for a Battle Lord or a War Hero here?*" Breaking the hug, she took her friend's hand in her own. "I will not leave without saying goodbye, Salva. I promise," she said.

Salva nodded noncommittally, turning away and retrieving her hand. "I know," she said with a sigh. "You know, you've been talking about leaving for the military for so long. Now that the time has come it doesn't seem real." D'Mique couldn't find a reply. Her silence caused Salva to frown and sigh. "I'll see you tomorrow," she said before starting toward her home. D'Mique sighed as well, watching her friend wend her way home before starting north.

She made her way to the post office. Dusty cobblestones baked in the summer heat, the twin red suns shining down mercilessly. Although the shops were open, there were no patrons. Few people walked the streets in the afternoon heat, having finished their business in the cool of the morning. The small post office squatted just inside the north gate while the gate itself sat open to the wilderness beyond. D'Mique slowed as she neared them. Beyond the gate the fields of wild flowers and short grass ringed the town, calling to her. She gazed longingly at the outside world for a few minutes. Those flowered fields formed a defensive perimeter around the village. Anything trying to fight its way into the town would have to cross a hundred yards of open space. And things did want to fight their way in. Monstrous things lived in the pine forest that loomed nearby, its deep green contrasting with the yellowing grasses.

The villagers called it the Dark Forest, and it was a known daemon stronghold. Why her ancestors had chosen to live here, in the heart of daemon territory, she did not know. The daemon's hatred wafted from the forest, carried by the breeze. It was as if the forest rather than its denizens hated the Children of Man. Only the bravest villagers ventured off the small dirt track that wound through the trees. Those who did not leave the trail simply hurried from one walled village or fort to the next until they reached either the Fanterra Plain to the north or the Great Desert in the south. A half-hearted breeze blew into town, not quite ruffling the pennants high up on the wall or the knee-length skirt of D'Mique's school uniform. Dragging her eyes away from the forest and the fields, she shuffled into the post office.

Small openings lined the walls of the quiet wooden building, the village's families' names printed in large neat letters below each one. Just as yesterday, the warm filtered sunlight fell across empty boxes. Disappointment filling her, she went back out and walked up to a gate guard, Ol' Thom she realized, closing the distance. "Isn't the mail late?" she asked. Thom nodded lazily, not looking at her. He scratched at the graying stubble that coated his chin, blue eyes dancing across the defensive fields. "It should have been here yesterday," she continued. "Is anyone going out to look for it?"

Ol' Thom eyed her suspiciously before answering, "Now, don't be getting any ideas, girl. Your mother wouldn't allow it," he said, assuming the direction their conversation was about to take.

"How do you know what my mother wouldn't allow?" D'Mique snapped before repeating, "Is anyone going to go look for it?" She cut off his reply adding, "What if the daemons got it?"

Ol' Thom paled at her words. "You should be home," he retorted, a hint of color blossoming in his cheeks. "Let the guards worry about it. Why anyone taught you to use a sword, I'll never know."

D'Mique glared, remembering how she'd pestered the guards into teaching her basic swordsmanship. Teaching a ten year old girl how to use a sword had been a game to the guards, something to do in order to fight off boredom. But she had continued her training well beyond the 'cuteness' stage and into the 'deadly' one. "*Here it comes,*" she thought, "*The Speech. The one about being only human and a girl and about staying in town and on her farm, going to dances, knitting clothes, cooking!*" She walked away.

"You should worry about finding a husband not fighting daemons!" Ol' Thom called after her. D'Mique did not turn around. She wished, not for the first time, that humans were daemon-spawn, that a Greater Daemon could be found in her ancestry. If there had been one, then her eyes would have blazed with red fire, proof of her anger and proof of her determination. "*I will leave this town!*" she screamed in her head, "*My mother has signed all the forms! She knows all about following your dreams! Only one form is missing! One form keeping me from my dreams! And it's late!*" As she fumed her steps grew faster, almost carrying her past her farm.

Her mother was out front hoeing a patch of peas. She looked up as D'Mique entered the yard slamming the gate closed behind her. Twin green eyes met, one pair ablaze, the other brimming with soft laughter. Anika sighed, "What's wrong, D'Mique?"

"The mail shipment is late and the guards are afraid to go look for it!" At her words, a soft smile smoothed her mother's wrinkled face.

"Oh, D'Mique, you're the only one brave enough to test the Dark Forest. You know that," her mother said, sarcasm lacing her words. "Fool guards anyway. I would tell you to ignore them but—" she trailed off and shrugged.

"That old geezer told me to find a husband!" D'Mique continued, waving back toward the gate. Anika laughed at her daughter's words. She shook her head when D'Mique's glare turned murderous.

"I hear that a lot too, D'Mique," she said. "I think that's why I chose not to remarry after your father died. But at least I was married once; at least I came back after studying with the elves. I had a child and I have a farm." She smiled, "They just don't know what to make of you. Your dream is bigger, even bigger than mine. Sometimes I don't know what to make of it either," she finished her smile turning sad.

"But the men being paid to protect us are afraid of their own shadows. What if a horde attacked? We'd all be slaughtered!"

Smiling, Anika returned to her peas, "Well, we'd have you to protect us, right?" she asked.

"Mom," D'Mique said with a hint of irritation.

Anika divided her attention between the peas and her daughter. "I know you think that you're the bravest of us all, but I think the guards can hold their own against daemons." Eyes twinkling, hoe working, she continued, "Don't forget who taught you. Just because they can't understand you doesn't mean they have nothing to offer."

"They taught me the basics as a joke," D'Mique scoffed, "The rest I taught myself."

"Yes, I know," Anika said.

"I'm going to find that mail shipment," D'Mique announced.

Anika stopped suddenly and looked up at her. "What, now?" A glimmer of fear entered her eyes. "It's nearly dark. You'll never make the fort!"

"No not now, first thing tomorrow," D'Mique said crossing her arms over her chest in defiance.

"And what about school?"

"School? This is more important than school! What if the daemons did attack? What if there are survivors? I could be their only hope!"

Anika laughed, shaking her head, "Okay, okay," she motioned for her daughter to settle down. "You're right. There could have been an attack and there might be a survivor or two waiting for a hero. The daemons have been growing bolder lately." She looked off towards the Dark Forest as if she could see it through the wall beyond their plot. D'Mique followed her gaze. If the daemons attacked the village, overpowering the guards and destroying them all, how long would it be before anyone found them? Would anyone beyond the forest care? "When you get to Olimidia, D'Mique, tell them about the daemons here. Tell everyone who will listen. They need to know. The goblins and elves seem to have forgotten their promise to protect us. Remind them of that," Anika said, interrupting D'Mique's thoughts.

"I will mom." D'Mique promised before adding, "I'll be able to catch up at school. I know I will. I'll only be gone a day."

"You'd better," Anika said with a hint of warning in her voice. "Now, before you rush off to save us all, go make dinner."

"Ha, ha," D'Mique said without humor as she headed for the house.

Sylus

D'Mique woke before the suns. Ignoring her school uniform, she dressed in combat armor instead, pulling on thick dark brown leather leggings, stout black boots made for traveling, a light gray cotton shirt with long sleeves, and a jerkin, lined with metal rings, green in color to match her eyes. She pulled a small sword from her wardrobe and strapped its worn scabbard around her waist. After pulling her hair back into a tight bun, she was ready to face the wilderness. But her first stop was her mother's room where she shook Anika awake, "Mom, I'm leaving," she said.

Anika's eyes flicked open and she smiled. "Be careful, D'Mique," she whispered, "Come back to me."

"I will, mom. I will," D'Mique promised as she laid a kiss on her mother's cheek. Then wrapping her determination around her, she left.

Despite the early hour, many villagers were already up and starting the day's work, hoping to finish before the summer heat grew too great. Col, the first red sun, was just beginning to peek over the horizon and its fiery twin, Nix, would follow shortly. Later this morning the system's third star, Rysk, also known as the Ghost Moon, would rise. Those villagers D'Mique passed in the streets slowed enough to look her way in disapproval. She ignored them as she always did. The guards had opened the gate at dawn. Although they barely glanced at her as she left, she could feel the same disapproval emanating from them that had followed her from home.

Beyond the gate, she pulled her short sword and took a quick swipe at the long grass beside the road. Her determination wavered despite this half-hearted attempt to rid herself of the town's rejection as she contemplated the mission she'd set herself. Beyond the walled village, the world seemed quiet, even lonely. Away from the bustle of the early morning, birdsong and insect hum replaced the clang of tools and creaking of machinery. As an optimistic breeze rustled through the tall grass and whispered in the distant pines, D'Mique heaved a deep sigh, trying again to push the villagers' disapproval away as she continued her trek down the small dirt road toward the trees.

She did not look back as she neared the huge pines. Instead, she stopped to stare at them, picking out the dappled sunshine at their edges and the deep shadows beyond. The trees demanded silence, reverence from those who traveled alone through them. The villagers were familiar with the vague sense of foreboding that drifted across the field and the stories that explained it. D'Mique grew up hearing stories of the fantastical monsters living just beyond the deepest shadows, legends and stories even worse than the daemons that actually lived there. But with the passing of childhood the myths lost their hold on her and she had been to the Dark Forest often enough to know that she was relatively safe during the day. It was only at night that the daemon's, like all daemon-spawn, came out. She paused at the tree line standing in the soft sunlight of the meadow, listening to the shushing sound of the wind in the trees and contemplating the distinct shadows underneath them. Beneath the boughs it was still nearly dark this early in the morning. But the forest's coolness reached for her as she stood there and she moved forward into the shadows' embrace.

Because the towering trees sheltered it from much of the weather, the road D'Mique walked through the forest was in good repair. Unseen birds chirped in the branches above her as buzzing insects and the rustle of small animals in the undergrowth accompanied her steps. Each stride took her further from the villagers' scorn, rebuilding her confidence and determination. The forest had always accepted her she felt. Every time she entered it, she felt as if she ought to just continue walking and this morning was no exception. "A day's walk between the fort and the next town and after that I will be out on the Fanterra Plain," she said aloud, her mind wandering. "Out of the village forever and never to return," she smiled until she remembered Salva and her promise. "*Perhaps not this time,*" she reminded herself silently, "*I promised to say goodbye. But soon. Soon I will just keep walking until I reach the Fanterra Plain.*"

She met no one else on the road as she walked, time passing slowly and uneventfully, the only change of pace occurring when the first pangs of hunger hit, and she strayed from the track just far enough to find a berry bush where she stopped to eat. Taking a swig from her canteen she peered up through the trees, trying to judge the positions of the suns. While dressing this morning, she had been certain that she would find the mail wagons just within the forest, creaking along, the drivers apologizing for their lateness and explaining how they had been victims of a broken wheel or a dead horse or one of a thousand other things. However, morning had turned to midday and there had been no sign of the wagons. Her confidence waned. She would have to spend the night in the fort she decided, hiding from the creatures that roamed the darkness craving human flesh. Returning to the road, she sighed, "Maybe the wagons are at the fort. For some reason they needed to stay there an extra day or two."

As she walked, the trees thinned, allowing a better look at the sky. Rysk's hazy blue disk had joined the Fiery Sisters, Nix and Col. D'Mique stopped, pondering their relative positions for a moment. The twin red stars were slipping toward the horizon and would be setting in about four hours, leaving just the Ghost Moon to light the night sky for a couple paltry hours before he set as well. Scowling she quickened her pace, racing the suns—she had to reach the fort before nightfall. The remaining hours of the day passed quickly, and near sunset the trail rose slightly as it climbed a small hill. Despite the imminent darkness, quiet ruled the fort that lay beyond the hill. "*It's likely that the only guests are the missing postal workers and this close to night they will all be huddled inside,*" she thought as she clambered to the top, a smug smile crossing her lips. She had reached the fort, one of many that lined the trade roads within The Dark Forest, with time to spare!

But as she looked down on the small indefensible clearing, her smile faltered, her mind grew blank. Her vision grew fuzzy around the edges and ice water poured through her. Then her eyes fell on the blackened smoldering timber that lay scattered around the clearing. The fort was gone! A massacre greeted her. A stray breeze danced against her skin, carrying the sickly sweet smell of rotten meat, meat that had once been horse and human, up the hill. Her hands tingled, adrenaline flooding her system. D'Mique turned from the sight collapsing to her knees, the tangible scent of death coating her tongue. Gagging, she closed her eyes, sweat breaking out across her brow and upper lip. She stayed there, on her knees, hunched over with her eyes closed, taking shallow breaths and waiting for her stomach to settle as the minutes dragged by. With her eyes shut, the glimpse she'd had of the ruined clearing became more defined. "No, no, no," she repeated as her mind's eye watched sharp jagged shadows and darkening pools of flesh and blood solidify, moving from unbelievable to real. The buzz of flies and the rustle of wings as scavenger birds took flight confirmed her worst fears. The fort had been attacked! *Everyone's dead,"* she thought.

She weathered the initial reaction but remained immobile, mind reeling as she tried desperately to think. Coherent thoughts refused to form. The voice in her head simply repeated over and over, "Everyone's dead!" "Everyone's dead!" Then it struck her, releasing a second surge of adrenaline. "*If they're still here,"* she thought, "*they'll be coming for me while I'm sitting here!"* Her eyes flew open head darting to either side as she quickly surveyed her surroundings and scrambled to her feet drawing her sword. No blades, no black-haired bodies and no daemons appeared. D'Mique lowered her sword and took a shuddering shallow breath, her free hand involuntarily covering her mouth and nose in an attempt to keep the offensive smell away. "A horde attack!" her mind screamed as her eyes fell on the carnage again. Songbirds still sang in the trees, the suns still shone across the world setting slowly on the scene. "*What did they care?"* she asked herself, "*Slaughtered humans were nothing to the birds or the suns."* D'Mique forced herself to move forward. "*How? How could a daemon horde take out the fort?"* she wondered as she took a slow step down the hill.

She thought again of the narrow clearing, envisioning daemons pouring from the trees at dusk, trees that hugged the fort walls rather than growing at a respectable distance. "And daemons are willing to challenge Rysk's waning light for a chance to harvest some human flesh," she concluded looking at the Ghost Moon. Nodding, she surveyed the clearing again. She was thinking clearly again, her panic channeled into something more productive. She had found the mail wagons of that she was sure, and somewhere down there, amidst the death, was her permission form. "*I have to go down there,"* She thought. "*I have to get closer!*" Swallowing, her throat dry enough to make the act painful, she forced herself to continue moving despite her shaking knees. She tried not to let her eyes linger on the carnage. Rotting remains in piles of red, black, white and gray, littered the clearing. Broken wagons smoldered in the blue light of the Ghost Moon along with the tall timbers of the fort, which had turned to ash and charcoal. "*I don't want to remember this,*" she pleaded silently, "*but I know I will.*"

She rounded a wagon bed that had been tipped on its side during the battle and stopped, pulling up sharply, bewildered. Lying in the debris was an elf. D'Mique shook her head, eyes closed, and then looked again. What she could see of the pale face was unblemished and she could just see the tip of one pointed ear between the limp strands of long wispy white hair framing the narrow face. "*Definitely an elf,*" she thought taking a step closer, trying to remember if she'd ever actually seen an elf or only pictures of them. "*Elves rarely come this way—they spend most of their time with the more important races,*" she argued with herself as she studied him. Although his lower body lay hidden under a cloak and a congealed pool of blood surrounded him there were no visible wounds on his thin bare chest. His upper body seemed well-muscled rather than soft. "*Not a merchant then,*" she thought with a smile, "*He's not flabby enough.*" That meant he was probably a warrior. Her mother's stories rose unbidden speeding D'Mique's heart. Although slight of build the elves were fierce. And the elfin villages beyond the Dark Forest specialized in hunting daemons. Anika had gone to live with those elves to learn medicine, the kind of medicine a human could do. And she had always had patients to practice on. D'Mique took another slow step toward the elf, leaning closer pondering his presence in that strange battlefield. Had he stood by the door while the daemons forced it open? Was his blade drawn and bloody when he fell by the wagon?

The elf's eyes slid open. D'Mique caught the surprised squeal in her throat but jumped backward safely out of reach. Her sudden movement focused the elf's eyes on her. The beetle black orbs—no whites visible and no differentiation between pupil and iris—glittered feverishly. "My legs are broken, human," he whispered after a moment. "Did you come to stare? Either help me or finish me." They stared at each other for a long moment.

When D'Mique remained motionless the elf scowled closed his eyes and dismissively turned his head away from her.

D'Mique studied him a moment longer taken aback by his words. Questions swirled through her mind but stuck in her throat. Instead she said, "The suns are setting, elf. My village, Dornak, is a day's walk south of here." She stopped, waiting for something more from him. He remained motionless and silent. "Perhaps," she continued, "a warm fire and food for the night would be a better option than killing you?" The elf turned to look at her again, an odd mix of anger and relief creasing his forehead. He nodded his agreement with her suggestion before his eyes slipped closed again. Cautiously, she sat down near him and rummaged through her pack looking for her fire kit. As she worked she continued to glance around the clearing. "Will the daemon's return?" she pondered aloud.

Her words caused the elf's eyes to flicker open. "They haven't yet," he whispered. She slowly unpacked the tinderbox, weighing his words, watching his face carefully. He stared back, emotionless.

"I'll get some firewood. A fire will have to be good enough for the night," she said, standing. Wood was plentiful and she found more than enough to last the night without straying far. Returning to her tinderbox she soon had a small fire crackling just beyond the rim of the wagon bed. As the warmth grew, the elf opened his eyes again and studied her. "I have food and water, if you don't," she said offering her canteen. The elf nodded, slowly, making a feeble attempt to rise. D'Mique shuffled around the fire and helped him take a drink. Then she handed over a packet of travel rations, dried meat and hard biscuits. She noted the calluses on his hands as he took the packet. "*Muscles and calluses*," she thought, "*Whoever he is, he's used to hard work.*" Despite her remaining unanswered questions they ate in silence, D'Mique helping the elf to a second drink as Rysk set, leaving the firelight alone to push back the darkness.

The elf continued watching her as she ate, his eyes reflecting the yellow-orange flames. "You mentioned your village," he began as she finished, "Dornak?"

D'Mique nodded, "yes." The elf studied her a moment longer before struggling to his elbows and pulling a small pack out from under his cloak.

D'Mique watched him but made no move to help. He rummaged through it a moment and then pulled out a small scroll tube.

"Are you D'Mique?" he asked, "Ah," he continued as she glared at him, "I suppose that's a yes."

"How did you know?" she whispered.

The elf smiled slightly. "I am Sylus of the Academy. Here," he held the tube out to her, "I was sent here to deliver this into your hands and escort you to your field class." As he spoke his voice grew stronger until the last words came out in a smooth baritone, carrying the edge of command, "It's your final permission form."

D'Mique leapt to her feet and hurried around the fire taking the tube from him and popping it open, shaking out the form to read it. The form dissolved her mother's parental obligations, making D'Mique an adult by law, if not by age, three seasons early since children could not join the military and she wouldn't reach full adulthood until the coming Harvest. With her mother's signature on this form, the final strand would be cut and she, D'Mique, would be free to leave the village forever. She looked up at Sylus. "Thank you," she said though it seemed inadequate. "*He's a soldier from the Academy,*" she thought to herself, all of her observations confirmed and some of her questions answered. Silence grew around them again and Sylus slowly lay back. "Will you be able to move in the morning?" D'Mique asked after she'd read the form again and returned to her side of the fire.

"I should be able to with your aid, Lady," he sighed, "I have lain here six days. I will survive one more night."

D'Mique studied him for a moment trying to reconcile his condition with the stories every villager knew about elves, the things her mother had told her. "Shouldn't you have healed by now?" she asked.

Sylus glared at her. "What do you mean?" he asked.

"Well, your elfin healing powers," she said, frowning in confusion and trailing off.

Sylus chuckled in response. "While we do heal faster than humans, I fear that any stories you may have heard regarding elfin healing are shamefully exaggerated. Although some who are specially trained can heal themselves and others, I am not trained as a healer and my powers are only able to heal the smallest of flesh wounds in three or four days. Broken bones, I'm afraid, take me several cycles to heal." She studied the elf a moment, her eyes traveling down across the cloak that covered his lower body. "But," he continued, "I'm sure you have other things to prepare before you leave your village. I will have time to regain the use of my legs."

D'Mique nodded slightly, "I have three more cycles of Primary Education," she informed him. "I must finish school before leaving."

"Three cycles?" A slight hint of surprise, perhaps fear, tinged the question but he nodded slightly and continued, "Yes, time enough to heal." They lapsed into silence again, the small fire crackling between them. "Sleep, Lady," Sylus said a moment later, "I will keep the watch and wake you if trouble comes." Pausing, he studied her, brow furrowed. "You do wear that sword as a tool, not a decoration?" he asked.

D'Mique smiled broadly standing and drawing her sword. The blade glinted in the firelight, deadly and beautiful at the same time. "The guards taught me the basics, Sir. Nothing pretty, but all of it effective," she responded.

Sylus nodded slightly, skepticism raising an eyebrow. "Call me Commander, not Sir," he said as an afterthought as D'Mique sheathed the sword and sat down again.

"Yes, Commander," she said, a thrill running through her as his previous words played through her mind. "*He was sent to escort me to my field class! I've already been accepted into the Academy and I won't have to petition for entry nor prove myself in battle first!*" she thought.

"Rest now," Sylus continued, interrupting her thoughts. Nodding, D'Mique stretched out beside the fire watching the flames dance between the branches and studying the elf until her eyes closed and her mind drifted away.

Sylus watched D'Mique until she had fallen asleep before he struggled to a sitting position. "What providence," he wondered, "brought this human to me? Any human would have saved me from dehydration. But one of the humans I came here to find?" He shook his head in a vain attempt to dislodge the disbelief that had sprouted. Quietly he lifted the cloak from his legs and peaked underneath. Bloody rags that had once been his shirt clung to his thighs, hiding the deep wounds and shattered bones. "Elf meat is best kept fresh," the daemon in his memory growled. As with so many other skirmishes, the battle for the fort was little more than a blur in his memory. *Finding himself on his back in the dirt Sylus struggled to regain his feet as two daemons closed in on him, one of them readying a killing blow. But its companion stopped the sword, a fang-laced grin on its face. Defiant, he met the grin with a haughty glare—a glare that gave way to screams of pain as the daemons cut his flesh from his bones, one holding him down while the other one worked. Somewhere in the pain his thigh bones snapped. Then a soft darkness claimed him.* When he had awakened the daemons had gone, his traveling companions slaughtered in their wake.

Pain creasing his forehead, Sylus dismissed the vision and gingerly removed a few of the linen strips. The flesh of his thighs was filling in almost visibly fast in order to stop the flow of blood, but his legs were still just so much raw meat. Seeing the wounds again brought a soft sob of pain from his throat. He closed his eyes tight and waited for the wave of nausea to pass. "They still won't be closed over before the girl sees them," he thought. "I'll have to warn her before she splints them." He covered the wounds again, first with the rags then with his cloak. Lying back he waited a moment for the throbbing pain to subside.

Despite the darkness and the feebleness of the fire nothing disturbed them during the night. Near dawn the fire sputtered and died. With the warmth gone and the suns' light an hour distant, Sylus pulled his cloak tight up under his chin. Slowing his breathing he retreated into meditation and as his mind quieted his senses sharpened. The pines surrounding him whispered into his head while the grass beneath him caressed away his pain. He sent his senses further afield sensing other plant life. Bushes of the undergrowth entwined together, forming a nest around him that mirrored the contours of the clearing. Below him in the cool earth, seeds waited, eternally patient. When he lost sense of himself as a separate entity, when he was one with all the plants around him, he sent his conscious mind drifting away from his physical body and into the Mage Realm.

As his mind superimposed the Mage Realm over the physical world, the rocks, trees, and wagon debris shifted color to muted blues, grays, and purples. A diffuse illumination lit the night, pooling hazy shadows under and around the drab objects. In his mind Sylus recreated his body, as he saw himself, standing, his legs whole, beside his real body. Just as with any other construct within the muted world, the Mage Realm body did not actually exist. Instead it served only to anchor the wandering conscious of the mage who chose to step away from the physical world and enter the Mage Realm, the first step to performing magic for most mages. Against the muted blues of the physical world Sylus' real body glowed bright green infused with the Life magic that defined elves as a species. But the whirlpool of green light that marked his real body wasn't the only bright color. Golden rivers of Earth magic coursed along the ground, one of them forming eddies near his glowing green body. The lady sleeping near him did not glow green. Instead her form in the Mage Realm was a nest of red sparks—Fire magic. Sylus lifted his gaze as if scenting the air. The sky above him was a miasma of pale blue and storm gray, a mixed cloud of Air and Water magic. Only when a mage could see the bright colors of the Mage Realm could he or she hope to influence them and perform magic.

From the flow of Earth magic near his feet he felt a familiar tug, as if something pulled at the center of his being, dragging him forward. It was a familiar sensation and relief flooded through him. "Master?" he called out in his mind. Even before the word had left his lips the Mage Realm dissolved around him, sending his consciousness spinning, falling into a close darkness.

The answer came, "I am here, Sylus." The deep thrum of the Earth Master's voice filled the dark void around Sylus. As he continued to tumble slowly through the endless dark, the Master's voice sank into his being. Despite falling into a sudden darkness, Sylus smiled. He had been in this pocket realm, a construct of the Mage Realm as real as his current body, countless times before. It was as comforting to him as his own home. But he was spinning uncontrollably through the dark and that was disconcerting. Despite his depleted magic he mustered what power he could, calling on the pocket realm to bend to his will. First he tried to stop tumbling, managing only to slow his speed to a lazy spin. Then hoping to create a floor in the darkness and stop by running into it, he tried again to force change upon the pocket realm. He might as well have tried to think his way through a boulder. The dark pocket belonged to one of the strongest mages in the world and it would not change for a mere elfin warrior. With an inward sigh Sylus gave up trying to change his surroundings and returned his attention to his Master.

Instead of words Sylus dug up his memories of the attack and sent them into the darkness. Remembered Black Daemons leered in the dark, torturing and killing; horses screaming, trampling humans and daemons; mornings filled with blood and thirst and pain; and D'Mique's sudden appearance, all traveled along the golden Earth forcelines in the Mage Realm unaffected by the appearance of the dark pocket. A moment later, a pink mist gathered around Sylus surrounding his constructed body, slowly dispelling the suffocating darkness. As the blackness parted and the pink mist expanded, a floor formed bringing him to a sudden stop. It was not his floor, not the soft rug he had tried to create. Instead stone tiles rubbed against his face and hands as he worked to right himself. The pink mist was another familiar pocket realm and Sylus knew without looking that the cloaked figure of the Earth Master stood before him. "Are you healing?" his Master asked with a note of concern, his deep voice gravely like grinding millstones.

"Yes, Master, slowly," Sylus answered, struggling to a kneeling position, keeping his eyes down and his head bowed as he answered. "Though death may yet come for me. Your Lady will try to help me to her village in the morning."

"My Lady?" the Earth Master repeated, surprise coloring the words. But he quickly changed the subject, "I've been calling, trying to find you Sylus."

"I know, Master. I felt your call but my magic was diverted to healing and conserving fluid. The Lady brought me water and my wounds are healing, so I felt I could finally risk a short contact."

"Indeed." The Earth Master faded as the word drifted around him, the Master's constructed body dispersing with the mist. A second later Sylus lost his own constructed body, his consciousness returning to his real body. In his mind's eye, the bright elemental magic of the Mage Realm faded as well, followed by the muted colors of the alternate realm. At the last moment, just as Sylus poured his consciousness back into his physical body, the Earth Master spoke again, "I will contact the magistrate in Trinik and let Marco know what has happened and that your arrival will be later than expected."

"I live to serve, Master," Sylus answered opening his eyes, doubtful that his Master heard. He lay quiet, listening to the awakening forest as the Fiery Sisters peeked over the horizon and started their long climb. For a moment he tried ignoring the dizziness and thirst that rolled over him, the toll his journey into the Mage Realm had taken on his body, but he could not. With an inward sigh he propped himself up on his elbows and called out to D'Mique, "Lady!"

"Wha—" she started, green eyes flashing open as she scrambled to her feet.

"It's morning, Lady," Sylus began, "and we have work to do." He put on a half-hearted smile, "I fear I will prove to be a poor escort this day. My legs need splinting before we can travel, and I should warn you," he hesitated, staring at her, measuring the strength in her eyes, "the daemons butchered my legs before leaving me for dead," he said at last. "Also I will need you to recover my blade before we leave."

She met his measuring look with a glare, "I am not afraid of blood, Commander," she said tightly, "I am a warrior and my mother is a surgeon, an elf-trained surgeon," she added with a small nod.

With a brief answering glare he pulled off the cloak revealing the old bloody bandages. D'Mique gasped at the sight, "Oh no." Rarely had she seen such a mess of a wound. "You should have shown this to me last night," she chided absently as she knelt beside him and pulled the bandages back with a soft wet sound. The wounds were still several inches deep, most of the muscle gone. White bone shone through the remnants of flesh. D'Mique returned the bandages to their place and sat quietly for a moment struggling again with her stomach as waves of nausea ran through her, leaving her sweaty and shaking. She stared at the ground, not wanting to add the wound to her memories.

"Well, Commander," she said after a moment, her voice only half as shaky as she felt, "we'll use your cloak and some planks from the wagon beds to make a stretcher. We'll have you in Dornak in no time." Her optimism sounded forced even to her ear. Swallowing she studied the elf for a moment before pulling her belt knife out and attacking her shirtsleeves. He watched silently as she sliced the cloth forming about a dozen strips. Once she'd finished, she steeled herself and reached for his legs, working quickly to change the bandages and bind the new ones in place. As she tied the last strips over the huge holes in Sylus' thighs she glanced up, catching her reflection in the elf's pure black eyes. "*I look so pale,*" she thought, swallowing.

When she'd finished, she stood, sighing, and checked the sky. Locating the twin suns, she judged it to be just short of mid-morning. There was still a great deal to do and the day was passing quickly. "*Thinking about it won't get it done,*" she chided herself. Grimacing she started on the wagon bed, straining against the nails that held it together and eventually wrenching two long planks from it. Propping them on the wagon tongue and surveying them she thought, "I need a saw." She looked around at the carnage-strewn clearing, her eyes glancing over the rotting forms almost growing accustomed to their presence, "*There should be one somewhere around here,*" she thought as she said aloud, "I'll be back." and started toward the blackened remains of the fort.

She made her way through the burnt timbers and piles of rubble, the remains of three more wagons that occupied the clearing. In the center, the walls of the fort had burned to the ground; only their stone foundations remained dusted with charcoal, the acrid scent of wood smoke mingling with the sweet smell of decay. Her eyes tracked along the ground trying to pick out the outline of a saw. She stopped to investigate every metal object that caught her eye, most proving to be only bits of silverware, while others, despite being larger, had no cutting edge. Finally she pulled a thick piece of black metal with a crescent-shaped blade from a pile of rocks. "Ah," she said, hefting the short-handled battle-ax, "A daemon weapon." She swung it experimentally, first with a one-handed grip, then with two. "Well, it'll cut wood," she whispered to herself though she couldn't see using it for any other reason. Shouldering the weapon she hurried back to Sylus.

Soon the wagon planks lay in four pieces, two smaller ones to splint Sylus' legs and two larger ones to use as a stretcher. Using the strips from Sylus' cloak to fashion the splints she gingerly tied the boards to his legs. Then she turned her attention to making a stretcher with the longer boards. When she finished she stood back, admiring her work momentarily. Smiling, she wiped her brow as she spoke, "Okay, Commander, we're ready."

She dragged the cloak and wagon stretcher next to Sylus who had managed to sit upright, and stood back waiting.

Sylus grimaced in reply while running a pale hand through his long white hair, "Suddenly a foot is a mile," he said, setting his jaw, looking at the stretcher next to him. Gritting his teeth he used his arms to lift his body from the ground and onto the litter, a small whimper of pain escaping. Gingerly D'Mique positioned his splinted legs on the litter as he took a shaky breath.

"Right. A quick look around," D'Mique said as she drew her sword, "and we're on our way."

"Lady," Sylus stopped her, "My elfin blade is somewhere out there. The daemons threw it into the brush."

"What does it look like?"

"It's an elfin blade," Sylus said after a split-second. "How many do you think you might find out there?" he asked sarcastically, brows furrowing. When she didn't move, he sighed, "The scabbard is blue and the hilt has a climbing rose set in it." With a single curt nod, D'Mique turned on her heel and walked away. First she made a large circle around the clearing finding no sign of life and no sword, then she left the clearing and searched the surrounding undergrowth staying just short of the forest. Near the end of her circle, she saw a glint of metal between the green leaves of a thicket. Smiling in both relief and triumph, she bent and retrieved the sword, picking it up by the leaf-covered blue velvet scabbard. D'Mique studied the sword. The leaves clung to the scabbard as she tried to pull them away but the plant held on tenaciously. She glared, studying it, following the plant's stem with her eyes as it grew out from the sword's hilt and wrapped around the pommels.

"Lady?" Sylus called from the clearing. With a shrug and a sigh, she started back toward him plant-covered scabbard in hand. A flash of visible relief crossed his face when she returned.

"Is this it, Commander?" she asked, handing the blue scabbard to him. He sighed as he took it from her, nodding. "I couldn't get the plant off it," she started as he grasped the hilt and drew the weapon, blood flaking from the blade. Sylus frowned at the dirty blade then smiled at D'Mique. Instead of returning the smile D'Mique watched the plant, its leaves shivering, its stems moving off the hilt and pommels as the vines caressed Sylus' hand. Then the plant withdrew and shrank in on itself wrapping tightly around the pommels out of the way.

"Thank you, Lady." D'Mique nodded absently eyes still on the plant. "We should get going," he goaded.

"Yes," D'Mique agreed, "We won't reach Dornak before dark, but we can make a start," she said with a bit of trepidation; the daemons would be out there in the dark. Sylus nodded, contemplating her as he returned the sword to its scabbard. He lay down as she picked up the litter near the elf's head and turned it toward home.

Maintaining a steady pace as she traveled the well-kept road took up all her concentration and the day passed quickly. At sunset she pulled off to the side looking for the Ghost Moon. Willpower alone allowed her to lower the litter to the ground instead of dropping it. Rysk stood at high noon his presence providing a slight respite before complete darkness fell. Weak though his blue light was it would likely keep the daemons at bay most of the night. She knelt beside the stretcher staring down at Sylus. His dark eyes surveyed her for a full minute before either of them spoke. "Do you need healing?" he asked.

"What?"

"Your back, your arms and your legs; do they need healing?"

"I'm sore, Commander, but I'll be fine without healing," she said, smiling and retrieving her canteen and travel rations from the litter. She helped Sylus take a drink and shared the rations with him. They ate in silence.

"When you've finished," he instructed, "find some wood and I'll start a fire; it may keep the daemons away after the Ghost Moon sets." D'Mique nodded and did as he asked. Soon a small pile of dead wood sat between them.

Sylus closed his eyes stepping into the Mage Realm. The rivers of Earth that engulfed the land glowed golden around him forming eddies at his feet. No pocket realms greeted him, he had entered the Mage Realm to work not communicate. Pulling at the sparks of Fire Magic that existed, almost lost in the maelstrom of green Life magic in his hands, he bent the magic to his will, directing Fire into the dry wood. Flames licked up from the center of the pile as he returned to the physical realm and opened his eyes. The fire that danced between them was a candy red in color.

D'Mique frowned at its color momentarily, wondering at it. "You just made a fire," she began her eyes remaining on the flames, "But you're an elf. I thought you only had healing magic."

Sylus nodded in reply, "Yes, it's true that Elfin magic is used for healing. My magic is all that has kept me alive since the attack; blood loss and thirst should have killed me days ago. But we can reach the other forcelines generally, although without a bonding our powers are limited." He paused a moment before adding, "calling Fire from your own hands is considered one of the basics, Lady. Most mages can do it, even when they can do nothing else."

With a nod she turned her attention outward, lost in her own thoughts on one level and straining to catch any sign of approaching daemons on another. Across from her Sylus lay propped on his elbows eyes closed. "Why did you apply to the Academy?" he asked at last opening his eyes.

She returned his gaze, the odd-colored fire reflected in the depths of his black eyes. "I just want to be a soldier. It's my dream," she shrugged.

"Humans have never before been accepted to the Academy. You do realize there is a great deal of pressure on you to succeed?"

"I have always held myself to a high standard Commander," she replied, but a sudden wave of uncertainty filled her. Silently she continued, "*It's true that no human has ever been accepted. Why would they be?*"

Sylus said with a smile, "My traveling companions had only good things to say about the Lady Warrior of Dornak."

D'Mique smiled wistfully but didn't reply aloud. "*People praise me? Not in my village*," she thought.

"Well, you seem strong enough," he added, "for a human." He paused a moment then added, "The fiercest fighters in the Black Lands are Vale Warriors—humans. It is said that the greatest thinkers up north beyond the Vast Wilds, are also humans."

D'Mique looked away and into the fire letting the silence grow around them as she pondered his words. "It's true we are the poorest species and unable to see the forcelines let alone touch them, weaker than goblins and Semians, and short-lived compared to your people," she said.

Sylus settled back on the litter, staring up at the stars glittering between the branches. "Still, there must be a reason we promised to keep your people safe, Lady," he replied after a moment.

D'Mique stared at him, jaw dropping, "You haven't forgotten the Promise?"

"Forgotten?" he returned her stare, honest confusion painted across his face.

"Yes," D'Mique said. "Many village elders claim that the goblins and elves have forgotten their Promise."

"We would never forget the Promise!" he replied, trying to sit up but failing as pain raced through him. He lay still for a moment settling for glaring at D'Mique until she looked away. He studied her for a time then sighed, "The reasons behind the Promise are lost to time Lady. But the custom of keeping the humans of the Nesting safe is an honored tradition."

D'Mique looked back at him, wondering silently, "*Was the Promise behind my acceptance into the Academy?*"

"You sleep first," Sylus offered at last. "I will wake you for the second watch." D'Mique nodded, lay down beside the fire, and was soon asleep.

Near dawn, shivering slightly from the early morning chill, D'Mique woke Sylus. She had spent the last hour of her watch cleaning the campsite and preparing for the final leg of their journey. "We'll make the village today Commander," she said, "and my mother will see to your wounds." She added with a smile, "She's elf-trained."

Sylus sighed, "Good news, indeed. Expending magic for the fire was a small necessity but it has weakened me."

D'Mique hoisted the litter and started for home as Sylus continued, "My Master was busy last night," he said, "He has given me extra magic to draw on in order to insure my survival, but even he cannot support me for very long."

"Your Master?"

"Yes. I am bound to the Earth Master," he said.

D'Mique stopped suddenly at his words a swell of panic washing over her. "He was here?" she stammered, fear dancing through her words.

Sylus chuckled. "No. He is safe in Dragon Ridge Fortress. We are joined together, servant to master."

"Oh," she said, though she did not quite understand the implication.

"It was Master Myrth," Sylus continued in an attempt to alleviate the fear he'd heard in her voice, "who secured your acceptance to the Academy. Although most fear the Masters, Master Myrth is your sponsor. You do not need to fear him."

"The Earth Master sponsored me at the Academy?"

"Of course, he sponsored both you and Marco. The High Generals at the Academy insisted he sponsor you since it was his idea to accept you. You can ask him more about it when we get to Dragon Ridge."

D'Mique's head spun as she tried to make sense of this new information. But before she could completely digest it she grasped onto the one thing that did make sense. "Wait, did you say Marco?" she asked.

"Yes."

"From Trinik?"

"Do you know him?" Sylus asked.

"I've heard of him. People say he's crazy."

"Not crazy, just magic."

"Really?" D'Mique asked, nearly dropping the litter. She looked over her shoulder, studying the elf, "A Mage of Man?" she asked, incredulous, watching for proof that he was joking.

"From what I've heard, I think so."

"But, humans have no magic."

Sylus shrugged. "I merely go where I am told to go," he said.

D'Mique shook her head and started again, thoughts chasing through her head, "*The Earth Master sponsored me? One of the most powerful Mages on the planet sponsored me!*" A second voice chimed in, "*His anger can shake the earth! A glare can sour a farmer's fields for decades!*" "*Why would he choose me?*"

"Commander?" she asked, stopping again, her muscles starting to complain about the work. "You said we are going to Dragon Ridge. Will we be going on to Olimidia afterward?" Sylus did not answer her immediately and she looked over her shoulder at him. He was lying with his eyes closed a slight grimace on his face.

"No. I'm a field instructor," he said at last, his eyes remaining closed. "You and Marco are assigned to my class at Dragon Ridge."

"Just the two of us?" she asked, sudden suspicion lacing her question. If they had chosen to accept two token humans, it would not surprise her to learn that they were to be segregated.

"No, you will be joining six others." D'Mique faced forward again and continued down the road. "If you had been other than human," Sylus continued, "I would have simply sent letters instructing you to report to Dragon Ridge. But Master Myrth knew two humans would need an escort."

"The Masters keep the Promise?"

"We all keep the Promise, Lady."

"But the Masters are Semians."

"Well, Master Marladon is a Mortak. But the Promise holds all."

"Hmm," she responded still not sure she believed him. More thoughts for the long walk home.

It was late afternoon when D'Mique sighted her walled village. As she came into view guardsmen left the gate and ran to her. They demanded to know what had happened. Two men gently took the litter from her and ran ahead with Sylus shouting for Anika. The remaining guards continued to pepper her with questions, why had she been gone so long, where had she found the elf, what had happened?

"Daemons attacked the fort. They torched the postal wagon and the elf is the only survivor," she informed them pushing through the growing throng toward town. Some guards stopped at the news glancing warily back at the Dark Woods while others continued trailing beside and behind her. She was so tired from dragging Sylus all day that she didn't feel up to reveling in their reaction. Instead she concentrated on following the litter while the guards carrying it, making their way to her house, shouted all the way to her front gate.

Reaching her house, the guards placed Sylus on the guest bed and Anika gingerly removed the makeshift bandages. "You," she pointed to a guard at random, "run and fetch Nico." D'Mique moved up opposite her mother pulling out a surgical tray—a well-practiced routine.

Sylus eyed the implements on the tray as Anika removed the last layer of bandages, "I don't know what good suturing will do," he said.

"I am the surgeon, I will decide what is needed," Anika replied. She gasped at the sight revealed by removing the final bandage and looked up at her daughter. "How old is this wound?"

D'Mique surveyed Sylus' thighs, "He's healing nicely, mother. The bones were visible the last time I saw the wounds. Also, this along the edges, is completely new tissue." Anika looked up at Sylus' face.

"I am healing as quickly as possible," he said, a note of affront in his voice. "The blood loss has been astounding. I am dehydrated and in shock. My legs are broken beneath the wounds, above my knees."

Nico, Anika's assistant, burst in followed by the guard that had gone to fetch him. He stopped beside D'Mique studying the wounds. Anika let him assess them before asking, "Any suggestions?"

"Was this just done?" he asked, looking from Sylus to D'Mique and back to Anika.

"Five days old, now," D'Mique supplied, finally answering her mother's question as well.

Nico gasped. "But he's an elf. Shouldn't he be healed?" Sylus sighed audibly in exasperation and Anika suppressed a giggle.

"He's regenerating about an inch worth of tissue a day," D'Mique continued. "He says the bones will take a couple cycles to mend."

Nico leaned over the wound his long brown hair almost dipping into the blood. "No sign of infection or rot." He pursed his lips as his eyes grew serious. "We should keep the splints in place while the wounds close. It will take approximately four more days," he eyed the wound, "The wound is too wide to close with stitches. The elf has lasted five days already." Straightening he continued, "We should support his healing efforts with food and water. Warmth and quiet for shock. If he was a human I would suggest a blood transfusion. I don't know if human blood can help an elf."

Anika smiled wistfully, "No, the bloods do not mix." She looked at Sylus, "Do you have any further needs elf? Other than what my assistant recommends?"

Sylus closed his eyes, "An old plant. One with vigor and strength."

"A plant?" D'Mique and Nico chorused.

"Elfin magic comes from plants," Anika informed them. The three sat in thought for a moment.

"Alva has a clux brush in a pot. It's about three years old," Nico supplied.

Anika nodded, "Take some guards and fetch it. I'm sure Alva will let us borrow it when she knows why." Nico and a couple guards ran off.

D'Mique surveyed the crowded room and stepped forward. "The elf needs quiet, time to go," she informed them motioning toward the door. Unwilling to leave, the crowd departed slowly, throwing furtive glances between Anika, Sylus, and D'Mique. As they left they simply joined the growing crowd on the road in front of the house. Salva stood near the gate a relieved smile flitting across her face when she spotted D'Mique. They exchanged nonchalant waves before D'Mique turned away. "*She thought I'd left for good,*" she realized, closing the door.

Marco of Trinik

Marco stared out the second story window. Outwardly he watched wistfully as two of the baker's sons chased each other on the green. But he had no real interest in their play. Instead he was studying a wisp—a flash of color that no one else could see. This particular wisp darted just out of the corner of his eye, flashing through a myriad of blue and gray hues as it flitted about. All his life he had tried to study them to catch more than just a flash of color before they disappeared. He had learned early on that chasing the golden sparks that he often found floating in the underbrush led to laughter and chastisement; laughter from the other children and chastisement from his parents. Proper boys, they had said, do not chase imaginary fairies. It was only when he'd entered school that he'd realized he alone could see the colored wisps and sparks. Of course by that time everyone already knew he was...peculiar.

"Are you going out today?" his mother asked from the table behind him where she sat with her pile of mending. He sighed and closed his eyes a moment then turned to look at her.

"Would you rather I helped around the house?" he asked.

"One last day of chores?" she asked with a smile. "Marco, go outside. It'll be good for you to take one more look around and visit your friends once more." He shrugged, his broad shoulders nearly touching the wavy black hair that concealed his ears. She knew no one would miss him when he was gone. Peculiar boys who chase imaginary fairy wisps and sparks of gold don't tend to have many friends. "Humor me," she said with a smile and a sigh.

Returning the smile he nodded, "Alright, I'll humor you." He made his way downstairs and out into the garden patch. The walled village lay around him, the palisade looming over the outermost ring of homes. As the younger boys noticed him they stumbled to a halt and exchanged whispers before laughing and suddenly running away. Marco sighed, dismissing them. Looking around he noted that few others could be seen; the heat of the afternoon having driven most people away from the sunny center of the village. As he stood by the gate his father and two members of the council came into view.

"Here he is," the Magistrate greeted, "my son." The council members nodded cordially in greeting but made no attempt at conversation. "The post has not arrived," the magistrate continued after taking his leave from the others. He stood at the gate with Marco watching them stroll across the green toward the bank.

"It's late," Marco replied, "but I'm sure it will be here soon."

"Yes." They stood silently for a long moment. "Did your mother send you out of the house?" his father asked at last.

Marco chuckled. "Yes, she thought I should say goodbye."

The magistrate smiled, offering his own chuckle before they fell back into a comfortable silence, lost in their own thoughts. Marco watched a small gold spark hover near his feet never looking directly at it. His father watched him until Marco felt the pressure of his gaze. With a knowing smile Marco looked directly at his father losing sight of the spark. "I expect," his father said, "you will remember what I told you. How to behave with the elves."

"Yes, I remember. And I will mind myself with them."

"Going to the Academy is an honor never before granted to a human Marco. Don't let..." he trailed off.

"Don't let them know about the fairies?" Marco asked, laughter dancing in his eyes.

"You and I both know you're not watching fairies," he said, his eyes turning to hard slate, killing his son's laughter.

"I'll be careful," Marco replied, "This is my chance to start over." As he spoke a small black bird glided to a landing on the fence next to them. It croaked a greeting then launched itself toward the messenger coop tucked up under the eaves of the house. "I'll collect it," Marco offered, pushing away from the gate, allowing his father to enter the garden. He hurried back in and upstairs again finding his mother pulling the message scroll from the bird's leg.

"It's from Dragon Ridge," she whispered, holding the scroll out to Marco, a tremor lightly dancing in her hand. For a split second Marco pulled away, as if the paper had suddenly sprouted fangs and tried to bite. Then he forced himself to take it and read it. "What does it say?" his mother and father asked simultaneously from opposite sides.

The magistrate closed the distance between them as Marco spoke, "It says my escort has been delayed. That I should wait patiently until the end of the season, and if I have not been contacted by then to travel as best I can to Dragon Ridge. Signed M." They all exchanged glances for a moment.

"Dragon Ridge, not the Academy?" his father asked reading over his son's shoulder. Marco nodded.

"What will you do?" his mother asked.

"I'll wait, as the note suggests," he replied.

Sylus fingered the deep green foliage of the clux brush leaning over to sniff a sprig of tiny, light purple flowers. "I'm leaving now, my friend," he whispered to the plant, "Thank you for your strength in my time of need." The cycles had passed quickly while Sylus healed, the sleepy rhythm of the isolated human village providing him with the perfect environment for working Life Magic and a welcome respite from the wearying world beyond the forest. He pushed magic into the plant calling forth more small purple blooms. "I return your strength to you," he said, letting the magic fade as he dropped his hand. While he had healed Anika had worked on replacing his clothing, and he stood on two strong legs, dressed in a new white wool shirt and stout trousers, a new travel pack sat on the floor beside his boots. His pale skin and white hair glowed vibrantly in the early morning half-light of the guest room.

"I'm ready Commander," D'Mique said entering, "packed and waiting."

"You've said your goodbyes?" he asked without looking around. She nodded as if he could see her. Part of her thought he could, part of her thought he just assumed she answered him. "And your form is signed?" he asked glancing up in time to catch her next nod. He sighed and smiled, "Then let's begin." He retrieved his travel pack from the floor and slung it over his narrow shoulders before striding out the door. D'Mique followed him a slight smile on her face. "He walks and talks like a giant, as if all will bow before him, trembling in his wake," she thought. At less than five and a half feet tall he barely reached D'Mique's chest. He was smaller than all the men in the village and even smaller than some of the women. "I think he's even short for an elf," she concluded.

Anika was waiting for them at the front door. She threaded her arm through D'Mique's and walked with her towards the north gate. "Now you be careful out there," she said.

"I will mom," D'Mique assured her.

"And write if you get a chance," her mother added. "And remember to tell them about the daemons."

"I will mom," D'Mique stopped and smiled at Anika. "I'll be fine," she said, hugging her close. Anika returned the hug, holding her daughter tight. After a long minute, they started forward again, a long sigh echoing between them.

At the north gate a crowd of people had gathered to see them off. D'Mique pulled Salva from the crowd and embraced her while swallowing back tears. Salva buried her face against D'Mique's shoulder trying to hold onto her childhood friend. Then she pulled away, a sad smile on her face. Sylus spoke quickly to the magistrate before stepping through the gate and starting across the fields leaving D'Mique behind. She watched him leave, grasping her mother's hand one more time. Then, without looking back, she followed him toward the Dark Forest. There were no cheers, no one running after them for one last word, only silent strength and unshed tears. D'Mique sighed and kept looking forward her eyes resting on Sylus' wispy white hair, while she worked to burn the image of her mother, standing in the gateway, her orange linen skirt dancing in the breeze, into her mind.

Again, the world beyond the village seemed too big and too lonely as they crossed the defensive clearing, Sylus walking a few steps in front of her, their footsteps the only sound. The Dark Forest loomed before them, its ancient whispering pines welcoming her as it engulfed them. D'Mique sighed again, "This is it," she whispered, "this is the last time I'll ever walk this road." Sylus turned, his dark eyes studying her.

"You don't think you'll be back?" he asked.

"I know I won't. Oh, maybe to visit but not to live," she added seeing the protest begin on Sylus' face. "My mother said so herself, my dreams are too big for a little walled village." Sylus adjusted his pace to match her own.

"So you think you'll succeed in the military despite being human, being female?"

"Other races have a strong tradition of fighting females," D'Mique said shrugging. "Goblin females have proven themselves for generations," she added, nodding at her own example.

"I know of many Semian females that wield the bow," Sylus contemplated aloud a few moments later. "However, I know of only one female who carries a sword and can use it."

"Well, I am human, female and I carry a sword," D'Mique said, stopping as a smile brightened her face.

Sylus stopped as well, "I'm sure Myrth had his reasons for accepting you into the Academy, and I will train you as I train every other recruit. But you must know that no one expects you to succeed," he said.

Her smile turned to a glare. "Then I will surprise them all by succeeding," she said, adding silently, "*I am used to scorn and disapproval.*" She let her eyes drift over him, "You can't tell me that you've never had a problem like that," she said aloud.

Sylus tilted his head slightly his eyes narrowing. "That was a size comment," he said with a hiss. "I've heard them all before and you're right. I have been dismissed because of my size. Woe to the ones who did the dismissing," he said with a decidedly evil smile. D'Mique returned a smile as wicked as his. "As long as you are prepared for the attitudes of others, Lady—,"

"I am," she interrupted.

"Then all will be well," he finished, continuing down the path.

Near sunset they reached the fort clearing. The horrors they had left behind four cycles ago were gone, bodies returned to their loved ones when possible. D'Mique knew several unidentified victims had been buried in an anonymous grave just outside Dornak, forever lost. For twenty-four days, groups of men from the surrounding villages had worked. After digging graves, they had hauled away the burnt timber and started construction on a new fort. So far, only the new lower walls had been built, sitting atop the old stone foundation—stone to deter the daemons. More wagons of stone were on the way and tomorrow more work would be done, but tonight, the clearing sat empty.

Sylus stopped at the foundation settling stiffly to the ground, his back against the new stone. D'Mique wondered if his legs were still not quite ready for a cross-country hike. He closed his eyes.

"Commander?" D'Mique asked, kneeling beside him, "Are you okay?"

"Yes," he said with a sigh, "The memories are still strong, my body still weak. I will set a ward so we can rest in safety tonight. You set camp while I gather wood," he said as he struggled back to his feet and started through the surrounding underbrush. While he was gone D'Mique unpacked their blanket rolls and travel rations. When he returned they ate dinner and then curled up beside the fire. Although Sylus' ward spell would keep out any daemon-spawn long enough for them to wake, allowing both of them to sleep, D'Mique spent the night fitfully tossing and turning. With dawn they cleaned up camp and started down the eastern road to the village of Trinik.

"Tell me Lady," Sylus began, "is Trinik also a day's walk from the fort?"

"No. It's only about five hours away."

"Good. We can be on our way back well before nightfall. I have already lost too much time on this errand." His words drew a frown from her but she said nothing as she followed him through the morning. Because her village lay along the trade road between the Fanterra Plain and the desert lands, regular caravans rumbled through Dornak on their way to the Stockade Mountains. But there was nothing beyond Trinik and the road between it and the fort was unkempt, large stones and deep mud pools lining it; some places nearly impassable for a wagon.

About halfway to their destination Sylus stopped beside a small creek. "Are all humans as slow as you, Lady," he taunted when she caught up. "Or is it just your delicate, feminine nature."

"What?" D'Mique asked, taken aback. Sylus studied her, mild curiosity dancing through his black-orb eyes. In answer to her question, he dropped his travel pack, his feet shifting slightly in the dirt. Something about the way he held himself sent D'Mique's skin crawling and she reached for the hilt of her sword.

"Do you entertain thoughts of besting me," he asked with a nod toward her hand on her sword.

D'Mique studied him a moment before replying. "Big words," she said with a smile, emphasizing the first word, relaxing slightly. She scoffed silently, chasing away her embarrassment, *"That was a test?"* she thought.

"That was a size joke," Sylus laughed. "Fair enough since I've taunted you for being female, but, as I said before, do not judge me by my size Lady. I am an elfin warrior." The earth trembled beneath D'Mique's feet and dirt suddenly piled up over her boots, pushed by invisible hands, burying her feet to her ankles. She gaped at the piles, trying to pull free, but the ground had a solid hold on her and she wavered, nearly losing her balance. Then the earth jerked her feet out from under her sending her backward to the ground. She landed hard on her back, the air leaving her lungs as stars burst across her vision and her teeth sank into her tongue, drawing blood. White-hot sparks of pain flashed through her mouth in reply. Sylus pounced on her chest, pinning her arms with his legs, constricting her chest even more. She struggled to pull her arms out from under his legs or roll out from under him, still unable to gain a full breath. But an unwavering strength held her in place. "An elfin warrior bound to the Master of Earth," he finished, his perfect black eyes staring into her angry, pain-filled green ones. "Now, shall I let you up and we can have a go with our swords?" he asked in a calm, almost disinterested, voice.

"This is still the test," D'Mique thought, *"It has to be."* She took a shuttering breath, releasing her anger and swallowing around the sudden humiliation that welled up inside her. "No, Commander," she gasped, "I do not wish to fight you."

"Good," he said, releasing her arms. He stood and helped her up, "Will we reach Trinik soon?" he asked. "Marco and his father have been waiting for us." She nodded in reply. "Good," he said as he started down the path again.

An hour later they emerged from the trees, dappled shadows giving way to a sun drenched clearing. Before them rose Trinik's walls, a mirror-image of Dornak. Like all the human villages within the Dark Forest its twenty foot wooden stockade was meant to keep out the daemon hordes long enough for the guards to dissuade them from attacking since daemons preferred easy meals. However, unlike Dornak, the main gates were closed, no crowd of weeping friends and family members greeted them. Instead a young man sat on a boulder just outside the gates while an older man paced beside him, eyes down. The younger man wore clothes similar to D'Mique's, brown and gray homespun, a worn travel pack next to his dark leather boots, boots that looked fairly new. His companion, like many magistrates, wore a plain white robe.

"Magistrate!" Sylus called as they neared. The older man stopped and turned, waving at Sylus, his bony arm drowned in the robe's sleeve. When they reached the pair Sylus continued, "I've come from Dragon Ridge; I am expected?"

"Good journey?" the Magistrate asked, bowing low as they neared, presenting them with his bald pate. "Yes, we received word to wait for you until the end of the season." Sylus produced a scroll tube and handed it to the younger man as the magistrate introduced him, "This is my son, Marco." Sylus bowed slightly in response as the young man stood. D'Mique eyed him warily. At six foot he was only slightly taller than she. His long, wavy black hair framed a tanned face, covering his shoulders. Pure brown eyes sized up D'Mique, taking in her sword and travel pack, the hint of a smirk curling his lips.

"My name is D'Mique," she introduced.

"Ahh yes, the Lady Warrior," the magistrate said, bowing low to her. Surprised, D'Mique took a step back. "We know you well by reputation, if not in person," he continued, bringing color to her cheeks.

Sylus studied Marco, "And we have heard rumors of you, Marco. A "peculiar" boy in Trinik, who talks to fairies." Marco's face soured and his father gaped. "Well, I suppose we should officially test you," Sylus continued, resignation and disbelief coloring his voice. Facing Marco he held out his hand, level with Marco's chest, before closing his eyes and stepping into the Mage Realm. For D'Mique and the magistrate nothing changed. Sylus stood immobile for a full minute, Marco watching him warily. But in the Mage Realm Sylus worked, studying the man and his surroundings.

The elf looked around. Golden Earth forcelines bypassed the village leaving the area bathed in the blue-gray miasma of Air alone. Fire sparks marked D'Mique and the magistrate but Marco was nowhere to be seen. Sylus gasped. Being masked in the Mage Realm was a common, self-taught defense from the power of magic. Being unable to find a person in the Mage Realm was one of the simplest ways to test for the innate ability to step between realms. Sylus moved toward where Marco should have stood. Three steps brought him up against an invisible barrier and white-hot pain seared through his head throwing him out of the Mage Realm and back into his body. Sylus opened his eyes with a gasp, pondering Marco as he stood before him and trying to quantify the pain throbbing through his head. "A barrier that hot..." he muttered under his breath. He massaged his temples for a moment and stood staring at Marco. At length he turned to Marco's father, "Magistrate your son is a mage," he said, his disbelief at his own words unhidden. He contemplated the painful shock he had received from Marco's wall once more, waiting for it to fade completely. "With training," he continued in a cautious half-whisper, "he will be strong enough to sit on the council or even serve as a Syra," Marco and D'Mique gaped.

"But he's human," D'Mique breathed. Marco glared at her.

The magistrate sighed with relief, "Well that's a load off my chest." He turned to the walled village, "Did you hear that?" he shouted, brandishing a fist at the closed gate. The three beside him jumped, startled. "Magic enough to be a Syra!"

"But he's human," D'Mique repeated.

Sylus nodded. "It does happen," he said. "One of the first Masters was a human. It is said that the Crown Cities to the North hold human mages."

"The first Masters ruled centuries ago," she protested. Sylus only nodded in reply.

Marco chuckled at his father. "Here father," he said, handing him the forms from the scroll tube.

"Ahh yes," the magistrate sighed as he signed them, reading each one briefly. Then he pulled his son into a brief hug handing back the papers, "Take care, my boy. Come home from time to time and write me."

"I will, father. Remind mother of my words this morning," Marco said. The magistrate nodded as he grasped Marco's hand, shaking it, before his son shouldered his pack. Then Marco started back the way Sylus and

D'Mique had come without waiting for them. As D'Mique had done the day before he did not look back.

She watched him walk away still trying to grasp the possibility that he really was a mage, "Impossible! Just impossible!" She thought. "Humans are not magical!" Sylus bowed to the magistrate once more and offered a farewell before following Marco, D'Mique trailing behind.

The trio returned to the fort that afternoon. Now workers from Dornak, Trinik, Scala, and other villages milled about, constructing new walls. They worked with a grim determination, each stone laid against the sinister creatures who hunted in the darkness. Those from Dornak waved to D'Mique when they saw her, a grudging acknowledgement of her role in discovering the massacre. She returned the greetings halfheartedly but did not stop, continuing westward toward Scala, the largest human village, which perched just on the edge of the Dark Forest and the Fanterra Plain. As the Fiery Sisters journeyed across the sky D'Mique worked to ignore the rumble in her stomach. Sylus looked like he had no interest in stopping before nightfall. She looked to the sky, searching for the Ghost Moon. Conventional travelers and most people she knew, counted day and night by the rising and setting of Col and Nix. It would be just her luck if Sylus were one of the few who counted "day" as when any sun was out, even the pale Rysk, and "night" as when no sun was out. Her heart sank. Rysk was nowhere to be seen, which meant he would be rising as the Fiery Sisters set. It could be a really long night. "Will we be stopping with the Sisters?" she asked, dreading the answer.

Sylus turned enough to study her but he kept walking. "Is there a reason to stop?" he asked, "If we push on we can make up for lost time. The Ghost Moon is bright enough to travel by."

"I'm hungry," she answered.

"Me too," Marco said, stopping abruptly and unshouldering his pack.

Sylus caught up to him and stopped as well. "Well it seems I'm out-voted," he said, looking between them. "We will stop now for dinner. Then we will continue until Rysk rides high."

Marco sighed with relief, dropping his pack at the side of the road, kneeling beside it, and throwing it open. "My father packed fresh food for my supper," he said digging through the contents. "I would like to share it."

"Only one meal's worth I hope," Sylus said as Marco handed him a meat filled pastry.

"Yes of course," he handed D'Mique one as well. "He did not pack it for travelling, he packed it while we awaited your arrival. We'd been waiting there every day since we received your letter from Dragon Ridge."

They ate quickly, finishing their meal in silence. Marco seemed lost in thought, his eyes and thoughts drifting randomly as D'Mique watched him. Sylus chuckled, "Are you curious Lady?" the elf asked.

Marco studied her darkly startling her out of her reverie. "I," she stammered. "Well, he can't be a mage, not really."

Sylus shrugged, "He is hidden in the Mage Realm. He has some power. We will know more once the barrier is down. For now, let's be on our way again," Sylus said, collecting his pack.

Soon the ghostly blue light of Rysk was all that remained of the day—the ghost of a sun, as the ancient stories claimed—and his blue light deepened the shadows around them. Hours passed, as Rysk climbed toward his apex, and the walking was starting to take its toll on D'Mique. Her knees ached, her thighs burned, her feet had gone numb. But neither Marco nor Sylus showed any sign of stopping. She focused on following them, glaring in anger and pain. "We will be stopping soon, we will be stopping soon," she repeated like a mantra.

Ahead of her Sylus suddenly stopped, looking thoughtfully at a clearing. "We'll camp here," he said. "Tomorrow we'll be in Scala. I can hire horses for us there."

"Why couldn't we have bought horses from my village or Dornak?" Marco asked. He sounded tired and grumpy, which made D'Mique smile as she dropped her pack in the center of the clearing.

"Well what fun would that have been?" Sylus asked. Watching the elf's face D'Mique thought she caught a hint of a smile as he answered.

Marco glared at him. "We would be sleeping in a bed at Scala Inn," he answered with a bitter edge.

"Soldiers in service to the Masters rarely sleep in beds or inns," Sylus replied. D'Mique lowered herself gingerly to the ground. "But really," Sylus continued, "There were no good horses in your village."

"You didn't even look in Trinik," Marco countered.

"True," Sylus paused, "There were no good horses in Dornak so I assumed there would be none in Trinik. Was I wrong?" D'Mique laid out her blankets and crawled into them as Marco shook his head, no. Sylus unrolled his blankets beside her and continued, "I suggest we sleep while we can," he said, lying down.

"I'm not tired," Marco argued.

"Then you can take the first watch," Sylus said. D'Mique opened her mouth to ask after wards, but Sylus caught her eye and his warning glare caused her to quickly shut her mouth again.

"Fine, I will," Marco answered.

A sharp shake woke D'Mique sometime later. Marco knelt beside her. "What is it?" she whispered.

"It's your turn to take the watch," he informed her.

She hesitated remembering Sylus' glare. "A watch?" she glanced at the sky. Rysk had set, leaving the night sky to the twinkling stars and the forest around them tense with anticipation, poised on the edge of dawn. "Okay," she said, climbing out of bed, draping a blanket over her shoulders. She watched Marco lay down beside Sylus then stirred the fire and looked around the clearing.

Small animals rustled in the forest. An occasional breeze blew through the trees. All was quiet. D'Mique settled back against a tree not far from the fire, her muscles and joint complaining loudly as she slid to the ground. With a sigh she rearranged the blanket, covering herself more completely, keeping out the cold early morning air. Yet despite the blanket, the cold settled into her bones, stiffening her limbs. Hours seemed to pass before Sylus stirred. D'Mique looked up at the movement. "Good morning, Commander," she greeted. Sylus stared at her for a moment then looked to the brightening sky.

"No one woke me for a turn at watch," he said, standing and stretching.

"It was only a few hours until dawn when Marco woke me," she answered. "But why did we even need to set a watch?" she asked studying him, "Last night you set a ward."

Sylus chuckled. "You won't always travel with a mage who can set wards. Besides Marco wasn't tired." D'Mique joined his soft chuckle. After their laughter died Sylus studied Marco a moment before shaking him awake. "Time to go," he said.

Marco struggled to stand, his face thick with sleep. D'Mique smiled to herself. "Bravado must always be paid for," she thought, standing as well. The pain piercing her thighs warned her that she should heed her own advice. Gritting her teeth against the discomfort she helped clean up the clearing and put out the fire. Once finished they started down the road again, eating as they walked.

Morning had not yet turned to afternoon when they came to the village of Scala, doorway to the Dark Forest, the trees fading away and the walled village springing from the grasslands at the edge of the forest. From here several trade roads snaked off through the trees leading to more walled human villages. Beyond the town and the forest spread a vast grassland, rolling out as far as D'Mique could see. Looking out at the plains it suddenly occurred to her that she had never been this far from home and had never seen so much open terrain. She hesitated as the forest fell away. Most of her wandering had been within the Dark Forest and never more than a day's journey from a fort. Distant mountains, the Dragon Hills, drew her eyes westward. On the highest peak the stories said, the marble palace of the Earth Master sat, its highest tower, the Tower of the Elements, piercing the sky. From studying her mother's maps she knew that further north beyond the Fanterra Plain and lost in the distance, the Quartz Mountains, the tallest mountains on the Southern Peninsula, reached skyward. *"Maybe one day,"* she thought, *"I'll get to see them."*

"D'Mique!" Sylus called, noticing that she had stopped, "Come. If we hurry, we will reach the Dragon Hills by sunset." He turned and continued down the road toward town digging in his pack as he walked looking for something. Marco fell in behind him as D'Mique hurried to catch up. The gate lay open before them and a pair of bored guards nodded them through when they reached it. Inside the wall a wide road ran the length of Scala. On either side dusty two-story buildings, most of them inns and taverns, greeted them. D'Mique slowed again, almost stopping as she tried to digest her new surroundings. In addition to the inns and taverns there was a bank and a large stable. But very few houses and no garden plots could be seen from the main road. Sylus led them to the stable pushing his way passed the crowds that lined the road. The trade route hub attracted people of all species and although most were human, lithe goblins, marked by their earthen skin tones, and elves, set apart from the rest by their white hair and pale skin, also milled through the town. A variety of Semians waited for the caravans. They were merchants and merchant-guards, wayward travelers, and fortune hunters. Scala, D'Mique decided, was less village than she had assumed. Instead it could best be described as a crossroad. Being with Sylus the last few cycles had numbed her to the existence of elves, but she found herself staring at the goblins, called Soil Children in the old tales. She could count on one hand the number of times she'd seen a real one. Only the richest merchant caravans could afford to employ them for the trip to the southern desert. But now her eyes fell upon their earthen skin everywhere she looked. With difficulty she forced herself to follow Sylus down the main road.

"Sir," Sylus called to a stable hand as they entered the building. "I need three good traveling horses." The stable hand looked over at them setting down the saddle and polish he had been working with.

He lumbered toward them before asking, "Where you headed?"

"Dragon Ridge," Sylus answered. The man almost choked at his answer, visibly working to regain his composure before nodding. Sylus didn't seem to notice the man's reaction.

This way sir Elf," he instructed, turning on his heels and leading them deeper into the stables, past the horses in their boxes, each step accompanied by straw and leather-scented air. "These are the horses for sale," the hand said bringing them to a large box at the back. "In my opinion any of them will get you to the Master's palace."

"Thank you," Sylus said entering the box. D'Mique's heart skipped a beat as Marco followed him, "Wait I don't know how to ride a horse," she thought. There were four horses tied in the box, two brown geldings, a large black stallion and a white mare. Sylus surveyed each in turn, running his hands over their legs, lifting their hooves and lips.

"How much for all four?" he asked at last.

The man eyed him for a moment. "Three hundred gold," he said finally.

Sylus laughed, a surprisingly deep sound. "Surely, you're joking, sir. They are good animals, true, but they are older, a bit worn," Sylus shook his head for emphasis.

"Two-fifty then," the man said.

"And you'll throw in the saddles?" Sylus prodded. The stable hand nodded reluctantly. "Then it's a deal," Sylus said reaching into his pouch and pulling out several gold bars and coins. After Sylus counted it out the man pocketed the gold and went to work saddling the three male horses.

"Commander," D'Mique whispered as the stable hand worked, "I don't know anything about riding horses."

"You'll learn soon enough," Sylus said with a smile before striding across the stable to the big black horse.

"I'm starting to hate that smile," she decided. With a scowl she watched the elf work, running a rope from the stallion's saddle to the white mare's halter. Then he clambered up onto the black horse's back and waited for D'Mique and Marco to mount theirs.

D'Mique studied the horse that the stable hand brought her, looking into its large, lazy brown eyes, patting it cautiously. "Put your foot here," the stable hand said with a patient smile, indicating the stirrup, "Then I'll help you up onto its back." With a grateful nod she did as he asked and, with his help, hoisted herself into the saddle. The horse took a tentative step forward and D'Mique quickly grabbed hold of it with both hands, squeezing her legs tight around its girth.

Sylus chuckled. "Take hold of the reins Lady," he said, moving his horse next to hers and showing her how to hold them. "Tap it with your heels to make it go, pull the reins to turn its head in the direction you want to go and pull back to stop." D'Mique nodded her understanding. Once he had given the same quick lesson to Marco, the three started through town at a slow pace, Marco and D'Mique bouncing in their saddles as they left through the northern gate.

As they traveled D'Mique stared out across the tall grass plain, her body jarring from side to side with each step the horse took. They traveled a vague road as it wound its way toward the Dragon Hills, Sylus setting a pace just slow enough to allow the novice riders to maintain their seats. They rode through the day stopping to eat and stretch their legs when the suns had reached the mid-point of their journey. Then it was back on the horses, Sylus pressing them into a fast trot, the jarring side to side motion replaced by a steady hammering. Watching them a moment Sylus suggested they try to move in rhythm with the horse. By sunset they had reached the edge of a cool forest which stretched westward blanketing the Dragon Hills. Behind them lay the lonely expanse of the Fanterra Plain. Here at the verge of the forest, the faint road divided, one continuing west, deeper into the forest, while the other road turned north. Sylus led them westward, passing beneath large, leafy boughs into the Dragon Hills Forest.

D'Mique noted the piles of leaf litter and pine needles covering the road, showing that few people traveled this way. At the first clearing they came to they made camp. Eager to be out of the saddle, D'Mique nearly leapt to the ground. Her legs aching and unwilling to hold her up, she sunk to her knees, grimacing as joints and muscles complained bitterly. Ignoring them Sylus left to gather wood and make the fire. Marco limped over to her and collected her horse. "I'll tend to them," he said. He eyed her, "Are you all right?" he asked. She nodded and glared as she made her way back to her feet trying to prove she was fine. Marco tilted his head and shrugged. As he unsaddled the horses and tied them out, he watched her unpack the bedrolls and lay them out glancing furtively about the camp as she worked.

When the fire was burning brightly, a golden yellow this time, they sat down to another dinner of travel rations, passing the time in silence. After dinner both D'Mique and Marco crawled stiffly into bed while Sylus offered to take the first watch. D'Mique eyed him but said nothing about setting wards. She closed her eyes and was soon asleep, Marco snoring beside her. Once D'Mique and Marco were sleeping, Sylus slipped into the Mage Realm and sent his mind drifting, looking for his Master's pocket realm construct. He opened his mind to his Master's call and listened. "Sylus," Master Myrth thrummed in his mind. "You are near?"

"We will arrive before sunset tomorrow Master," Sylus informed him, his Mage Realm body coming to rest in a kneeling position surrounded by the familiar pink mist. "Master, I must warn you, the human Marco is highly magical, easily as powerful as any Syra. However I cannot truly test him as he is shielded within the Realm."

"Really?" The connection to the Earth Master faded suddenly before Sylus could answer the question. The pink mist construct winked out of existence. He opened his eyes returning easily to the physical realm. He sat watch for a few minutes contemplating Myrth's reaction to the news. Then he set a safety-net ward and went to sleep.

As the suns' light brightened the sky D'Mique woke. She moved slowly, testing her body for aches and pains. Her limbs protested loudly as she climbed out of the bedroll, muscles agonizing over the movement. "All I did was ride a horse," she thought, "and walk a few miles." She surveyed the campsite. Beside her the fire had died leaving the camp cold. Her eyes rested on Sylus, sleeping beside the dead fire instead of keeping watch. She limped over to him and cautiously shook him awake. "I didn't think you would stay awake for a watch, Commander," she accused with a smile after he'd opened his eyes and focused on her.

Glaring, Sylus struggled out of bed. "Wake Marco," he said, dismissing her remark, "We must hurry."

They packed quickly, the stiffness remaining in D'Mique's legs as they worked. When it came time to remount D'Mique stared up at the saddle, contemplating the distance between the horse's back and the ground. "Do you need help?" Marco asked, stopping on his way to his own ride.

"I hate horses," she thought, "I'd rather walk on my own feet, thank you." She nodded and Marco helped her up into the saddle. From where she sat she watched as Marco fumbled his way onto his own horse. When he finally sat upright atop the horse he smiled at her, a friendly and open, if hesitant smile, and the first real one she'd seen from him. As the suns cleared the horizon, they ate breakfast as they traveled. For hours D'Mique's muscles protested every harsh step her horse took. The road wound through gullies and over hills, never taking them up into the surrounding mountains. As the day wore on the track grew well-worn, proof that more people traveled it. The feel of the surrounding forest changed as well, shifting from lonesome isolation to cheerful companionship. Marco hummed as they traveled, the sound drifting around them, floating outward through the trees. D'Mique glanced at him occasionally trying to place the tune—its familiarity nagging at the corner of her mind. Each time their eyes met he smiled at her. At first she ignored his overture, but soon she caught herself smiling back, shaking her head.

"Here we are," Sylus announced late in the afternoon. Marco's humming died. A massive white marble wall rose before them. There was no defensive clearing around the palace, the pine trees growing in a dense thicket all around and up against the walls. D'Mique studied the walls, "There aren't any ramparts or even any arrow slits," she thought incredulously, "but the gate seems stout enough." She said aloud, "It's not very defensible, really." She pointed toward the trees growing against the walls. "You have no warning; any enemy could sneak right up to the wall, even climb a tree and gain access without anyone noticing. There are no ramparts, no arrow slits, nothing!"

Marco and Sylus looked at her. "Well it is the Earth Master's home. I doubt many would attack it," Marco pointed out.

"Master Myrth can manipulate the stone as he sees fit," Sylus added. "He can stretch the wall higher or push it lower. He can add ramparts, towers or arrow slits and balconies. He can even seal the wall completely so that there is no door." Sylus dismounted and led his two horses to the closed gate. By the time D'Mique and Marco followed him the gate was opening, allowing them into the palace grounds.

The Master of Earth

Beyond the gate lay a dark gray cobblestone courtyard graced by a large fountain, all of it framed by the blinding white marble walls. The fountain rose in three tiers, each one a jumble of rollicking carved statuary, glittering rubies and emeralds forming the eyes of each stone beast. Framing the courtyard and stretching beyond it toward the buildings of Dragon Ridge grew a verdant rose garden. Red, pink and yellow blossoms relieved the coldness of the surrounding stone. The buildings of Dragon Ridge were understated. The Earth Master's "Palace" consisted of a long, single-story structure made from the same white marble as the palace walls crouching opposite the gate. An identical building ran along the wall to D'Mique's left. Stone paths led from the courtyard to the buildings fanning out to create verandas in front of each one. Slightly off-center, between the fountain and the back wall, a large white tower reached for the sky.

D'Mique stared at the soldiers milling about in front of the building to her left. They were all goblins and fit the same mold as the merchant guards she had seen in Scala—tall, lanky bodies, earth-tone skin and long black hair. Their faces were a series of sharp angles and edges, high cheek-bones, short pointed ears, and sharp chins. When they smiled or laughed fangs caught the sunlight, and each gesture drew D'Mique's attention to their shiny black claws. Each one wore the same uniform: leather bracers and ring mail jerkins, similar to the one she owned. Many also wore padded leather armor on their thighs, although most had only thick wool trousers and knee-high boots. While a number of soldiers hailed Sylus when they saw him, the majority of the Earth Master's soldiers cautiously studied her and Marco, their faces unreadable.

A human in black and white livery—a black doublet and hose with a white shirt—came for their horses, speaking with Sylus for a moment before leading the four animals away to the right. There didn't appear to be a stable in that direction, but other horses were tethered along the right-hand wall. "Come you two," Sylus said, "The Master is waiting." D'Mique followed slowly, resurveying the buildings around her. "This is the palace?" she asked herself, "Calling Dragon Ridge the Palace of the Earth Master was a joke! This is a fort at best!" Shaking her head she hurried after the diminutive elf following him across the courtyard, past the fountain and around the base of the large white tower to the entrance of the building along the back wall.

Two goblin guards also dressed in black and white livery instead of armor, flanked the door, saluting Sylus as he approached before opening the door for them. Within, another human servant took their packs and disappeared back the way they had come, closing the door behind them. D'Mique waited for her eyes to adjust to the sudden dimness. She could just make out two more doors, one of sturdy oak on her right and the other of stone on her left, leading from the entrance hall. Sylus knocked on the stone door and waited for it to open. Then he motioned for them to enter the dark room beyond. "Welcome," a low, thrumming voice greeted as they stepped from the light. D'Mique jumped at the sound. Sylus' brows furrowed in warning, demanding silently that she enter the room. With a deep breath, D'Mique squelched the sudden wave of panic that threatened to engulf her and stepped into the soft, deep shadows beyond the stone door. Sylus followed them through the door closing it behind them.

Before them two torches suddenly came to life, illuminating a hooded figure sitting on a stone throne—the Earth Master. The cloak's hood covered his face completely, just as it hid his body. The only visible features were his three-fingered, clawed hands as they rested on the arms of the throne. She watched fascinated, as he reached up and scratched the head of a small dragon that lay draped over his shoulders, his claws combing through the dragon's feathery mane, threading between the dragon's pearly horns. The small, sinewy green and blue reptile wound around the Earth Master's shoulders, snake-like in its attitude, its tail lashing like an angry cat's, its red eyes glaring at the people who dared to interrupt. D'Mique averted her eyes fear creeping through her. "This is the strongest mage on the planet," she repeated over and over. Sylus knelt about ten steps from the throne and D'Mique imitated him, kneeling a step behind him and to his left. She caught sight of Marco head bowed, kneeling beside her. "The most powerful Mage on the planet!" she thought again, heart racing. She caught herself surveying the room, looking for the exit. Oil lamps and torches began burning along the walls, pushing the shadows further away. Four more goblin warriors stood along the walls, hands on their swords or folded across their chests. She could see no door although she assumed there was still one behind her.

"Welcome back Commander," greeted the Master, his voice so incredibly deep D'Mique could almost feel it vibrating in her bones.

"I have returned to you, my Master, at last. My mission has been a success."

"Rise please, my friend," the Master instructed.

D'Mique started to stand. "Not you human," a goblin snapped—the warning in his voice clear. D'Mique froze then sank back to her knees.

"Master, I am pleased to deliver your Man Children from the Nesting. This is the Lady Warrior of the village Dornak," he paused, "And this is Marco of Trinik. I have tested him and found the ability to work the forcelines strong within him."

"Rise before me Marco of Trinik and Lady of Dornak," the Master bid. This time the goblin guards remained silent as she stood. She tried to meet the Master's eyes but a fine tremor ran through her as she stood and she could only glance at him intermittently. The Master leaned forward allowing the firelight to penetrate the shadows beneath his hood. Warm light danced across the bronze hawk's beak that dominated his face. Small, coppery feathers surrounded the beak, framing large pearl gray eyes and black lips, which pulled back in a fierce smile at the corners of the beak. "Welcome, Children of Man," the Master spoke, forming the words in his throat and barely moving his thick lips or beak. "I am Myrth, Master of Earth, Keeper of the Dragon Hills and all lands surrounding them. Be at ease in my home."

"Thank you Master," Marco said bowing his head; D'Mique imitated him.

With the welcome over Myrth dismissed the humans and focused his attention on his elf servant. "Sylus," he continued, "the remaining guards are below ground. All in all they have been well-behaved. However, I am glad you are here to set their energies toward more productive tasks." Sylus gaped at him for a second and then glowered over his own thoughts but he offered no rejoinder. "The three of you may go," Myrth concluded sitting back, sinking into the shadows again. In unison they bowed again, and backed a few steps away from the throne before turning and leaving.

Once they had returned to the antechamber Sylus stared at the closed door for a moment before looking between Marco and D'Mique. "Come," he said. He led them out of the room and across the rose garden to the door of the second building where the goblin soldiers were milling about. As they moved through the area activities stopped, conversation ebbed, and glittering eyes followed them. D'Mique caught more than one set of steely eyes resting on her, traveling to the sword and drawing a smirk from thick black lips before returning to her face. She set her jaw and glared at the back of Sylus' head as they moved through the goblins' ranks. Inside the building there lay a large, sparsely furnished room, where half a dozen goblins lounged about on mismatched wooden furniture. They hastily regained their feet when Sylus entered each doing a double take at the sight of the two humans following him, eyes of green and gold resting longest on D'Mique. In the center of the room ringed by large flagstones, a wrought-iron spiral staircase led down into the earth.

Sylus started down the staircase but D'Mique stopped. Marco peered around her curious. "We're going underground?" she asked before the elf disappeared.

"Well it is the palace of the Earth Master, Lady," Sylus replied looking up at her. "You didn't think that two little buildings made up the entire palace," he finished with a smile that simply failed to be innocent as sarcasm touched its corners. Appreciative goblins chuckled around her. Glaring D'Mique followed the elf down the stairs Marco laughing quietly at her back.

Myrth's Honor Guard

They descended into a stone fortress and each floor they passed through was airy and well-lit despite being underground. A variety of people—mostly uniformed goblin soldiers and liveried human servants—formed the crowds who lived within Dragon Ridge. "This first level," Sylus began, as he stopped at the landing between spiraling flights, "is where you will find the barracks and servant quarters. When your training is complete you will be given rooms on this level." They moved quickly to the next floor, leaving D'Mique with an impression of the first floor consisting of plush red and molten gold. The next level was more sedate, decorated in hushed greens and mottled browns. "This level is where the officer's quarters are, both military and state officers. My quarters are here," Sylus added without stopping. On the third level there was a sudden drop in activity. The walls were brushed stone, undecorated, and only a few random human servants wandered past as Sylus continued his tour. "The third level is full of storerooms," he said, "and the fourth," he held out his arms coming at last to the bottom of the stairs which ended in a dirt floor, "is your new home."

D'Mique looked around briefly then back up the spiral tunnel to the surface. She swallowed hard. They were in a small, square room with two doors and a shuttered window. "To your right is the classroom; to your left your quarters," Sylus directed.

"And the window?" D'Mique and Marco asked together, looking at it and then at each other.

"Ah, it's enchanted," Sylus said, crossing to it and pulling the shutters open. Beyond the window the Dragon Hills could be seen in the distance, surrounded by grassy plains that waved in a gentle breeze. It was an aerial view of the Fanterra Plains as the land would look from somewhere above the Dark Forest.

"Cute," D'Mique said, realizing that she had stared out the window a bit too long to be nonchalant.

"One of Master Myrth's and Mistress Jay's more interesting tricks," Sylus said before closing the window's shutters again. "Well, come on. Let's meet the rest of our group." He led them to the left throwing the door open without ceremony.

"Commander Sylus!" a goblin guard just inside the door barked upon seeing him. D'Mique jumped and noted that Sylus did as well. In addition to the guards, three lanky forms occupied the large room, one lying on a bed while two others lounged in a couple wooden chairs. They flew to their feet with the guard's announcement forming a rigid row as Sylus entered and crossed to them.

Stopping just inside the door D'Mique eyed the guards on either side before taking in the room and its other occupants. Bordering on starkness, the room held little more than a pair of tables, each surrounded by four chairs, and two bunk beds. Even this far underground warm dry air filled the room. Sylus surveyed the people before him. The first two in line were goblins, both nearly a head taller than D'Mique and Marco, looming over the short elf, and both with typical goblin features—long black hair, long pointed noses, and sharp-tipped ears. The skin of the taller one was a burnt red-orange, the color of wet sandstone, while the other was a sickly olive-green. The green one smiled hesitantly, flashing great white fangs in their direction.

The third person, who stood even in height with the goblins, had pale milky white skin, his hair falling in a long thick mane as pure white as new-fallen snow. His ears, their length adorned with three golden hoops each, came to narrow points nearly three inches above his head. His eyes were the bright pink of a tropical flower, a startling splash of color amidst the chiseled whiteness of his complexion. D'Mique stared at him, frozen, mouth open. "He's a Land-Nymph!" she thought. "He can't be, but he is! They're practically extinct!" For a moment the improbability of his existence stunned her. Then she thought, "I wonder what he's doing here."

"Names?" Sylus asked, interrupting her train of thought.

"Tierren," the red goblin croaked harshly, eyes never dropping to the commander.

"Rogan," the other goblin said, his voice holding a slick oily coating, his smile faltering as he looked down on Sylus.

"Clippen, Commander," said the Land-Nymph, barely above a whisper.

Sylus glared at them for a long intense moment, drawing a nervous fidget from the Land-Nymph. "This is Marco and D'Mique," Sylus introduced. Tierren and Clippen glanced at them, barely flicking their eyes toward the humans. Rogan smiled again and a troubling wave of discomfiture crawled through D'Mique. Sylus turned to the nearest guard, "I should have six guards here. Where are the other three?"

"Through the other door Commander," the guard supplied, gesturing, "Master Myrth ordered them separated."

"Separated?" Sylus repeated. The guard nodded once and Sylus turned to eye the three cadets in front of him. The Land-Nymph blushed, his face turning a delicate pink to match his eyes. No explanations were offered. With a glare Sylus stalked to the next door and opened it, Marco and D'Mique following him.

"Commander Sylus!" another goblin guard barked as they entered. This time neither D'Mique nor Sylus jumped at the sound. Although this room was identical to the first, the three people who rushed to stand at attention formed a less-uniform line than the previous three had formed. The first figure in line, another Land-Nymph, brought an audible gasp from D'Mique. "Two extinct creatures in one place!" she thought, shaking her head. His curly, hot pink hair and angry, emerald-green eyes, were bright gashes of color against his milky white skin. His high pointed ears held no adornments, but she guessed that he matched the other Land-Nymph in height and his chiseled features were so similar to the first one they could have been brothers. An elf stood beside the pink-haired Land-Nymph, his pale skin only slightly pinker than the Land-Nymph's. He smiled at Sylus. "Commander Sylus, I am Genow," he introduced, his deep, black-orb eyes smiling as well, traveling from the Commander to Marco and D'Mique without faltering. He stood shorter than either human but taller than Sylus. Sylus did not acknowledge the greeting. Instead he moved on to the third person in line who stubbornly looked down at the floor, his black hair hiding most of his face. "He seems human enough," D'Mique thought studying him, "He could be Marco's younger brother. But he can't be human, can he?"

"A Mortak?" Sylus asked, surprised, stopping in front of him and answering D'Mique's unspoken question.

"Commander," the Mortak said, raising his head, his solid silver eyes—similar to an elf's with no whites, no pupils, and no irises—focused on the mid-distance. "I am Kryoso," he said in a lilting, nearly falsetto voice that belied the male perfection of his body.

D'Mique bit her lip, worrying. "Land-Nymphs and Mortaks?" she thought, "At home, they're both creatures of legend, and now I'm standing in the same room with three of them!" The absurdity of the thought brought on a sudden urge to laugh, chasing away the worry that haunted her.

"And you?" Sylus asked the curly-haired Land-Nymph.

"I am Trillip, Commander," he answered noncommittally. Sylus nodded.

"This is D'Mique and Marco," the Commander introduced again.

"Humans?" Genow asked.

"A lady?" echoed Kryoso, his black eyebrows raised and his pupil-less eyes wide. D'Mique felt the scowl deepen across her face.

"Yes," Sylus answered. "Now," he walked to the wall separating the two rooms and laid his hands against the stone closing his eyes. A moment later the wall melted away disappearing into the ceiling and floor accompanied by a sibilant sound. The guard closest to Sylus grabbed the wooden door before it could fall. The commander dropped his hands watching as the two rooms became one.

"I hope that we will not need to separate again," he said to the entire room, "We will conduct some basic training beginning tomorrow morning to assure you are all fit for duty. Until then you are confined to quarters." He glared at each one of them before leaving, the goblin guards trailing behind him, lugging the superfluous wooden door.

Once they were gone, all eyes turned to D'Mique and Marco.

"Humans," the green goblin said with a disdainful sneer on his black lips.

"Perhaps Master Myrth is, you know—" the curly-haired Land-Nymph said, tapping a clawed finger to his temple, smiling just enough for his sharp little fangs to shine between his lips.

The elf gasped, "Do not say such things, Trillip. Master Myrth hears all within these walls."

"If that were true," said Clippen, the white-haired Land-Nymph, "Then he would not have left the two goblins together." He smiled wide, his own razor-sharp teeth glinting between full lips.

"Just as you would not disobey a direct order from the Water Master, we would not disobey a direct order from the Earth Master," the red goblin said with a note of offense in his gravelly voice. D'Mique blinked, trying to follow their conversation.

"Lady," Kryoso interrupted, "You may choose one of these last two bunks."

She turned and smiled at the Mortak, "Thank you," grateful for an excuse to move away from the main group.

"Surely, as improbable as it is you are mages?" Genow asked, also dropping the subject of the Earth Master. "I can think of no other reason to include humans in our group, especially female ones."

D'Mique's scowl burrowed into her features, hot anger seething through her. "I am a warrior," she spat, "I have studied the sword since I was a small child! If you have a problem with me being here take it up with the Earth Master!" The elf took a step back and she passed her glare onto the next in line until she reached the two goblins.

"I'm a mage," Marco supplied, his words dropping behind hers like a stone. A collective gasp whispered through the room and they all stared silently at him.

D'Mique knew what they were all thinking, "He can't be! There are no magic humans!"

"I am also a mage," the Mortak said turning to Marco, the first to recover from his remark, "As is Clippen."

"I meant no offense Lady, truly," the elf replied once the silence had been broken. The goblins and Land-Nymphs turned to study her again. "I just thought magical ability was the only reason to include either Mortaks or humans in a military unit," the elf continued. The goblins and

Land-Nymphs chuckled adding a harshness to the elf's words that D'Mique suddenly realized the elf did not mean to imply.

Kryoso's eyes shimmered as his brows drew down. "Believe what you will elf," he hissed, almost snake-like, "My presence here is a gift from Master Marladon, Master of Fire, Keeper of the Black Lands and a Mortak!"

"I do not doubt your abilities, Kryoso, nor Master Marladon's. I merely comment that magic is the only reason to include you," Genow tried to explain, his voice plaintive, honest surprise at Kryoso's and D'Mique's anger painting his face. He looked between them almost frantic.

The red goblin smiled as he made his way over to stand in front of D'Mique. "Let it be, Genow," he said coming to the elf's rescue. "I think we have a very well-rounded unit. Two archers," he indicated the other goblin and himself, "two swordsmen," the Land-Nymphs, "you, Genow, a healer, with two Mages, despite their origins," he nodded to Marco and Kryoso, "and a toy," he finished with a suggestive sneer at D'Mique. Dark male chuckles crawled through the room.

"Toy!?" D'Mique shouted.

Tierren nodded smugly. "I see no other use for a human female," he said, folding his long arms across his chest, shifting his feet to an open stance. D'Mique's sword flashed from its scabbard.

"No, Lady!" Kryoso shouted, reaching for her arm, but he was too late. From out of nowhere, Tierren caught her upstroke with his own blade sending a harsh clang echoing through the room.

"Oh, Tierren," the white-haired Land-Nymph sighed, shaking his head.

As quickly as the fight began it ended. The floor erupted between D'Mique and Tierren, knocking them backwards to the ground. The air escaped her lungs as stars burst in front of her eyes. "Not again," she thought, recalling the brief scuffle she'd had with Sylus. Beneath her the earth continued moving, piling up around her, encasing her in a stone prison. "No!" she screamed, trying to rise in a blind panic, but she could not lift more than her head, and that, only as far as her hair would allow. Her eyes found the goblin first marking his position. The earth had grown up around his prone form embedding him in stone as well. Seeing him trapped as surely as she was D'Mique took a shuddering breath in an attempt to refill her lungs and regain control.

The door at the far end of the room crashed open startling most of them, and Sylus entered, a small white blizzard storming across the room. He seemed more than tall enough from the floor as he glared at all of them, "To bed, now!" he roared. Everyone able to do so scrambled to their beds lay down and closed their eyes. For a moment Sylus stood, fists clenching and unclenching at his sides. From the floor near him D'Mique watched the muscles of his arms work under his skin. A full minute passed before he sat down beside her head, anger glittering in his eyes. "How is it that you are causing trouble Lady?" he asked, his voice straining for calm. "Can you not hold your temper? Tierren's remarks are hardly the worst you will encounter."

D'Mique swallowed hard, her chest constricted by the stone. "Yes Commander," she breathed.

"This fight is finished," he said voice lowered, "but no swordsman you meet will take you seriously Lady. You are out of your league from their point of view. You are just a silly little girl," he said, emphasizing every word. "If you rise to the bait every time, you will have no peace and you will prove them correct." Their eyes locked for a long minute Sylus waiting for her to digest his words. She nodded slightly in reply before he passed a hand along her body causing the stone to melt back beneath the dirt floor just as he had done before with the wall, releasing her. Freed, she sat up quickly, scrambling away, backward, from the still prone goblin. Sylus contemplated her for a moment more head tilted to one side. "Go to bed Lady." he instructed, "And remember what happens when a sword is drawn in the Earth Master's residence."

"Yes Commander," she said, standing, eyes still glued on Tierren as she crossed to the back of the room. Marco had taken the bottom bed so she climbed to the top bunk and lay down on her side watching Sylus where he sat beside Tierren's head.

The goblin lay calm in the stone prison—a Child of the Soil returned to his home. "Master Myrth has been less than enthused by your behavior since arriving, goblin," Sylus began, his voice low but carrying in the silent room. "I find that hard to believe. You are his creature to command, he could stop your heart on a whim, and yet, you provoke him. I do not know why he has not sent the lot of you away as I would have. Honor guards are easy enough to assemble."

"I have not defied a direct order. He can end my life for nothing less," Tierren answered. "Truth be known Commander, I do not wish to be here. My wife awaits me in Hawkethorne Valley."

Sylus sat contemplating his words for a moment before answering. "If I have no more trouble from you I will send for your wife in three cycles." When Tierren acknowledged the deal, he continued, "Either way, Master Myrth is determined to retain you, all of you, for his guard." Sylus looked around at the others raising his voice, "Making yourselves unwanted is not going to change his mind." He released the goblin as he had D'Mique. "Now go to bed."

"Yes Commander," Tierren said. He rose easily and made his way to the top bunk near the door. Sylus stood a minute more eyeing them then he turned on his heels and left, shutting the door quietly behind him.

Genow lay on the next top bunk over. He turned to look across at D'Mique. "I would like to offer you my apologies Lady. I did not mean to provoke you in any way. I," he paused, "I believe you are a warrior. Only a warrior of top quality could have stopped Tierren's thrust. Masterfully done," he smiled at her in the slowly dimming light.

Before she could reply the torches and lamps winked out. "Magic torches?" she thought, staring at the one remaining lamp, its light cheery in the darkness. "Are you a swordsman?" she asked the elf.

"No. Although Sylus is one, most elves prefer the bow as we tend to be too slight for swords." D'Mique chuckled at the thought of Genow being too small for a sword but Sylus not. Genow glared at her until she explained her merriment then joined her in a quiet chuckle. "Do not judge Sylus by his height," he warned, "He is an Earth Blade, mixing Earth Magic with his sword techniques, making him truly a terrible force. Re'Ana, the elf servant of the Wind Mistress, is his only equal with the blade. And she also must mix magic and steel." Genow's smile saddened as the silence grew around them. "There is another elfin Blade. Like you she is not a Mage. I hope you will be able to meet her one day. She is with the Water Master now." He lapsed into silence again and D'Mique's eyes closed. "I was hoping to be bound to the Water Master before Master Myrth sent for me," Genow said with a sleepy sigh.

"Nepo isn't strong enough to bind an elf," the next person over said. Genow turned his head towards the speaker and, opening her eyes, D'Mique sat up high enough to see the voice's owner, the white-haired Land-Nymph, Clippen.

"Oh really, Clippen?" said Genow, "Tell me, are all Land-Nymphs experts on the Water Master?" Genow's voice held a bitter edge.

Clippen rose up on his elbow facing them, mirroring D'Mique. "No. Only the ones who are cousin to his apprentice," Clippen returned.

"Water's Chosen is your cousin?" Genow asked, sitting up.

"All Land-Nymphs are cousins," said Kryoso from the bunk beneath Genow, interrupting their conversation. "At least, that's what we say up north. They are so terribly inbred."

"Hush, Mortak!" hissed Tierren, who lay on the top bunk beyond Clippen, closest to the door. "If Sylus must return again tonight we will not be sent to bed but to the classroom instead."

"HOW DARE YOU!" roared Trillip, drowning out the goblin's words and rolling out of bed landing between his bunk and Kryoso's. "Only approved unions are allowed and we sacrifice much to keep from inbreeding!" He swung a clawed fist at the Mortak with a shout of rage. Kryoso fled by rolling off the other side of the bed.

"Get back to bed both of you!" shouted Tierren. Instead Trillip chased after Kryoso, circling the beds. D'Mique gaped, sitting up to watch. "Sylus comes!" Tierren pleaded. "I can feel him! Please! He warns us! To bed!" His words brought no end to the chase. Trillip lunged in blind fury as Kryoso skirted around the far table.

"If your punishment is lacking, Mortak, I will skewer you!" shouted the other goblin, Rogan. "Tierren's wife will be lost!"

"Feign sleep, Lady Warrior," Genow said, "and you, Marco. Perhaps Sylus will spare those who are trying to follow his commands." With that he lay down, closing his eyes.

"Trillip, leave him!" Clippen shouted as the door burst open. Sylus took in the scene and flung his arm in a semi-circle. An explosive earthquake tore through the room flinging the guards from their beds and toppling furniture against the far wall. Beds, tables and chairs clattered to the ground, leaving a vast open space in the center of the room. For the second time that evening, D'Mique felt the stone encase her where she had fallen, leaving only her face free and barely enough room around her chest to breathe.

"I do not believe this!" shouted Sylus once the room had grown still, "If you aren't tired I guess we might as well start our training tonight." Silence lay over the room. Just as suddenly as she'd been encased the stone crept away allowing D'Mique to stand. She looked around. Sylus' quake had decimated the room. Kryoso and Trillip remained embedded in the floor. Trillip lay on his side crying, great, heart-wrenching sobs filling the room while Clippen knelt over him, whispering in his ear. Kryoso had fallen face first to the floor when the quake hit. In order to avoid his face, the earth had pushed him up, bowing his spine. Pain mingled with guilt across his face. The two goblins knelt beside each other, bowing their heads to the floor, facing Sylus, while Genow stood silently beside D'Mique, Marco at her back.

"Peace, Trillip," Sylus said releasing him.

The Land-Nymph curled up into a protective ball, his head on Clippen's thigh, where his sobs slowly quieted. Sylus waited for him to regain control before asking gently for an explanation. "The Mortak was...was mocking us..." Trillip said before trailing off, hiding his face against Clippen.

"Trillip and his love were denied marriage privileges. Their bloodlines are too similar," whispered Clippen as he hugged the other Land-Nymph close to him.

D'Mique looked from them to Kryoso. The pain had left his face and only guilt remained. Sylus considered the Mortak a moment and then released him. Kryoso hurried across to the Land-Nymphs kneeling before them. He touched his head to the floor, "I was wrong. Please forgive my outburst and my actions," he blurted, remaining bowed to the floor, waiting, for several minutes. But his only answer was Trillip's quiet whimpers and the sharp, painful anger in Clippen's pink eyes. When they remained silent Kryoso rose and turned to Sylus, "I will accept the punishment for all of us Commander. It is the least I can do."

Sylus nodded, "Very well Kryoso. Come with me. The rest of you, clean this room then go to bed."

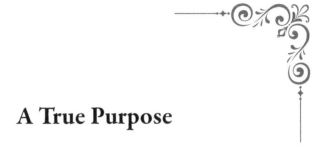

A True Purpose

For D'Mique, it seemed that only a few moments passed between crawling exhausted into bed and being violently shoved awake by Tierren. As she sat up, blankets falling away, a liveried human servant entered with piles of clothing in her arms. She set the pile down on Marco's bed, telling D'Mique, "for both of you," before disappearing as quickly as she'd come. D'Mique riffled through them identifying her three outfits, two beige linen tops with brown trousers, the same uniform the others wore, and a black and white outfit, which she quickly identified as the same livery the servant had been wearing. Draping the beige and brown uniform over her arm she looked around for a place to dress. But there was only the single bathroom the others were lining up to use. "Great," she thought, heart sinking. Sylus' warnings returned replaying in her head, "Don't be a silly girl," she chided herself, taking her place in line with the others.

In front of her, Rogan and Tierren conversed in low guttural whispers, speaking a native goblin dialect, while their eyes wandered toward the door at the far end of the room from time to time. Genow joined the line behind her a yawn splitting his face in two. "Good morning to you, Lady," he greeted. She returned the greeting but did not offer anything else. While Tierren disappeared into the small room to clean up for the day, Rogan stood guard—arms folded across his chest, back to the door, beady eyes taking in the rest of them. D'Mique met his gaze with her own steely look. She congratulated herself silently when he looked away. She expected them to switch places when Tierren exited the room but instead both goblins moved toward their bunks, Rogan taking up their conversation as if there had been no interruption. She entered the bath locking the door behind her before surveying the room. It was dominated by a glass shower stall on her right joined by a small stone bench-like toilet against the far wall and a deep basin on her left that was adorned with a simple mirror.

Although she hadn't showered in days, Genow was still waiting to use the room and she was unsure how long they had to get ready before Sylus expected them for training. Regretfully she chose to wash off quickly in the sink before changing into the clean clothes, checking her reflection briefly after pulling the linen shirt tight around her, tying it closed, and doing her best to ignore a call from Rogan for Genow to force the bathroom door open and expose her. The D'Mique in the mirror looked tired, worn from days on the trail away from home. Tears threatened at the corners of her eyes for a split-second brought on by the thought of home. "Thoughts I can't afford to have," she chided. Dismissing them, she rushed through the rest of her routine, doing her best to tighten her braid up without undoing her hair, before stepping back into the sleeping quarters with her best withering glare in place for Rogan, who only chuckled in reply. Once Genow had dressed and rejoined them Tierren led the way across the hallway, past the shuttered, magic window, to the classroom.

Opening the door, they entered an arena as large as a village square. Polished weapon-racks, loaded with an assortment of blades and pole-arms lined the walls. A vaulted ceiling topped the stone walls, the area noticeably absent any seating meant to accommodate a cheering crowd. Sand, bordered by a pitch-covered track, formed the circular floor they stepped onto as they entered. Against the wall opposite the entrance a stone patio decorated with small wooden tables and chairs, similar to those in the sleeping quarters, occupied a large alcove. Lamps lit the room, chasing the gloom into the far corners of the alcove. As with every other room D'Mique had encountered underground, the air was fresh and dry. In the center of the room Sylus sat on a chair, boredom emanating from him. Kryoso knelt before him digging a hole in the sand with his hands. The elf watched them, silent and unmoving, as they trudged through the sand toward him, Tierren in the lead. "Commander," the goblin greeted, coming to a stop.

Kryoso paused when Sylus stood but the elf glared down at him and barked, "You're not finished yet." The Mortak quickly returned his attention to the ground while Sylus addressed the rest of them. "Every morning," he said, "at the bell, you will report here and run ten laps around the classroom before being excused for breakfast. Breakfast will be brought fifteen minutes after the morning bell. If you hurry your food won't be cold. If you dawdle you risk going hungry. Breakfast will be cleared away thirty minutes after the bell." He studied them for a moment then shouted, "Well? Begin!" Jumping at his command they hurried over to the track and started to run.

"Ten laps," D'Mique thought, "That's not so far. Just pace yourself." But the Land-Nymphs and goblins, their long legs eating up the ground, quickly outdistanced her, Marco, and Genow. She ignored them and concentrated on her breathing and the mechanics of running. With one lap down she found herself pulling even with and then running beside Genow and Marco.

"Surely you are holding back, elf," Marco commented as they jogged together.

"I could go faster, yes," Genow answered, "But this is a very good pace for me. Does the pace suit you, Lady?" he asked looking at D'Mique, his tone taking on a cordial lilt as he spoke to her.

"Yes," she answered. After a few more steps, she asked, "Where are you from Genow?"

"I am most recently of Sea Spray, though I was only there a day."

"Sea Spray, the palace of the Water Master?" Marco asked, panting between his words, not used to running long distances.

"Yes," Genow answered, offering nothing further as they completed their second lap. They jogged in silence for some time, accompanied by the sound of their pounding feet and strong breathing.

"Why were you only in Sea Spray for a day?" D'Mique asked, starting on their third circuit.

Genow hesitated before answering, "I was supposed to join Nepo's honor guard," he spat, "However, Myrth instructed the Land-Nymphs and me to come here and Nepo could not refuse." He added, "On our way through Olimidia, Mara was taken from Trillip." The elf swallowed hard and lapsed into silence, a scowl on his face as memories played through his mind.

D'Mique passed a look over the elf's head to Marco, who had ducked his head, eyes on the track in front of him. She thought, "Sounds like Myrth went out of his way to collect most of us here, not just me."

"Mara is his love?" Marco asked.

Genow nodded. "It's really his story to tell not mine," he said curtly, "Ask him if you wish to know more." Marco nodded his understanding unable to answer aloud.

Tierren and Rogan ran past as the three lapsed into silence. "Humans are so slow!" they called over their shoulders in unison chuckling as they sped away.

"Are you teaching them to run, Genow," Clippen asked as the Land-Nymphs also passed by.

Genow glared after him for a beat before looking to D'Mique and Marco. "If you will excuse me," he said politely. They nodded, smiling as he quickened his pace, pulling away from them. Before half a lap had passed Genow caught up to the Land-Nymphs. He ran alongside them in silence for half a lap before pulling away. Accepting the elf's challenge, the Land-Nymphs picked up their pace, pulling even with the goblins just as Genow left them behind as well. By Genow's fifth lap all five were sprinting around the arena and threatening to lap D'Mique and Marco a second time. As they came up behind the humans Genow increased his pace once again, easily staying in front of the others, flashing by D'Mique and Marco, little more than a white blur with a smug smile on his face.

"He's not even breathing hard," D'Mique noted as the goblins and Land-Nymphs passed them again. Marco watched them go. "How many laps is that for us?" he asked, ignoring her remark.

"Six," D'Mique answered, "Maybe five."

"I think it is five," Marco agreed. Then he laughed breathlessly, "Look," he said, pointing across the room. D'Mique followed his gesture and chuckled too, watching the Land-Nymphs and goblins stagger to a halt, doubled over and out of breath. Noticing what had happened Genow slowed, showing no sign of weariness.

"You really must pace yourselves," Marco said as he and D'Mique caught up to the Land-Nymphs and goblins.

"You know what they say about Fae Folk, Marco," D'Mique added, laughing over her shoulder.

Marco looked at her, puzzled, "What do they say about Fae Folk?" he asked.

She shrugged and laughed again, "I don't know, it sounded good." Marco chuckled appreciatively.

As they caught up to Genow, who had slowed to rejoin them, the elf laughed, "That ought to keep them quiet for a time."

"I don't understand why they're so rude," Marco panted, glancing back at the goblins and Land-Nymphs.

"None of us want to be here," Genow answered, "It's safe to say that we felt if we caused enough trouble Master Myrth would change his mind and send us back."

"I want to be here!" Marco and D'Mique said in unison, identical looks of astonished defensiveness on their faces.

"Well, no one else does," Genow corrected himself. "Master Myrth took most of us from Master Nepo's field class. We chose to serve the Water Master not the Earth Master. Of course we all have our own reasons. As I said before, I was hoping for a bond with the Water Master. If Clippen's cousin is Nepo's apprentice, Clippen was probably hoping to use that influence to win his own apprenticeship. He is highly magical and already fully trained. You," he said turning to Marco, "and Kryoso will be going to Master Island together in twenty-four days to complete the same training." After a moment he continued, "Apparently, Tierren had to leave his wife behind. I think Rogan is Tierren's blood brother." Noting their confused looks he explained, "He owes a debt to Tierren and was obliged to come. Because of that debt Rogan will support Tierren in all things until it is repaid."

"And Kryoso?" Marco asked. D'Mique looked to the center of the room where Kryoso still knelt, digging his hole.

"I don't know exactly," Genow admitted. "Marladon and Myrth had a huge argument a few days ago. Then Kryoso showed up. He says he's a gift from Marladon." Genow stopped suddenly, abruptly ending their conversation and facing Sylus. "I count ten laps, Commander." His sudden halt caused D'Mique to falter as well, nearly stopping beside the elf. Instead she forced herself to keep moving, her lungs beginning to complain, her legs growing heavier with each step.

"As do I, Genow," Sylus returned. The Commander's gaze rested on D'Mique, following her progress, goading her to run on. Glaring, she hurried to catch up to Marco and continue their laps. Just as Genow reached the tables and sat, liveried servants brought in trays of food. Hot, sweet spices filled the air, drawing a noisy complaint from D'Mique's stomach and reminding her that she had not eaten since breakfast the previous morning. Her mouth watering she turned her attention to finishing her laps.

"My count is one more lap for Clippen, Trillip, Tierren and Rogan," Sylus supplied, "three more laps for Marco and the lady, and ten laps for Kryoso." D'Mique looked over at the Mortak. He was still digging in the dirt.

"Does it seem fair to you to make him run laps?" she asked Marco.

He laughed. "Lady we're in the military. Nothing is fair anymore."

"He hasn't slept all night. He's probably been digging all night." Just then the Land-Nymphs passed them running at a near sprint. Tierren ran past as well. Rogan pulled up short, jogging slowly, almost a fast walk, beside D'Mique.

"I agree with you Lady," the goblin said. She looked up at him, "The Mortak is stuck digging a hole that fills itself, a Filling Hole. I've seen Nepo and Marladon use similar punishments."

"What do you mean?" Marco asked.

"Kryoso has been told to dig until he hits a large stone slab. It's actually quite close to the surface. But Sylus uses his magic to move the slab every now and then so that Kryoso will never reach it. He will stay there digging until he collapses from exhaustion. Despite his attitude, he is a Mortak and a race does not live in a volcanic valley without gaining strength and stubbornness." D'Mique looked between Kryoso and Rogan, who continued, "I am satisfied with his punishment, as is Tierren. Are you?"

"Satisfied how?" Marco asked cautiously. D'Mique echoed him.

"Satisfied that it need not continue," the goblin said with a wink. D'Mique gaped at his words, studying his expression, which was carefully blank.

"I'm satisfied, but—" Marco began.

"Good!" Rogan cut in, clapping him on the shoulder with a black-clawed hand. Then he explained, "The Land-Nymphs are still angered by his comments. I don't know how Genow feels, but he is already eating. Tierren cannot chance Sylus' anger. Therefore, that leaves the three of us. I wouldn't be able to do it alone, but you'll help me." The goblin smiled down at them, wide enough to show off large, black incisors glinting between harsh white fangs.

"Help you do what?" D'Mique asked, her stomach shrinking at the thought of doing anything with the goblin.

"Ease his punishment and end it," Rogan said slowing to a walk. D'Mique and Marco slowed beside him. "When I finish my lap, I have time enough to eat breakfast before our next training session begins. Although we are supposed to use the entire time to eat, it belongs solely to us and we can use it as we see fit. When you finish your laps, the same free time rule applies. Instead of eating we can help Kryoso dig. With all three of us working we will be able to outpace the magic and reach the slab."

"But the Land-Nymphs and Tierren won't be helping us?" Marco asked as a puzzled frown erupted on his face.

Rogan shook his head. "As I said, they have their reasons."

"But they will be angry at us for helping him," Marco protested.

Rogan shook his head, "No. Well, the Land-Nymphs maybe but not Tierren."

"It means going without breakfast?" D'Mique asked, her stomach complaining again. Rogan shrugged.

"And Sylus will be mad at us," Marco added.

Again, Rogan answered with a shrug. "Nepo laughed and walked away, knowing that we would win." Rogan paused. "Master Marladon changed the task. When the class succeeded he sent them all out into the Black Hills to dig, the only goal being to not stop." The goblin smiled, as if recalling a cherished memory before asking, "You'll help?"

Marco nodded slowly. D'Mique sighed, "Can I eat something first?" she asked. Rogan smiled at her and nodded before leaving the track and heading for the center of the arena. D'Mique and Marco started jogging again, their attention on the center of the room.

"What game are you playing?" Sylus asked as the goblin approached.

"My time is my own," Rogan answered, "I choose to help Kryoso." The goblin knelt beside the Mortak and started digging.

When D'Mique and Marco finished their final lap they sprinted for the breakfast tables, grabbing fruit, eating without sitting. Genow studied them curiously from where he sat while Clippen and Trillip glared at them.

"Are you helping the Mortak?" Clippen asked watching them.

Marco stopped eating long enough to answer. "We haven't eaten since yesterday morning."

"So you're going to eat and then help him?" Trillip spat. D'Mique nodded. A cloud of hatred drifted from the Land-Nymphs, engulfing her and Marco as they finished their fruit. With just enough in her belly to stop its rumbling, she left the alcove and started for the center of the classroom.

"You are giving up your time as well?" Sylus asked, a thread of anger in his voice.

"Yes, Commander," she answered.

"So be it," he said, not looking very pleased. Heart in her throat, she knelt opposite Kryoso and Rogan and started digging as well. Marco was soon beside her, digging fast, flinging wet sand from the hole as if his life depended on finding the buried slab. In contrast D'Mique found herself working in tandem with the goblin. As his thick claws scored the earth she pulled the mounds of sand from the hole allowing him to concentrate on breaking new ground. Beside the three of them Kryoso continued to dig seemingly unaware of them, his movements mechanical and almost dainty. D'Mique watched his hands as he worked, bright red blood mixing with the sand. "He took this punishment for all of us," she thought, grimacing. As far as she was concerned, she decided, he was forgiven.

"Hah!" Rogan cried after almost ten minutes, "I've found the slab, Commander!" Sylus peered into the hole, skeptical. Kryoso moved the dirt away from Rogan's gashes and touched the solid rock. He looked up at Rogan his silver eyes gleaming, a small grateful smile touching his thin lips.

"Good. Ten laps Kryoso," Sylus said standing up. "You should hurry if you want to eat this morning." He turned and made his way to the tables where he dished up breakfast for himself, watching the group at the center of the arena as he chewed. The Land-Nymphs finished their meal and made their way to the center of the arena, their cloud of hatred still floating around them.

"Can you run Kryoso?" D'Mique asked, ignoring the newcomers as best she could.

"I may be slow, but I can run forever," Kryoso answered, staggering to his feet and starting toward the wall. Clippen and Trillip glared at him as he left.

"He has bled into the earth for his comments, Trillip," Rogan said. "I'm amazed it wasn't more blood. Perhaps he has worked with his hands before. Truly an oddity for the palace whelp he claims to be."

The bite of derision in his voice sat at odds with his recent actions, painting confusion on D'Mique's face. "He helps him but insults him," she thought, pondering the goblins' character.

"There isn't enough blood in his whole body to satisfy me," Trillip countered his words scalding. "Mara refuses to choose another for marriage. Her family may force her into it."

"What?" D'Mique snapped, rising.

"Childless females are no longer an option we can afford," Clippen supplied in response, shielding Trillip from her glare by stepping between them.

"How many Land-Nymphs are left?" she asked.

"There are only a few thousand of us," Clippen supplied, "Combined with a declining birthrate."

"If you're as rare as that," Marco asked, voicing D'Mique's question from the day before, "why are you two here instead of home?"

D'Mique nodded, "We are training to be soldiers."

"But this isn't a combat position," Trillip answered his anger seeping away.

"We're an honor guard. We just travel with the Masters when they must go somewhere. We shouldn't see any fighting," Clippen added.

D'Mique gaped at them their words echoing through her heart. A nasty metallic ball of worry and fear formed in her stomach, sinking low in her gut. For a moment the world seemed to spin around her, blurring along the edges of her vision. The Land-Nymphs' words reverberated through her, "We're an honor guard...we shouldn't see any fighting."

"You didn't know that, did you?" Rogan said looking at her, watching the progression of emotion across her face. She shook her head without speaking suddenly finding it hard to breathe. "It is a wonderful chance to meet people," the green goblin continued, "Many who live in the northwest area of the peninsula have never even seen a human." Tierren mirrored her glare, shaking his head at Rogan.

"Thanks," she croaked, "That makes me feel better." She stood up, shaking, and made her way over to Sylus who was conversing with Genow, walking through a strange, gauzy world, the lights too bright, while the sounds remained muffled. "Commander," she started, trying to keep her voice even as she interrupted his conversation, "I still have nearly ten minutes of my own time?"

Sylus eyed her suspiciously before answering, "Yes."

"Would it be possible to see Master Myrth?"

Sylus' black eyes widened and Genow gaped at her.

"Apparently it's an unusual request," she thought.

"He doesn't concern himself with this training and rewards or punishments, I promise you," Sylus hissed.

Taken aback by his retort it took a moment for D'Mique to answer. "I—I only wish to speak to him for a moment. I have a request."

Without a word Sylus closed his eyes. For a full minute D'Mique watched him, trying to decide if she had been dismissed. Then just as she moved to shake him, he opened his eyes again, refocusing on her. "Master Myrth says to come up. Do you remember the entry to his throne room from yesterday?" She nodded, "The stone door leads to the throne room, knock on the *wood* one and he will answer."

"Thank you, commander," she said before hurrying out of the classroom.

She made her way up the spiral staircase chewing on her lower lip, lost in thought as the Land-Nymph's words ran through her mind. She climbed through the bustling levels of the underground palace without earning a second glance despite the fact that all other humans were servants. At the top of the staircase she entered the outer barracks, pointedly ignoring the myriad goblin eyes that fell on her, some full of curiosity, others contempt.

Although they stared they said nothing. Relieved by their silence she hurried on.

Outside, the morning sunlight dappled the rose garden and cobblestone courtyard, filtered by the close-growing pines. Light danced across the white tower, the Tower of the Elements, and it glinted as if newly washed. Unseen horses neighed and birds chirped in the forest beyond the walls, their voices joining the babbling of the large fountain. For several steps D'Mique took no notice of the bright morning around her, wholly involved in practicing the conversation she was about to have with the Earth Master. But as she walked the world seeped into her thoughts and she looked up. Stopping in the center of the palace grounds she took a deep breath of fresh air, finding it exhilarating after being below ground, and closed her eyes, face to the sky. The bright freshness of the morning bolstered her courage. *"How do you decline the hospitality of a Master,"* she wondered. *"How do you tell him no?"* The excitement she had felt over being accepted into the Academy dwindled. *"Did he sponsor me just so he could have a pet human?"* The questions whirled through her head and settled in her gut. Then she was standing at the entrance they had used yesterday and her courage faltered.

She expected the guards to challenge her but they just nodded and opened the door for her, closing it behind her as she entered, leaving her alone in the entrance hall. She glanced at the stone door that led to the Master's throne room before staring at the large wooden door opposite it. "What am I doing?" she screamed in her head. A long minute crept by, then, "I came all this way, I can't just turn around!" she berated herself. Heart pounding, she knocked on the door, the sound reverberating through the small stone anteroom.

"Come," commanded the Earth Master's deep voice. She hesitated, her questions forgotten, the conversation she'd practiced on the walk over, lost; all of it drowned by a swelling, irrational fear of the mage behind the door. As she stood struggling against the tide, the fighting from the night before invaded her thoughts, accompanied by Sylus' warning to all of them that Myrth would not send any of them home for misbehavior. "But this is different," she chided, "I don't want to go home, I want to go on!"

Swallowing hard and clearing her throat she opened the door and bravely pushed onward.

The room beyond lay bathed in morning sunlight. Expecting more darkness D'Mique blinked at the light, confused. After yesterday's dramatic throne room interview the warm, even cheery, space that greeted her seemed anticlimactic. Every picture and presumption she had about the Earth Master came crashing down around her. The Earth Master was the strongest mage on the planet! He belonged in a stone room filled with darkness. A deep-voiced, cloaked figure who belonged in a candlelit sepulcher! The Earth Master she carried in her head did not belong in the sunlight, or—she looked around—a workroom. The far wall housed an enormous workbench cluttered with vials and jars of strange powders. Dried leaves and flowers, seemingly tossed at random, dotted the surface as well and hung from various pegs in the rafters. Jars of murky substances sat on shelves against both the left and right walls, each set of shelves topped by a large plate glass window. The Earth Master leaned on a tall stool, back to the door and his visitor. In addition to the darkness, he had shed his hooded cloak which lay draped across the stool, trailing to the stone floor.

Hesitantly she studied the avian Semian, unsure if she should be kneeling in his presence or even looking at him in such a state of undress. The stray thought brought a flush of color to her cheeks, but she did not drop to the floor or avert her eyes. Master Myrth's head and torso lay bare of clothes, his body covered instead by bronze-red feathers, short and downy along his head and neck, but growing larger and stiffer as they made their way across his shoulders and back. Those on his upper arms hinted toward bird wings but quickly grew downy as well. The feathers stopped at his elbows where the skin on his lower arms became the thick, gray scales of a bird's feet. His hands had only three fingers each one ending in a black, cruel-looking talon, though they seemed dexterous enough to allow him to hold the beaker and phial he was working with as D'Mique entered. The only clothing the Master wore was tight-fitting black pants tucked into soft black, knee-high palace boots. Along his back the feathers disappeared into his pants but when he turned to address D'Mique she saw that the feathers of his stomach turned to pale human skin just shy of his waistband. She pulled her eyes quickly to his face. "D'Mique please sit," he said with a smile as he waved to a smaller stool near the door.

"You used my name," she blurted out startled. Then she gasped and clapped a hand over her mouth, taken aback by her audacity.

Myrth's smile grew, pulling at the edges of his beak, "Indeed," he said. "Please, Lady, sit," he corrected. "I was not aware that you followed elfin name custom." Again he motioned to the stool.

"If you don't mind, Master, I would rather stand," she said declining his offer. Her heart shriveled, fearing the mage's reaction to so many affronts in such a short time.

Myrth shrugged his bony shoulders, "As you wish." He sat watching her, expectant but patient, his eyes alight.

"Press on bravely," she thought. Swallowing a few times she forced the hard ball of fear further down her throat then said, "I wish to make a request. Respectfully, I wish to transfer out of your honor guard, Master. I would like to continue on to Olimidia and the Academy." She held her breath thinking, *"There! I said it!"*

"Why?" he rumbled.

"Well," she paused, trying to remember her rehearsed conversation, trying to find the words needed to convince him, "I have spent five years forcing gate guards to teach me the sword. I have gone against village elders and traditions to become a soldier, and my dream is to command a unit in the army. With respect Master, I don't see how being the human ambassador to the world will fit into my plans. Traveling around with you to tea parties will not accomplish my goals despite all the honors," she said.

Master Myrth chuckled unexpectedly. He set the vial he had been working with down on the bench then stood and squarely faced her. "Oh you must give me permission to use your name, Lady Warrior," he said, the depths of his voice lightened by his laughter.

"He's definitely laughing at me," D'Mique thought, scowling.

Her reaction brought another bubble of mirth from him, his deep voice shivering in her bones as it echoed in the small stone room. "Please, let's start at the beginning. First I don't recall ever being invited to a tea party." D'Mique winced as glass jars tinkled along the shelves and the length of the workbench sure the sound of his voice would knock things over. "Second, as for the issue of command," he continued, "you know that in three cycles Sylus will take the mages and leave for Master Island?" D'Mique nodded. "A commander-in-training will take his place. I had bet on Tierren as that was his rank in Hawkethorne. But if you prove yourself better equipped it could be you." Myrth smiled at her, hopeful.

She contemplated that last bit of information but sighed resignedly, "As nice as that sounds, Master, I would still be in charge of a...a status symbol."

"Status symbol?" Myrth repeated.

"I want to be in charge of a combat unit!" She shouted suddenly causing the Semian to pull back sharply. "I want to patrol the forests!" She spun away from him and began pacing the length of the room, "I want to fight daemons! I want to see all the places my mother talked about! I want...I want to save people!" she shouted, throwing her arms into the air.

"Calm yourself Lady," Master Myrth said, grabbing her arms, holding them down at her sides as he forced her to face him. Concern pulled the corners of his beak-mouth downward. "Am I to understand that you feel the Honor Guard is not any of these things?" he asked searching her face.

"How can it be? Trillip and Clippen are some of the last of their kind! They would never be assigned to a combat unit!"

"They told you this?" he asked, ignoring her shouting, a half-smile creeping back onto his face. D'Mique nodded breathing hard and glaring at him. Myrth stared at her a moment then released her. "Sit down Lady," he said, leading her back to his stool and helping her onto it. "Please give me permission to use your name. I am a Semian and you are human. What do we care for elfin customs?"

D'Mique perched on the stool and studied the Master. The simplicity of his request pulled her away from her rant. "I don't care if you use my name," she said after a moment.

"Thank you D'Mique," Myrth sighed before smiling at her. "Let me tell you a story," he said, stepping away from her folding his arms across his chest. "Once long ago, a Greater Daemon came into this world."

"A history lesson?" she asked, her mind clicking over from anger to worry.

"Yes," Myrth said pointedly.

"Is this about the breaking forcelines and the Hero Masters?"

"No." Myrth waited studying her until she felt the urge to squirm. "This event," he continued, "happened after the Masters were well established. When the daemon appeared the peoples turned to the Masters to save them. They were, after all, the best mages on the peninsula." Myrth stopped expectantly. D'Mique stared at him. "This is the part where my class usually says, 'Four against one, poor daemon,'" Myrth prompted. She mirrored his smile.

"But that's not true" she said remembering her own history lessons, "The Masters always have an army with them."

"Correct. The Masters took a small army into battle against the Greater Daemon. That army was the first Honor Guard. And every army afterward has retained the title, even you and your fellows today."

"But combat roots don't change what it has become," she replied, "It may have started life as an army, but it's just an entourage now."

"True most Honor Guards do not see combat. Trillip and Clippen did not lead you astray. However," Myrth stared hard at her, "sometimes the unit must be returned to its original purpose." Silence fell about her following the Master's words. D'Mique felt her mouth go dry, the room seemingly holding its breath.

"What?" she asked in a whisper, an electric shock traveling along her limbs.

Myrth pulled away from her and turned back to the workbench head down. "For most of the time the Honor Guard acts as a status symbol. They parade around in fancy uniforms, attend tea parties," he glanced at her with a smile at the last words. "And every year or two, we rotate the soldiers out of the Master's army and back to their original positions, so they won't become too complacent." He paused again and took a deep breath.

"Six cycles ago, the Sea of Dreams reacted to the presence of a Greater Daemon entering the Void," he whispered, voice almost so low she could not hear him. She gasped, the world melting away. Haltingly he continued, "The next day I dismissed my honor guard and picked out the eight people that the seers said had the best chance of defeating that daemon." Myrth let the silence sit undisturbed between them awaiting her reaction.

D'Mique counted cycles in her head. "That was around the same time I received my admission to the Academy," she said aloud, inside she screamed, "eight people to hunt a Greater Daemon! They're mad!"

Myrth nodded. "Yes. I had to pull a few strings to get hold of the two humans on my list. The High Generals were not pleased." He smiled at the memory.

"The two humans on your list," D'Mique repeated, catching her breath as a fine tremor ran through her.

"Last night," Myrth continued quietly, "those eight people met each other for the first time and this morning they ate breakfast together. My Honor Guard has returned to its original purpose," he finished, looking at her.

D'Mique slid to the floor, hitting hard, and stared up at the Master. Myrth blinked down at her. "Daemon Hunters?" she squeaked. Myrth nodded and held out a hand. She stared at it not taking hold. "When were you going to tell us?" she asked, anger trying but failing, to replace fear.

"True, I wasn't going to tell you for a cycle or so. Plenty of other things to do," he admitted, still holding out his hand.

"Does Sylus know?" she asked, taking his hand at last and standing. The Master's grip was warm and sure, his avian skin soft and dry, as he helped her first to her feet and then back onto the stool.

"Of course he knows."

"Master? Is my cadet still there?" Sylus' voice, as if on cue, rang through the room. D'Mique jumped, looking around, though Sylus was nowhere to be seen. Sudden anger spilled across Myrth's features; his open joviality swallowed in a fierce glare that he turned to the ceiling. D'Mique swallowed hard at his transformation, shrinking defensively into herself, her stomach churning as the room swayed slightly.

"Are my conversations less important than your schedule now, Commander Sylus?" the Master shouted, the room vibrating with his voice, glass vials tinkling as the earth shifted slightly. D'Mique closed her eyes and took a deep breath steadying herself against both the Master's emotions and the small earthquake.

"Of course not. Forgive me Master." Sylus answered.

"I will send her along shortly. Have her tell the others why they are here," he added.

There was a moment of silence before Sylus answered, "Understood, Master."

Myrth looked back at D'Mique. "Will you be staying then D'Mique?" he asked. She nodded slowly. "Good, now run along and tell the others that they are a combat unit. No tea parties for them," Myrth added with a smile, his anger gone again as suddenly as it had surfaced.

She made her way back to the classroom lost in thought. "Daemon Hunters!" she repeated to herself in an attempt to make the thought more real. But the words echoed through her. She could almost feel the world shift around her as reality tilted. When she entered the classroom Kryoso was eating. Everyone else, including Sylus, stood near the tables, watching her as she walked over and stood before them. Words wouldn't come only the thought, "I'm going to die!" Silence stretched out between them.

"Lady?" Genow whispered breaking the spell.

"I went to Master Myrth to request a transfer to Olimidia," she started. "I want to be part of a combat unit—that's my goal in life. And sitting around here didn't seem the best way to fulfill that goal." She stopped, the words stuck in her throat trapped behind an icy lump of fear. Sylus nodded at her, she took it as a sign of encouragement. "As it turns out I already am a part of one," she said, pausing again as she tried to think of the right words. The others were scowling at her, waiting. "Master Myrth explained to me how the Honor Guard began, how its original purpose was fighting Greater Daemons." Others were nodding remembering history lessons of their own. "Well, we have been recruited to carry out that original purpose," she finished quickly. For a split-second they all stared at each other, then the others drew back, surprised, before they started talking at once to both her and each other.

"What?"

"I beg your pardon?"

"Combat unit?"

"Greater Daemon?"

"Quiet!" Sylus barked. Mouths snapped shut, and they all turned to him, waiting. "Six cycles ago the seers felt a Greater Daemon enter the Void.

They contacted Master Myrth with a list of people they had seen defeating the daemon. You are those people," Sylus clarified.

"We spent three cycles making trouble," Tierren said, looking from Sylus toward the door, "Forgive us, Master." The others followed his gaze. Master Myrth stood framed in the doorway. He had left his cloak upstairs and his bronze feathers seemed to burn in the light of the arena. Sylus bowed to him.

"You are forgiven," Myrth said as he strode into the classroom. When he reached them the goblins dropped to their knees. Myrth ignored them and continued, addressing Sylus, "Oracle has just contacted me. He has confirmed the daemon's approach." He looked at D'Mique, "If there had been no confirmation we could all start practicing our table manners. However, time is now exceedingly short. The daemon attack on you Sylus, and your subsequent delay, has strained our timetable. In one cycle the mages will journey to Master Island," Myrth looked at all of them, "The rest of you will stay here; ready to move when the daemon comes."

"In one cycle?" Sylus asked confirming the timeline.

Myrth nodded. "Yes Oracle has narrowed down the arrival point. Will that be a problem?"

"One cycle is quite possible if there is no more nonsense," Sylus said glaring at his charges.

"There won't be," Myrth assured him, glaring at them as well.

Arrivals and Departures

For the following cycle D'Mique and Marco pushed themselves to match the Land-Nymphs and goblins in all their training regiments, the days passing in a blur of pain and exhaustion. To make up for the shortened schedule Sylus changed their training—forcing anyone who finished running before breakfast was delivered to run another five laps. By pushing themselves Marco and D'Mique reached fifteen laps, though breakfast was served before they finished. At the same time Kryoso's laps never increased. Despite his lean sculpted frame, it seemed that his muscles were of little practical use. The nymphs and goblins, long of leg and fast by nature, earned twenty laps some days and fifteen on others. Often on the days when they did only fifteen, it was because Marco, Clippen, and Rogan ran together, deep in conversation. D'Mique ran just behind them, listening as they talked of treasure and adventures they'd had, while Tierren kept pace a few strides ahead of Rogan, trying to ignore them all. As the running trio bonded as only single males could, Trillip remained aloof, especially when Clippen ran with Marco and Rogan. He often ran alone, lost in thought, half a lap behind D'Mique. Genow also ran alone through the cycle, but only because he proved to be the fastest of them all. Buoyed along by his natural healing magic, which would not allow his muscles to tire or his breath to shorten, he often ran twenty-five laps, sprinting the entire way.

After breakfast the guards worked on strength training which D'Mique had missed the first day. It involved carrying piles of rocks from one end of the classroom to the other, the piles growing larger each morning, forming from the arena floor in an endless stream. Once they had moved the entire pile lunch was served. During the one-hour lunch break they talked about the lives they had left behind and the circumstances they found themselves in now. Tierren's wife, Samsha, entered the conversation most often as Tierren read her letters aloud to Rogan and the rest of them. Samsha's undeniable enthusiasm, brimming over in each letter, brought a smile to D'Mique's face, and she found herself looking forward to the goblin's arrival nearly as much as Tierren. But the pride that shone from Tierren's face as he spoke of his wife and her imminent arrival acted as a sharp, hot slap to Trillip, who continued to pine for his lost love, Mara. If anyone asked about her, he would quickly finish his lunch and leave. With his departure they turned to Clippen for information. Through the other Land-Nymph they learned that Mara had been forced into marriage, and if she did not choose to consummate the relationship, she would be forced into pregnancy as well. D'Mique often left these conversations as fast as Trillip, her blood boiling with impotent rage at the thought of a woman being forced to marry and bear children.

Leaving the classroom she wandered up to the surface, more often than not unintentionally trailing Trillip. From a discrete distance she watched him, and each time he trudged out into the center of the rose garden near the base of the white tower and hunkered down. Motionless between the bushes, only his bright, hot-pink hair marking his position. He stayed there for the rest of the lunch break and D'Mique watched him without approaching him not knowing what she could say or do to alleviate his pain.

When their midday break ended the others wandered above ground as well and started their afternoon training session, working with Myrth's goblin soldiers and some elfin archers from a nearby village who came at Myrth's request to help with bow work. From the first day the goblins and Land-Nymphs proved they needed little training and that any "lessons" given by the goblin soldiers or elves were merely exercises. Although self-taught, D'Mique showed the first day that she had a good understanding of the basics. She could slash, thrust, parry and block. Her strokes were deliberate and varied enough to remain unpredictable. Sylus even praised her for not signaling where the next attack would come from, keeping her shoulders and hips straight and using her elbows and wrists to change her attack.

The first evening Sylus paired her with Tierren for a sparring match, the elf's deliberately infuriating smile back in place. Armed with real swords rather than the wooden practice blades they had been using throughout the day, Tierren and D'Mique circled each other cautiously at first. "I stand by my remark, Lady," he warned, "You don't belong here, no matter what the seers say." Angry, she moved to attack first, launching a series of sweeping strokes that Tierren deftly parried. He didn't attack in return, preferring to simply defend the entire time, leaving her unmarked. Yet her best efforts could not completely break through the goblin's defense and she managed to nick him only twice before Sylus called for them to stop. Tierren saluted her before leaving, his bearing filled with contempt, and as he walked away D'Mique's heated glare followed him.

Frustrated and embarrassed, she consoled herself by watching Marco, Genow, and Kryoso in their sparring matches. Proving that there was a limit to Sylus' deviousness, he paired Kryoso with Rogan instead of one of the Land-Nymphs, leaving Marco to take on Clippen and Genow facing Trillip. *"So, maybe I'm not so bad,"* she thought, watching Clippen turn Marco into a series of bloody gashes. The man could barely hold a sword even after practicing all day with the goblin soldiers. Kryoso fared little better, unable to block a single thrust. Halfway through the match, Rogan feigned boredom and changed tactics, mimicking Tierren's defensive strategy. Only when Kryoso was so winded he could no longer swing the sword did Sylus call for a stop. Laughing, Rogan sheathed his sword and took the Mortak by the arm, helping him toward the barracks.

The Fiery Sisters touched the horizon as Trillip and Genow faced each other, the elf blatantly ill-at-ease with the sword in his hands. "I'll go easy on you tonight Genow," the Land-Nymph said, a hint of smugness on his face.

"Will you?" Genow asked, suddenly thrusting the sword at the Land-Nymph's stomach. With a humorless bark Trillip caught the stroke and moved into the elf, crowding him and forcing him backward.

"Why Genow," Trillip breathed, "You've been holding out on us. You do know how to fight." Genow's parries, while less skillful than his opponent's, remained effective, and several minutes passed before Trillip's flashing blade found its mark, drawing blood. The elf hissed at the Land-Nymph, pulling back momentarily with his free hand cupped over the wound. He wavered, as if on the verge of losing his balance, causing Trillip to hold his next attack. Then Genow's blade leapt forward nearly burying itself in the Land-Nymph's upper arm. Trillip dodged, spinning away from the elf, a surprised laugh erupting in the attack's wake. "Hey, you're not bleeding anymore," the Land-Nymph noted as the pair faced each other again their defensive stances set.

Genow scoffed, "I'm a combat healer in training, Land-Nymph. Why would I let myself bleed?" With another sharp laugh Trillip attacked again. They fought on through dusk until it grew too dark to see. Then with Rysk's rise still an hour away, Sylus called for them to stop and report to the classroom for dinner. D'Mique walked with Genow impressed by his lack of visible wounds. When she mentioned it the elf chuckled. "Trillip is a strong fighter and," he admitted, "he was going easy on me. I had to heal myself five times."

Three days into their training further proof of the Land-Nymph's fighting prowess presented itself. During the early afternoon session D'Mique found herself watching Clippen and Trillip spar with staves, the wood poles dancing in their hands, flashing around their bodies so fast she lost sight of them. In awe she stood mesmerized by the skillful dance and the rhythmic clacking of the weapons. Every movement flowed into the next with a precise, potentially deadly, beauty. "I'll never be that good," she thought suddenly frowning. "How could I ever think I was good enough to join the Academy?" Her sudden self-doubt grew as the rest of the cycle passed, compounded by the fact that when she did spar, she tended to draw a crowd of curious onlookers, soldiers interested in passing judgment on the human warrior, each one unafraid to offer loud criticism. By the morning of the eighth day her change in attitude had become obvious and Sylus took note, pulling her aside.

"Are you well, Lady?" he asked.

She nodded in response.

"I think you are not. What troubles you? Are you homesick?"

She hadn't thought of her home or her mother for days! "No Commander. I'm—I'm worried about facing the daemon," she said, unable to voice her true feelings, settling for the plausible lie.

Sylus studied her, eyes narrowing, before answering, "The seers chose you, D'Mique. You may not be the strongest or the fastest here. You are, after all, only human. But you will serve a purpose."

"As a toy," she added silently, mimicking Tierren's taunt from the first night. Still concerned Sylus dropped the subject with a weary shake of his head, sensing that she would offer nothing more.

That evening while they trained a deep gong sounded from the high outer wall, signaling the approach of unknown riders. Everyone stopped, turning toward the front gates as they swung open admitting two figures mounted on large black horses. The hoods of their traveling cloaks were down revealing them to be Semians, one feline and one canine. A reverent hush fell over the assemblage as the visitors crossed the grounds, stopping near the fountain. Whispering, the goblins gravitated toward the Semian riders forming a semi-circle around the horses. Sylus pushed his way to the front, bowing low to each visitor in turn as he spoke, "Greetings sent from the Master of Earth, Grand Syra Palo. Greetings to you as well Seer Oracle," he intoned formally, facing first the feline then the canine Semian. The crowd bowed their heads as the visitors dismounted and nonchalantly handed their huge black horses to a human stable hand.

As the feline approached, unclasping his cloak and draping it over one arm, Sylus bowed again, remaining in that position while he spoke. Aside from the cloak the feline-Semian wore loose-fitting pants and calf-high boots with no shirt. A long tail trailed behind him. Like the fur on his face, chest and arms, it was a mottled black, gray, and white—the splotchy, spotted pattern of a snow leopard. "Where is your master?" the feline asked in a low baritone, studying the crowd with gold-green cat eyes, his high-set, cat ears twitching.

"He is in the tower, meditating, Grand Syra," Sylus answered.

"The Grand Syra?" D'Mique whispered eyes wide, "the leader of the entire Fanterra Plain?"

"He's come to escort us to Master Island," Marco returned, his voice low. D'Mique glanced at him before looking back at the snow-leopard.

The Grand Syra smiled, revealing large white fangs, "Will you take us to him?" he asked.

Sylus actually paled before answering. "That is more than my life is worth, Grand Syra. Myrth bids you enter his residence and refresh yourselves from the long journey." As they conversed the other Semian joined them his cloak now pulled back over his shoulders. He wore little in the way of clothes, only a matching loincloth belted around his waist, the plain gold adornment glinting in the afternoon sunlight. His body, from head to toe, was wolf. Paws replaced his hands and feet while his leg bones formed a smooth sweeping curve along his knee. A shaggy tail peeked out from beneath his cloak, and the face that surveyed the crowd bore a sharp wolf muzzle and close-set canine ears. D'Mique caught herself staring at him—he was the rarest of Semians—one with no visible humanity. She swallowed hard as his gaze fell on her, an odd expression lingering in his alien, amber eyes.

"It will suffice," the leopard-man said as the two Semians followed Sylus into the Earth Master's residence, the crowd parting before and closing behind them, whispers breaking out in their wake.

That evening passed quickly. D'Mique ate dinner mechanically and retired early to her bunk. The others followed her though they lay awake, whispering long after the lights had gone out, leaving the room bathed in a soft yellow half- light. She stared down at Kryoso's bags, packed and ready to go, darker shadows at the foot of his bed. Marco's bags sat beside his bunk as well. A sudden wave of loneliness washed over her, bringing a lump to her throat as she contemplated their departure. "Soon I'll be both the only female and the only human." Next to her Genow stared at the ceiling, ears twitching as he listened to the conversation two beds away where Rogan and Tierren whispered together in their native tongue.

He translated what he could hear, "Rogan thinks that Tierren will be named commander of the forces remaining here," he whispered, "sorry," he added, remembering that D'Mique had been hoping for the honor. She shrugged as he continued, "He, Rogan, feels that you will be Tierren's second...Well, that's good." Genow smiled, pausing, then shook his head, exasperated.

"Well?" D'Mique prompted.

"He, Rogan, hopes you will give him permission to use your name while we are here." The implied sexual innuendo housed in the remark was not lost. For most Fae Folk permission to use a person's given name was tantamount to foreplay. Tierren and Rogan broke into a fit of stifled laughter.

"And now? Are they laughing at that?"

"No. Lady, there is a reason they are using the goblin tongue," he cautioned. She glared at him. "I will tell you if you give your word not to hold it against them." He waited until she promised to hold her temper before saying, "Tierren said it would be wise for Rogan to switch to human females since all the goblin-maids have rejected him." D'Mique forced a smile across her face which made Genow chuckle and sigh, "I've said enough," he concluded. Once the goblin's conversation subsided Genow turned over facing her. "Do you think we will still run before breakfast?" he asked.

She nodded. "Those of us staying will probably have to carry stones as well." Genow nodded as she added, "I thought you would be going with them. You're a mage; why are you staying?"

"I'm training for healing in battle; I can do that more easily here with soldiers. Besides it is a natural elfin ability, the Potentate at Master Island cannot train me as they only work in elemental magic." As she nodded her understanding he continued, "What are you specializing in?"

"Master Myrth wants me to learn tracking and scouting," she said. "I have some experience in that already."

"Yes, that suits you," Genow said before closing his eyes and drifting into sleep, a small smile on his face. D'Mique watched the elf sleep, listening to Kryoso snore. Just as she began drifting off as well movement caught her eye and, looking across the room, she noticed Clippen hanging down from the top bunk, his mane of white hair aglow in the gloom as he whispered to Trillip.

Tierren woke them the next day for laps and breakfast. "Ten times around for all," he instructed, "Today, we run together." Suspicious but willing to comply D'Mique started her laps surrounded by the others. Marco and Genow ran beside her while the long-legged goblins and Land-Nymphs took the lead and Kryoso brought up the rear. After one lap D'Mique sprinted until she caught up to Tierren.

"If I am to be scout," she asked, "shouldn't I take the lead in this formation?"

He thought for a moment and then nodded, "Indeed. And Genow should run in the center."

"Excellent," Rogan commented as D'Mique took up a position in front of him. She scowled but forced herself to focus on running.

"The rear is weak," Clippen said after another lap. "Trillip or Rogan should run between Marco and Kryoso or even behind them."

"I will guard the rear," Trillip volunteered falling back. They held the formation for ten laps keeping pace with Kryoso, Sylus watching it all from the tables a small smile on his lips.

Once they'd completed ten laps they slowed to a walk and made their way across the arena to the tables. "There will be no stones after breakfast," Tierren announced, "When we are through eating we are to report to the courtyard. Clippen, Marco and Kryoso, bring up your packs."

"Clippen?" D'Mique thought, *"But why? He's already trained."* She contemplated the Land-Nymph before asking aloud, "Why are you going to Gaity? I thought you were already trained."

Clippen chewed deliberately for a moment before replying, "Why would I not want to go to Gaity given the chance?"

"That doesn't answer—" she began.

"I do not wish to go to Gaity," Kryoso interrupted, carefully avoiding Trillip and Clippen's murderous looks. "I am a gift from Master Marladon and when I was sent here it was on the condition that I would remain here. Being sent to Gaity is betrayal on Myrth's part and disobedience on mine," he explained.

"Well, I'm excited about going to Gaity," Marco interjected. "I am the first human Mage in over a hundred years," he added unnecessarily, swelling with pride, "I can't wait to go." He finished his porridge in a gulp and grabbed a handful of berries, tossing them into his mouth as he stood and left. Odd glances jumped across the table in his wake, but no one spoke. With a heavy sigh, Kryoso took another bite then followed Marco without saying another word.

D'Mique finished soon afterward, but waited on Genow as he ate delicately, savoring every bite as though it were a gourmet meal. While he ate she watched the others. Rogan and Tierren started talking once again in the guttural goblin tongue, their conversation sounding urgent. She caught Genow's eye but he shook his head slightly. *"Maybe he knows,"* she thought, *"But he isn't going to tell me."* In contrast Trillip and Clippen ate silently, sitting so close to each other they touched. *"I wonder if Clippen's touch is comforting to Trillip. I wonder if he will miss Clippen,"* she thought. Once Genow finished D'Mique followed him up the spiral stairs to the courtyard. "Was the goblins' conversation important?" she asked after they'd left the arena.

"No Lady, do not trouble yourself. They spoke of Samsha nothing more."

Outside horses and riders waited for them. When D'Mique arrived the Grand Syra, Palo, sat his great black horse while Marco and Kryoso sat beside him. Marco mounted on the brown beast he had ridden from Scala and Kryoso on the white mare Sylus had bought. The elf waited beside them mounted on his own black while an older palomino waited for Clippen. "Genow do you know why Clippen is going with them? He's already completed his training," asked D'Mique.

"I do not know Lady. He spent many years with the Potentate. Perhaps he is going to visit his friends."

"Visit his friends with a Greater Daemon on the way?" D'Mique asked, a hint of disbelief in her voice. With a look Genow acknowledged the absurdity. Myrth's arrival cut their conversation short. The canine-Semian trailed behind Myrth eyeing the mounted group, one claw idly scratching an ear as he bent in close to Myrth's head whispering. Myrth answered with a dark glare but said nothing. The wolf-man shrugged and sat down on his haunches, pointedly ignoring the Earth Master's continued dark looks. Clippen finally emerged from the soldier's quarters and tied his pack onto the golden horse before mounting.

"Fare well on your journey, Grand Syra," Myrth intoned, holding up a hand in salute once the party was assembled.

"We shall, Master Myrth. I will return your guard in four cycles. I pray that it is soon enough," Palo answered, holding up his own black, padded palm to the Master.

"If we must leave," the wolf-man growled, "You will come along, Palo." The Grand Syra smiled flippantly, nodding. "You will," the wolf-man insisted, rising to his full height. Myrth glanced between the two of them but said nothing.

"We might leave without our mages?" Genow whispered, his voice trembling with a hint of fear that jumped from him and echoed through D'Mique. "Suddenly I don't like this plan."

"Come Sylus," the Grand Syra commanded, starting for the gates, forcing his horse straight toward the wolf-man who stepped aside with a snarl. Myrth shook his head and rolled his eyes as the Grand Syra passed. Marco waved to D'Mique as he left, his horse following the Grand Syra's. Kryoso rode directly behind him while Clippen and the commander brought up the rear, the massive gate swinging shut behind them.

As one, the crowd watched the closed gates in silence for a full minute. Then, as Myrth moved again, turning away from the portal, the goblins awoke, breaking apart and returning to their morning routines. In their wake they left a tangle of new people flanking the remaining honor guard, Myrth, and the wolf Semian. D'Mique eyed them suspiciously as Tierren introduced them, Sildona, a falcon-Semian, two elves, Karl and Crella, and a goblin named Shry. Sildona bowed low, her feathered arms forming pseudo-wings with long black and white barred feathers. Her deep blue eyes, twinkling with challenge and merriment, perfectly matched the sleeveless cotton shirt she wore accompanied by black pants tucked into rugged mid-calf boots. As she straightened, dropping her arms to her sides, the feathers revealed a delicate-looking crossbow hooked to the belt at her waist. D'Mique dragged her eyes from the weapon long enough to glance at Genow.

Beside her Genow gaped, staring at the elf, Karl, trembling. "Genow?" she asked, concerned.

Her voice broke through whatever held Genow and he turned to her with a mixture of panic and excitement on his face. "That's Karl!" he hissed. "We'll be learning from Karl!" D'Mique studied Karl. Dressed in yellow and brown leather he stood slightly shorter than Genow, his wispy white hair pulled back into a severe ponytail. Two sword hilts rode across his back, their plant-covered hilts high over his shoulders. Genow continued,

"Karl is a Wind Blade, like Re'Ana! I didn't think Herdan would allow him to come!" Karl smiled at him, bemusement fighting with embarrassment. D'Mique realized that Genow had shouted the last line and motioned for him to be quiet while Tierren cleared his throat. Genow blushed and fell silent.

"And Crella will be working with you Genow on combat healing," Tierren said, indicating the elf that stood beside Karl. Smiling, she nodded at Genow, the white curls piled atop her head bobbing as she did so. She was the first female D'Mique had seen wearing a highly stylized gown instead of armor. Its white satin, plunging neckline and flowing skirts better suited a real palace rather than the serviceable fort she currently stood in. But Crella seemed unperturbed by her dusty surroundings.

"Shry," Tierren motioned behind D'Mique to the goblin, "will be teaching you to track and scout Lady." D'Mique turned and greeted her new tutor. The goblin stood slightly shorter than her his long gray hair braided with black ribbons and bones. Black eyes glittered in the shadows below his brows surrounded by gray skin only slightly darker than his hair.

"Lady," he croaked with a nod. He wore a homespun deep green tunic and baggy black pants. His feet were bare, the stubby black claws of his toes glinting in the sunlight. "Come, we start now," he directed, turning and walking away, his heel spikes, black claws growing from the back of his foot, clicking on the cobblestones with every step. D'Mique watched him for a moment.

"The heel spikes only grow in dominant males," Rogan whispered beside her startling her. "He won't be kept waiting, Lady." Nodding, she followed after the elder goblin.

The rest of the day she worked with Shry, absorbing every lecture he gave, some of his information familiar and some of it new. Her only break from this work came when they stopped for a quick lunch in the early afternoon. During the break she was joined by Genow who had been working with Sildona and Crella. After lunch she returned to Shry and continued working. Only as the Fiery Sisters set did he dismiss her with instructions to return to him tomorrow morning after breakfast. Exhausted, D'Mique worked her way through dinner thinking only of her bed. However after dinner, Karl collected her and Genow for sword training which continued into the darkness, blades clanging together in the torchlight. As she made her way back underground D'Mique resigned herself to the new schedule, drawing strength from the thought that it would only last four cycles until the mages returned to Dragon Ridge.

When she reached their quarters Rogan was just asking Tierren where he had been. "I was with Master Myrth," the red goblin answered.

Taken aback, Rogan asked, "You were with Master Myrth? Why?"

Tierren shrugged. "A history lesson," he said. "We discussed the Promise."

His words brought a startled gasp from D'Mique and she stopped to stare at him. Her mother's concern over the forgotten Promise wafted through her memory. "The Promise to keep humans safe?" she asked. Tierren nodded. "Sylus said the Masters kept the Promise, that they all keep the Promise."

"Yes we do," Rogan answered.

"There are people in my village who feel that the humans have been abandoned and the Promise forgotten," she continued.

The others looked stunned, suddenly speechless. "How can it be?" Genow asked.

"The daemon hordes have grown more bold and numerous over the last few years. Many believe this is because the other races no longer hunt them. Also, Sylus was the first elf to enter my village in nearly a decade," she explained, "If we never see the Fae Folk and the daemons are increasing, it is a natural conclusion to make."

The others passed a look between them before Tierren answered, "I will speak of this to Master Myrth at our next session. We know that the daemons have grown more numerous of late. And I know several soldiers personally who have pulled patrol duty in The Nesting, the Dark Forest, as you call it."

"I know several as well," Rogan supplied, "some who patrol the Nesting more than once a year." D'Mique studied him. An oily smile crossed his face, "Even I have gone on patrol there. My unit dispatched several dozen daemons while we were out." D'Mique nodded before turning away, an acknowledgment of their words. As she climbed into bed troubled thoughts followed her. *"If they know that the daemons have grown more numerous, why don't their patrols account for that?"* she thought at last, *"The human settlements are at the mercy of both daemons and fae. The elves had promised to keep us safe, to patrol the Dark Forest for as long as humans lived within it. But it seems others keep the Promise as well. And yet, we still feel forgotten."* She drifted to sleep, a familiar worry over the safety of her home weighing her down.

The next morning as they ran laps and moved stones before breakfast Tierren disappeared. When they sat down for breakfast he reappeared, dropping onto the bench across from D'Mique. He smiled, "Myrth was surprised by the sentiment you expressed last night Lady," he began. "But he agreed with you that something had to be done to rectify the situation. So he is sending a diplomatic unit to The Nesting to speak with all the villages. They will go in your name," he added.

D'Mique gasped, "In my name?" she repeated. He nodded, smiling, as he ate.

"Congratulations," Genow said laying a hand on her wrist, a suddenly intimate gesture.

"Thank you," she said to him and then to Tierren as well.

The goblin waved it away and continued eating for a moment before continuing, "There's more," he said. "The Wind Mistress will send units to patrol the forest visibly, swinging through the villages and following the trade routes. Of course the Earth Master's patrols will continue to be non-intrusive—searching and patrolling the deeper forest."

She chewed on his words as she ate. *"Why are they non-intrusive?"* she thought without asking aloud. Tierren quickly finished eating and watched her until she noticed him. She forced a smile and added, "Well, that's good. Better than I'd hoped for, honestly" she added. Tierren returned the smile; somehow, his seemed more real than hers.

"Myrth will be joining us for lunch," he said to the table. "After a shortened training session we are moving to our permanent quarters on the first floor, suites surrounding Master Myrth's residential quarters. Before you all leave I have roommate assignments," he announced. "Clippen and Trillip will be together, Genow with Kryoso, and Marco and Rogan. I'll be with my wife, of course, when she arrives tomorrow, and the Lady will be on her own."

As he finished speaking, Genow finished and stood. D'Mique followed him to the surface where they met Sildona. "You are working with Karl D'Mique," she informed them, "Genow, follow me." D'Mique fought off the sudden gloom that fell around her as she watched Genow leave. Karl came up beside her, arms folded across his chest as he looked between her and Genow. She glanced down at the Wind Blade who met her eye and gave her a small knowing smile. At his full height he came up to her chest. But Sylus had taught her how grave a mistake it was to judge elfin warriors by their size, especially those who dual-wielded sword and magic.

"Want to fight?" he asked, the smile lingering, glittering in his black-orb eyes.

"Not really," she said, crushing a nervous laugh as a trickle of fear ran down her spine.

"I choose to hear a compliment rather than recalcitrance," he replied. A cold lump sunk into D'Mique's stomach and she blushed. Karl looked away, "Come Lady. Let's go over by the Tower so we'll have enough room." She followed the elf across the courtyard watching his hands, waiting for them to move to the hilts that rode above his shoulders. As he neared the Tower of the Elements she fell back, increasing the distance between them, and rested her hand on her own sword hilt ready for Karl's attack. Yesterday evening's battle remained fresh in her mind. He had attacked her outright, without warning, flinging Genow to the far side of the courtyard. It was all she could do to keep the Wind Blade from burying a sword deep inside her. Still, by the time Genow returned to her side, blood seeped from a dozen wounds on her arms and torso. Genow healed her, dodging random sword attacks as he worked. If the same thing happened this time, she'd be on her own.

Karl stopped in front of her and D'Mique drew her sword falling into a crouch. The elf's ears twitched toward the sound but he kept his back to her, his swords sheathed. "Control your breathing, Lady," Karl said, "Then think, how long can you hold that stance? What will you do if I don't move?" He fell silent for nearly a full minute. "You're still breathing too loud, too harsh," he said. He glanced over his shoulder. D'Mique tensed but he still didn't move. She swallowed hard and focused on her breathing, slowing and deepening each one. "Good." Karl pulled his left sword from its shoulder scabbard and spun on his toes, adopting an upright, direct stance. "Will you rush me before your muscles tire?" he asked. "Or are you waiting for me to make a first move?"

She studied him for another few seconds. Both hands rested on the single sword hilt but she knew how incredibly fast he could be. She edged toward him, flanking slightly to the right, treading on the balls of her feet. He watched her but made no move to follow her or spin to meet her flanking action. Their standoff attracted goblin guards from the nearby barracks and several meandered toward them, a cautious curiosity engulfing them. Those who had witnessed Karl's lesson the night before were torn between being close enough to the action and maintaining a safe distance. D'Mique ignored the gathering crowd and focused on circling Karl. When she reached his side she lunged forward, aiming to drive her sword through his chest. She expected him to spin and block her thrust but instead he stepped out of her path and slapped her back with the flat of his blade.

"You over-committed to that thrust, Lady. You could not know how I would react," he said behind her. She turned quickly, just in time to see the second blade clear his shoulder. He smiled and started toward her blades pointed away from his body, leaving him defenseless.

"Ha! Not likely," D'Mique countered remaining where she stood. Before the last word cleared her lips Karl moved. He lunged forward, bringing his right-hand blade up toward her stomach. D'Mique dropped her blade to block his swing, leaving the rest of her body open to the following down-stroke of the left blade. The metal bit into her shoulder, sinking deep then pulling free. Gritting her teeth, she spun away from the pain of his attack. However Karl's two quick strokes merely formed the opening movement. He chased after her and she spun back toward him just in time to catch another descending blade, the loud clang echoing off the marble walls.

"That was close, Lady. Did you actually take your eyes off your opponent? Do you not respect my skill?" he taunted, pressing her with a quick series of hacking attacks. She deflected each one just short of them reaching her skin, backing before his attack. The goblin watchers backed away as she neared them and the outer wall. "You're running out of room,

Lady." Karl noted. With a cry she twisted her blade beneath his right sword and lunged for him. His own forward momentum brought him into her sword, cloth tearing beneath her blade. He twisted sideways away from her attack and the sudden cessation of his own attack caused D'Mique to fall forward. She caught herself and moved toward him hoping to take advantage of his defensive maneuver. A solid gust of wind barreled into her lower legs, knocking them out from under her, dumping her face first to the ground and stunning her.

Adrenaline surged through her and she rolled over bringing her sword up into a defensive position without knowing where Karl and his blades were, her vision slightly clouded from the rush of unexpected movement. A harsh clang, accompanied by a sharp jolt of pain up her arm, proved the timeliness of her block. She continued rolling away from the last place she had seen Karl. Her eyes cleared as one of Karl's blades sunk into the ground stopping her roll. She sensed more than saw him out of the corner of her eye and kicked up and outward aiming for his groin. Solid flesh met her boot drawing a pained grunt from her opponent. She scrambled up and away from him, blade ready to block his next attack. When no attack followed her, she blinked and charged forward to meet him.

Pain covered his face as he parried D'Mique's first charge and her following flurry. Karl backed away from her along the outer wall, more goblin soldiers moving out of their way. This defensive posture nagged at D'Mique. *"I was never on the offense yesterday,"* she thought. Slyly she studied Karl looking for the injury she had given him. *"Where did my kick land?"* she wondered. *"His right knee? His ankle or groin? Maybe I hit his stomach?"* She watched him shuffle backward pain slowly draining from his face to be replaced by a haughty determination. Then she saw it in the tracks he left behind as he moved. His right foot dragged heavy on the outer edge, *"He's lame!"* she thought triumphantly.

Without thinking she spun to Karl's right side and swept his right leg out from under him. Karl dropped to the ground landing on one knee. A throaty cheer went up around them as the audience reacted. With an answering roar, Karl wrapped D'Mique in an unyielding cloak of air, violently flinging her away from him. She flew through the air, landing hard on her rump about ten yards away. The Air magic dissipated as Karl charged toward her, now obviously limping on his right side. She hurried to her feet and ran to meet him, trying for another offensive streak against him, aiming for the weakness in his right leg. But Karl's double-blade attack foiled her attempt, and she quickly found herself back on defense, doing her best to block each attack. The grim snarl on Karl's face remained painted in place as he worked to slip through her defense. Every third or fourth swing found D'Mique's flesh, and soon she was bleeding from a dozen wounds. Blood running down her arms soon coated her hilt and each block compromised her grip on the weapon as the force of Karl's attack conspired with the blood, making it harder to keep hold of the sword.

Then her sword was gone, and Karl's blades whirled together before the right one cut into her side and the left one stopped just short of her neck. Appreciative applause erupted from the goblin crowd. Karl met her eyes, his breathing heavy but controlled. "Your breathing, Lady," he said, his blades remaining where they were. D'Mique swallowed hard and steadied her breathing, not taking her eyes from the elf. Karl smiled and withdrew his blades, pulling the one from her side as quickly as possible. She gasped in pain and shrank from the elf. Karl studied her for a long minute. "I feel better about your chances Lady," he said at last. "You're getting better every day. I like how you ferreted out an opponent's weakness and exploited it." He turned away from her, cleaning his blades off on his shirt before sheathing them. D'Mique collected her own weapon and cleaned it as well. "You're dismissed, Lady. Go find Genow for healing."

"Thank you," she offered before leaving. Goblins smiled at her or nodded in acceptance as she moved through the crowd. For the first time she allowed herself to consider the cheer they had voiced—a cheer for her, for a human.

Genow fluttered around her for a moment once she found him near the stables, studying each gash in turn. Sildona watched him work, patiently waiting for him to finish. Once he'd inspected each wound, he rested his hands on D'Mique's shoulders and closed his eyes. A stomach roiling wave washed over her, beginning where his hands touched her and moving outward along her extremities. At each gash, the power pooled and sunk deep inside her, pulling flesh together. She shivered in reaction to the elf's work. When he'd finished, his hands dropping to his side, she thanked him. "You're most welcome, Lady." Unspoken words sat between them.

"What is it?" D'Mique asked.

"I think you have fewer cuts today," he said, meeting her eyes and smiling. D'Mique nodded noncommittally and walked away.

There was still an hour until lunch and Shry was sure to be loitering around the barracks; there was time to work with him fulfilling his request that she meet him for another lesson. She found him sitting with five other soldiers near the back wall where she had been sparring with Karl. He smiled as she approached. "You want to work?" he asked, already knowing the answer, and she nodded. He mumbled something in his own language to the goblins nearest him then stood. "Let's go outside," he said glancing toward the Fiery Sisters nearly directly above them. "It will be cooler." D'Mique followed him across the courtyard and through the open gate. For a time they walked beneath the cool, close-growing pines unspeaking. D'Mique glanced at the ground from time to time, a habit Shry had asked her to develop. Deer, horses, foxes and birds had left signs of their passing in the dirt and underbrush. "How did you know about Karl's ankle," Shry asked as they walked. D'Mique noted his knowing smile before answering.

"You know. I saw his tracks. He stood heavier on the outer edge of his injured foot."

Shry nodded. "There may be hope for you yet," he said. He glanced around the forest. "How many deer were here today?" he asked, dropping his gaze.

"I—I didn't count," she stammered.

"Then go back and count."

Determined to answer the question D'Mique retraced their steps working slowly. She found a soft patch of soil that held several hoof prints along with hers and Shry's tracks. Perhaps three deer had passed along the trail, moving slowly, browsing on the brush. Near the main road she found several more tracks, *"But how do I tell if they were different deer than the other three?"* she asked herself. She counted again and came up with two deer. *"Five or three? Or were there always only two?"* Fretting she returned to the trail's prints and studied them—three deer, she decided. Then she returned to Shry.

"Well?"

"There were five deer here this morning," she said.

"What makes you think so?" Shry prodded.

"There were three in the forest and two on the road." Shry started to ask another question, but she moved to head him off, "The two on the road did not move into the forest because there is no trail showing a third deer joining them. Nor is there a third deer out on the road. Therefore there were two groups of deer, two on the road and three in the forest making five deer total."

Shry smiled, "you are correct as far as it goes. There were two deer at the front gate this morning and a group of three on the trail we followed as we walked." He paused, "but how many were on the other side of the road?" D'Mique gaped for a moment before closing her mouth. She had no answer. "Myrth wanted you to be on time for lunch today," Shry said dismissing her. She glanced up through the trees trying to judge the time. It felt later than midday. With a sigh she hurried back.

When she entered the training arena Myrth was seated with the rest of the cadets. Although he appeared to be at ease the others ate bathed in a tense silence. "Ah, D'Mique," he boomed on seeing her, "thank you for joining us."

"My apologies, Master," she said, bowing her head.

"Please sit," he responded. Obediently D'Mique found a spot between Genow and Rogan, opposite Myrth and Tierren. Trillip, his eyes fixed on his food, sat between Genow and the red goblin. Myrth looked from one to the next, pearl-gray eyes alight with merriment. "This is wonderful," he opined. Fork in hand, D'Mique picked daintily at her food unsure how to behave around the Master.

The stiff silence troubled her, *We can't be like this all the time,"* she thought. Taking a deep breath she spoke, "Thank you, Master, for sending the diplomats to my village."

"A trifle, D'Mique," he acknowledged her thanks with a wave of his hand.

Genow gasped, "Master Myrth uses your name?" he whispered to D'Mique, scandalized. Brows knitted, Rogan also reacted to the revelation, throwing her a glare before returning his attention to his meal.

Tierren took in their reaction, chewing slowly, although Myrth pointedly ignored them. Then, following D'Mique's lead, Tierren offered the breadbasket around the table also trying to break the ice. "Thank you, Tierren," Myrth said, taking a roll and continuing to eat. Several silent minutes passed before he set his fork down and chortled, "Well this is lively." Tierren chuckled and Myrth smiled.

"We do not deserve the high honor of eating with you Master Myrth," Genow whispered.

"Yes you do," Myrth countered, "Perhaps in your hurry to train and the upheaval of half our number leaving you haven't thought much about it, but you can't have forgotten why you're here." They sat in silence. "It may have escaped your notice, but there is a Greater Daemon on its way. Seer Oracle has positioned himself in the Tower. Although the daemon felt him watching and hid its presence from him, Oracle assures me that he will know when it breaks through into our world. And when it does...I am asking the eight of you to risk your lives for our world. At the very least I can call you friends—even call you by your names. At the very least we can enjoy our time together." These words were also met with a deep silence.

"If I am traveling to my death," D'Mique replied after a moment, "I want my last days to be with friends not strangers."

"Traveling to your death?" Myrth repeated, "Oracle named you to the group that has the greatest chance of succeeding."

"Succeeding without casualties?" she challenged. "How many of us will die killing this daemon?" Silence engulfed the table once again.

"Myrth," Tierren said into the silence, "We accept this fate."

"Such fate is a lie," Myrth responded, "Tell me, when the moment of death comes will you fight against it?" he asked, studying them in turn.

"I am forever a fighter, Master. Death will take me only after it beats me into the ground," D'Mique said glaring.

"Good. But call me by my name D'Mique."

"Of course Myrth," she said and his lips twitched into a smile.

"See, not too hard to do," he said.

After the food was gone Myrth stood, "Come along then, I will show you your new rooms," he said. They followed him out of the classroom and up the stairs to the third floor. Halfway up the spiral to the next level, a horrendous churning, rumbling noise began behind them. D'Mique looked back in time to watch a maelstrom of earth fill in the hole to the fourth floor. She stopped in her tracks.

Trillip shook his head and followed Myrth without a word, passing around D'Mique and Genow. "Just like that and our classroom and quarters are gone," the elf said awe and fear mingling in his voice, "It was so easy for him," he continued. "There are tales of War Masters. Have you heard them?" he asked looking up at D'Mique.

"I know the one about an army that came against the Water Master in the desert and drown, and the one where the Earth Master pulled a mountain down on his enemies," she half-whispered, eyes still on the fresh-scarred earth.

Rogan, who stood two steps above her, interrupted them, "Come on," he said, "Myrth doesn't want to wait." He talked as they walked, joining their conversation, "How about the one where the Fire Master called to the friction heat generated by a charging army and burst them all into flames, or the Wind Master who stole the air from everyone in a valley suffocating hundreds of people."

"We are indeed lucky we live in peaceful times," Myrth rumbled from where he'd stopped to wait for them, Trillip and Tierren beside him. D'Mique and her companions pulled up short startled by his interjection. They looked at Myrth, his words hanging heavy around them. D'Mique's heart fluttered in her chest, a sudden fear bolting through her. Remembered horror stories clamored for attention as the realization dawned—a Master stood before her. According to the stories he was a creature who could encase her completely in stone and walk away, humming, leaving her to suffocate! He could call stones from the ground and throw them with his mind faster than the eye could see, or take the sand from an hourglass and send it streaming across the room, glass shards exploding in its wake. Souring a farmer's fields was the least of her worries. She could feel the stone around her, over her waiting to drop, under her waiting to leap up and engulf her. The stone only waited for a word from this hawk-man to collapse on her, crushing bones and life from her fragile human body. "I call you my friends," Myrth continued, meeting each one's eyes in turn. "I have never used my powers to take the life of a stranger or a friend. There should be no fear between us—the goblins will tell you my heart." He added nodding to Rogan and Tierren.

They returned the gesture as Tierren spoke, "The stories scare you as much as they scare us," he added.

Myrth glared at him a moment. Then he nodded slowly, "Indeed. Those are not the words I would use, but they are true enough."

D'Mique swallowed. "I'm sorry, Myrth," she said, "When you hear so many stories...."

"I know D'Mique," he interrupted, "There's no reason to apologize. Come, let me take you on a tour of your new chambers. Tierren your wife is waiting as well." Wide-eyed Tierren rushed forward.

"One last unpleasant question Myrth," Genow said as they walked across the first floor, one level down from the barracks. They stopped and looked back at the elf. "Well," he glanced nervously from one person to the next, "Umm... . It's been said that you are strong enough to influence metal objects."

"Metal?" D'Mique asked aloud before thinking, *"Metal is unnatural, beyond the reach of any Master!"*

"Metal is made of purified minerals, the basis of all earth and stone. It is theorized that a strong enough Earth Mage could influence metal," Genow explained looking at Myrth. D'Mique studied the Earth Master waiting for his answer.

His face was carefully blank as he contemplated the question. "It isn't the metal itself," Myrth spoke at last, "but the impurities within the metal." He smiled before turning and leading the way to a set of large doors. Servants and soldiers made way for him and the trailing Honor Guard, bowing low before their Master.

"He didn't really answer my question did he?" Genow observed quietly. D'Mique chuckled under her breath, pondering the answer Myrth had given.

As they followed the Earth Master, he treated them to a tour of the underground palace. "This is the thoroughfare," he said as they walked down a wide, well-lit hallway. "It runs from the barracks to the throne room." At the end of the thoroughfare sat a large stone door, two huge goblins standing guard before it. They bowed and stepped aside as Myrth stopped before the door. "Beyond lies my private residence and this door is the only way in or out without me or the ability to use Earth magic," he added offhandedly as he opened the door and led them into a carpeted hall.

The floor covering was a muted red, the color of rust, with white fringe around the edges. It matched the curtains that hung at regular intervals along the left wall, and between each set of curtains sat an enchanted window depicting the same setting D'Mique had seen before, a distant view of the Dragon Hills. From where they stood the hall branched to the right and ran straight before them for about fifty feet before turning right again. Myrth left the doorway to the thoroughfare and headed down the right hand hallway. At the end it turned left, forming a large square with the previous halls. The evenly spaced windows continued their parade around the inner wall of the square while thick wooden doors occupied the outer walls.

"This first room is Genow and Kryoso," Myrth recited as he walked the corridors, "This next one is Rogan and Marco." They reached the second left turn in their trek along the square, opposite the large doors from the thoroughfare. Halfway along this stretch they came to a staircase on their right. "These stairs can be made to open into my audience chamber," Myrth said waving at them as he passed. At the end of the hall they made another left. The room opposite Rogan and Marco's belonged to Tierren and Samsha, his wife, and the next to Trillip and Clippen. Another left turn brought them almost back to the doors of the thoroughfare. Two doors sat opposite each other in the center of this hall. "On your right is D'Mique, on your left is me," Myrth said opening the door to his room at the center of the square and gesturing for them to enter.

They crowded into a light, airy room. "Please, look around. The balconies are enchanted, like the windows, so you shouldn't try to go out on them." Myrth sat down on a nearby padded chair, watching as his guards explored the area. There were three more chairs ranged around a large oval table laid with food trays. The guards spread out as he instructed, exploring. Every wall, including the one with the door, held multiple balconies and large arched windows. What little wall space remained between them was white with gold flecks.

A huge canopy bed sat in the center of the room on a raised dais. The rust brown gauzy curtains surrounding it matched Myrth's feathers. Between the bed and the table sat a sunken bath of white marble. Opposite the bath, taking up most the rest of the room, stood a series of low shelves, ringed around a large square table and chair. The shelves held hundreds of books and scrolls and upon the table sat three large glass jars. D'Mique stared at the jars, remembering stories she had heard of them. There was one for each Master, full of the corresponding element, and they allowed the Masters to communicate with one another.

"Is this your home Myrth?" Trillip asked, waving to the scene beyond the balconies and windows. D'Mique looked out the balcony windows where he was standing. The ground fell away steeply, covered in snow or rubbed raw by the passage of ice. Clouds drifted by, far below. They were on top of a very high mountain.

"This is Imperial's Summit, a place I often visited in my youth," Myrth answered.

"You're from Hawkethorne?" Trillip asked surprised.

Myrth chuckled. "Ages ago, Trillip," he said. He stood in one smooth motion. All eyes turned to him. "Now before you retire to your rooms there are a couple things I should tell you. All the rooms have the same floor plan. That way you'll know each room perfectly even if you have to enter it in darkness. If you would like a different scene in your windows or balconies just ask. I picked places close to your original homes. Finally, consider this your haven, the doors are sealed while I sleep and none may enter nor may any leave," he added. Also, your roommates will be back in a short time so share nicely." He sighed and shrugged, then smiled, "Dismissed," he finished. They nodded their heads in unison and turned to leave.

The others filed out past D'Mique leaving her in the doorway. She hesitated, staring across the hallway at the door to her own room. A room she would have to herself. She turned back to Myrth, "Myrth is there a reason I am closest to your door?" she asked, her mind jumping to a variety of conclusions.

"Are you insinuating something?" he asked, an amused smile pulling at the corners of his mouth.

D'Mique chuckled nervously, "Not really, not from you," she said, although his words caused her stomach to flip over. "But ..." she trailed off.

"I shall consider that a compliment," Myrth said. "I placed Tierren and Rogan at the most vulnerable entrance. Also Marco my most powerful mage. Samsha is with Tierren because they are married. If there were a breach in the outer wall the invaders would reach this stronghold through the audience chamber and down those stairs. The goblins belong to me and will fight to the death for me." He paused and D'Mique nodded her understanding. "My first thought was to split the Land-Nymphs, but then I saw how fragile Trillip has become. You know about Mara?" D'Mique nodded again as he continued, "So I decided to put them together. This leaves my healer guarded by a mage instead of a sword."

"It didn't really matter which room I put those two pairs in so I chose the outer ones. That left only one place for you. I also noted how close you and Genow were—friends mind you," he added when she glared, "so I put you as close to him as I could."

"To protect him?"

"Yes, if there is an invasion." He stood in thought for a moment. "Are you worried about unwanted attention?" he asked cocking his head to the side.

"A little," she admitted. Although as she said it, she realized that, for the most part, her fellow honor guards had stopped eyeing her and chuckling darkly behind her back. *"Does that mean they have accepted me?"* she thought. Only Rogan caused her heart to skip a beat from time to time. But she had to agree with Myrth, her friendship with Genow had grown in leaps and bounds. Myrth closed his eyes for a moment. She waited recognizing the long pause as a sign that the mage was working with the forcelines.

"I changed your door," Myrth said when he opened his eyes. "It will now only unlock for your hand. You need only fear three unwanted guests. I am Semian and old enough to be your grandfather so no worries there. Sylus is elfin and has not been given permission to use your name, so you are safe from him. That leaves Marco. We'll see to him when the time comes."

"Wait," the mention of Marco brought back something, "did you say that Marco is your strongest mage?" Myrth nodded. "What about Sylus?"

"Sylus is bonded. Most of his power is borrowed from me."

"But Marco is stronger than he is?"

"They are evenly matched now. If Sylus was set free from his bond Marco would be stronger." D'Mique stood a moment in thought.

"Thank you Myrth, for the door," she added. He nodded and smiled seeing her out. She walked across the hall and entered her room, Myrth's door closing behind her.

The room mirrored Myrth's in layout. The curtains on the bed were deep green, highlighting her eyes. Her bed was not quite as big; her oval table was not as grand, only two chairs sat beside it. The sunken bath was black marble streaked with gold veins. Her desk and low shelves were empty and seemed lonely. The platform which her bed sat on held several drawers. She opened them. All empty. However the travel pack that she had brought with her from home sat on her bed.

Her balconies and arched windows were less numerous than Myrth's and looked out into a close-growing forest. "The Dark Forest," she whispered, noting the wood paneled walls. Moving her pack she lay down on the bed and fell asleep staring out a window, wondering if any animals would wander past.

Into the Mage Realm

For several hours after leaving Dragon Ridge Palo rode at the back of the group conversing with Clippen, while Sylus led the way through the Dragon Hills Forest. Once the road left the woods Palo and Clippen urged their horses forward, taking the lead, and increasing their pace. For Marco the first day passed in a blur of tall grass, horses, and hasty meals. That evening they stopped to set up camp as Nix and Col touched the horizon. Once the bedrolls lay around the crackling fire Clippen spent half an hour leading Marco and Kryoso through several breathing exercises meant to calm their minds, allowing them to step into the Mage Realm. Afterward the Land-Nymph sent them to bed. For some time after Marco crawled under his blankets he lay watching Clippen and Palo as they conversed in low whispers, in a language Marco did not know, leaning close to each other and laughing from time to time. Sparks drifted around him, toying with him as they gleamed in and out of existence. He had been ignoring his fairies, he felt, quite successfully while training at Dragon Ridge. Sleep overcame him soon after he lay down.

Clippen startled Marco awake, gently shaking him before smiling broadly and moving on to wake Kryoso. Marco sat up, yawning and stretching as he clambered to his feet. Light streaked the sky, the Fiery Sisters just peeking over the rim of the world as the night dissipated. "It's time to practice," Clippen called. He sat near the fire pit, the coals cold within it, waiting for Marco and Kryoso to join him. As they did so he continued, "This time work on seeing the world without opening your eyes." His cryptic instructions brought a frown to Kryoso's face, but Marco closed his eyes, clearing his mind, eager for another attempt at entering the Mage Realm. He fell back on the novice skills learned during yesterday's brief session, focusing on his breathing until he felt centered, then envisioning the world around him, trying to remember what the campsite looked like without peeking. As he worked sparks suddenly flared behind his eyes startling him. Gasping, Marco lost his concentration. "Marco?" Clippen questioned, noticing. Shaking his head, Marco returned to the exercise, curious but not willing to explain. While they worked Sylus packed and when all was ready Clippen called an end to the session and ordered everyone to mount; they would eat as they rode.

As the Fiery Sisters reached their zenith the group stopped for a short rest. Sylus tended to the horses as Clippen and Palo sat with Marco and Kryoso, retreating into meditation once again. This time Palo walked them through a series of mind-clearing exercises and tricks designed to help them enter the Mage Realm. Marco embraced each word of advice and threw himself into the session determined to break through into that other world, the only place where he could learn to control the elemental forcelines and work magic. As he sat, thinking of nothing, the darkness retreated, pulling away from him. With closed eyes, suddenly he could see the world around him as a gray, shadowy version of the original. Everywhere he looked vivid colors slowly appeared. *"Oh!"* he thought, *"This is the Mage Realm!"* Marco shouted in his head, his elation engulfing him. Above him blue and gray wisps grew from the fairies he'd grown up chasing to an expanse of color. The gold sparks around him joined together to form ribbons of light. "It was here all the time," he breathed.

Palo growled in his ear, "Mount up!" startling him. The gray world winked out of existence and Marco opened his eyes, the lost glimpse of his goal floated in his mind. Frowning he stood slowly, Palo rising beside him. They eyed each other for a moment, Marco smiled at the snow leopard remembering the Grand Syra's easy friendship with Clippen. But Palo only stared, waiting.

"Come. We will be in Olimidia tonight," Sylus called.

"Actually, no," Palo said, turning to the elf, "We are leaving the road. I'll take Marco and Kryoso straight across the plain—it will save an entire day of travel—if you'd like to go to Olimidia on your own." Sylus glared at the Grand Syra without speaking. Palo shook his head, "Myrth insists on having his mages trained by the Potentate but time is short. As much as I would love to sleep in a warm bed tonight, I can't justify staying on the road and detouring to Olimidia." The Grand Syra collected his horse and mounted before continuing, "Will you be joining us, Clippen?" he asked.

The Land-Nymph surveyed the plains looking west across the grassland and north along the road before replying, "I must go with Sylus, Palo. I promised Trillip that I would check on Mara."

Palo nodded his understanding, "A good journey to you both then," he said. "Come on, Marco," he turned his horse westward. Kryoso, already mounted on his horse, followed the Grand Syra into the grass as Marco hurried into his saddle moving quickly to catch up with them.

They followed Palo through the tall grass until sunset when they stopped and set camp—Palo working confidently but silently beside them. Once the fire burned brightly the Grand Syra motioned for them to sit in meditation. "Yesterday and this morning we worked on clearing our minds, entering the Mage Realm," he started, "Tonight we will enter the Mage Realm." His words carried a determined finality. "I'll give you a few moments to do the work yourself, but after that time I will have to pull you into the Realm." He paused, "I'd rather not do that by the way." He sat back and closed his eyes. Swallowing, Marco threw a nervous glance to Kryoso, whose expression confirmed his fears. If Palo had to pull them into the Mage Realm it was not going to be pleasant. However, heartened by his earlier glimpse of the elusive realm, Marco brushed aside the twinge of fear and confidently closed his eyes, centering himself and envisioning the gray-washed world he'd seen before.

The Mage Realm manifested around him, replacing the inner darkness of his centered mind with a dusky version of their campsite. In front of him, smiling and as vividly colored as he had been in the physical realm, sat Palo. "Oh good," he said, "You did step into the Mage Realm this morning then." Marco nodded. "If you concentrate a bit harder you will have a more solid body," he said, motioning toward Marco's center. Marco looked down at his form. Rather than the vivid solidity of Palo's form, his form looked as if it were made of glass and filled with smoke. The sight broke Marco's concentration, and he fell out of the Mage Realm, dropping back into his physical form. He opened his eyes and stared down at his chest for a moment before looking back up at Palo.

The Grand Syra sat across from him with his eyes closed and face blank. Marco hesitated just a second longer before closing his eyes and stepping back into the Mage Realm. The transition was almost instantaneous, like slipping in and out of a pool of water. This time Kryoso stood beside the fire, his 'body' slightly more solid than Marco's had been the first time. "He can stand," Marco thought, before turning his attention to his own body. As he had done with the world around him, he worked to remember what his body looked like in the physical realm. The smoky glass solidified and grew vivid. Happy with his work Marco looked up at Palo smiling.

"Good," the Grand Syra said from where he sat. "We will start with the study of forcelines and sources. Kryoso sit back down. There is no reason to gallivant around."

"Yes Grand Syra," the Mortak said, sitting again.

"The basics are easy enough to understand," Palo began, "Earth power flows in currents along the ground. Air and Water form billowing, intermixed clouds. Fire exists within source points almost like sparks in the darkness. I want you to search for these elements. You are not to touch them, merely study them," he said, his voice confident that he would be obeyed. "If you cannot see the powers you cannot work with them," Palo chided.

Marco studied the sea of wisps above him, "No," he thought, "Not wisps, not fairies. Water and Air. And the sparks," he swallowed around the lump that suddenly formed in his throat, "All this time they were Earth." He relaxed, the colors growing more pronounced. A thick golden current of Earth traveled east to west, cutting through the middle of their camp. As he watched the power eddied around them, whirling against their half-formed bodies. There was nothing to feel as it brushed against his knees and lapped over his ankles. He looked at Palo and Kryoso. Amidst the vivid colors of Palo's Mage Realm body, he could just make out thousands of tiny red sparks, all of them Fire sources.

"Very good, Marco," Palo said with the hint of a smile. Marco looked to Kryoso expecting the same forest of red pinpricks. Instead his fellow student remained smoky and somewhat transparent. Marco frowned. "Sometimes," Palo said catching Marco's reaction, "Mortaks are different. No one knows why." Palo looked at Kryoso, "I dare say you do not know."

Kryoso shook his head. "Elves are also different, being pools of Life magic. If Sylus were here you would see him as a whirling green source point rather than a series of red Fire points. The Fire exists, of course, but they are lost in the Life."

Marco returned his attention to the river of Earth magic coursing around him, reaching out with his will, pondering how hard he would have to think to move it. It roiled away from him! Surprised Marco dropped out of the Mage Realm, his eyes snapping open. An astonished Palo greeted him, eyes wide, feline mouth agape. At seeing this reaction a bolt of fear flashed through Marco.

The snow leopard recovered quickly, "I remember telling you not to touch the forcelines, Marco."

"But I—" Marco stopped, swallowing hard as Palo's scowl deepened. "I apologize, Grand Syra," he finished.

"Go to bed, both of you. Our next lesson will be more taxing," he said, dismissing Marco's transgression. With a sigh—partly of relief—Marco retired to his bedroll.

"Patterns work with all types of magic," Palo said, "and every pattern will produce a different effect depending on what it's made from." Once again, they were seated in the Mage Realm after a few fitful hours of sleep. Palo continued, pulling ephemeral wisps of green light from the world around him, willing them to coalesce into a solid, woven pattern that hugged the ground around them. "The Net," Palo introduced, "When woven from Earth it creates a quake sphere, which will cause the area to explode when the pattern is disturbed." Kryoso gasped beside him as Marco froze, his eyes wide. Palo smiled, "But, if the Net is made with Life, as this one is, it forms a ward against daemon-kin. When disturbed by daemonic forces it explodes as well, although it doesn't cause any physical harm."

"When we set a ward we have to monitor it to make sure it remains undisturbed?" Kryoso asked. Palo nodded. "But wards are set in order to allow everyone to sleep. How do you monitor a ward while sleeping?"

"Practice," Palo replied, "Which is what I'd like you to do now. Practice making the Net out of Air and Life magic." He looked pointedly at Marco, "Not out of Earth." He waited for Marco to acknowledge the command before continuing, "While you practice, I'll pack." Palo winked out of existence leaving Kryoso and Marco to stare at each other. With a small shrug Kryoso turned his attention to the fleeting wisps of Life magic that rippled off the plants surrounding them.

Marco concentrated, trying to pull the green Life magic into a workable braid. Yet the golden Earth Power overwhelmed his senses, the river running through the center of the campsite, pooling around him and piling up against his knees. He fought through the Earth flow, searching for the elusive green strands. Looking outward toward the grassy plains, he noticed for the first time that the golden Earth power also sunk into the ground, forming a diffuse cloud beneath everything else, mirroring the diffuse cloud of Air and Water above him. Surprised, Marco turned to Kryoso for his opinion.

Kryoso screamed and fell out of the Mage Realm as the red Fire sources sparkling in his arm flared suddenly. A split second later pain exploded through Marco's head and he fell out of the Mage Realm as well, toppling to the ground as he slammed into the physical realm. The pain continued, thundering from his temple to his jaw. Marco looked around, glaring when his gaze fell upon Palo, who stood over him, snarling. "Never again, Man Child, never again!" Palo shouted. Marco's glare softened into confusion. "To bed, Marco, now!" Palo ordered.

He sat up slowly, his head spinning and his face a swath of red agony. *"What happened?"* Standing, he stumbled to his bedroll, his whole body shaking. After crawling into his blankets, he felt his cheek gingerly. Shallow gashes started in the hollow of his cheek and ran all the way to his eye, blood flowing freely from them. He scooted around until he could reach his pack without getting out of bed and pulled out a linen wrap, holding it to his face to stop the bleeding. He lay quietly for some time applying pressure to his wound. Thoughts chased around his head, *"Why had the Fire flared like that? Did I do that?"* He felt his wound again, realizing that Palo had pulled his punch, *"He could have shredded my cheek easily and it would have been even easier to take my eye."* Marco soon fell into a fitful sleep none of his questions resolved.

When he awoke the next day it was still well before dawn and he thought he'd be the first awake but Palo sat before the fire. Its flames danced eerily in his gold-green eyes, his leopard nose twitched as he turned to watch Marco join him. Marco knelt before him head bowed. "I have come to apologize, Grand Syra. I am not sure what happened, but I have to know, is Kryoso okay?"

"He's fine," Palo whispered, "It is only a mild burn. I know you didn't mean to touch the Fire sources," he continued, "Which is why you will not be scarred or blinded for life," he finished with a smile, turning his head sideways to study the wound.

Marco digested his words before replying, "I don't understand how I touched the Fire source without meaning to Grand Syra," Marco said.

"It happens Marco, particularly with strong mages. Tell me what you were doing, and we can figure out how you touched the Fire unintentionally." Marco gathered his thoughts before answering. "Well, I was studying the Earth flow and noticed that it forms a cloud within the ground, the same as the Air forms above us." Marco looked over at Kryoso, "Then I looked at Kryoso and the Fire sources flared." Marco returned his attention to Palo. The Grand Syra was gaping at him, obviously surprised. Marco returned the surprised look, "What?"

"The Earth Cloud?" Palo asked, his voice barely more than a whisper.

Marco shook his head. "What is that?"

Palo clamped his mouth shut and closed his eyes. Marco sat waiting confused by the Grand Syra's reaction. A long minute passed before Palo opened his eyes and continued, "It took an enormous effort to see the Earth Cloud, Marco. When you looked at Kryoso your effort did not diminish. Thus, you flared the Fire sources."

Marco nodded. "Yes, that makes sense."

Palo nodded with him, "An accident was bound to happen," he sighed, "Normally these first lessons are conducted by a skilled Potent, but we are sorely pressed for time. You may not have noticed yet, but Master Myrth shares many qualities with his elemental familiar." Palo smiled.

"His what?"

"His elemental familiar, the stone," Palo replied. Marco choked on a laugh as the Semian continued, a hint of nostalgia coloring his voice, "Myrth can be very stubborn and thick-headed at times, and he insists on the Potentate training you. Both Oracle and I are against it, of course, but Myrth often gets his way."

"Oracle is the seer that came with you to Dragon Ridge?"

"Yes. He watches the Void for the daemon's approach. He stayed at Dragon Ridge to gloat over Myrth when the daemon enters our world and you are still with me."

"Really?"

Palo chuckled, "No. The Tower of the Elements holds a gateway into the Void. Oracle has a better chance of an early warning there."

"Oh."

"Wake Kryoso, Marco, and pack, then it is time to meditate again," he instructed after a moment of silence.

"Yes, Grand Syra." Marco hurried to obey. Palo watched him the entire time with a calculating look on his mottled face.

Just before dawn they sat together, meditating. Now that Marco knew about the golden cloud it was easy to see, hovering beneath them. In places it erupted into tiny golden rivers and the power spilled outward, joining the current that traveled west. This morning he felt compelled to join it, and allowed his consciousness to be pulled along by the river of Earth. He rode it across an uninhabited stretch of the Fanterra Plain to the Sea of Eternity, the sea to their west. After crossing a small channel the power descended into a whirling vortex. *"This is Master Island?"* he thought. Before he could drop into the maelstrom he opened his eyes, his vision snapping back to the Physical Realm where the Fiery Sisters lit his face, dragging his consciousness back to his body.

"Mount up," Palo commanded rising and heading for his own horse. "We'll be in Gaity this evening," he said, the encouragement in his voice only slightly forced.

Training with the Potentate

The suns were setting when they neared the ocean shore. Marco glanced at the sky, looking for Rysk, but it was futile. For the first half of the night there would be no Ghost Moon, only stars. He returned his attention to the world before him. Here the grassy plain eroded away into a stony, shallow bay. Across from them a large, wooded island glistened in the dying light. *"My entire village would fit between the shore and that island,"* Marco realized. The maelstrom of energy from last night flashed through his mind, *"I guess I've seen this place before,"* he mused. Several ferries plied the rough water of the channel, carrying all manner of peoples, cargo and animals. It took Marco a moment to realize humans were absent from the throng. He lowered his head rounding his shoulders as he retreated, *"I'm alone at the end of the world,"* he thought. Unbidden his horse started toward the water, following Palo.

A well-worn but sturdy pier extended into the water and, as the ferries pulled up alongside it, their passengers disembarked followed by their crews. As the suns set the few boats crossing to the island were nearly empty and those coming to shore seemed full to the brim. After disembarking, a short walk to the north brought passengers to a small town that, if pressed, the residents would say was called Gaity Banks, though most travelers never asked. It was little more than a collection of inns, pens and stables serving the needs of those who could not find shelter within Gaity or who missed the last ferry.

"We are too late for the last ferries," Kryoso said pointing across the channel where several white flags, adorned by black crosses, unfurled along the cliff face, signaling the end of the day's travel across the channel.

Scoffing, Palo tossed his head, "I am the Grand Syra. I will not be kept off my island," he said scanning the arriving ferries. "There," he said,

"Four Potents are on that one." Marco looked where he had pointed. At the back of the crowd stood four soldiers, an unmistakable aura of command and self-confidence emanating from each. Even more obvious than their bearing, their unrelieved black uniforms set them apart from the merchants and workers around them, while their small black caps, each one decorated with two narrow red feathers, bobbed above the crowd.

Palo urged his horse toward the pier, eyes set on the four red-feathered soldiers. "You there!" the dock master growled as Palo passed his stand, "Can't you see the flags? The far side has closed!" Palo turned in his saddle and glared at the elf who had addressed him. The elf squeaked in response, "Grand Syra!" and fell to his knees in the dirt. Palo continued to the pier a slight smile on his feline face. At the shore he dismounted and waited for the various farmers and merchants to clear a path, most bowing reverently as they passed him.

The soldiers disembarked before Palo reached them and he shouted, "Members of the Potentate! Re-embark! You shall accompany us back to Gaity—I have a job for you!" The four soldiers stopped, shielding their eyes in the light of the setting suns, as they searched for the owner of the voice.

"Who speaks to four Potents in this manner?" a gruff goblin countered.

"I am called Grand Syra by most, Char," Palo answered.

The three other soldiers bowed at the waist remaining bent over as the goblin chuckled, replying, "But I remember calling you 'ignorant whelp' on more than one occasion." Palo laughed as he closed the distance between them and embraced the goblin, old friends reacquainted.

"Rise Potents," Palo said absently. "I have brought two trainees from Dragon Ridge. Will you take them in?"

"Have you no modesty?" one of the Potents hissed at Marco, "How dare you strut about, your humanity visible to all!" Marco gaped as the Potent crowded close to him, noting the thin black veil, held in place over his face by an elaborate, beaded band. Marco struggled to make sense of the veil and threat.

Kryoso leaned close, "By custom Semians hide the parts of their bodies that look human and flaunt—within the bounds of modesty—the areas that are animal."

Marco tossed him a grateful smile but it faded quickly as he stared at his accuser, thinking, *"He's a Semian with a human face and he thinks I'm Semian too!"* Marco bit back a laugh, his jovial reaction stoking the Semian's obvious anger and indignation. "But I'm human," he replied, swallowing his mirth. The Semian drew back, his shock so obvious Marco chuckled again.

"Impossible! The Children of Man have no magic," the Potent replied.

Char, the goblin, eyed the pair and turned to Palo.

"There is enough time tomorrow to prove both that Marco is human and a mage," the Grand Syra answered. "Take us now to Gaity. I am weary of the road."

"By your command," Char bowed his head slightly before turning on his heel and leading them back to the ferry where the crew was preparing to go home for the night. "One more crossing, by order of the Grand Syra!" Char barked, halting their work. The crew bowed low as Palo stepped aboard, leading his horse, with the others following behind. As they boarded a Potent took a position beside each of them as an escort or, in Marco's case, a guard. For a few minutes they stood quiet as the crew positioned themselves. Marco fidgeted under the harsh gaze of his Potent guard, the veil an ineffective barrier against the Semian's hatred and suspicion. As the ferry pulled away from the pier, Marco took stock of the other Potents, striving to ignore his. In addition to the veiled Semian and Char, a dark, brown-skinned goblin the color of loamy soil with large heel spurs and over-sized fangs, they were accompanied by a second goblin, a willowy goblin-maid with white skin and sunny yellow hair, and an elf.

"That's a strange color combination for a goblin," Marco thought, staring at her while the elf spoke quietly to Kryoso. Unable to ignore his guard Marco spent most of the journey across the channel watching him from the corner of his eye, taking in his defiant, arms crossed, stance. The crew, though tired from their day's work, rowed the ferry smoothly through the water and mere minutes passed before they reached the island pier. The dock jutted out from the cliff face and a pair of soldiers dressed in the same black uniforms as the Potents—the only difference being the white feathers in their caps—stomped down the length of it to meet them. They looked ready to turn the ferry back until they saw Char and Palo at the front and, gaping suddenly, bowed low at the waist. The ferry pulled alongside the

pier and a flurry of orchestrated movement by the crew soon had it tied off long enough to unload its passengers and their horses before it started for home at last. The Potents and their guests followed Char and Palo down the pier. As they neared the cliff face Marco noted the deep, shadowed scar that offered access from the pier to the island.

Beyond the pier and the cliff scar a well-traveled path led up into the forest. As they climbed to the top Marco noticed several square towers and black pennants rising above the treetops, visible against the gathering night, a short distance from where they would emerge from the scar. Leaving the cleft, the forest embraced the path and its travelers. There was no underbrush to speak of; the massive trees had stolen too much sunlight. The trees grew flush against a granite wall that melted from the gloom as the party approached the city of Gaity, where a sturdy wooden gate barred their path.

Char pounded on it until a small window opened and a disgruntled, white-feathered goblin guard peeked out. "We escort the Grand Syra," Char informed him. Palo leaned in close, crowding Char out of the way, and smiled at the guard. Any protests died under Palo's gaze and the guard quickly disappeared, swinging the gate open a moment later. Beyond the wall a city stretched outward, encompassing much of the island's interior. The houses, neat and compact, did not rise beyond two stories. They were all off-white stone, their window shutters and doors painted in a variety of colors. Here at the gate, the path became a proper road running straight to a large palace at the city's center.

Palo led the way, the only noise falling between the storefronts lining the main thoroughfare was the whispered conversation between him and Char and the solid steps of their horses. Upon reaching the palace, a white wall matching the one surrounding the city barred their way. Rising above, the palace within sported four square towers and a bright white dome at its center. At the palace gate they once again had to stop and knock. Palo waited for the window to open before saying, "I am unaccustomed to being locked out of my own house!" The white-feathered elfin guard apologized through the window as the gate opened, saying over and over again that there had been no notice of Palo's arrival. Palo glared angrily the whole time. Once they were all in and he had stalked off away from the gate, the

Grand Syra chuckled. "Had him hopping," he confided to Char. The goblin gave a throaty laugh as Marco frowned at the Grand Syra's back.

When they reached the huge white dome liveried elves came forward to take their horses and Palo turned to the Potents, "Settle them into the camps," he said regarding Marco and Kryoso, "We'll meet tomorrow and assign each of you a mentor," he glared at Marco, adding, "No trouble tonight."

"Of course not Grand Syra," he answered. Nodding and taking Char's arm, Palo headed for the main dome leaving them with the Potents.

"Come," said the goblin-maid, a lilting voice in the near dark. She seemed well built, her hair flowing around a rugged face. "The Potentate quarters are around back."

"I've never seen a blonde goblin before," Marco noted as they trudged around the dome building. She looked over at him.

"She's a sun goblin from the Misty Realms to the north," Kryoso answered, "Many of them serve Marladon."

"You are correct Mortak. I am Lien," she introduced as they stopped. Before them a low hedge separated the courtyard from a lawn of short grass. In turn the lawn gave way to an open packed dirt area surrounded on three sides by low wooden barracks.

"As I told Kryoso before," the elf began, "The Potentate is comprised of three encampments: elves, goblins, and Semians. Since neither of you fall into those camps you are free to choose. I will say however, that there are three Mortaks living with the elves."

Kryoso glanced at Marco, a brief apology on his brow and shrugged his shoulders, "Take me to the elf camp then," he instructed, "I should be with my own people."

"This one will come with me to the Semian camp!" the veiled guard shouted, "He will also be with his own kind."

"I am not Semian!" Marco tried again.

"We shall see." Venom dripped from the Semian's words.

Marco, shocked by the Semian's vicious tone, stammered a series of near-incoherent denials. In response to his stammering the Potent held out a gloved hand palm up. With a small pop, a ball of fire appeared above his hand.

"Marco be careful," Kryoso cautioned, "he's a Fire Mage. Maybe you should humor him and go to the Semian barracks."

After a moment's thought Marco concurred, "Fine," he said, "I'll go to the Semian camp, but I am not a Semian." With a curt nod the fireball winked out of existence. The veiled Potent motioned for Marco to lead the way and directed him to the building on the left; Kryoso and the elf disappeared into the center building.

Inside, the Semian barracks was one large room with sleeping compartments, stacked one above another, lining the walls. Two wooden chairs and a small table accompanied each pair of beds. Three long tables with accompanying benches dominated the center of the chamber. Near the back an unmarked door led into the bathroom. Small groups of Semians, ranging in type from avian and feline to stag, occupied the room; there were about twenty of them total. Their conversations died as they sighted him and his escort, their eyes following him to the center of the room where a black-furred feline Semian sat laughing with his companion, a stag.

Once Marco and his guard reached the table, the feline left off his conversation and studied his visitors, unspeaking, while his gloved hands deftly shuffling a deck of cards. What Marco could see of the feline Semian's black fur was slashed with white stripes. He wore thick cotton trousers and a gray linen shirt with long sleeves. His companion, whose velveteen horns sprouted from a human forehead, gazed suspiciously up at Marco with inhuman goat-like eyes atop a muzzle that pushed out from the deep-bronze of her face, a face covered in the same velveteen fur as her horns and arms. Her hands ended in two thick-skinned fingers—dexterous cloven hooves—and held a fan of cards. "Well, hello Almira," the black tiger said at last, addressing the veiled Semian, "What have you brought us today?"

"Almira?" Marco turned to the covered Semian, "You're a girl?"

"I am a lady, not a girl," she spat from behind the veil. Now that he knew the veiled Semian was female he could hear the dusky lilt in her voice. The black tiger chuckled and the veiled Semian turned back to face him. "Pyko, I've brought a new Semian trainee," Almira said, "He claims to be human," she added. Eyebrows were raised and whispers chased through the crowd that started forming around them.

"And you don't believe him," Pyko observed.

"Well there hasn't been a mage human in ages! It's far more likely that he is Semian and pretending to be human."

The tiger-man sniffed the air. "He smells human." The stag chuckled at his remark and Marco's scowl.

"If you haven't noticed, I smell human too," Almira hissed from behind the veil.

"Well, what do you propose?" Pyko looked to Marco. "What's your name?"

"Marco."

"See? A Semian name!" Almira shouted, her voice suddenly triumphant.

"Almira, you have an elfin name. Names mean nothing." The stag bent over in silent fits of laughter at the exchange. Pyko studied Marco for a moment. "Where are you from?"

"The Dark Forest, the village of Trinik."

"The Dark Forest? I do not know it," Pyko said.

"The Nesting?" the stag asked, awe breaking over her face as her laughter died.

"The Nesting?" Pyko repeated. A murmur ran through the onlookers.

"That changes nothing," Almira said. Pyko studied her for a moment. He looked back at Marco.

"You're on your own here, she is very stubborn," he said at last. "Perhaps you can prove you are a mage? That would be simplest."

"I don't know what I can do? I don't think I'm allowed to touch the forcelines tonight," he admitted, absently running his fingers across the scabbed-over scratches on his right cheek. Pyko and the stag followed his gesture and understanding lit Pyko's face. *"Maybe he knows how I got them,"* Marco thought.

"Strip down! Let us search for animalia," Almira spat, breaking the tenuous bridge between Marco and Pyko.

Marco gaped at her. "Are you out of your mind? I will do no such thing! I am human!" He floundered about for a believable reason, "The sight of my humanity will be distressing to some of you." Laughter, some of it nervous, erupted around the room.

"Better to be embarrassed than suffer through someone fooling the Potentate," Almira responded ignoring the laughter that ringed them.

Marco wracked his brain, *"There has to be a way out of this,"* he thought. An idea flashed into his head. With a sly smile he looked at Almira and said, "I'll show you mine if you show me yours." A wave of dark laughter rippled through the crowd.

"Very well," Almira said pulling herself up to her full height, the top of her head coming to Marco's chin.

She pulled off her black gloves, dropping them to the dirt floor. Her hands were a delicate bronze, completely human. She undid a catch at the bottom of her veil, hooking a delicate gold chain to the bottom of it. Then she lifted the veil showing her face for the first time. Her smooth brown skin covered high cheekbones and a broad nose. Her full lips were drawn out in a sneer. Perfect, dark eyes glared at him. She removed the veil and cap. They joined the gloves on the floor. Short black hair curled around human ears, falling around her delicate neck.

"You're... You're beautiful," Marco stammered. The angry sneer on her face disappeared for a moment replaced by astonishment.

"You speak too soon, Marco." She started on the clasps of her uniform.

"Umm,"

"What!" she snapped. "You asked to see my animalia, I'm showing you." She turned her back to him and lifted the bottom of her shirt. Her bare back melted from perfect brown skin to an iridescent blue-green stripe down her spine that started just shy of her neck and disappeared into her pants.

Unconsciously Marco stepped closer, studying the iridescent, four inch wide fuzzy stripe. He could not be certain but it looked like downy feathers. "You're avian?" he asked.

"Yes," Almira lowered her shirt. She turned around. "Now it's your turn."

"What?"

"I showed you my animalia. Now it's your turn."

"But I'm human. I have nothing to show."

"Prove it."

With a sigh, Marco set down his pack. "Human hands," he held out his hands. "Human face."

"Open your mouth," she instructed. Marco did so. He stuck out his tongue.

"Human teeth, human tongue," he said.

Almira folded her arms across her chest. "Take off your clothes."

Marco eyed her. "Seriously?"

"I've never been more so."

"All right," he said undoing his jerkin and dropping it to the floor. Then he unbuttoned the shirt. Fanning it out, he spun in a slow circle, letting it fall after he'd done a complete turn. "Human," he said, crossing his arms over his broad chest, mirroring Almira.

"Now the pants," she said.

"You didn't take yours off!" he snapped. The crowd laughed.

"My animalia is on my back!"

"And I have none to see!"

"Enough of this," Pyko interrupted. "Much longer and you'll both be naked." Laughter accompanied his words but the crowd took them as a cue to disperse, the show was over. "Almira, ninety-five percent of all animalia is found on the upper body and face. Another three percent are tails only. There is only a two percent chance that he has animalia on his legs or... other lower areas." The stag Semian chuckled at Pyko's choice of words. "Leave him be. If he's a trainee he'll be here long enough for you to foil any plan he may have." Glaring at the black tiger she picked up her things and marched off without another word.

Pyko smiled at Marco, "Please, Marco, sit with us. I am Pyko, High Water Mage. This is Collen," he indicated the stag, "She is testing into the Potentate next cycle."

"Hello," Collen waved a hoof at him. Marco returned the wave, retrieved his clothes and pulled up a chair. "So," she began, "What's your story. You're a human mage?" Pyko turned eager gold eyes on him.

With a sigh Marco started. "I am one of two humans assigned to Master Myrth's Honor Guard. He sent me and a Mortak here to train with the Potentate."

"And the other human?" Collen prompted.

"She stayed at Dragon Ridge. She isn't a mage."

"She?" Pyko interrupted, "I didn't realize that human females took to the arts of war."

"Human females are free to choose. Most choose quiet safety," Marco supplied. They lapsed into silence.

"I expect you are tired from your journey," Pyko said at last. "I hesitate to tell you that there is only one empty compartment. We are running at capacity right now. High summer will soon be over and those here who fail to become members of the Potentate will depart."

"Oh," Collen laughed again, a look of shock crossing her brown eyes, "The only free bed is above Almira." she said, "Oh Pyko, that's too perfect!"

"I could force someone to move," Pyko offered ignoring Collen.

Marco shook his head. "It'll be fine, High Mage. I suspect Almira will not be far from me while I am here. I might as well share her space."

"It's straight across, next to the door you came in." Pyko pointed.

"Thank you." Marco stood, shouldering his pack and turning back the way he had come. As he walked he noticed that most of the Semians were drifting toward their own beds; the night felt heavy, the day used up.

When he reached Almira's compartment she lay in bed, her face uncovered, reading. "Hello again," he tried. She glanced at him then returned to her book. "Is there a place to store my stuff?" he asked.

She sighed before looking up at him. "There's a door at the head of the bed. Push on it and it will pop open." She demonstrated with her own.

"Thanks." Marco used her bed to climb up into his own. He popped open the storage space. It was as wide as the bed, around three feet, and about two feet deep. He stuffed his pack, shirt and jerkin in and then shut the door.

The thin mattress, almost comfortable beneath him, had been made up with a thick woolen blanket. Marco laid back. "What happened to the last person to sleep here?" he asked.

"I ate her," Almira snapped.

"What?"

"She kept interrupting me while I was reading."

"Oh, sorry," he apologized. He lay atop the blanket a moment, listening to the low shush of sound in the room before wriggling under the blanket and crawling out of his pants.

"Lights out!" Pyko shouted from across the room and the lights faded. Marco heaved a sigh and closed his eyes. Suddenly his blanket disappeared! His eyes flew open and he saw Almira standing over him, his blanket hanging from one hand, a large ball of flame in her other one.

"What?!" Marco shouted. She studied his legs and skin-tight shorts ignoring his outcry. "I'm human! Even beneath my shorts!" he added.

"Almira! Leave him be!" Pyko shouted from his own bed followed by laughter ringing the room.

"I see that now," she said to Marco, ignoring Pyko.

"Almira," the high mage warned. With a grimace Almira handed Marco his blanket then disappeared, clambering to the floor. As she touched down a globe of water appeared out of thin air and splashed over her. She gasped her fire winking out. "Bedtime!" Pyko roared. Marco swallowed his own laughter as Almira climbed into bed, soaking wet, while others chuckled in the dark. With a sigh Marco snuggled into his blanket and drifted off to sleep.

It was early morning when Marco awoke. Almira smiled at him as he rolled over to survey the barracks. "Good morning," she said. Marco reached for the cupboard door at his head as he returned the greeting. "You have a uniform, here, human," she continued. Marco lay back down and stared up at the soft wooden ceiling. Then he leaned over the bed watching unabashedly as Almira dressed, donning her black uniform over her thin black shorts and no-sleeve top. Another uniform sat folded on the table near their beds. Marco slid to the floor and crossed to the table, fingering the thick dark cloth. The pants were black, sturdy cotton, and judging from what he'd seen yesterday, fit baggy around the knees and thighs and tight on the calves. He slid into them and then into his old boots. There were two shirts. Almira had put on both of them and Marco copied her example: First a light cotton shirt, black in color, then a thick leather vest, also black.

"Is the Grand Syra's livery black? Or is it just the uniform?" he asked.

"Palo's livery is black," she answered. "Otherwise the vest would be a different color." She set her cap on her head, piling her loose curls up into it before donning her veil.

Marco stared at his featherless cap before using his fingers to comb out his shoulder-length hair and tie it back into a ponytail. Almira watched him patiently until he set the cap on his head, adjusted the brim and smiled down at her veiled face. "Hmm," she began, "I am to escort you to Palo's audience chamber," she said. "But I also have a class to teach. Do you think you can find your own way? The Grand Council Building is that dome we passed last night. Take any door in and walk to the center of the dome. You'll come out in the Pit where the council meets. There is a glass door leading out of the pit to the Grand Syra's audience chamber."

"Easy enough. I can find it," Marco assured her.

"Good." She nodded and walked away. Marco watched the Semians around him preparing for the day. Many of them had featherless caps as well, and it dawned on Marco that these were his fellow trainees. *"High summer began two cycles ago,"* he thought, *"After the tests are over next cycle I'll be the only one in here without feathers."*

With a sigh he left the barracks and made his way to the huge dome. The morning suns lit the practice yard and he glanced at the trainees—elves and goblins who had beat the Semians to the yard—working with weapons and magic. Groups stood with their eyes closed deep in the Mage Realm, while others worked with bows and swords. Marco smiled to himself as he left the yard behind. *"I'll be out there soon enough!"* he chortled as he walked.

Sylus and Clippen rode down to the ferry at dawn leading their horses along the pier to an empty boat where they waited quietly for Gaity to furl the banners and open for the day's travel. The ferry crew worked quickly around them preparing to sail. As the suns rose higher a few farmers, loaded down with crates of animals or sacks of vegetables, joined the queue. The ferry's captain stood barring entry to his barge until the huge black and white banners that hung from the shores of Gaity started to crawl upward, disappearing as unseen workers took them in. Then he moved aside and beckoned Sylus and Clippen aboard.

"Shoving off!" the pilot shouted once the barge was full and the ferry started forward. It was only a few minutes across the channel. Sylus fought the urge to pace as they traveled, mastering his impatience. Beside him Clippen remained silent, as silent as he had been since his brief meeting with Trillip's family. Within minutes the ferry reached the island where guards in white-feathered caps and elfin dockworkers scurried along the pier helping travelers disembark. Sylus looked up at the guest towers, just visible above the forest, and the black pennants playing from their tops. He waited until the last farmer had disembarked before leading his horse to shore, Clippen trailing behind. He did not bother remounting the horse, as it was only a short walk along the path to Gaity and the palace. The gate into the city was just swinging open when they reached it. The farmers had to stop, listing what they brought with them into the island city but Sylus and Clippen passed through unquestioned.

The city too, was just waking. Most of the inhabitants here were Semian, representing every variety and form, although a spattering of elves could be seen among them. They reached the Palace gate without incident. The white-feathered elf guard looked them up and down before addressing them, "State your business," he intoned, bored.

Sylus studied him thinking, *"All the elves here know me...he must be new."* With a patient smile that did not touch his eyes he answered, "I am Sylus, the Earth Master's lieutenant, and have come to confer with Grand Syra Palo."

"Of course," he said his boredom replaced with excitement. "I have been instructed to send you straight to the Grand Syra's Audience Chamber." The guard bowed allowing them through and a stable hand hurried forward to collect their horses.

"Are you coming with, Clippen?" Sylus asked.

The Land-Nymph nodded yes. When the Land-Nymph did not offer anything further, Sylus nodded, turned, and headed for the dome. They met no one within the dome until reaching the Pit. Twelve Syraes milled about, their elaborate robes denoting their region by color and pattern. Opposite the door they had entered sat the glass door to Palo's residence. "I'll wait here," Clippen offered, lowering himself to the floor near the door.

Concerned, Sylus hesitated before nodding, "Alright, Clippen," he said before crossing to Palo's door, ignoring the Syraes who called a greeting to him. Through the door he entered another round room, a mirror of the Pit outside, with a white stone floor and painted white walls. A large, round dais took up much of the floor. Scowling Sylus climbed the three steps that gave access to the top of it where he found Palo laying on a white couch at the center. Palo smiled languidly when he saw Sylus.

"What are you doing?" Sylus asked him.

"Relaxing," Palo answered.

"How can you lounge here? There is a Greater Daemon coming! Maybe already here! Your Syraes need instructions!" Sylus shouted gesturing toward the Pit.

Palo scoffed, "I told the Syraes about the daemon. They are notably worried but can work on their own."

"And my trainees?" Sylus asked.

Palo sat up his ease evaporating, replaced by an edge of anxiety. "They are well but..." he took a deep breath, "I think you need to know. I can't train Marco."

"What?!"

"Marco can see the Earth Cloud."

Sylus' jaw fell. Palo made room for the elf beside him and patted the cushion. Sylus turned and fell onto the lounge. "I knew he was strong but—"

"He doesn't realize that no one else can see it," Palo continued.

"How did you find out?" Sylus asked.

"He had a small accident," Palo said. "Don't worry there was no permanent damage." Sylus glared until the Grand Syra elaborated, "He accidentally burned Kryoso's arm—a minor burn."

"What did you tell him about the cloud?" Sylus asked.

"I told him that it took a lot of will to see the Earth Cloud." Several minutes passed before Palo continued, "But you do realize I can't teach him anything." Sylus nodded, continuing to stare at the floor.

Then he looked up and smiled, "But he can still learn pattern magic here."

"Well yes," Palo agreed, meeting his eyes. "We can teach him that. But there's only one person on the peninsula who can teach him about the Earth Cloud."

"You don't think Myrth sent him here for some reason other than training?" Sylus seemed scandalized as he said it.

"No," Palo laughed at his tone, "But he will never be more than half-trained here. If he had stayed with Myrth he could have learned true Earth Magic."

Sylus nodded. "I don't think Myrth knew," he said. "I told him that Marco was strong enough to make the Potentate. Even win Syra. But I don't think Myrth took the time to test either of them for extreme limits." He shook his head, "And that's something I can't do."

"Myrth isn't going to like this. He's so dead-set against an Apprentice," Palo said his words coaxing a chuckle from Sylus.

The door opened and Kryoso entered escorted by a female Mortak, a Syra. Her long black hair framed solid silver eyes and fell to mingle with the black and orange of her ceremonial robes.

"Syra Jeniladona," Palo greeted. She bowed before him.

"I have come to offer my services in training this young Mortak, Grand Syra Palo."

"What of the daemon and your preparations?" Palo asked.

"It is my understanding that the daemon will surface on the lower peninsula. Kryoso's training will be a great contribution to the fight, and with luck the daemon will not even reach my lands," she stated.

Palo nodded. "I will grant your request Jeniladona," he replied.

"Thank you, Grand Syra. We will start immediately." She backed out of the room, taking Kryoso with her. As she left a large, black-tiger Semian entered.

"Pyko," Palo greeted.

"You sent for me?" he asked.

"Yes. Wait a moment," Palo waved toward the corner. Pyko hunkered down against the wall, near the door, mirroring Clippen in the Pit. They sat in silence until the door opened a third time and Marco wandered in, alone.

"Marco," Palo greeted with the same enthusiasm he had used with Pyko. "Did you sleep well?" he asked.

"Once I got to sleep it was pleasant," Marco answered. He bowed to Sylus, "Commander." Sylus nodded once at him.

"I'm having a difficult time deciding what to do with you Marco. No one here can train you to your fullest potential," Palo bluntly admitted. Sylus caught Pyko's sudden interest in the conversation.

Marco glared at Palo. "I don't understand," he said.

"Well. You can see the Earth Cloud. It is not a very common ability. None of the Potents can do so. Nor can any Syra, including myself." Marco went very still. "There is only one person capable of teaching you to use the Earth Cloud and that is Master Myrth."

"So you're sending me back?" Marco asked, his voice full of bitterness, his face painted in disappointment.

"No. However we can only teach you pattern magic. Now, there are a few strong Earth Mages for you to choose from."

"Grand Syra," Pyko interrupted from the back of the room. Marco jumped, noting Pyko's presence for the first time. "Might I suggest a trainer for the human?"

"Certainly," Palo said with a shrug.

"Almira," he suggested.

Marco glared at the Semian.

"Almira is a Fire Mage," Palo said.

"True. But she has a certain way with him."

Palo chuckled at his words and Marco's glare deepened. "All right. We'll try it." Marco spun around and gaped at Palo.

"I'll fetch her," Pyko said, standing.

"Not yet Pyko," Palo said, stopping him. "I want you to do some extra work with Clippen. He needs to refine his combat skills."

"A Land-Nymph training for combat?" Pyko asked.

"Master Myrth has insisted," Sylus added.

Pyko bowed at the waist, "I would never second-guess a Master."

"Good," Palo said, "Remember to train well but train quickly," he said dismissing them. With another bow Marco followed Pyko out of the room and across the Pit, which was now full of bickering Syraes, to stand with Clippen near the exit.

Sylus waited for the door to close before questioning Palo, "A Fire Mage?"

"It's pattern magic; he'll be fine working with her. Besides, she's one of my best trainers."

"So," Pyko started, as the trio made their way out of the Dome, Marco looking between them and trying to follow their conversation, "What are you doing here? I thought you were with Nepo," he asked Clippen.

"Myrth drafted me," Clippen explained. "Trillip and Genow too."

"To fight a daemon? He's out of his mind," Pyko said with a gruff chuckle.

"Maybe. But we were hand-picked by Oracle."

"Really?" Pyko studied Marco before continuing. "But even Oracle only sees potential and possibility." Clippen nodded at his words. "And you were hand-picked as well, human?" the tiger asked eyeing Marco closely. Marco answered with a nod and Pyko turned away, chuckling, "What did Nepo say to Myrth when he stole you away?"

Clippen's laugh lacked humor, "He's still furious! I think he talks to Myrth every day asking after his honor guard."

"Well, I don't blame him."

They entered the training grounds where the morning's flurry of activity had given way to quiet meditation. Many sat or stood in lines and groups with their eyes closed. "One moment, Clip," Pyko instructed, "Come, Marco. There's Almira." Marco passed a smile to the Land-Nymph before following the Semian over to a group of trainees sitting in a row. One was Collen, the goat-lady. "Here's a new trainee, Almira," Pyko interrupted.

Almira turned her veiled face to them. "No! This is a review class! These are the eight most likely to pass the tests! I'm not teaching a beginner at this stage!"

"The Grand Syra has ordered it. Just put him at the end of the line and let him watch the others work."

"I'm a fast learner Almira," Marco added. She turned on him. He could feel her glare through the veil.

"I've already said you'd do it," Pyko supplied, smiling.

"What? Why?" she shouted.

"He needs a strong hand," Pyko said, waving at Marco.

"What?" Marco squeaked.

"Hmph," Almira huffed. She sat looking at Marco. "Fine," she said at last. "Sit over there," she waved at the end of the line opposite herself. Smiling he did as he was told.

From the Void

It was a round room eight feet in diameter. Four windows adorned the white stone walls, located at each of the four compass points, depicting four different, incongruous, scenes. A meadow in high summer appeared in the north window, while the southern looked out into a magma pool. The east window sat on the edge of a high, sheer cliff with no visible land, and the window opposite it looked out into a deep blue ocean. Between the Earth window and the Air window stood a Gateway. Most of the time it appeared to be a wall—the same bare, white marble as the rest of the tower. Only mages and seers could find the keyhole and open the Gateway. Today it stood open. The edge of the door glowed pink as if rimed with cotton candy, while the rest of the door looked out into a starry depth.

Oracle sat on a mound of pillows staring out into the Void beyond the Gateway. The wolf Semian rubbed an amber eye with his paw. There was a Greater Daemon out there, somewhere in the Void. He dreamed of it rending reality and crawling into their world every night. The urgency of his visionary dream drove him in his search for the daemon. He had scoured the streaming timelines until he found it...found it in the future. But the Greater Daemon felt Oracle's search and vanished in the present. It may have hidden itself from the timelines but Oracle could still feel it out there—he could still feel its malevolence closing in on his world.

Behind him the regular door into the tower room opened and the goblin housemaid Samsha ducked in, whispering in greeting, "Seer Oracle? I was hoping to clean around you." He nodded his consent without turning around. "Thank you," she said and hurriedly bustled around the room, straightening the couch and dusting the table behind Oracle before watering the plants that hung from the ceiling. Oracle glanced up at

Tierren's wife as she passed near him, her deep olive skin soaking in the lamplight that fell across her sturdy frame.

Oracle looked back out into the Void where a green light cut through the stars, shattering the blackness and fading slowly. With a snarl, "Foul Fae!" he bellowed, startling Samsha. Taking a deep breath he closed his eyes, sending his conscience down along the forcelines and into Myrth, pulling on the lines that embedded themselves in the Master's brain.

A jolt of agony wracked him and with a high-pitched shriek Myrth woke. His vision exploded with white stars, his heart leapt to his throat, suddenly beating so fast he nearly choked on it. As his vision cleared he looked out from his bed, taking in his room and working to slow his heart rate before the Earth forcelines responded to his sudden agitation. The white marble walls and floor glowed a ghostly blue in the moonlight that streamed through the enchanted windows and balconies.

"Myrth!" Oracle cried in his head.

"Oracle? The daemon!" he guessed, talking to the Seer in his mind.

"He has breached our world!" Oracle continued. Myrth gracefully rolled out of bed, grabbing his robe as he rose, conversing with the Seer. *"Your forces are divided!"* the wolf continued.

"Stop yelling. I'll contact Sylus. He can bring them back."

"Call Jay first!" Oracle continued yelling, *"It emerged in the Broodlands in my vision."*

Myrth pulled two saddle packs out from beneath his bed, *"Fine, I will call Jay first."*

"Tell Sylus I'll meet them in Olimidia!" Oracle added.

Myrth sighed. Only Oracle would dare yell at him. *"I will,"* he said. With the saddlebags ready he shifted the enchanted balconies to look out at the Broodlands. The lava desert stretched out away from him, prickly shrubs clinging to life in the red sand and black rocks.

Myrth closed his eyes breathing deep and stepping into the Mage Realm. Underground, the Earth Cloud floated around him, swaddling him. An upwelling near the center of his room, churned the golden sparks of dust into a lazy dance. Myrth sent his thoughts out, up the current, to the surface river where the current pulled him toward the Tower of the Elements and the Gateway there. Exerting his will he moved against the current, away from the Tower, until he was free of it and the Earth power coursed westward toward Gaity and the next Gateway. "Sylus!" he called as he neared the swirling currents of Master Island. *"Sylus!"*

Sylus' voice echoed through the Mage Realm, *"I hear, Master."*

"It is time Sylus. The daemon is here. Bring my mages and meet Oracle in Olimidia."

"Of course Master," Sylus said, *"There is some—"*

"I will contact you again. Wait for my instructions," Myrth interrupted.

"Yes, but Master—" Sylus tried again.

Myrth opened his eyes, slamming back into the physical realm. He sent a call down the forcelines to the goblins, searching to wake Tierren. His second in command was already awake, listening to his wife as she helped him sort through supplies. Myrth backed away, returning to the physical realm and starting to dress, confident that the two goblins had things well in hand. *"So very few marshals can organize a household and an army,"* he remembered the Warlord saying as he resignedly signed Tierren's transfer. *"Do not ruin my best warrior with your Honor Guard flippancy Myrth."*

"My parting gift!" Oracle shouted in his head again, interrupting the memory. The Seer's vision echoed through the room and through his head. Myrth suddenly stood in the Broodlands staring at the river of lava that split the desert. A sickly green light ruptured the sky and birthed a daemon.

The Hunt Begins

T he ground under her boots crunched as she walked across the charred embers. Stopping, she turned slowly surveying the horizon. All around her lay the scorched land of a red-rock desert. To her north five mountain peaks loomed—the two largest belching huge clouds of smoke and ash. A sudden rumble shook the ground and D'Mique dropped into a crouch, waiting for the quake to pass. Acrid steam burst through the thin crust to her right, startling her and covering her with a fine layer of dirt.

"I'm in the Broodlands," *she thought.* "The trade roads run close to the volcanoes, and I can reach them in less than a day." *Only after the thought finished did she add,* "That wasn't my thought! I don't know where the trade routes are!" *Her heart skipped a beat but she stood and started north, walking quickly, lightly, across the volcanic crust.* "Whose thoughts are in my head?" *she wondered,* "Who's making me walk this way?" *Topping a rise she stopped, her path blocked by a rift of bubbling lava meandering across the valley floor.* "He comes from the Broodlands," *the alien voice spoke in her ear, rather than her head. D'Mique spun around vainly searching for the owner of the voice, but she stood alone in the desert. Swallowing her terror, she turned and started walking parallel to the crag. No plants grew here and there were no signs of any animals passing. There was only D'Mique and a growing sense of foreboding.*

As she paralleled the river of lava the skin on the back of her neck crawled and she stopped, staring at the opposite bank. A hazy, sickly yellow light sliced diagonally through the air about a hundred feet ahead of her. Instinctively she threw herself to the ground, landing hard, as a huge, clawed hand pushed through the line of light, widening it by thrusting downward on the edge of reality. When the light had widened into a ten-foot hole, a monstrous insect-like head forced its way into the world! Blazing red eyes turned toward her.

D'Mique woke with a startled shriek. She was in her room safe in bed at Dragon Ridge. She surveyed the room, eyes wide, the monster insect daemon still residing in her mind. There were no breakfast trays on her table which meant that it was still early, and that Myrth was probably still sleeping as no servants or guards could enter their private quarters while the Earth Master slept. He sealed their chambers shut before retiring and the seal remained in place until he awoke. This procedure had annoyed her for two cycles now, making it impossible for her to leave before the morning bell. Of course she could leave her room and visit the other suites within the box, but if she wanted to see the sunrise she would have to settle for the enchanted one coming through her windows. Now she took comfort in the fact that no one could disturb her. "It was just a nightmare," she chided herself, looking out at the Dark Forest, checking the time. The world beyond her enchanted windows sat in utter darkness, the Ghost Moon yet to rise. Yesterday it had risen just after dawn and today Rysk would be even later into the sky.

With a sigh she climbed out of bed, grabbed her sword off the desk, and crept across the room, opening her door. The hall beyond glowed with lamplight, flickering shadows dancing on the wall. D'Mique padded across and knocked on Myrth's door. Like her own door it could only be opened from either side by the occupant's own hand.

A half-dressed Myrth cracked opened the door a moment later startling her with his swift reply. "D'Mique," he whispered, equally startled. He wore a shimmering blue robe open across his chest, and short white shorts but nothing else. He was human in form from the waist down, his skin slightly scaly like his forearms, but bronze in color. He caught her eyes wandering and pulled his robe closed.

Blushing she returned her eyes to his face and the reason she'd knocked. "Can I come in? I...I had a strange dream just now," she asked.

He studied her, taking in her black shorts, sleeveless nightshirt and sword. Only after a full minute did he open the door wider asking, "You were in the Broodlands?"

She nodded, "I think so," she said as he turned away making room for her to enter. He'd changed the scene outside his windows from the mountains of his home to a desert land, similar to the scorched volcanic world of her dream. D'Mique stopped, staring wide-eyed at the river of lava from her dream bubbling in the middle of each window and balcony. She looked at Myrth for an explanation but did not disturb him as he studied the scene before him.

There was another knock at the door. Myrth glanced at it before rumbling, "It's open, come in." Tierren and Rogan entered cautiously both wearing the same outfit as D'Mique. Samsha followed them an air of restrained excitement roiling around her.

"We came to your call Myrth," Tierren said concern coloring his voice.

Myrth nodded at their arrival. "Samsha, finish your preparations," he said, dismissing her before turning to her husband, "We need to find the daemon, but I see no sign of it," he said, gesturing toward the windows and balconies.

D'Mique turned her attention to them. Each one was empty, devoid of life. "We're looking for what I saw in my dream?" she asked. Myrth nodded. D'Mique walked around the room going from one window to the next. There was no mottled green, giant insect in any window or balcony and no sign of the yellow hole in reality it had made. "Nothing," she conceded.

Myrth took a deep breath retying his robe closer over himself. "Agreed. Wake the others while Samsha finishes packing for travel," he ordered. "I must speak with Sylus," he said dismissing them.

"I'll get Genow, you get Trillip," D'Mique said to Tierren, as they left Myrth's quarters. She didn't wait for his reply before starting toward the elf's door.

At Genow's door she knocked but there was no answer. *"He's probably asleep,"* she thought. She tried the door handle but it was locked. Just as she was about to knock again Genow opened the door.

"D'Mique? What is it?" he asked.

"It's time to go," she said.

"Hunting?" She nodded and Genow turned back into his room. "Hunting," he breathed, looking around. "We need to pack."

"Samsha is packing, just get ready." At her words the elf refocused on her.

"I had a dream," he whispered.

Her own dream flashed across her mind in response. The praying mantis head topped with steer-like yellowed horns that sprouted above burning red eyes, eyes that looked through time and space and saw her. Her stomach clenched and a sudden wave of sickness swept over her and she sat down hard on the stone floor.

Genow dropped beside her, "D'Mique! Are you well?" As he clasped her hand she reached up and pulled him close, hugging him.

"Genow," tears filled her eyes.

He stiffened in her arms, "It's okay D'Mique," he whispered, a tentative hand on her shoulder. Staring up into his eyes an awareness of their bodies grew between them and Genow pulled back.

"Genow," she pulled back too, "I'm sorry." She struggled back to her feet wiping tears from her cheeks that she did not remember shedding.

"It is I who should apologize, Lady," Genow said, rising beside her and bowing formally. "Are you well?"

"I will be," but even to herself she sounded unconvinced. "Did I imagine that?" she thought, "Or did it really look at me."

"I will see you upstairs then," Genow said. She nodded before returning to her room.

Samsha was in her room pulling together her travel pack. "I am nearly finished here, Lady," the goblin maid said as she added tan cotton shirts and black sturdy pants to the pack. D'Mique donned the outfit that Samsha had laid out for her beginning with the same tan shirt and black pants and ending with her green, ringed jerkin and her boots. "I have your travel rations, food kits ... oh I don't know what else," Samsha said, her flurry of movement ending with a sigh. She watched D'Mique drop her sword belt across her shoulder, the blade sitting comfortably across her back, and pull her hair close to her head, preparing it for a bun. "We should do something with your hair," she said. "Goblin Hunt-maids often cut theirs short."

D'Mique protested, "Goblin Hunters don't cut their hair. Rogan and Tierren both have long hair."

"True," Samsha shrugged. "It was worth a try," she said with a smile. "I'll pull it back and wrap it for you then," she suggested. D'Mique nodded in agreement and Samsha worked quickly, creating a thick, snake-like braid

LADY WARRIOR, MAGE OF MAN

that hung down her back wrapped in a thick green ribbon, which the goblin-maid knotted at the end, adding a feather and small bell to the end.

"The feather and bell? It's a goblin luck charm, right?" D'Mique asked.

Samsha smiled. "Take any luck you can get, Lady," she said before leaving. D'Mique draped her pack over the shoulder opposite her sword and followed the goblin out.

At the stairway that led to Myrth's audience chamber she found the Master surrounded by the rest of his Honor Guard, all of them dressed similar to her, the goblin's thick leather armor more battle-worn than hers. Beside them Myrth paced, dressed in plain black pants and knee-high boots, a white, loose-fitting shirt draping over his shoulders, its buttons undone and its tail left hanging out of his pants. It billowed around him as he furiously paced up and down the corridor, carrying out a fervid debate with a glass jar he held in his clawed hand. "Look again," he insisted, the world swaying slightly with his emotion.

"I did look Myrth," a lilting voice said from the jar. It instantly brought the twitter of baby birds to mind. "Every Eye is open. I saw him come through. The moment he was here he vanished from sight," said the jar. " Myrth, I can still feel him on the forcelines. He pulls at my soul!"

"What about your griffins?" Myrth asked.

"My griffins?" the jar shouted, startling Myrth who nearly dropped it. "Of course I sent my griffins! My aeries are empty!" The hallway's swaying grew more noticeable. Myrth stopped pacing noticing the quake for the first time. Sighing he closed his eyes, mastering his emotions. "Myrth?" the voice asked as the silence stretched outward. It had also returned to its calm lilting.

"We're coming Jay; we're leaving now," he said as he set the jar down at his feet. D'Mique watched, breathing forgotten, as the floor erupted, flowing over the jar, and formed an egg-shaped shell of stone around it. Myrth picked up the stone egg and wrote on it with a claw, the letters etched into the stone by magic. He dropped the egg into a bag and slung it over his shoulder before meeting D'Mique's gaping stare. He smiled mischievously before starting up the stairs followed by the goblins and Trillip. Genow lightly pushed her shoulder to start her moving. When she looked back at him he smiled broadly. At the top the stone opened and they poured into the shadowed throne room, just to the left of the throne. Myrth grabbed his hooded cloak from the massive stone chair and put it on. Then he grabbed a sword and a large black pillow from behind the stone seat and headed for the door.

Five horses waited in the dark courtyard. D'Mique did a quick head-count. "One of us is walking?" she asked.

"Don't be silly," chided Tierren as he mounted a nearby horse. "Myrth will be riding Jerrold." The others followed Tierren into their saddles as Myrth set the pillow on the cobblestones. D'Mique could just make out the dragon that was embroidered on its surface. Its multi-colored, serpentine body wound around the pillow, almost aglow in the near-dawn light.

"Wait," D'Mique started, *"I've seen that dragon before."* She continued in her head, *"Only it can't be the same dragon. The one I saw was draped over Myrth's shoulders when we first arrived."*

"Come Jerrold, it's time to ride," Myrth commanded the pillow. D'Mique stared at him then back at the pillow. The stitching shimmered and rippled as a soft ripping sound emanated from the surface. Beginning with its horned and whiskered head the dragon pulled away from the black satin, filling out as if inflated by an unseen pair of lungs until the dragon she had seen before coiled on the ground before them. Wriggling his red-scaled toes the dragon started growing in size until his head reached as high as the horse's withers. "Thank you, Jerrold," Myrth said. The dragon bowed its head to the ground, kneeling so that the Earth Master could mount. As he climbed up, D'Mique hurried for her horse, mounting awkwardly. *"All those cycles of training and none of it had concerned riding horses,"* she thought bitterly.

Sylus lay with his eyes closed for a moment replaying his conversation with Myrth. *"That was less than successful,"* he sighed, opening his eyes and staring at the ceiling. *"How am I going to tell Myrth about Marco?"* he thought. Then he smirked, chiding himself, "The daemon is here and I'm worried about a half-trained Earth Mage." He threw off the thin cotton blanket, sat up, and surveyed the guest room Palo had given him. Near-dawn light filtered into the vaulted room's arched windows. High up in the tower closest to the sea the open windows also let in a salt-tangy breeze that played fitfully with the curtains around Sylus. Frowning in determination he stood, dressed and packed. Taking his equipment with him he marched down to Palo's room, the Night Watch noting his passage but allowing him to continue on.

He entered the dome and then the Pit without meeting anyone. Palo's audience chamber with its raised dais was empty as well. Sylus hurried around the room to another door which opened into Palo's private room. He knocked but there was no answer, so he tried the knob and the door swung open silently revealing the snow leopard sound asleep in bed. "Palo!" Sylus called loudly. The Grand Syra remained motionless. Sylus tapped him sharply on the forehead then jumped back, falling into a defensive crouch as the Grand Syra flew awake, leaping from the bed.

He quickly scanned the dimly lit room for enemies, his cat-eyes aglow, until he took notice of the elf. "Sylus," he greeted as the elf relaxed. "What is it?" he asked looking around again.

"It's time to go," Sylus answered.

"The daemon?" Palo tensed again and Sylus nodded. "Well, two cycles are better than none," Palo concluded turning away and beginning to rummage through his bedclothes.

"Yes. Myrth insisted we hurry," Sylus added.

"We?" Palo looked up surprised, the shirt he'd been searching for clasped in one hand. He grimaced at Sylus' frown. "I'm not going," he informed Sylus, petulance creeping into his voice.

Sylus started, "But—"

"But what?" Palo interrupted. "Your Mages have nearly mastered pattern magic in only sixteen days. And Marco! You are taking my only High Earth Mage away from me."

"He can't be named High Mage for a year. Besides, he took the Potentate test on a dare! He only passed because of luck!" Sylus fumed.

"Fine," Palo sighed, "But you don't need me. Not with the three you have. I'll stay here and organize the Syraes."

Sylus' glare deepened as Palo squared his shoulders folding his arms defiantly across his chest. "I wouldn't presume to change your mind, Grand Syra," Sylus hissed at last, bowing formally before turning to leave.

"You told Myrth about Marco? What did he say?" Palo asked calling after him.

Sylus stopped in mid-stride. "I didn't tell him," he admitted, turning around again. "He didn't give me a chance." Palo chuckled shaking his head as Sylus left.

The elf made his way back outside and toward the Semian camp, crossing the lawn where they had held the Potentate try-outs eight days before, where Marco had surprised them all as an argument with Almira led to him taking the exam—and passing. "And now he's a Potent and a Presumptive High Earth Mage," Sylus stewed, "And only half-trained at best!"

He entered the Semian building unchallenged. Before the tests, there had been nearly fifty hopefuls here. Now there were only eighteen. Pyko, High Water Mage, sat alone at a table in the center of the room. He looked up at Sylus acknowledging him with a nod which Sylus returned. He remembered the black tiger who had tried for Water Master's Apprentice about eighteen years ago, his skill nearly that of a Master's. But the Water Master had chosen Nepo instead. Sylus stopped in front of the bunk where Marco slept. Despite all the now empty beds, he had remained above the veiled Semian, final proof of their growing friendship; a friendship that seemed at odds given the fiery exchanges they had in public. Sylus shook Marco awake. "Marco," he hissed, trying not to wake Almira.

"Hmm," Marco moaned.

"Wake up." Sylus shoved him hard on the shoulder. "It's time to go," he said pushing him again.

Marco rolled over looking blearily up at the elf. "I'm up," he whispered.

"Get ready. Myrth wants us to meet Oracle in Olimidia," Sylus said.

"The daemon?" Marco asked. Sylus nodded.

"Ready the horses," he whispered, "We'll meet at the palace gate."

"Yes Commander," Marco replied as Sylus turned making his way back toward the Pit, steeling himself for one last attempt at convincing Palo to join them.

Marco clambered out of bed dressing in his Potent uniform and pulling his hair into a ponytail before adding his two-feathered cap, the red feathers bobbing in the dark. As he gathered his things into his travel pack Pyko wandered over silently observing him. Marco stomped into his boots before the tiger said anything. "Good luck, Marco. Remember, you are always a Potent and will always be welcome here."

"Thank you Pyko," Marco replied, straightening, grasping the tiger's thick warm hand in friendship. Then he looked to Almira and was surprised to see her watching him with large, dark eyes. "You're awake, sorry," he said.

"Weren't you about to wake me anyway?" she asked knowingly.

He smiled at her, "Of course. I have to go. Myrth wants us back now."

"But you're a Potent like Pyko said. You belong to Palo's forces now," she whispered.

"But I'm not really a Potent," he stressed. "I came here to learn pattern magic from the Syraes. I was part of Myrth's Honor Guard before I took the Potent exam."

She smiled, "There are two red feathers in your cap. You are a real Potent even if you belong to Myrth." Marco knelt beside her bed and she rolled closer to him her eyes never leaving his face.

"I want to see you again," he whispered.

"You will. Honor Guard assignments only last a year or so. Potent is for life," she said with a smile.

"I mean, I want to see you. I—"

"Shh," she interrupted placing a finger on his lips, "I know what you meant Marco."

"I wouldn't expect you to wait for my return," he continued.

"I wouldn't. But I'm too human for most Semians and too Semian for most humans."

"Not for me," he whispered. He closed the distance between them giving her a quick kiss—their first. Pulling away, afraid she would lash out and smack him, he smiled at the surprise blossoming over her face. Standing he said, "I'll see you soon." A small smile was her only reply. Shouldering his travel pack he hurried from the barracks, working his way around to the stables near the palace gates.

The sky was lightening as dawn approached and the horses in their stalls began to stir. The grooms were starting their chores. "I need my horse," he said to the stable hand at the tack room door.

"Which is yours, Potent?"

"That chestnut brown," he pointed. "I also need my companions' horses, the white mare, the palomino and Commander Sylus' black."

"As you command, Potent," the stable hand hurried to collect the horses and saddle them.

Marco's heart flip-flopped in his chest, *"They listen to me,"* he thought, *"Why? Because of the feathers?"* Once he had the horses Marco made his way to the front gate where the others were waiting. They collected their mounts and started for the pier without a word, each one still half-asleep and only half-aware of anything beyond the fact that they were going out to hunt a daemon.

At the pier a non-magical guard stopped them, his single white feather gleaming in the near-dawn. "We have need of a ferry," Sylus said. "It is light enough to go."

"We aren't supposed to start until dawn. The korsks are frisky in the pre-dawn light," the guard protested.

"I have no time for korsks. I am commanded by the Earth Master," Sylus demanded. "If he is angered by my delay I will return that anger to you!"

"We can handle a korsk," Marco said stepping forward. The guard noted his red feathers as Marco ordered, "Ready a ferry."

"Of—of course, Potent," the guard stammered backing away.

"It is the feathers," Marco thought, his mind drifting back to his village and the children who had always laughed and pointed and run away.

Sylus glared at Marco as the guard hurried off, his black eyes resting on the red feathered cap. Taking note Marco shrugged at him, fighting not to squirm. "When we are off this island you will change back into your other uniform," the elf growled.

"Yes Commander," Marco acquiesced. With a nod Sylus started after the guard impatiently demanding the ferry. Beside Marco, Clippen and Kryoso shook with silent laughter. "Come on," Marco said glaring at them before following Sylus. Shortly they boarded a ferry at the end of the pier, the workers still preparing it for the crossing.

Marco took up a position in the bow. He closed his eyes, stepped easily into the Mage Realm, and focused on the Earth Cloud. He could see it shimmering beneath the blue cloud of water under the boat. Behind him the earth currents formed a whirlpool over the dome of Gaity Palace before diving into the Gaity Gateway and disappearing into the Void. One of the first things he'd learned to do was ignore the currents and focus on the Earth Cloud instead. Whereas the currents drove inexorably into the maelstrom of the Gateway demanding he join them, the Earth Cloud remained constant. So to work his magic he pulled Earth power from the Cloud beneath them and willed it first into a golden strand, and then into a tight crisscrossing pattern around the boat's hull—an endowment that strengthened the craft. With the endowment in place he started on a shield, gathering the miasma of Water into a current as he had done with Earth before forming a smooth bowl of power roughly three feet from the hull of the ferry.

Marco opened his eyes slowly keeping the patterns in sight. He now stood between realms, his body in the physical realm and his thoughts in the Mage Realm—one Realm superimposed over the other, allowing him to monitor his work, maintaining both the shield and the strength endowment while continuing to react to the physical world. Clippen came to stand beside him as the ferry shoved off, his staff at the ready. Having trained in pattern magic before, the Land-Nymph had spent his time training as a Mage Defender, charged with protecting Marco while he worked in the Mage Realm.

As they cleared the shore and the bottom dropped away to form a deep channel, the water before them parted, birthing a sleek-furred black shape, a korsk. Clippen moved between Marco and the aquatic daemon-kin. The ferry rolled upward pushed by the monstrous animal's body as it explored the craft's underside. Marco stumbled and Clippen caught him, steadying him, and Marco forced his will into the shield, holding it against the beast's explorations. The korsk rolled back under the dark waves its head never breaching the surface, and the ferry returned to a level position. Marco checked his patterns. The shield held but it had not discouraged the curious korsk. Disappointed he let the pattern fade. "If it's not going to stop them, it doesn't need to be there," he thought, putting all his will into keeping the hull's earth endowment strong.

Beside them the water churned as another korsk surfaced. Clippen fell into an on-guard stance facing the beast, ready to dissuade it if it also rolled toward them. Marco took a deep breath, watching the daemon-kin's length slip from the deep, dark water, its blunt snout and oval head leading the way. Glistening fur fell away from its eyes—eyes aglow with daemon-fire that bathed the ferry in red—exposing scaly black skin. Marco swallowed hard as the beast rolled sideways, away from the ferry. Its seal-like flipper cleared the water next exposing a huge pike of bone at the tip, just one of the korsk's weapons. In front of the ferry, only an arm's length from Marco, another korsk surfaced opening its mouth and hissing through a forest of fangs. Marco and Clippen spun toward it and Clippen jumped in front of Marco.

Marco closed his eyes trying hard to breathe and concentrate. *"Clippen has me covered,"* he told himself, pulling more Earth from the sea floor, strengthening the endowment as he slid into the Mage Realm to work. Once he'd finished, he stayed there, establishing his presence beside his endowment pattern. Looking around he picked out the red sparks that denoted Clippen and the ferrymen, the shadowy, half-there form that was Kryoso, and Sylus, who swirled green in the washed-out world. Floating through the blue miasma of the water beneath him, korsks loomed, hazy black pools circling the ferry. *"Shadow magic, daemon magic,"* Marco thought. As the water grew shallow again and they neared the shore they left the curious creatures behind. Marco breathed a sigh of relief, opened his eyes, and let the endowment fade. Around him the ferrymen tied off the craft before they disembarked, mounting their horses and starting down the road toward Olimidia.

The Winds of the Broodlands

D'Mique climbed off her horse gingerly stretching as each joint creaked. "Cross-country rides will be my undoing," she thought. From the corner of her eye she caught Rogan smirking and replied with a glare before turning her back on him and staring out across the plain. Her eyes wandered skyward, picking out cloud formations as they raced westward pushed by the mid-afternoon breeze. Since leaving early this morning Myrth had set an easy, ground-consuming pace. Now finding themselves on the lonesome edge of Dragon Hills Forest, he had called for a short break.

"Are we stopping for the night?" Genow asked.

"No. We need to hurry," Tierren answered. "The greater the head start the daemon has the harder it'll be to find it."

"We will rest again in Scala," Myrth added as he dropped his large black pillow and sank onto it, his legs folded delicately under him, closing his eyes in meditation. D'Mique took this as her cue and threw herself down on the grass near her horse startling the animal. Using her arm as a pillow she tried to rest and stretch-out, staring up at the sky, while the soft whisper of the tall grass around her lulled her into a light doze.

"Where is Oracle, Myrth?" Tierren asked, his gravel voice startling D'Mique awake.

"The Master is meditating, Tierren," Genow admonished.

Tierren scoffed, "Myrth has been with us for some time. The feel of him beside me changes when he is truly meditating." D'Mique swiveled her head toward them. Tierren and Rogan sat motionless beside Myrth while Genow hovered near the horses fidgeting with the tack.

"Oracle has gone to fetch our missing members," Myrth said eyes still closed, seemingly unaware of the exchange between the elf and goblin.

"This is an advantage to belonging to a Master I suppose?" Genow asked, ignoring Myrth in turn.

"Hush Genow," Myrth said, eyes flashing open as he stood easily and stooped to retrieve the pillow. "Do not judge the goblins; they serve me well, as they have served all Earth Masters." Genow bowed his head, standing motionless until both Tierren and Myrth had collected their horses.

D'Mique struggled to find her feet, forcing her arms and legs to work despite their protests. Once upright she stood beside Genow watching the others remount before grabbing her own horse. *"I'm doing it right,"* she thought with a sigh as she studied their mounting techniques, *"It's just something I need to practice."* Stiffly she scrambled into her saddle, Genow smiling at her encouragingly, reaching up to steady her until she plopped down into the saddle with a painful grimace.

"You're getting better," he lied, climbing aboard his own horse. Turning to follow Myrth's dragon toward the next town, he asked, "Will we stay long in Scala?"

"Only until dawn," Myrth answered. "At dawn we move again." True to his word they rode until reaching Scala then stopped for the remainder of the night, taking three rooms in the first inn they came to—one for D'Mique, one for Myrth, and one for the rest of the Hunters. She had barely fallen asleep when Tierren shook her awake. Bleary-eyed, she dressed and stumbled out into the morning mist, clambering onto her horse and wending her way through the merchant caravans and guards automatically. With Myrth in the lead they spent the day skirting the Nesting, leaving the well-traveled roads behind on their way to the volcanic desolation of the Broodlands.

Near sunset the plains died away, the grass growing sparser as the land rolled downward along a gentle descent. The Hunters stopped for the night just as the last blades of grass died away and the valley floor leveled out. Before them the black and red desert of the Broodlands fanned outward reaching the far horizon, the last light of the suns setting it ablaze. There were no roads for them to follow; no cities had been founded in the

Broodlands—no farms and no mines. There were only the volcanoes known collectively as the Brood, and the red rock desert strewn with lava flows. From where they surveyed the land the tallest peak of the Brood rose just above the horizon, and near it ran the lava-filled crag D'Mique had seen in her dream. *"The place where the Greater Daemon entered,"* she thought with a thrill of panic remembering the vision. *"Was it a vision? Was it my imagination?"* The only other thing out there in the desert, lost in the growing darkness, was the Floating Castle, palace of the Wind Mistress.

Rysk joined the Fiery Sisters the next morning, and all three stars started across the sky as Myrth led his Hunters into the volcanic desert, their only company the spiny plants and cacti that found purchase and the insects and birds hunting amongst the black boulders. They set a course straight across the valley floor toward the tallest peak, the dormant volcano Wyrm. D'Mique rode behind Myrth one eye on the ground, searching for signs of passage by anything larger than a horse. The land was scrubbed clean. "Maybe I just don't know what I'm looking for," she muttered.

"Peace, D'Mique," returned Myrth. "Shry taught you much in the time he had. If you can find no signs, then there hasn't been any traffic here." He pulled Jerrold to a stop interrupting himself, "Well. The castle is going to be hard to reach." D'Mique followed his line of sight picking out the Floating Castle near the top of the volcano, glittering like a monstrous gem as sunlight refracted off its surface. True to its name it floated in mid-air. Rogan and Tierren hesitated, falling behind as Myrth started forward again. D'Mique waited with them watching them as they stared up at the castle, noting the fine tremble that settled in Rogan's hands. She looked back up at the castle as her horse started around the goblins following the dragon. The walls and spires were planted solidly atop a giant chunk of earth as if the entire castle and its foundation had been scooped up by a shovel and then flung into the air where it drifted to a halt instead of crashing back down to earth.

Near sunset, the Castle now looming in the sky above them, Myrth stopped again, pointing to a dark winged beast that had launched itself from the building far above. They watched cautiously as it fell in a series of banking dives until it closed the distance between them, and D'Mique could pick out its black-furred lion hindquarters and the bright white wings erupting from its huge shoulders. The griffin screamed defiantly, startling the horses. As the wings worked D'Mique noticed for the first time the elf who rode between them, using the leather reins to fight with the beast. When they landed a few feet in front of Jerrold, the griffin screeched again, snapping at the dragon and glaring defiantly at them with fierce red eagle eyes.

"Easy Storm," the elf chided as she dismounted keeping one hand on the reins. The griffin raked the sand with its clawed forefeet. "Greetings to you and your party most generous Earth Master," the elf said bowing low.

"And greetings to you, Re'Ana, servant of the Wind Mistress," Myrth answered.

"My Mistress has taken the castle away as you can see," she said waving behind her. She was wearing blue and white livery, her forearms covered in leather bracers, with a heavy crossbow riding across her back. Re'Ana bent and scooped up a fistful of sand then straightened and smiled. "But the way is prepared," she said throwing the sand into the air. It landed before it hit the ground easily outlining the first several feet of an invisible staircase.

"A staircase made of Air!" D'Mique's breathed, her throat seizing suddenly.

"Regretfully there is no way to bring your horses," Re'Ana sighed. "Perhaps Master Myrth, you can construct an appropriate shelter?"

Myrth dismounted, nodding as he took several steps away from the stairs before holding out a clawed hand. At his gesture the earth leaped upward, boiling and spewing great seamless stone walls, streaked red and black like the land around them. As they grew upward they leaned inward to top the structure off with a peaked roof. Myrth dropped his hand and the ground settled back into complacency, the new building an organic part of the scenery.

After surveying his handiwork Myrth pulled the large black pillow from Jerrold's saddlebag, and called to the dragon, "Come, friend, a palace or a stone hut?" He set the pillow on the ground and stood back. Jerrold studied the stable before tossing a glance toward the castle in the sky. Then he shrunk to his serpentine form and coiled up on the pillow. Shimmering in a heat-haze that flowed from his own body, the dragon's tail suddenly flattened, shrinking further and changing from scales to stitches. The magic traveled up his body embroidering his coils around the pillow until only his head remained. Then he winked at them, a silent laugh lighting his face as the spell caught up the last of the physical dragon, stitching his head to the pillow, caught in mid-wink, trapping the smile in stitches.

D'Mique let out a breath she hadn't realized she'd been holding. "Did that hurt?" she asked the pillow.

Myrth chuckled, "Of course not." He grabbed the pillow in one hand scooped up some sand in his other and marched toward the staircase. At its base he threw the sand higher along the stairs than Re'Ana's had gone, continuing to outline the steps.

Rogan gathered the horses, waiting for each rider to dismount and collect their saddlebag before taking the animals into the newly constructed stable. As he worked Tierren and D'Mique stood together, staring at the invisible sand-lined stairs. They appeared wide, sweeping grandly through the sky. If they had been made of anything other than solidified air the horses would have been able to climb them two abreast D'Mique judged.

Myrth stared at the steps for a moment then bent and grabbed another handful of sand before starting up. When the sand outline ended he threw his second handful, continuing to mark the stairs. Genow and Trillip each took two handfuls of sand and followed Myrth, throwing their sand when it seemed their nerve had given out.

D'Mique stood at the base of the staircase flanked by Rogan and Tierren, all of them watching the steady progress of the others. Re'Ana watched them with her head tilted in curiosity. "Is there something wrong?" she asked.

Rogan and Tierren looked down at her, "We do not wish to leave the earth," Tierren said. "We are Soil Children."

Re'Ana nodded then gestured toward the griffin, "Storm may let you ride him, but he can only carry two riders. The third one will have to walk anyway." The three honor guards exchanged quick glances and Re'Ana continued, interpreting their looks as hesitation over who would ride the griffin. "I will stay with the one who walks; I will not let you fall for I am bound to Air. If we slip, I will catch us."

D'Mique replied, "I am a Child of Man. I'm not afraid to climb the stairs. The goblins can take the griffin." Relieved Rogan and Tierren hurriedly took the reins, clambered aboard the beast and turned its beak toward the castle. With a shriek, the downy white wings unfurled and the lion hind legs launched it into the sky. Re'Ana tracked their progress until they reached the castle. Then her black eyes returned to D'Mique.

"Ready? Grab a couple handfuls of sand so we can mark the way," she said stooping to follow her own instructions. D'Mique copied her and then stood at the foot of the invisible staircase. Above her the others continued their ascent, maintaining a steady pace. Determined she started up the sand-strewn stairs Re'Ana lightly holding her upper arm.

As she climbed D'Mique focused on the sand. When it disappeared, she scattered first one handful then the other, bringing more of the steps into view. Beside her Re'Ana did the same. She kept her eyes on the steps, a strategy that worked until her gaze moved below the sandy outlines. The desert sprang forward and a fuzzy warmth suddenly engulfed her, settling in her head. Re'Ana's grip tightened around her arm as she slowly sunk to her knees. "Lady?" Re'Ana asked, an edge of concern in her voice. D'Mique looked up focusing on Myrth where he sat several steps above her.

"Don't look down, don't look down," she whispered repeatedly, closing her eyes and waiting for her head to clear. She concentrated on her heartbeat and the gritty feel of sand beneath her knees.

"Are you all right?" Re'Ana asked kneeling beside her.

D'Mique nodded and opened her eyes. "Gods," she breathed, staring through the grains of sand and down at the desert nearly a hundred feet below where the ground formed a patchwork quilt of volcanic sand, slick rock and lava flows. She closed her eyes again focusing on her breathing.

"I'll help you Lady," Re'Ana coaxed. She laid an arm across D'Mique's shoulders lending support.

D'Mique tilted her head upward and opened her eyes again. The castle filled her vision and with a deep breath she rose again and continued on.

Then there was no sand, the stairs seemingly ending in midair. Heart sitting in her throat, threatening to jump from her mouth, she took another step forward, focusing on the others ahead of her. *"The steps are still there,"* she told herself, *"because the others still climb."* Her foot found the next step easy enough, then the next and the next. As she climbed her heart settled back into her chest, beating too fast but satisfied to stay inside her body. Her world narrowed to the firm weight of Re'Ana's arm across her shoulders and the feel of solid steps beneath her feet.

It seemed they had climbed for an hour when her concentration was shattered by a voice near her waist, "Well hello." Startled, a small half-squeal erupting from her lips, she sank to her knees, landing on the invisible steps in front of Trillip who smiled condescendingly down at her. "Afraid of heights?" he asked.

"I didn't even see him!" D'Mique chastised herself.

"It is a common fear," Re'Ana said beside her.

"I can do this," she hissed at Trillip glaring up at him. He nodded and looked out over the side of the steps. D'Mique looked down through them. They were about halfway to the castle. The volcano loomed near them, its massive black flanks rising beneath the stairs, slightly decreasing the distance to the ground.

"I do not fear the heights," Trillip whispered, a pensive note on the air. D'Mique gazed up at his sharp features, his skin alabaster in the clear sunshine. A stray breeze played with the candy-pink hair as he returned his attention to D'Mique.

"We are nearly there," Re'Ana announced. "Come, friends of my Mistress. Jay is holding a storm at bay for us." They stood and Trillip turned back toward the castle. He laid a hand on D'Mique's shoulder as they started up the steps, "Come, soon you will be on solid ground," he said.

D'Mique looked up toward the castle. Its brightly shining walls stood in contrast to the dark treetops growing behind them, their branches dancing in a strong breeze. She glanced at Trillip as they started climbing. His curly hair, just long enough to graze his shoulders, danced as the breeze tickled through it. *"I wonder if it's as soft as it looks,"* she thought. Horrified by the sudden random contemplation she swallowed hard and forced herself to concentrate on the steps. Twenty minutes passed before they closed on the castle. From this close, the walls no longer shone. Instead they proved to be an opaque white crystal, sparks of gold and rainbows glinting across the surface.

"It's a good wall," she thought measuring the height in her head, *"And guards, that's good,"* she continued, noting the people on patrol along the structure's top. The castle's gate lay open before them welcoming them. Five towers rose above the walls, the outermost on either side reaching twice as high as the wall, while the two inner towers doubled in height again. All four were decorated with several large, dark windows.

At the center of the castle surrounded by the towers, stood an imposing crystal spire, stretched high and thin, the balcony ringing its tip nearly lost in a bank of clouds high above the tallest towers. D'Mique swallowed hard as her stomach sank. "That balcony is probably the Wind Mistress' Audience chamber," she thought.

"Lady?" Re'Ana asked lightly touching D'Mique's arm as she stopped walking. Trillip also stopped, and looked to her.

D'Mique looked back at Re'Ana. "That balcony," D'Mique asked pointing skyward, "is it the audience chamber?"

Re'Ana smiled, "No Lady. That is the Mistress' observation point. The audience chamber is at the base of the Spire." Nodding D'Mique continued climbing, reaching the top of the stairs a few minutes later. She looked around, startled by the distress that seemed to drain from her upper body as her feet found solid ground. The Floating Castle was perched in the center of an earthen disc, its edge jutting out from the wall creating a narrow space between the castle and air. The goblins lay flat on the ground stretched out on their backs just outside the castle while the griffin Storm stood quietly near. He screeched a greeting to Re'Ana when he saw her and pawed the ground happily as she hurried to him. Myrth and Genow were nowhere to be seen. Trillip paused just outside the gate watching the goblins as they slowly sat up.

A sudden strong wind blew around the castle, playing with their clothing, howling past them as it rushed through the trees. The griffin screeched again, stretching his wings nervously as the blast threatened to carry them all off into the nothingness beyond the island. Gasping, D'Mique hurried toward the castle. "Come on," she shouted at the goblins, "We can't stay here." She hurried through the gate. Inside the wind suddenly disappeared and she pulled up short. A desert garden rolled away from the crystalline walls ringing the five gray towers. White rock paths branched

out from the gate, snaking through the garden, enticing her to explore.
Along the paths ornamental plants dotted the desert landscape—black lava
rock accented cacti and thorny trees while weathered bushes grew from the
red sand.

Myrth was just disappearing around the central Spire and D'Mique
hurried after him, her boots crunching along the path, echoing in the deep
silence of the castle grounds. At the back of the spire D'Mique stopped
again beside a frosted glass door that led into the structure. Hesitating, she
glanced around furtively looking for Myrth, before concluding that he'd
disappeared through the door. Trying the handle and finding it unlocked
she quickly slipped inside. Myrth had stopped just beyond the door frame
and D'Mique nearly ran into him as she entered. He took a single step
forward, making room for her but gave no other sign that he knew she was
there. Leaning to her left she peered around the Earth Master and found
Genow standing in front of him. They filled the entrance to an open, airy
room. To her right a staircase of blue stone hugged the wall as it rose up
the Spire disappearing through an opening in the vaulted ceiling. Small
windows dotted the walls, while green and gold cobblestones made up the
floor beneath her feet. Throughout, the structure glowed with a faint inner
light. A golden throne sat centered along the back wall, framed by a frothy
white waterfall that sang gently as it fell into a pool. From where D'Mique
stood the pool looked cold and deep as it rippled behind the throne.

A small figure burst from the water startling D'Mique, and rushed
toward Myrth, throwing itself into his waiting arms. Scowling D'Mique
dropped her hand from her sword hilt. *"If she'd had a weapon,"* D'Mique
scolded herself, *"Myrth would be dead."* D'Mique studied the crying willowy
female folded against the Earth Master's chest. She had a flowing red crest
of hair that stood about three inches high on the top of her triangular head
and trailed, wet, down her back, falling to her knees. The skin along her
head and arms was a dull light gray, blending and fading to white on her
neck, underarms and hands.

She wore a diaphanous turquoise top and a short matching skirt, both
wet and clinging to her muscular form—every inch of her skin visible
through the cloth. Startled and suddenly embarrassed, D'Mique averted
her eyes for a moment before realizing that there was nothing to be

embarrassed about. "She's a shark Semian," D'Mique thought taking a second look at the newcomer's asexual form. Shark Semians had no human parts to hide, and any clothing they chose to wear was for an observer's comfort.

The small figure pulled away from Myrth allowing D'Mique to see her face. Her narrow, triangular eyes glinted like solid gray chips of granite, two shades darker than her skin. "Oh, Myrth. I'm so glad you made it," she breathed. Her voice was the same wind chime tinkle D'Mique had heard arguing with Myrth from one of his jars.

"This is the Wind Mistress, Jay," D'Mique concluded, then added incredulously, *"The Wind Mistress is a shark?"*

"All is well Jay?" Myrth asked.

"No Myrth! There is nothing well!" the Wind Mistress shouted, stomping a bare narrow foot. "That daemon is gone, completely hidden from all my senses!" She paused choking back a sob as she regained control. "It taints the Wind, drawing storms to cover its trail! And we can't stop it from doing so! Nepo can't take the water from so far away, and I'm struggling to steady the force lines. The winds heed only the daemon's word!"

"Powerful daemons have come before Jay. We will defeat it," Myrth reassured her, holding out a hand.

Jay shook her head refusing both his hand and his words, "No, Myrth, this daemon is no more powerful than any other Greater Daemon." Her voice grew hysterical as she ran through her litany, "It should not be able to keep me from my Wind! It should not be able to hide from the Eyes! It turned an entire pride! Myrth! Ten griffins! They attacked us! My griffins attacked me! They were torn apart in the sky above us!" she screamed. The emotion she had been holding at bay rushed over her again and she crumpled to the floor crying. Taken aback by her sudden outburst Myrth hesitated before hunkering down beside her.

"What are you saying?" he asked holding her by the shoulders.

"I'm saying that there is someone helping it! Someone in our world called this daemon, granting him added strength!" she shrieked.

The room grew cold as the Wind Mistress' words died away and Myrth stood, staring off into the mid-distance thinking. D'Mique swallowed hard as thoughts raced through her head, *"If someone called the daemon that means it's on a mission,"* she thought. *"It isn't just exploring a new land, warping the forcelines on accident and behaving badly. It's here for a reason—it's after someone or something and it's heading for a specific target with a specific goal in its evil mind."*

Myrth pulled his cloak tightly around him before speaking, "How can this be, Jay? Daemonic control is a lost art. There is no one who could call a daemon and control it."

"How would it know to hide Myrth?" Jay continued regaining her feet and her composure. "It hid from us the moment it came through. Oracle barely felt it. Even in the void it was hiding from us!" the shark-woman grew hysterical again.

"Jay, peace!" Myrth commanded.

She pulled up sharply, biting down on her next words, small triangular teeth clamping audibly shut. Her eyes grew hard glinting. "We are wasting time, Myrth," she said with a forced calm coloring her voice, "The pride that was turned against me was patrolling the northern plain near Ragnis Peak."

"When?"

"Yesterday morning."

"D'Mique," Myrth turned to her, pausing as he noted Trillip's presence. "Go get the goblins we need their eyes."

"Yes, Myrth," she said, turning on her heels and pushing past the Land-Nymph who had joined them sometime during Jay's rant. Outside she rounded the base of the Spire and stopped. Tierren and Rogan looking shaken and sickly pale were making their way toward her. She waited for them to close the distance before speaking.

"Myrth sent for you," she said as they stopped in front of her.

"What of the daemon?" Tierren asked.

"The Wind Mistress thinks someone called it here for a reason."

"What?" they exclaimed. But before she could elaborate Tierren held up a hand and a sudden stillness engulfed them.

"Myrth is scared of this idea," Rogan murmured a moment later and Tierren nodded. Silent, the three made their way back around the Spire and into the audience chamber, D'Mique trailing behind the goblins.

Myrth looked up as they entered barking orders to everyone, "Spread out and check the Eyes," he waved toward the wall.

"I have already checked the Eyes!" Jay exclaimed.

"We may see something you did not," he answered nonchalantly, unaware of the hurt that erupted on Jay's face at his words.

D'Mique turned to the closest wall noticing for the first time that the windows held the same enchantment as those in Dragon Ridge—although at the moment they all seemed to be looking out at the Broodlands rather than bringing a variety of locales into the throne room. She fanned out with the others scanning each window in turn. Sand, rocks and scrub stretched outward, each window showing the same scene from a slightly different angle. There were no tracks or broken plants or disturbances in the rocks. *"Nothing seems out of place,"* she thought. *"I couldn't have missed him. In all the stories Greater Daemons are bigger than a house. If one had passed through the desert before it would have left some sign."* She noticed Trillip climbing the stairs and followed him, pausing at each window she came to, with the same result. On the next floor she found a library. Rather than disturb the windows along the outer wall, the bookshelves sat in the center of the room facing outward, with a ring of small tables around them. Trillip moved around the room glancing at each window. D'Mique trailed him, looking as well, chiding herself, *"Maybe he missed something."* The others slowly worked their way up the stairs, Myrth and Jay bringing up the rear.

D'Mique made her way around the room. Just as the spiral started to climb to the next floor the windows along it became black.

"All the Eyes beyond are closed," Jay said noticing D'Mique's glance. "They were open at first," she added when Myrth turned on her too.

"Open them back up," the Earth Master hissed. "Do you know where your pride was when you lost them?"

"Near Ragnis Peak," Jay said again, a bitter edge coloring her lilt.

"Turn the Eyes there Jay. All of them," he instructed walking away, ignoring the Wind Mistress' bared teeth and hurt scowl. With a cleansing sigh, Jay closed her eyes and the windows came to life. D'Mique watched as the view out the window nearest her pulled up into the sky and swirled northward. Red sand and black rocks streamed past as a black mountain peak drew near. Around her windows staggered and stuttered as each one stopped at a slightly different angle, focusing on a slightly different object, some showing the mountain's flanks while others swooped over and around the volcanic peak. When the movement stopped Ragnis Peak spread out before them, a disjointed portrait. D'Mique's window stopped far enough from the mountain that it sat in the center of the view. In the foreground a faint path ran over a small rise before disappearing into the distance.

"What has to happen for a daemon to turn an animal?" D'Mique pondered speaking aloud, staring hard at where the path rose over the hill and out of sight.

"The strongest can do it with a touch, others need to take blood from the animal they're trying to turn," Myrth said joining her at the window.

"So our daemon probably did it by touch. Otherwise he couldn't have turned the whole pride," Trillip whispered over her other shoulder. She turned quickly toward him finding his sharply chiseled profile just over her shoulder, less than a breath away. She pulled back slightly as he looked at her, his deep green eyes penetrating and intense.

"We should not assume anything," Genow added, staring out his own window, "There may be other ways to turn animals."

"We have to start somewhere," Trillip said straightening.

"We will start downstairs," Myrth said, "While you, Trillip, and Genow continue upward." He went back downstairs followed by Jay and the goblins.

Genow looked at D'Mique. She looked at Trillip who was looking back at her as well. *"They're waiting for me,"* she realized, a cautious thrill tracing her spine, *"They're waiting for me to lead."* With a shrug she said, "You two recheck the ones on this floor first and then catch up to me." They turned and started scanning the windows around the library. *"They listened to me!"* she thought daring to let the thrill leap from her spine to her heart. She watched them a moment longer before mounting the stairs and climbing upward studying each window she passed.

The next floor was the Wind Mistress' private chamber. A round bed surrounded by frothy blue-green curtains dominated the space. The room also contained another pool, this one running around the perimeter giving way only to the staircase. About five feet wide and a yard deep the pool traveled along the outer wall just under the windows. Its sides, along with the floor D'Mique stood on, were formed from a jade-colored stone polished to a dull shine. At the bottom of the pool the walls disappeared beneath black sand. Here and there rainbow-hued corals and sponges grew up from this sandy bottom. Where the pool disappeared behind the bed the side dipped slightly, allowing the water to overflow, forming the waterfall on the floor below. Beside the bed, between it and the pool, was a small table on which sat three jars, two of them identical to Myrth's. The third jar filled with rocks and soil, had to be the one Jay used to talk to Myrth.

D'Mique started slowly along the edge of the pool looking out each window. Halfway around the room she stopped and stared. Through the window directly across from her a path came over a small rise and meandered into the foreground. She'd seen the path so many times in so many other windows, she almost knew it as well as she would have if she'd walked along it. It was the same path as the window she'd first looked through downstairs, only there was something more, something that caught her eye as she turned her head. A half-lit hint of white flashed again in the wind, "There's something there!" she shouted, jumping into the pool and thrashing over to the window churning up the sandy bottom in her wake. "Myrth!" she screamed. Sounds of people storming up stairs and throwing themselves into the water next to her were lost in the pounding of her heart.

At the top of the hill, just visible, a harsh furrow marred the path and there. "A white feather," she breathed pointing. Jay's gray head crowded into her vision and Myrth leaned close over her other shoulder.

"Change the eyes Jay," Myrth whispered after a silent study of the window. Jay straightened, closing her eyes as she concentrated on the windows. All around them the scenes changed as Jay centered the Eyes, ringing the feather on the hill.

"There's blood on the feather," Rogan said, his pointy nose nearly touching the Eye before him as he squinted into the image.

"Something about the furrow too, Myrth," Tierren added from where he stood looking at his own version of the scene. D'Mique looked from one to the other, all of them soaked, standing in the chest-high water intently scrutinizing a different window.

"The rock is fused, melted together," Trillip said from across the room. D'Mique looked toward him noting that his window looked down into the furrow.

Myrth climbed from the pool awkwardly, cloak soaked, water pooling in his wake as he squelched across the room. He splashed back into the pool beside Trillip and studied the image. "This is from a daemon claw. The fire within them sometimes heats their body enough to affect the outside world." Myrth turned back to Jay, "Where is this?"

"The Nest Trail. It travels northward from the brood over Ragnis Peak's foothills and out onto the Plain."

"Will the storm affect this evidence?" Genow asked.

Jay scowled in thought. "I can construct a dome over the hill and surrounding area. It will keep everything out until I say otherwise."

Myrth nodded. "Will the storm last until morning?"

The Wind Mistress nodded. "I kept it off until you reached the castle. It will be fierce. Storms don't appreciate being held captive."

"We will weather it here then. As soon as it lets up we will fly down to our horses and study this site in person."

"Do you want me to come with?" the Wind Mistress asked.

Myrth stood in thought for some time, frozen and silent, before replying, "Can Re'Ana undo the dome?" he asked at last.

"Yes," Jay swallowed hard, "but I do not wish to part with her."

"Now is not the time for selfishness, Mistress," Myrth chided.

Jay glared at him. "I was merely stating my feelings Master," she hissed, the last word dripping with anger.

Myrth studied Jay for a moment as if really seeing her for the first time. Then he smiled softly and his tone changed, enfolding the room in decadent velvet, "If someone called the daemon here, we must move quickly Jay. We will catch him, and we will avenge your Pride and your Aerie." He paused as he climbed out of the water. "We will call Nepo and have him collect the other half of our army. He can then escort them here and meet up with you." Myrth paced around the bed, puddles in his wake. "I will take Re'Ana with us to undo the dome. I will keep her safe, Jay," he promised, slipping the sodden cloak from his shoulders and letting it slump to the floor in an untidy pile.

"And Marladon?" Jay asked.

Myrth looked over at the fire-filled jar. It pulsed and flickered. "You should warn him," Myrth muttered, "he won't believe me."

Jay nodded after a moment. "Re'Ana show our guests to their suites please." Re'Ana acknowledged the command with a bow. "Formal dinner in an hour," Jay added turning in a slow circle, "or I can have food sent to you," she added, a frown growing across her forehead as each Honor Guard climbed from the pool adding their own puddles to Myrth's. With another bow Re'Ana ushered them down the stairs. As she left D'Mique glanced back at the Wind Mistress. Jay was standing in the pool still removing her clothes as she sank into the water. Throughout the room all but one Eye turned black, closed to the outside world. That single Eye remained open, showing the feather close up, flecked with dried blood, engulfed in darkness as the storm descended.

Leaving the Spire of Eyes they crossed to the next closest tower on the right. Re'Ana let them through into a lavish dining room. The mingled scents of cooking food wafted from a double wooden door directly across from them. D'Mique's mouth watered, her belly rumbled, and she swallowed hard, suddenly aware of how little she'd eaten. The room was a semi-circle of glass, enchanted windows showing a vast seascape. Thick white carpet covered the floor and in the center sat an ebony table large enough for twenty people. The place settings were black and white echoing the table and carpet. As a finishing touch a gold cloth adorned with seashells and plants ran the length of the table.

Re'Ana continued through a door on the right and D'Mique followed her, reluctantly, along a spiral ramp that conveyed them to the second floor. A hallway bifurcated the tower, lined with four doors—two per side—standing ajar. At the end of the hall a fifth door sat closed, unwelcoming.

"These suites house up to three guests each. You are our only visitors. If you don't show up for dinner we will send you food," Re'Ana explained. "Sleep well," she added before leaving them in the hallway staring at the rooms.

They all looked at D'Mique. "Who are you rooming with?" Rogan sneered drawing an indignant gasp from Genow.

"Rogan," Tierren hissed, "Apologize."

"I will not apologize because you say," Rogan answered.

Tierren glared, "It was an order, Rogan, not a request."

"No, wait," D'Mique held up a hand to Rogan facing Tierren. Mind racing she said, "Thank you Tierren, for your concern, but after all these weeks Rogan no longer offends me." Tierren pulled back, studying her, a hint of disbelief toying with his eyes. Heart pounding, unsure where her rebellious tongue would take her, D'Mique looked up at Rogan. "I will be rooming alone, Rogan. Given no other choice, I would room with Genow." Behind her Genow made an affronted strangling sound, but she ignored him, staring instead at Rogan whose eyes hardened as his sneer faded.

Tierren nodded curtly and then assigned them to their rooms, "Myrth will stay with me and Rogan in the back room, D'Mique in one of the side rooms and Trillip and Genow in the other." With a nod of her own and without another word, forcing herself to walk at a deliberate pace, D'Mique took the closest left-hand room closing the door behind her. Safe inside, hands shaking, she leaned against the door, deliberately unmoving while the sudden rush of adrenaline subsided. "That should sort him," she thought at length.

She studied the room. As with the hallway and the dining area below its decor was a sharp contrast between black and white. The black floor and white walls seemed to be made of marble, the white polished until it was nearly translucent. Three modest beds sat against the far wall, their soft gray covers acting as mediators between the walls and the floor. At the center of the room lay several overstuffed comfortable chairs, also gray in color, and a couple tables both black. On her left, white wooden screen partitions separated the bath area from the main room. With a sigh she pushed away from the wall and peeled out of her wet clothes, changing into a clean dry set from her pack before hanging the wet ones over the screen and stretching out across the center bed.

D'Mique started awake. The room was dark, a single lit candle throwing back the shadows around Re'Ana's face. Her black elfin eyes reflected the pinprick of flame as she smiled down at D'Mique. "The storm is abating Lady. It is early morning, the suns yet to rise. When you did not come to dinner we sent dinner up. The servants reported you sleeping. I have a sack of biscuits here if you are hungry." D'Mique nodded, taking the bag of still-warm biscuits from Re'Ana and falling on them, ravenous. She ate as Re'Ana stuffed her nearly dry uniform back into her pack then waited patiently by the door.

"We'll have to re-do your hair tonight," she commented as D'Mique stood. D'Mique ran her wrapped braid through her hands glancing at Re'Ana's own white hair, which lay in small cornrow braids gathered into an ebony clasp at the nape of her neck. A sudden chuckle swelled inside her as she realized how perfectly Re'Ana matched the room. Swallowing the laughter D'Mique took her pack and followed the elf out the door and down the spiral.

Outside the storm was over yet clouds still lingered, although they failed to obscure Col and Nix, who were just peeking over the horizon as the Masters and honor guard filed out of the tower. At the gate two griffins waited for them, Re'Ana's Storm and a second white-feathered and tawny furred one. Myrth greeted the white griffin, patting its beak as Storm enfolded Re'Ana in his wings. "Hello Puck," Myrth said before climbing up on the second griffin and taking a seat behind Jay. Just as they settled onto its back the white griffin launched itself into the air, disappearing quickly over the edge of the floating island. D'Mique watched as it fell, unfurling its snow-white wings, gliding and banking to the ground below where the night's storm had transformed the desert into a lush green carpet.

Re'Ana climbed onto Storm. "Tierren you're first," she said.

The goblin paled. "Flying again?" he squeaked.

Re'Ana struggled to hide her smile. "Well, we can't swim down," she said, "There's one griffin for each of you," she indicated eight newcomers: four more griffins, ranging in color from deep brown to almost white, each one accompanied by a uniformed avian Semian.

Rogan bent and picked up a small rock. He handed it to Tierren who nodded closing his hand over it. With a grim "I go to my death" look around, the orange goblin clambered awkwardly up behind Re'Ana, barely falling into the saddle before Storm launched himself out into the lightening sky. D'Mique mounted the nearest griffin as Tierren's shriek faded in the distance. The soldier in front of her had long striped feathers instead of hair, and she forced herself to focus on the black and green bars of color two inches in front of her instead of the terrifying drop that was about to happen. Beneath her the half-lion beast gathered itself as if about to pounce, and its deep gray wings unfurled as it leapt from the island.

A yelp tore from D'Mique and she grabbed the soldier, clinging to him as a wave of panic washed over her. She shut her eyes molding herself to the soldier's back. For a short eternity they fell like a stone, the wind tearing at clothing and feathers alike. Then the griffin pulled out of its dive and the wings thrust forward and upward, working on either side of her. She felt the large wing muscles moving beneath her and dared a small peek as her fear overshadowed her curiosity. One huge wing stretched out to her left. Beyond spread the ever-nearing ground. In a few moments they pulled up for a landing. The wings pumped almost horizontally and the griffin jolted to the ground. Only when they'd stopped moving did she dare release the soldier—who seemed nonplussed by her behavior. Only now did it seem awkward to her.

"Thanks for the ride," she managed as she half-fell off the beast, sitting hard on the ground.

"Anytime," the soldier replied, his voice a cultured half-whisper.

Around her the others began sorting out the horses. Gratefully she found her gelding and replaced her saddlebags before mounting. A brief whispered conversation ensued between Myrth and Jay. When it ended Jay abruptly urged her mount into the sky and, followed by her soldiers, she returned to the castle, leaving the rest of them to begin their journey northward Re'Ana in the lead.

Olimidia

O*nce, long ago, before any of you were born, the great society of the Land-Nymphs lived throughout the Fanterra Plain. They built great cities far and wide each one surrounded by a wall of polished stone. These cities were known as the Shining Cities, and people came from all around to gaze upon their splendor. Then the Greater Daemon, Darmorg, first of his kind, breached the barrier between our realm and his. He destroyed nearly all the Shining Cities and the Land-Nymphs in his quest for power. But once the Hero Masters had disposed of Darmorg, the city Olimidia—its walls of white crystal, stained but unbroken—held all that remained of the Land-Nymphs and their once-vast civilization."*

Marco gazed down the hill to the Shining City as the remembered history lecture replayed through his head. Though beautiful, the view brought a hollow sadness with it. This city was all that remained of the Land-Nymphs and it should have been a bustling, lively place. Instead death rattled about the streets. The city sprawled along the bottom of a weathered ancient crater, its sides engulfing the city, sheltering it from the rest of the Fanterra Plain. White single-story buildings climbed up along a high rolling ridge at the center of the basin, with the two largest structures in the city—the Palace and the Academy—fighting for dominance at the top of the central pinnacle. Every member of the armies of the Southern Peninsula spent some time training here at the Academy. Through it, even a human farmer could rise to greatness. After completing his initial work here the young soldier would be assigned to one of the provinces and from there he could go anywhere. Not for the first time Marco pondered being assigned to a province without setting foot in the Academy, *"There's something odd about that,"* he thought, glancing at Sylus' back. Then the second large building caught his eye. "Who lives in the palace?" he asked, realizing he had never heard of a Land-Nymph king. The others stopped their horses and turned to look back up the hill to where Marco had stopped.

"It is the Mother's Palace," Clippen answered, "the leader of our people."

"She acts as the Magistrate of Olimidia," Sylus added.

Nodding his understanding Marco followed after them, his movement bringing his feathered Potent Cap to Sylus' attention. The Commander's eyes narrowed dangerously, but he said nothing. Marco rode onward, trying to ignore the itch between his shoulder blades that signaled the elf's continued concentration. *"This game,"* he thought, *"could get dangerous in the city...or the Academy."* Just after dawn yesterday Sylus had demanded Marco wear the tan and green uniform of the Academy threatening to set fire to the Potent uniform if he saw it again. Angrily Marco had complied but he'd stopped short of removing his Potent Cap and defiantly continued wearing it through the rest of the long ride. After an initial hiss of fury Sylus had pointedly ignored Marco's hat resorting to furtive glares in Marco's direction often enough that the man had prudently decided to ride behind the elf today. Now as they neared the western gate, Marco removed the cap and stowed it in his saddlebag with the rest of the Grand Syra's black livery. *"This is Sylus' world,"* he thought, *"and I'm just visiting."* He nodded to Sylus as the red feathers disappeared earning a suspicious snarl in return. Marco pointedly turned away, ignoring him and taking in his new surroundings.

The sheer size of the city seemed to demand the presence of a great bustling crowd. Instead just inside the shining walls a serene glade, nearly deserted in the afternoon heat, greeted them. *"A park,"* Marco thought. But even the park felt deserted. *"A park full of ghosts,"* he corrected. The road they followed wound through the park and was dotted from time to time with neat two-story houses. Here and there Land-Nymphs played and talked or read quietly. Two young children chased each other around a large tree. *"'Ghosts' wasn't far wrong,"* he thought as his eyes passed from one pale form to another, a near copy of the one before, chiseled alabaster bodies highlighted by tropical splashes of color.

Beyond the park the road entered a sedate neighborhood where the houses grew closer together. Passing through this district they came to a marble plaza, and here the road diverged and continued east, entering another residential district and turning north to wind through another park. Several benches ringed the plaza, facing the fountain at its center, providing the statue atop the fountain with the possibility of an audience. But no one sat here. *"Perhaps the Land-Nymphs have lost interest,"* Marco thought taking in the statue, recalling the history it represented. Carved from a plinth of dark marble it depicted the four Hero Masters who had saved Olimidia. A human and a stag Semian stood proudly at the back, framing and protecting a goblin-maid—Syra by name. The fourth Hero Master, an elf, sat at the base dangling stone legs into the water around him. Marco couldn't remember the other names. Like most he only remembered Syra because she had created their current form of government lending her name to the official position she'd envisioned.

A sadness settled over him as his eyes rested on the human at the back. *"The last known Mage of Man,"* he thought. *"Why don't people know your name?"* he asked the statue. Then, *"Will they remember mine?"*

Between them and the statue Oracle sat astride his tall black horse. They stopped as the Semian dismounted and glided toward them. "Seer Oracle," Sylus greeted from his horse. Oracle nodded his own greeting. "Myrth instructed us to meet you here," Sylus continued.

"Indeed," Oracle replied shifting his cloak over his shoulder. "Myrth tracks the daemon with his fighters."

"He has no way of winning without us!" Clippen interjected.

"Peace, Clippen," Oracle chided the Land-Nymph. "I do not think he means to fight it. Rather, I think, he plans to bring it to ground or follow it to its lair."

"We will continue on to Dragon Ridge," Sylus said, "and catch up to him."

Oracle looked at him, studying him. "I see you in Sea Spray," he said at last, blinking his amber eyes.

"Sea Spray?" Clippen asked. Oracle nodded.

"No, we should hurry after Myrth," Sylus said.

Oracle shrugged. "I can only advise, Sylus," he replied. "I must go now. I see myself elsewhere." He turned and remounted, spinning the black horse northward and urging it to a slow trot. Sylus watched the Seer leave before shaking his head and closing his eyes. Projecting himself outward he called to Myrth but there was no answer. After a moment he opened his eyes frowning. "No Myrth. Let's go up to the Academy and settle in. I'll try again from there."

"Could I contact him?" Marco asked.

"No," Sylus said smiling sadly. "Conversing across forcelines is only possible between servant and Master." They too turned north, leaving the plaza in Oracle's wake.

The houses gave way to clean storefronts as they climbed the central hill; the crowd of Land-Nymphs never increasing or decreasing there was always someone present, but never more than a couple dozen in sight at any given time and children were strangely absent. There was an almost imperceptible sense of defeat about the city, *"a defeated people waiting for the axe to fall,"* Marco decided.

At the center of the crater the buildings disappeared and the road started up the sloping pinnacle. On either side, green terraced fields opened up and at the top of the hill, to their left sat the white stone palace. The palace grounds seemed empty though red liveried guards walked the perimeter at a measured pace. On the right was the Academy, its grounds bustling with activity as a huge crowd watched two swordsmen sparring. Another nearby group practiced with a variety of bows. As Sylus and the mages approached, the clang of swords greeted them, mingling with the cheers and cries of students. The riders reached a drive leading up to the front steps and turned into the Academy grounds. Two elfin stable hands, dressed in the same tan and green uniforms the cadets wore, came for their horses.

"Commander Sylus," one of the elves greeted, "You left on Miky and you return on a Palace Black."

"Miky gave his life defending me from daemons in the Nesting. I have yet to name this one, but put him in Miky's stall," Sylus instructed.

"Of course," the stableman said, "And these are your students?"

"Some of them," Sylus answered. Is there an empty barrack for us?"

"I fear not," the stableman continued. "High Summer has nearly ended. Our barracks are full of hopefuls."

Sylus grimaced. "Alright," he said dismounting. "Come," he called to the others and they clambered out of their saddles grabbing their packs before hurrying after him. Sylus led them up a set of steps and into the red brick building. Inside spacious halls, wide enough for wagons to fit down, greeted them. They trooped down the cavernous main hall to the end where a bright office welcomed them. A thin human sat behind a large wooden desk.

"Commander Sylus," he greeted.

"I need three cots brought up to my private suite," Sylus said, "My students will be staying with me."

"Of course commander," he replied, ducking his head.

Without a second thought for the human clerk Sylus left the office and led the group up a nearby flight of stairs. At each floor two halls branched off in opposite directions. When they reached the third floor they took the left hallway, moving back toward the front of the Academy, stopping at the last room on the right. Closing his eyes the elf placed his hands on the door, concentrating until a thick click echoed through the hall and the door unlocked. The commander opened the door and let everyone in behind him. The room within was dusty and unlived in. "Light the lamps please," Sylus commanded. Clippen did so as Sylus sifted through a closet, reemerging with a stack of towels, which he passed out before setting Marco and Kryoso to dusting the room. They worked quickly, exposing the cherry-red wood beneath the gray fuzz. A knock on the door interrupted their work and a huge clay-gray brute entered. He carried three folded cots in and set them down before saluting the elf and departing.

"Was that a mud goblin?" Kryoso asked. "I've never seen one on this side of the Crest."

Sylus nodded adding, "We have many people serving here." He continued, "You are free to go where you wish and do as you wish within the city walls. I will stay here and await Myrth's call."

When they finished dusting and setting up their cots Marco followed Clippen out into the city leaving Kryoso and Sylus behind. "Where are you going?" Marco asked. Clippen glanced at him but did not reply. "I'd like to help," Marco added. Marco followed his silent companion down the hill and through the residential district until they had reemerged in the park. Here Clippen left the road and crossed a field leading them onto a tree-lined street. The Land-Nymph stopped and studied Marco a moment.

Resigned he answered the man's question, "I have a message to deliver...to Trillip's love, Mara." He turned and continued down the street. The gravity of the Land-Nymph's mission hovered over Marco and for a moment he considered turning back unsure if the Land-Nymph would want an audience. But Clippen stopped and looked over his shoulder. "Are you coming?" he asked.

"I...do you want me to?"

Clippen pondered the question for a moment then nodded. "I see no reason why you shouldn't come. It will be better with another there." With a nod Marco followed Clippen down the road and up a well-maintained walkway.

At the whitewashed door Clippen knocked solemnly. After a minute an elderly male Land-Nymph answered. He was shorter than Clippen and Marco. His hair carried a hint of the bright, sky-in-summer blue it had once been although now it was mostly gray. His green eyes, though surrounded by a wrinkled face, shone happily up at them. "Well hello Clippen," he greeted.

"Hello, Elder. I was hoping to see Mara, may I?" Clippen asked.

The elderly Land-Nymph thought a moment before replying, "My son has gone to his work and I cannot gain his permission. His wife still refuses him and he hasn't the heart to force her. However he has deprived her of nearly every non-essential part of life. Visits with old friends surely fall into that category."

"When may I see her? I have brought her a message from the love she pines for. I feel that the message may help her accept your son," Clippen explained, his voice carrying a distinct edge.

The old Land-Nymph thought some more, "Okay. I will grant you a visit."

Clippen smiled, "My thanks, Elder." The old Land-Nymph stepped back and let them into the house. A small entry hall fell before them. On the left the space opened up into a library housing two tables, an assortment of lamps and hundreds of books. Clippen turned right and Marco followed him deeper into the house. They went through a sitting room and into a large kitchen. Near the back of the house a narrow staircase rose along the back wall.

Leaving the elderly Land-Nymph in the kitchen, Marco followed Clippen up the stairs to another door. Clippen knocked again and waited but there was no answer. With a sigh he tried the handle and opened it slowly. Stepping through he called, "Mara?"

"Clippen?" a soft voice answered. Marco followed him in. Mara stood near a window along the right wall. The room, tucked in under the eaves of the house, garnered little sunlight and the short lean Land-Nymph seemed deathly white in the gloom. Her hair was a wistful yellow, her eyes a pale melon green. Aside from the varying hair and eyes, and her short stature, Clippen and Mara looked exactly alike, their chiseled features mirror images of one another.

"Who is this?" she asked, her soft green eyes falling on Marco.

"This is Marco, my friend," Clippen answered.

"Then welcome, Marco, to my prison."

"Mara—" Clippen started.

"No, Clippen. This is a prison." Mara turned away from them choking back a sob.

"As you say, Mara," Clippen acquiesced.

"And you, Marco," she continued not looking around at him, "Are you a friend to my Trillip?"

"I call Trillip friend as well," he said after a momentary pause.

"And would you call this a prison?" she asked, turning and looking straight into his eyes.

"I," he looked at Clippen, who offered no help, then back to Mara. "I disagree with what your leaders have done to you and Trillip."

"I bear a message from Trillip," Clippen interrupted. "He says that the Elders can't force you to love Timmil. You will always love Trillip and he will always love you. But that you must...that he must," he paused, searching for the right word, "continue," he said at last his voice holding some reluctance. "If we leave no children behind, then we are done. You and me and Trillip, we are the last generation. Without children from everyone, there will be no more Land-Nymphs." Clippen paused and took a shaky breath. "He begs you to have a child and name her after him, honoring your eternal love," he finished his voice catching slightly.

"And Timmil?" Mara asked in a whisper, her own voice thick, "What does he say to this?"

Clippen shrugged, "I have not spoken to him of this."

"He isn't here?"

"No. Elder Hamma let us in."

"Then you have given me more than a message, Clippen. You have given me a bargaining tool. I will honor Trillip's wishes and I think, perhaps, that I shall name my second child after you, dear Clippen. But you must hurry away now."

"I shall be honored, Mara. And I will tell Trillip of your decision when next we meet." They crossed the room and embraced. Then Mara showed them out. "It was a pleasure meeting you, Marco," she said before closing the door behind them.

Clippen wiped at his eyes and took a shaky breath before descending the narrow stairs. Elder Hamma sat at the table in the kitchen working on a bowl of stew. He looked up as they entered. "Tell your son that Mara is agreeable. She will bear his children if he will allow her to choose their names."

The elder Land-Nymph chewed thoughtfully for a moment. "That is a small price to pay," he said.

"I thought so too Elder," Clippen said. Elder Hamma set his bowl aside and started to rise. "No, dear Elder. I can see myself out. Thank you," he said before backing from the room and hurrying away. When they were back on the street Clippen turned to Marco. "I thank you for the part you played in persuading Mara to give in to her husband."

"Thanks, I think," Marco said.

"You think?" Clippen stared at him curiously.

"Well, I understand that Trillip and Mara are too closely related to wed but there ought to be another way." Clippen nodded in reply. Marco continued after a moment, "Why is being able to name the child such a big deal?"

"Females naming their young?" Clippen laughed. "It's just not done."

Marco studied him closely, "My mother named me," he said.

"But how can you trust a female to choose a strong name?" Clippen asked.

Marco gaped, "I can't believe you just said that," he said.

"Sorry," Clippen apologized without conviction.

"How can you have such an opinion of women? Your Magistrate is female," Marco pressed.

"The matriarch is the oldest mother in the city. Her sons advise her. When she passes away the next oldest mother takes her place and her sons advise her," Clippen explained. "Our females are prized possessions that must be cherished and loved. And who better to rally around than the most dignified female in the city?"

"And your mother?" Marco asked.

Clippen waved a non-committal hand. "She is only thirty-seven summers. Nowhere near old enough." Marco laughed at his friend.

"And you feel the same about your mother as you do about the other female Land-Nymphs?" he asked, trying to gain an understanding of such a foreign viewpoint.

"Yes," Clippen answered; he too was becoming defensive. "My mother deserves my protection and advice. She deserves my obedience and attention for she sacrificed much to bear me and raise me."

"But your father chose your name," Marco pointed out.

"No. My father died before I was born. My uncle chose my name. We lived with them. Still do, actually."

"Your uncle?" Marco thought a moment. "That would be Chosen of Water's father, right?"

"Yes. Of course," Clippen started toward the Academy again, Marco following him. "Tekalo is my cousin. My uncle gave me a sensible Land-Nymph name and then lost his mind and named my cousin Tekalo, 'Tek' for his favorite horse, and 'alo' for Palo, Grand Syra."

"Your cousin's named after Palo?" Marco asked with a chuckle.

"Yes," Clippen said. He shook his head, lost in thought.

"Much better than anything your aunt might have chosen," Marco finished.

Clippen opened his mouth to answer and then clamped it shut. He glared at Marco. "I tire of this conversation," he said quickening his pace. Marco's laughter died. He hurried to keep up with the Land-Nymph.

"And how about D'Mique?" he asked, not yet willing to give up on the argument.

"What do you mean?"

"Would you trust her to name her own child?" Marco asked.

"I will not discuss this further, Marco," Clippen huffed, "She's not even a Land-Nymph."

"Better yet if you were the father, do you think D'Mique would let you name her baby?" Clippen did not answer him. "Clippen?"

The Land-Nymph turned on Marco, "If you insist on having this ridiculous conversation," he shouted waving his hands in frustration, "then, yes! I would expect D'Mique to name her child. She is human, not a Land-Nymph."

"But what if it were your child?" Marco asked, laughing.

Glaring, Clippen rejoined, "What if it was your child? That is a more fitting question as you are also human."

"I already know. If I have children, then I would like to name my sons. But my wife could name my daughters."

Clippen studied him. "I suppose that might be a solution," he said at last. Marco nodded. "But that is a solution for two humans," Clippen continued a hint of scorn riding his voice. "Our culture is different," he said dismissively turning and walking away.

Frowning, Marco hurried after him again, "I did not wish to offend you Clippen, I apologize."

"All peoples move toward a better understanding of their neighbors," the Land-Nymph replied.

"Now you sound like an advertisement for a cultural fair," Marco said.

Clippen smiled, "I suppose so," he said with a chuckle. They had reached the Academy.

Marco frowned up at the three-story building. "How long do you suppose we'll be here?" he asked. Clippen shrugged as they ascended the front steps and disappeared inside.

The Feather on the Hill

D 'Mique stayed just behind Myrth and Tierren on the long ride north while Trillip and Rogan rode behind her flanking Genow. Griffins proved awkward on the ground, their mismatched legs to blame. Storm would waddle along awkwardly beside them from time to time, his lion hindquarters padding gracefully, his eagle forelegs mincing along gingerly or hopping lightly. Then he would leap into the sky and return to scouting the land ahead. Yesterday the land around them had been dead. With rain, a large amount trapped in rock-formation basins, a sense of urgency had overcome the desert as if the plants and animals knew the water would not last long and an abundance of life had poured forth. Everywhere cacti bloomed, insects hummed and toads called for mates. But there was no road to follow through the newly green desert, and there was no sign of the daemon's passage.

The party stopped to rest in the early afternoon Re'Ana and Storm joining them. D'Mique dismounted leading her horse to a pool of water as Re'Ana reported to Myrth. "If you continue on straight you will come to a trade road," she said, "It bears north-west. Follow it for a time then turn north again."

"When will we reach the peak road?" Myrth asked.

"Once you turn straight north off the trade road you have only a couple miles until you reach the peak road. I must say Master, the most direct route is not the safest."

"I am Earth Master, Re'Ana. I can feel how thin the crust grows beneath our feet. I can keep it strong enough for us."

"Of course Master," she said bowing her head, "I spoke in error." Myrth nodded. D'Mique downed a travel ration of dried bread and meat before feeding her horse, gathering rations from a bag the griffin carried. When the food was gone they remounted, following the route Re'Ana had described and reaching the peak road near sunset, Col and Nix just touching the horizon and Rysk about three hours behind.

The narrow rolling path matched the images in the Spire of Eyes exactly, including a distinct lack of new vegetation. D'Mique surveyed the wide circle of undisturbed land until Re'Ana interrupted her, "The dome has been removed, Lady. Please continue." Nodding, D'Mique stepped onto the road, a mix of trepidation and excitement washing over her, while the others remained behind. She rode slowly scanning the ground. She easily picked out the lion and eagle footprints gouged into the mud, many of them rimed in blood. The griffins had fought here but they had not died here—there were no bodies. At the top of the next rise the white wing-feather they'd all seen in the Eyes practically glowed in Rysk's subtle light. D'Mique stared at it and the ground. She looked out at the surrounding desert, rolling lava-rock foothills that promised to keep secret anything they knew. The only tracks were those of the griffins. Shaking her head she looked back at the rest of the party, "There are signs of battle, but it looks more like the griffins were fighting among themselves rather than fighting a daemon."

Myrth bowed his head in thought for a moment. He started growling, "The daemon is cloaked by a local mage. It has left signs; they are merely hidden by a spell."

Genow inched forward, "I feel the workings of a spell. It covers the ground." He closed his eyes. D'Mique watched the ground for a minute. Genow sighed, "I can't unwork it," he said, "The mage who laid it is not elfin. He is very powerful, Myrth."

"A spell that hides a Greater Daemon doesn't come from any natural element, Genow," Myrth murmured attempting words of comfort that simply made the elf glower at the ground again.

"It is Shadow magic," Re'Ana whispered.

Myrth sat in thought contemplating the possibility. "Shadow magic is only done by daemons," he said. "We are chasing the only one on the plain. Whoever is helping this daemon isn't a daemon himself."

"There are related magics Master, are there not?" Re'Ana continued.

Myrth shrugged. "Shadow magic and its secrets are long-lost to us," he said closing his eyes to study the spell on the ground. "I cannot undo the spell either," he said after a long minute, "but I can see where it leads."

"North," Tierren guessed.

"Of course," Myrth stared northward. "There are three populations in the north: Hawkethorne Valley, The Gemm Hills—"

"The elves would never!" Genow cried turning red with outrage.

"And the Black Hills," Myrth finished. He turned around eyeing the bag that held his communication jars. "We can contact Marladon and ask after the Black Hills. That will help us narrow down the possibilities." He removed the Fire jar melting the rock shell with a thought, revealing its flickering glow, warm in the half-light. Myrth spoke to the jar, "Marladon." He waited for an answer but the only one he received was the lazy pulsing of the golden light within. "Marladon." Again there was no answer.

"He is away from his chamber," Tierren concluded.

Myrth nodded returning the Fire jar to his saddlebag. "We will follow the spell," he announced. "It is undoubtedly the path the daemon is following." They started north Myrth directing them based on the spell he saw in the Mage Realm, the faintly glowing black lines staining the earth.

The desert slowly turned to a prickly scrubland as they journeyed north, lava rock giving way to hardy thorny plants. Tomorrow they would leave the Broodlands behind and return to the Fanterra Plain with its sweeping grass fields. Just before nightfall they stopped to make camp. Myrth tried Marladon's jar again without reply before dropping onto his pillow in the center of the camp. With arms and legs folded, the Earth Master sat motionless, eyes closed, studying the shadowy spell that hid the daemon. D'Mique and Genow tended to the horses behind him while Re'Ana fed Storm. D'Mique watched the griffin eat as she brushed Trillip's horse. From the corner of her eye she caught a gleam of white beyond the firelight. Her hand stopped and she stared out into the night searching for movement or another gleam.

Genow saw her and looked out into the darkness as well. After a moment he spoke, "What is it, Lady?"

"I think I saw something."

He studied the darkness for a minute, then spoke, "I don't see anything. An animal in all likelihood," he concluded.

D'Mique studied the darkness a bit longer before agreeing, "Yes, you're probably right," she said. Giving the horse near her a last pat she started for the fire. Genow followed her and they sat down together on the ground beside Myrth.

A cold chittering broke through the quiet murmurs of the party. D'Mique looked back toward the horses, at the darkness beyond them. Myrth's eyes slid open. Tierren and Rogan stood slowly, crossbows at hand scanning the darkness as Trillip pulled a thin blade from the scabbard at his hip. "What was that?" D'Mique questioned, her gaze darting between the other party members. The strange call brought images of cold darkness and soft wetness to mind. She drew her sword mimicking the others. *"It wasn't a bird, it wasn't a man, it wasn't a cat,"* she thought. The feel of the blade in her hand chased away the fear that suddenly blossomed in her chest.

"Stay put," Myrth whispered closing his eyes. Genow moved closer to the Master as the ground rumbled beneath them. A stone wall erupted around them, enclosing their encampment and startling the horses who pulled against their tethers. After rising ten feet the stone curved inward, forming a domed ceiling above them. As it formed more chittering echoed through the darkness, several distinct voices rising from the depths, bringing fear with them. When a small smoke hole was the only way in or out of the enclosure Myrth opened his eyes again. The horses milled nervously, shying away from the new walls while Storm hunkered down, still crunching his rabbit bones, unconcerned by either the Master-made cave surrounding him or the approaching danger.

Claws skittered along the outside of the wall. "What is it?" D'Mique asked again, her whisper brimming with fear.

"Can they dig in?" Trillip asked studying the rocky ground.

"The walls come up from the bedrock," Myrth answered, "They can't dig under them."

An ear-piercing screech sliced through the stone room and all eyes flew to the smoke hole. A pair of snow-white eyes surrounded by wrinkled black skin and an upturned fleshy nose glared down at them. D'Mique caught a yelp of fear and surprise in her throat as the creature screamed again, its red slit mouth lined with sharp white teeth as it tried forcing its head through the small hole. D'Mique jumped as a twang beside her signaled the release of a crossbow bolt. Red fletching replaced one of the creature's white eyes and with a shriek of pain and fury it vanished. Rogan reloaded the crossbow.

"What was that?" D'Mique asked for the third time, breathless.

"A scalawag," Rogan answered.

"They're myth," she replied automatically.

Rogan spared her a condescending look. "Well I think I'll shoot them on sight just the same," he said.

"I would hate for any mythological creatures to tear you to pieces Lady," Trillip added, scoffing.

D'Mique glared at him then Rogan. *"Could they be right?"* she thought, *"Scalawags are supposed to be scavenger daemon-spawn, but everyone knows that Black Daemons are the only real daemon-spawn in the world."* Claws scratched at the wall behind her as another creature climbed up to the smoke hole. Rogan, Re'Ana and Tierren took aim again waiting for it to appear. Large black claws explored the edge of the opening, digging into the stone, drawing furrows at the rim. The three archers held their fire waiting for the scalawag's head to appear. With a deliberate slowness the claws worried the edge of the hole, the furrows sinking deeper each time they flashed in the darkness until the hole began to grow bigger. Seeing this Myrth gasped and shut his eyes, setting to work repairing the damage. The furrows filled again and the scalawag shrieked. Chittering, it dug faster its claws flaying the stone. D'Mique turned to look at the walls. She could hear more digging, claws scraping away at the stone, although none had yet successfully breached their protective dome. Above them more claws crept over the edge of the hole and started pulling at its edge, fighting to widen it against the will of the Earth Master. Re'Ana sent a bolt flying through the hole, reloading quickly as the scalawags outside grew louder their shrieking taking on a maniacal tone.

D'Mique studied the hole above them and glanced down at Myrth, the goblins and Genow. The elf seemed pale, almost frightened. Remembering herself, she closed the distance between them hoping to comfort him by her presence. *"I am your protector,"* she thought. The others remained steady, poised for action while Myrth stood motionless in the center, eyes closed, brows knitted together in concentration. The furrowed smoke hole filled with new stone as quickly as the scalawags dug it away. *"What is the limit of a Master's power?"* D'Mique wondered. *"Can he stand here all night filling in the claw marks?"* A sudden shriek brought her around to face the wall behind her. A small hole had appeared and black claws flashed around its edge working to widen it. "Myrth!" she shrieked. Eyes flying open he looked where she pointed a sharp intake of breath acknowledging his understanding. Scowling he closed his eyes again and the hole grew steadily smaller...but it never quite closed. D'Mique glanced up at the smoke hole again, noting its diameter.

"Myrth," Trillip called, "There's another here."

"Genow come to me," Myrth replied holding out a hand to the elf.

"Master," Genow bowed his head and hurried to obey, taking hold of the clawed hand, closing his own eyes as he worked to push extra strength into the Earth Master.

"That answers my question," D'Mique thought as a cold pit of fear developed in her stomach. *"He can't keep this up. Even the Masters have limits."*

"Let us help you, Master," Tierren volunteered, "take our strength." Myrth and Rogan nodded in unison. For some time they all remained motionless, watching the holes, waiting for the scalawags to peer in at them before one of the archers fired at their attackers. Almost imperceptibly the holes started to shrink but as they did an air of exhaustion settled over the goblins and Genow.

"We still can't stay like this," D'Mique thought. *"Can he let the holes get bigger? Maybe he can repair them one at a time."* She spoke, fear driving her to voice her concern, "Myrth, there has to be something else we can do."

Deep in the Mage Realm Myrth noted D'Mique's words, the edge of panic they carried, but he threw them aside. *"The Earth obeys,"* he thought willing the golden power to fill in the holes as they appeared around him. *"But it won't for much longer,"* a tranquil remembered voice whispered through his head, *"You are still mortal."* Grudgingly he acknowledged the truth behind his Master's voice. The goblins were failing and he dared not take any more strength from them. *"They're meant to defend me and they can't if I take everything from them."* He pulled away from them. Genow felt him falter and pushed more strength toward him. "No friend," Myrth said, his physical words sounding distant and dreamlike from where he stood in the Mage Realm. "Save your strength for the night ahead. D'Mique's right, we have to do something else before...," he trailed off, finishing silently, *"before everything is gone."*

Pulling away from Genow Myrth sent his consciousness outward, westward. "Sylus!" he summoned. And then the elf was there standing in his quarters at the Academy, staring eastward toward his Master.

"Master," he started.

"I am sorry my friend," Myrth said before reaching out and wrenching strength from the elf; stealing what he had always asked to borrow before. His servant's confusion and pain chased the strength back across the Fanterra Plain as it flowed into Myrth buoying him upward. He saw Sylus drop to the floor Marco and Clippen hovering over him just before closing the connection between them. With the influx of power the holes grew steadily smaller before Myrth pulled away from the Earth Cloud and the Mage Realm. He opened his eyes and called to Jerrold, "We can't stay here. We have to run." Grimly Tierren ordered them to ready the horses. "We haven't much time," Myrth added. D'Mique ran to obey the order while Re'Ana leapt for Storm, pulling him to his feet. Trillip doused the fire as they clambered onto their mounts, filling the cave with smoky darkness. In the dark the scalawags drew closer their shrieks triumphant. "There's a small tunnel beyond the wall, here," Myrth breathed from the darkness to D'Mique's left. "It's not long, but it will give us a small head start. Rogan, Re'Ana, Trillip, you're first. I will follow with Genow and D'Mique; Tierren last." Their orders just registered as the Master added, "Ride north, stop for nothing." Then the wall before him melted into sand disappearing, the new-formed opening taunting them, daring them to leave their protective dome.

Rogan kicked his horse, leaping forward with a scream of rage. Re'Ana followed on Storm. Trillip waited a moment before urging his mount forward followed by Genow and Myrth. "Go now D'Mique!" Tierren screamed. Startled she kicked the horse, aiming for the darkness the others had disappeared into. Tierren followed her with a yell of his own, and for a moment all she could hear was the blood in her ears and the ringing echo of the goblin's rage. Ahead of her the tunnel gave way to open air, the night slightly brighter than the earthen dome they'd left. Her breath caught in her throat, and she tugged her sword from the scabbard as she burst out of the tunnel. Large winged shapes closed in on the riders ahead of her. Fighting against the threatening wave of panic she focused on Genow and the scalawag that landed on his shoulders, its clawed hands tearing at the elf. D'Mique screamed—her battle-cry more fear than defiance—as another scalawag leapt at Genow landing on the horse's neck. She caught up to them and her blade flashed toward the scalawag atop Genow aiming for its neck. The galloping horses threw off her aim and her blade caught the scalawag's wing instead, narrowly missing Genow's back. Shrieking, milky eyes narrowed in hatred, the creature collected itself for a leap to her horse. She swung again, this time trying to time her swing with the bouncing horses, and her blade cut across the scalawag's face, slicing its fleshy nose. Blood flew as the creature dropped to the ground and disappeared into the night.

Ahead, a chittering winged wall closed off their escape route. D'Mique's heart sank but the others charged forward. White eyes glowed in the dark on both sides as more scalawags closed in. From the west Storm suddenly stooped through the night screaming as he plowed through the creatures, the slight scalawags no match for the massive griffin. Shrieks from the east brought D'Mique's attention back around. More scalawags were falling unceremoniously to the ground as Myrth faced them arm out-stretched. She spun her horse around looking back the way they'd come. More white eyes appeared closing off any hope of retreat. Tierren flew past her joining his fellow goblin on the front line, leaving her alone at the rear. With a deep breath she urged her horse back toward the mound, protecting the rear, hoping to meet the daemon-spawn before every direction was cut off.

As she charged, screaming her fear, blade outstretched, scalawags dove toward her. She caught the first one across the stomach, entrails spilling to the ground as it fell with a shriek. Her back swing caught another in the wing just as it crashed into her toppling her from the saddle. She flew backward, ridden to the ground by the wounded scalawag and hit the earth rolling over and over, her sword pinned neatly between their bodies. Face to face the scalawag strove to sink its teeth into her, trying for her eyes, her throat, while its claws tore into her chest. The pain was immediate shooting through her. She screamed as they came to rest in a thorn bush the scalawag on top. D'Mique brought her knee up hard into the scalawag's body. The creature shifted enough for her to turn her blade edgewise, and she pulled it down across their bodies, sending hot blood spilling from the shallow cut. The scalawag's scream mingled with hers as the sword broke free and D'Mique hacked into its unprotected back, pulling shrieks of pain from it, its attack morphing into a struggle to escape. D'Mique released it rising to her own feet. They stood glaring at each other, both of them breathing hard. It chattered at her, its claws flexing in anger. Sword ready, D'Mique charged. Surprised the scalawag turned to run, its stocky legs useless on the ground. It launched itself into the air but its injured wing could not carry it. D'Mique ran her sword through its chest, pinning it to the ground as it fell back to earth. She twisted the blade as she withdrew it, sure to hit a vital organ. The scalawag flopped helplessly on the ground blood gurgling in its lungs, drowning as it bled.

Exhilaration ran through her, *"I'm alive!"* she thought. She turned looking for her horse and more scalawags. Back near the stone tunnel she found them. The horse was down covered in winged bodies. It wasn't moving. She swallowed hard. Turning from the horse she looked for the others. *"No one!"* Cold dread gripped her heart, "I'm alone," she whispered. The army of scalawags was gone as were her companions. *"Where did they go?"* she thought listening to the growing silence—no sounds of battle, nor cries of fear or pain. *"It won't be long before they notice I'm missing,"* she told herself, starting north.

As she walked she came upon dead scalawags brought down by her companions, but no other sign of them. For a moment she stopped and closed her eyes. *"Should I wait for morning?"* she thought. Without an answer she trudged on exploring her wounds tentatively as she walked. The slices were deep, cutting across the side of her ribcage from her armpit to her belly, just missing her breast. Pain punctuated every deep breath, but panting shallow ones allowed her to keep going. With a few miles between her and her fallen horse she lowered herself to the ground, studying the darkness that engulfed her. There was only the night, no hint of a griffin in the star-spangled sky, and still no sign of the others.

Her eyes slipped shut for a moment, an exhausted sleep beckoning to her. *"I can't sleep here,"* she thought forcing her eyes open. They fell on an orange glowing pinprick in the darkness before her. *"That's a fire!"* she thought starting to her feet, gasping with pain as her wounds protested the sudden movement. She stared at the fire, "It has to be them!" She pictured Myrth and Tierren huddled together over the fire, Genow frantically searching the surrounding gloom, pacing as he waited for her; she started toward the light.

Each step accompanied by a sharp intake of breath, she steadily closed the distance between the light and herself. After a hundred yards her side grew numb and she lost herself in the rhythm of her footfalls. The world narrowed to just the orange light, growing ever larger ever closer. A dull ringing grew in her ears, and for a number of steps she felt as if her heart would fail. When nothing came of it her panic subsided and she stopped a moment closing her eyes, focusing on the hint of a breeze that ghosted past her. Focused, centered, she moved again pain tracing outward from the wound in her side. For an hour she limped forward, stubbornness giving way to determination before blind instinct took its place. Suddenly, as she approached her goal, Rogan stepped out of the shadows startling a scream from her before she collapsed before him. "Easy, Lady," he said. She sobbed once before letting the darkness engulf her.

The goblin picked her up with a small smile and carried her to the fire, laying her down near Genow. "She has a nasty wound," Rogan said as Genow placed his hands over her side pouring magic into her flesh.

After a moment he sighed letting his hands fall away. "The cuts are healed and there is no infection, but I'll have to re-treat it in the morning so that it won't scar."

"And her horse?" Myrth asked.

Rogan shook his head. "I saw no sign of it; she's walked a long way given the amount of blood on her clothes."

"We will have to share a mount now," Trillip observed. "My horse is the best suited for double-riders."

"You would share with the human?" Rogan asked glaring at the Land-Nymph.

"I keep the Promise, goblin," Trillip hissed.

Wakefulness crawled over her and D'Mique slowly opened her eyes, sunlight streamed through the overhanging branches piercing her head. Wincing she closed her eyes again, returning to the darkness and turned over. A wave of nausea engulfed her as she shifted position, and for a few moments she focused only on breathing. Once she was certain she wasn't going to vomit, she opened her eyes again and took in her surroundings.

Trillip sat nearby working with a knife and a pile of sticks. He didn't seem to notice her as she watched him, the sunlight playing through his pink curls as he sighted along a piece of wood he held in his hands. After a moment he set the stick in a smaller pile on his other side. The next stick he picked up went straight into the fire-pit. He stopped, suddenly sensing her, and turned to look at her. She stared back not knowing what else to do. Trillip returned to his sticks without comment.

D'Mique looked around. The camp was empty. Her heart skipped a beat, "Where is everyone?" she asked.

"They went back to salvage your saddlebags."

"Oh. Why didn't they wake me? I would have gone with them."

"It was decided that you should rest," he said derision coloring his voice.

"We are losing ground to the daemon," she said after a moment, half to herself.

"It was my opinion that we should split up, drawing lots to see who would stay behind with you while the rest of us continued the hunt," Trillip said. "It is cruelly ironic that you share this opinion." An uncomfortable silence grew between them broken at last by D'Mique's stomach rumbling. She thought of her food rations in her pack, *in all likelihood, spoiled by the scalawags last night,* she finished silently. She glanced up at the Land-Nymph, her eyes meeting his own shards of green.

With a sigh Trillip rose, gliding smoothly over to the big bay horse he had ridden from Dragon Ridge and rummaging in his packs, pulling two packets from them, one of them food which he threw to D'Mique. "You sound hungry," he said as she picked up the travel rations—hard biscuits and smoked fish she noted as she opened it.

"Thank you," she said.

Trillip dismissed her and returned to his place by the fire. The second packet turned out to be feathers and a phial of glue. D'Mique watched him as he worked notching the smaller sticks, stripping the bark from them and gluing fletching to one end. He looked up at her from time to time as he worked, at last saying, "I cleaned your blade last night."

"My blade?" She asked. He nodded toward it and D'Mique turned over to see it lying next to her. Pulling it from the scabbard she inspected the gleaming metal noting the intricate gossamer etching that marred the metal. "Daemon-spawn blood really is acidic?" she asked.

"A bit, "Trillip said. "The damage is slight to my eye," he continued, "We will have a smith study it as soon as we reach a town."

"Thank you again," she said returning the sword to her side. Trillip studied her carefully before nodding and returning to his horse. He came back with a small metal box. Inside arrowheads gleamed against red velvet. Using twine and glue he secured an arrowhead to each stick. Then he laid the dozen new crossbow bolts before the fire to dry. He pointedly studied them ignoring D'Mique.

The sound of approaching horses came to them. D'Mique gripped her sword as she shifted to face the sound ready for anything despite being flat on the ground. Trillip moved to stand just in front of her slightly off to the right. Rogan rode through the surrounding brush smiling at them. Storm, Jerrold, Tierren, and Genow followed his horse.

"D'Mique," the elf greeted, "it's good to see you awake." He dropped to the ground beside her and handed over a saddlebag. There were some gashes in it, but it was basically intact. "We did our best for your mount," he added.

D'Mique checked the pack inventorying the remnants. She took out a food packet and one of her spare uniforms. Standing, unsteady at first, she tossed the food to Trillip who caught it easily as she headed for the nearest bush. She checked her side while changing, running tentative fingers over the new skin. There was no sign of any trauma. When she returned to the fire everyone was milling around, settling in for the day it seemed. Rogan was starting on his own replacement crossbow bolts. Trillip had laid down eyes closed, asleep, and Myrth had joined him. Genow sat stirring some vegetation into a pot of water on the fire while Tierren tended to the horses removing Trillip's and Genow's saddles.

"What's going on? We're losing time," she said.

Tierren turned to her. "We have decided to move at night and rest during the day," he said.

"Why?"

"Daemon-spawn are masters of ambush. If we camp at night we'll get caught again. It's best to camp during the day so we can see them coming," he explained as he removed the last saddle.

D'Mique studied him for a minute before asking, "And how is moving at night safer?"

He glared at her, "There is no safety only tactics," he replied.

"And where are we headed tonight?" she asked.

"North for another night, then west to a small village," he answered. "I forget its name," he said moving to sit beside the fire.

"An elfin village?" she asked.

"Semian I think."

"We're going there for a new horse I suppose," she muttered. In her mind she saw her horse covered in scalawags again, fighting for its life in the dark.

Tierren nodded, "Yes, and supplies."

"And what about the daemon? We're losing ground on it."

"It's still out there. Myrth tried again to break the shadow spell with no luck. He did get Marladon to answer his jar finally. The Fire Master says there is no sign of daemons or shadow magic in the Black Hills."

D'Mique thought about this for a moment. "So is it going to the Gemm Hills?" she asked. Tierren shrugged.

While they talked Re'Ana and Storm reappeared lumbering into camp. The she-elf handed Genow a couple plump dark feathered birds before turning to smile at D'Mique. "Let's rework your hair Lady," she suggested. With a begrudging nod D'Mique sat, submitting to the elf. Re'Ana worked in silence creating a complex pattern of small braids to hold D'Mique's hair tight against her skull. Once she'd finished, hesitantly adding the goblin charm to the final tail end, D'Mique returned to her bedroll and tried to sleep, her conversation with Tierren replaying through her mind.

The day melted into late afternoon and as the suns set they ate Genow's stew and packed, leaving the copse of trees by the light of the Ghost Moon, Genow and D'Mique sharing Trillip's great bay horse while he rode Genow's. As they rode Myrth kept watch on the shadow magic trail, drawn dark, paralleling their course just east of the path they followed. True dark found them picking their way through a scrub oak forest and by midnight they reached the flat grassland of the Fanterra Plain. When dawn neared they set camp and rested, the day passing slowly as they took turns dozing and keeping watch.

For another night they journeyed west and as they rode D'Mique studied the ground from the bay's saddle, Genow lightly clinging to her back. *"There's nothing to find,"* she decided with a sigh, resigned to the fact that Myrth would have to track the daemon by the shadow magic trail. Then she pulled up short startling her horse. The others stopped beside her. In the path before them a monstrous three-toed print was plainly visible. Her heart skipped a beat and she dismounted quickly, studying it closely, trying to make out details by the Ghost Moon's light. The edges were fringed, the ground burnt. It measured five feet in diameter, deep furrows at the tip of each toe showing the claws. Plants in the area had turned black, rotting as they watched. The hair at the back of her neck stood on end, and for a moment the world around her faded. Eight feet further along the path, on the other side, another print confirmed the direction the creature traveled. Swallowing hard D'Mique turned to look back at Myrth. "We've found him," she whispered, fear drowning the triumph from her words.

Myrth closed his eyes studying the Mage Realm. "The spell continues north," he said, his voice carrying his own fear and a hint of perplexity, "The daemon has strayed from the path."

"Meaning?" Tierren asked.

"We can track it now," D'Mique offered.

"Also, whoever laid the spell has lost control of the daemon," Myrth added.

"The village," Genow breathed. Staring in the direction of the tracks, "The daemon is going there."

"Smelt?" Trillip added.

"Sawelt," Myrth corrected. "We must hurry," he said suddenly kicking Jerrold forward, leaving the rest of the hunters to follow behind.

Sawelt

They hurried along the daemon's path following its charred footprints through the tall grass of the plain and onto a wagon track. As they ran the grass changed to crops and soon, dark one-story buildings loomed out of the night signaling their arrival in Sawelt. As the track they followed entered the town, other roads branched off from it. Myrth pulled Jerrold to a sudden stop, upsetting the dragon, who tossed his head indignantly. Ignoring him Myrth closed his eyes and studied the Mage Realm. "There is no change," he said after scanning the forcelines, "The daemon is unprotected. Go slow, search everywhere." He motioned for Re'Ana to follow him and started forward again keeping Jerrold to a silent walk. Tierren and Rogan swung their horses left, flanking the center of the village. Trillip watched them go and then headed right, motioning for Genow and D'Mique to follow him.

They passed by a series of fields before reaching the first farmhouse. Trillip stopped, waiting for D'Mique to pull alongside him before motioning to the house and yard. In the darkness it took a moment to comprehend the sight before her. Then the animals melted from the night around them. They lay strewn about the yard freshly slaughtered, feathers and fur glowing gray. The house's wooden door stood ajar beckoning them inside, an informal welcome belying the horror in the yard and the heavy silence surrounding them.

"Genow can you tell when they died?" Trillip asked motioning to the dead animals.

Frowning Genow climbed down and checked the nearest corpse, gingerly hunkered over it like a reluctant bird of prey. "They are freshly killed, perhaps early this morning," he said after a moment, gratefully standing, a relieved sigh punctuating his words as he turned away from the scene. D'Mique and Trillip gazed at the farmhouse, the unspoken necessity of exploring it hanging between them. Frowning Genow looked at the farm again, this time very aware of the thick silence around them. Fighting the dread that screamed and clawed at the back of her mind, D'Mique climbed off the horse, drew her sword, and crept deliberately toward the low silent building. Reluctantly, Genow followed at a safe distance leaving Trillip with the horses.

They crossed the yard without incident. Inside the farmhouse the soft gloom hid all but basic shapes. D'Mique sidled in, despite the darkness, leaving Genow in the doorway. As her eyes adjusted she picked out shapes on the floor and in the corners of the room. *"Everyone's dead,"* she thought stepping to the nearest lumpy shape. Hunkering down she poked it with the tip of her sword, confirming her suspicion as flesh gave way before the blade. Hurriedly she rose and stepped back rushing for the doorway. Genow gave way but did not follow her as she crossed to Trillip. "The farmer's dead," she announced to the waiting Land-Nymph. With a curt nod Trillip swung his horse around and started for the next farm. Genow and D'Mique climbed back up on the bay.

They made their way past fields that would never again be cared for, harvested or replanted and soon stood in front of the next farm looking over a similar scene of abandonment and slaughter. With a grim set to her jaw D'Mique climbed down and started through the farmyard, noting that the bodies here were half-eaten, the last course of a huge feast. At the thought her stomach knotted threatening to vomit. There was no sign of survivors so she remounted behind Genow and they moved on quickly not bothering to stop at any other farms. The story would be the same. Dark silence smothered even the center of town as they reached the village square. Across the way Rogan and Tierren appeared nodding to Trillip as they converged. "Everyone's gone," Trillip said knowing their report would be the same.

Before Rogan could reply, a darker shadow moved to their left. Swords sang as they leapt from scabbards and the five hunters turned toward the sudden movement. D'Mique's heart tripped into her throat as a creature emerged from the gloom along the building's lee side. Its beaked, reptilian head bobbed slowly, hypnotically swinging from side to side atop the long leathery neck as first one milky glowing eye focused on them then the other. Powerful shoulders and a svelte, horse-sized black body followed the head, its four padded feet silent as it stalked toward them. A low hiss cut the air as it approached, tail lashing excitedly behind it. Movement to their left caught D'Mique's eye and she saw another creature slowly swaying between the buildings nonchalantly hunting them. The first creature let out a throaty croak shattering the quiet night, as it squared off in front of them. It suddenly charged.

Trillip's blade met the creature, parrying its slashing beak. The lithe neck twisted, the head reaching around for Trillip's face, its snapping beak missing by a breath as the Land-Nymph threw himself backward, laying back in the saddle. The goblins launched toward the second creature leaving Genow and D'Mique with Trillip. Genow urged the bay closer bringing D'Mique within range and distracting the creature. D'Mique swung for the serpentine neck as the sharp beak snapped closed just shy of the elf's throat. Her sword bit deep into the creature's flesh drawing a squeal from it. The pain staggered the creature and it suddenly slumped against the bay. The big horse kept its footing, screaming in fear as the creature shoved the horse sideways before crumpling to the ground. "I got it!" D'Mique shouted above the sound of her racing heart.

Genow turned in the saddle his hand on his neck, disbelief and relief mingling across his face. "My thanks, Lady," he breathed.

Just then the center of town exploded in light and noise. D'Mique turned to look, shielding her eyes from the sudden brightness. Rising above the single-story structures the Greater Daemon roared at the sky. Its huge, milky white eyes mimicked those of the daemon-spawn. The wedge-shaped, insect-like head seemed top-heavy, over-balanced by two curving horns above its eyes. Green fire rimed its dark body, bathing the town square in an eerie half-light.

The world fell away around D'Mique, her vision narrowing to the insect head, its wrinkled skin, and the strings of saliva dangling from its mouth as it screeched. "That's how I die," she thought suddenly, each word a dread finality as it looked at her, fear flowing down around her heart and long minutes passing before the world returned. Then noticing movement around her once again D'Mique pulled her attention from the daemon and focused on her fellow hunters. Storm and Re'Ana flitted wildly about the daemon, trying to wound it while dodging in and out, ducking the clawed hands. It roared again—the slit-mouth at the point of its head parting to show huge knife-like fangs—as a barrage of rocks flew through the air and exploded in the green fire leaving the daemon untouched. The goblins shouted at each other, their guttural language streaming up from somewhere beneath the daemon. The daemon's head swung around and a fireball flew from its mouth. D'Mique screamed, shielding her eyes with her arm as the flame engulfed Storm and Re'Ana. They disappeared within the mottled orange ball for a split second before a burning Storm plummeted to earth.

"No!" D'Mique screamed. Genow shouted and started toward them urging their mount toward the side of the buildings that stood between them and the daemon. As they raced forward another reptilian beast leapt from the shadows. The bay reared in surprise, lashing at the daemon-spawn with its front hooves. D'Mique slid backwards off the horse hitting the ground hard. Stars burst behind her eyes as her head cracked on the cobblestones. Above her, the reptilian beast stopped its charge, screaming at the horse.

"Genow!" Tierren screamed. D'Mique struggled to sit up as the sounds of battle engulfed her. Trillip slashed at the creature in front of her as Genow fought with the horse. She managed to sit up, looking around still half-stunned. Horses thundered past, followed by Jerrold, swinging west out of town. Behind them the daemon leapt over the row of buildings, giving chase to the horses. The ground shook as it disappeared into the night.

"Genow! Go to Myrth!" Trillip shouted, the reptilian beast now dead at his feet. "To Myrth!"

"But the Lady!" the elf shouted, looking down at her from the prancing horse.

"I keep the Promise! Now go!" Trillip shouted shoving the bay. With a dark frown Genow nodded then urged the horse forward following the daemon into the darkness. A sudden silence engulfed the town square.

Trillip stood by D'Mique helping her up with a strong, thin hand. "Lady, you are very unlucky around horses," he said. D'Mique's eyes narrowed but a croaking roar cut off her reply. "This village is full of mange!" he hissed looking around.

"Mange?" she repeated aloud, thinking, *"That's a second daemon-spawn myth come to life!"* Another of the reptilian beasts came around a building. D'Mique stood to face it, sword at the ready but Trillip stepped in front of her.

"I've got this one, Lady," he said. "You watch our backs." She turned to see another mange slinking out of the shadows.

"I've got our backs," she said with a smile as it croaked at them.

Running From the Daemon

Jerrold's strength ebbed as they ran, the horses beside Myrth thundering through the darkness. "Genow!" Myrth shouted for the second time. Genow's cold healing waves passed over them sapping the animals' weariness and returning their strength. "Just keep them running," Myrth thought. The daemon lumbered behind them each step shaking the ground, whipping the horses with fear. Jerrold renewed, quickened his pace but the effort had taken its toll on Genow who slumped forward in his saddle, nearly falling. Tierren reached for him helping him stay seated while their horses galloped together. The crashing steps of the daemon suddenly stopped. Startled by the sudden silence Myrth spun around where he sat and looked back. The daemon roared its frustration as they disappeared into the night.

When next the horses tired he allowed them to slow until they reached an ambling pace. Then without warning Jerrold stopped and shrank on the spot, unceremoniously dropping Myrth to the ground with a loud thump as he resumed his normal size. Myrth looked up from where he sat. All around him the horses hung their heads, muscles shivering. Tierren and Rogan watched him pain, fear and anger engulfing them. He stood slowly, smiling wanly down at the dragon fairy. "Thank you, Jerrold. I owe you my life," he whispered. Jerrold bared his fangs in a vicious grin, a more civil response than Myrth had been anticipating.

Myrth turned to scan the horizon in the direction they had come. There was no visible sign of the daemon. He closed his eyes stepping into the Mage Realm. The blue and gray miasma of the sky glowed with a suffused light, dispelling the darkness of the real world. All around them the Earth Cloud glowed brightly, forever imperturbable, and a river of golden light trailed southwestward heading toward Gaity. Far below he could feel the fiery core of the planet. Knowing that the daemon would send out eddies of blackness as it approached, he watched the Mage Realm for a long time. He was half-aware of the others climbing down from the horses making camp around him, leaving him undisturbed in the middle of the field. For an hour there was no blackness in the forcelines no Shadow magic taint.

"Myrth," Genow interrupted. Myrth focused on the whirling green Life magic beside him in the Mage Realm before opening his eyes and returning. "I left D'Mique behind. She's with Trillip," the elf breathed.

Myrth digested the information slowly. When he did not react Genow retreated to the others. *"I am now without humans,"* Myrth thought. The Seers' verse haunted him, Sage's words cutting into his heart, "The two most likely to succeed are lost," he said with a sigh, moving for the first time since Jerrold dumped him to the ground. *"Still, we must continue. What else can we do?"* He asked aloud, "I'm right in assuming that we are near the Gemm Hills?" Genow nodded. "Let's head for Gemma then." He hesitated looking across at the horses and down at Jerrold, where he'd returned to his embroidered form stitched on his pillow. "Tomorrow," he added. "We will go to Gemma tomorrow. I will contact Sylus and tell him to meet us there." The others nodded in response their relief palpable.

"If only I could also be relieved," Myrth thought sinking onto the pillow and removing Jay's jar from his nearby saddlebag. For a long moment he stared at it composing his thoughts. *"This night has not gone well at all,"* he sighed to himself. Without looking he fumbled the pack open and pulled out the rest of the jars. *"Not just yet,"* he thought, feeling along the forcelines, calling Sylus, his voice strumming the Earth currents. Myrth envisioned laying a hand on Sylus' head and the elf was there, before him in the Mage Realm. The Earth Master sent a stream of images to his servant, starting with their departure at Dragon Ridge and ending with them huddled alone in the dark south of Gemma.

Sylus sent images in response—his travels to Gaity on Master Island, Marco far exceeding all expectations and their rooms in Olimidia. "What do you command, my Master?" Sylus asked as the last image faded.

Myrth stood a moment in thought. "Bring my remaining hunters to me Sylus. Go to Sea Spray first and collect Nepo and his honor guard. I will contact him next."

"As you command. Master, Marco—"

Myrth opened his eyes cutting Sylus off. *"Perhaps...one more thing, just one more thing...maybe two. And then Jay,"* he admonished himself, *"And then Jay."* He reached for Nepo's jar calling aloud, "Nepo." When the Water Master did not answer he called for his apprentice, "Tekalo."

"Master Myrth?" the apprentice answered almost immediately a bit breathless as if he'd run to answer.

"Where is Nepo?"

"I'll go get him," he said the jar flickering softly with each syllable.

After a time Nepo replied, "What do you want now Myrth," hostility coloring the honey-rich, baritone voice.

"We have found the daemon. I need you to come with Sylus and my honor guard,"

"Your honor guard?" he asked, anger thrilling along the forcelines.

Myrth glared at the jar, "Yes."

"Perhaps you mean my honor guard,"

"I am not going to argue with you Nepo. When Sylus gets there come with him to Gemma and bring your honor guard."

"I will come. My honor guard will already be there." The jar was suddenly dark. Myrth glared at it for a moment wrestling with the urge to call him back and have the last word. He closed his eyes breathing deep, sighing as the emotion rolled away. He set the jar down and stared at Marladon's jar pointedly ignoring Jay's.

"Marladon," Myrth called.

"Yes?" Marladon answered, the sharp sides of his voice softened by sleep.

"We found the daemon, Marladon."

"Where?" asked the Fire Master, lethargy dropping like a stone from his voice.

"In Sawelt. Meet us in Gemma. It will be a few days before Nepo gets here with Sylus."

"As you command, Myrth," he said.

Myrth stared at the jar as the light faded wrestling with the last task, wanting the words he had to say to change; but the past would not rearrange itself for his convenience. He picked up Jay's jar and stopped hunching over, pulling inward as the pain engulfed him, *"Re'Ana."* He set

Jay's jar back down a lump caught in his throat. *"How am I going to tell her? How can she lose her shadow?"* He'd known Jay and Re'Ana all his life, their visits to Herdan's Castle often overlapping. There had never been one without the other. A silver tear slid down his cheek, his eyes seeming to leak color rather than his body losing fluid. "I shall shed tears for both of us, Jay," he whispered, picking up the jar and caressing it with a single claw. Nature had been too cruel to grant the Piscian Semians the ability to cry. *"If only they had been left heartless as well,"* he thought. For a second time he took a deep breath and let out a slow sigh releasing emotions into the miasma around him. "Jay," he called aloud, forcing himself not to dwell on things, but to begin. He sent the call along the forcelines that tied the jars together, "Jay?"

"I'm here, Myrth," she said from the jar.

"Sit down, Jay," he said, quietly.

"Gods, Myrth," her voice clouded suddenly, "How dare you start that way!"

"Jay, Re'Ana has fallen. She's ... she's gone," he choked.

"No!" Anguish filled the air around him Jay's sorrow manifesting through the forcelines. For a second it was hard to breathe as she pulled the power away. The brief thought that all across the planet people would be gasping for breath crossed his mind. But he waited, eyes closed as the tears fell.

"Jay," he whispered, pushing past the panic that settled on him as the air thinned.

"How?" Her voice held the tears that would never fall.

"It was the daemon," he said, a slight gasp echoing the words. "We were going to Sawelt for supplies. The daemon was there. It ... It lay in the village square. We didn't see it until.... She saved us. She saved me," he finished. His words felt hollow next to the pain and so much more needed to be said.

"I'm coming to you Myrth," Jay said softly after a very long silence. The air returned allowing a deep cleansing breath.

"We are going to Gemma," he answered. The jar was suddenly dark.

Myrth sat with his eyes closed for a long minute swallowing back his tears, pushing the sights and sounds of the village green from his mind, focusing on the thick air around him and the solid earth beneath him. He felt the goblins approach and opened his eyes, looking up at them, knowing that they felt his sadness, grateful for their stalwart faith.

"What of D'Mique?" Rogan asked.

"And Trillip?" Tierren added.

"As long as they get out of Sawelt they will be fine. Gemma is the closest haven. I'm sure Trillip will catch up in a few days."

For three days they rode north across the plains the mounts cutting a path through the drying, knee-high grass. As they traveled the plains gradually rose, the bowl they described almost unperceivable unless you looked back toward the devastated town of Sawelt. Foothills grew around Myrth and his companions, stretching northwest, rising ever higher until they gave way to the Quartz Mountains. From this side the range was not nearly as impressive as from the western end. Of the five monolithic peaks that made up the Quartz Mountain range the two rising before them, Majesty and Perrin, were the least impressive, towering over the plain as their companion peaks did, but covered in mossy green and gray brush, instead of the barren quartz rock of the others. Starting into a valley between two hummocks they stumbled upon a well-used road and followed it through the Gemm Hills winding ever-closer to Perrin's flank. The mountain soon filled the northern horizon, the mounds on either side grown to small mountains in their own right, and the road marching toward it, cutting through steeper hills until it found its way to the mouth of a large cave.

Just inside the cave four elfin guards dressed in vivid blue stared out at them, startled by the riders' sudden appearance. They remained unmoving as Myrth and the others dismounted leading their mounts the few feet to the cavern entrance. Only when Myrth stood before them did the elves react kneeling formally. "Master of Earth we have made ready for your arrival. Please follow us," the nearest guard said.

"Made ready?" Myrth asked his eyes adjusting to the cavern's gloom.

"Oracle arrived earlier today," the elf said by way of explanation.

"Oh," Myrth continued, "Take my guards to the quarters you have prepared. I will see Oracle immediately," he directed.

"As commanded, generous Master," the guard intoned standing and forming an escort with his fellow guards. Grabbing their packs and leaving the horses behind, they followed the elves to the back of the cavern and around a corner into a narrow passage. Passing single file through the choke point they entered a broad thoroughfare, the cavern walls pulling far from the road they walked leaving a wide, rock garden verge between them and the constructs occupying the cavern walls. Everywhere pale-skinned elves bustled through the bright tunnels—every few yards of ground lit by mirrored lamps, their magical flames glowing in a variety of colors. The road wound through a shopping district where stores had been carved deep into the walls, large windows open to the thoroughfare. Above them a second tier of alcoves, reachable by wooden walkways and ladders, served as homes for the storekeepers.

Beyond the airy shopping district these alcoves grew spaced out changing from stores to houses, the fronts of these recesses partitioned from the main thoroughfare by brightly colored, wooden walls that ended half way to the ceiling as the rock garden verge disappeared. Here life and light still filled the cave, but a furtive intensity had replaced the jingle of commerce. Where the shops had been well kept, the dwellings here held the weight of time within them and seemed closer to tumbling down—not an easy task for solid stone cavern walls. Soon even the houses disappeared and the tunnel opened up into a huge, city-sized cavern, a dark bowl so large that the ever-present lanterns could not drive all the shadows away. Lights twinkled in the distance, mirrored across the glassy surface of an underground lake that filled the lower half of the bowl. At the heart of the lake a tower of stone, the keep of the magistrate of Gemma, rose from the glittering water and strove to reach the ceiling far above.

The elfin guards led them to a fleet of small skiffs and ferried them across the lake to the monolithic structure. Once they reached the keep they separated, one guard showing his companions to their prepared quarters while the other three accompanied Myrth to the Magistrate's audience chamber. Myrth led the way along a spiral of rough stone steps to the room at the top of the tower. The guards stopped at the door letting Myrth enter on his own. Despite the soft gray stone walls, bright colors drenched the room - reds, golds and greens exploding from tapestries and carpets festooned across the walls and laid upon the floor. The Magistrate came down from his throne when Myrth entered. Draped in the same vivid colors, red and gold silk that flowed around his limbs, contrasting with his pale white skin and large black eyes, he floated across the green carpet and stood before Myrth dignified and silent but expectant. His wispy white hair had been pulled up into a topknot and decorated with faintly twinkling gems. After the door closed leaving them alone he knelt, bowing his head, "Master Myrth," he greeted in a voice as darkly secret as the cavern surrounding his tower.

"Magistrate Arlan," Myrth said taking hold of the magistrate and helping him up, bowing at the waist as he did so. "I thank you for your welcome," he started. "I hear that Oracle is also here, so I assume you know why I am here as well. A daemon has come from the Void. Even now it terrorizes the Semian towns of the Plain."

"I have heard this news and I give my blessings to you Master Myrth. May your hunt prove successful," the magistrate said.

"Thank you, but for now my forces are divided. We will be gathering here with your permission."

"Of course Master. Your hunters are always welcome," said Arlan bowing again. "I will take you to Oracle," he said turning and leading the way through a side door to a small room.

Gold and red lanterns lit the area bathing it in a soft glow. Several small tables surrounded by chairs furnished the sitting room. "Master Myrth, Seer Oracle," the magistrate introduced before bowing out. Oracle looked up from his cup as the door closed. He had draped his white cloak over his chair and sat drinking in his loincloth and belt. Myrth removed his cloak as well laying it across his lap as he sat down opposite the Seer.

"Myrth," the wolf-man growled in greeting as the Master sat. A young elf entered carrying several cups on a tray. Kneeling beside their table she held it out for Myrth waiting while he chose a small mug, dismissive of its contents.

"You saw what happened?" Myrth asked as the servant left, referring to the seer's special vision.

"Indeed," Oracle said. Myrth sipped from his cup wincing at the tangy orange liqueur waiting for Oracle to continue. After a moment he did, "I sent you out to face this daemon with two humans Myrth," he said, a slow, deep anger turning the words dark.

"We've had this argument already, Oracle," Myrth hissed, his own anger subtly hidden beneath the surface. "I sent Marco to Gaity for necessary training. You can't expect an untrained mage and a warrior who can't even sit a horse to defeat a daemon." The room rumbled around them, the Earth Cloud responding to the Master's emotions.

"Their condition was a nonissue Myrth. I told you not to hunt this daemon without those two humans." Oracle leaned toward Myrth across the table, snout to beak, amber eyes glaring into gray. His clawed hands balled into fists on the tabletop. "Two humans, Myrth," he hissed, "Not one! Not even any two! Those two!" The room reverberated with the Seer's deep voice, a counterpoint to the barely contained quake that continued to shake the room. They stared angrily at each other for a few long seconds before Myrth took a deep, calming breath, the quake fading as he released his emotions. Oracle leaned back as well eyeing the master.

`"What is done is done," Myrth stated matter-of-factly. "I don't want to talk of it," he finished with a sigh resting his head in his hands and closing his eyes for a long moment.

"Where are your humans, Myrth?"

"Marco is on his way to Sea Spray." Myrth answered. He was quiet for a long time.

"And D'Mique?" Oracle prodded.

"She's with Trillip," Myrth answered. Oracle stared at him and Myrth felt the Seer searching the Time forcelines.

Understanding dawned and Oracle growled low. "You don't know where she is!" he snarled.

"I am Master of Earth!" Myrth snapped fists pounding the table as his anger flared again. Facing down the Seer's anger, the tower shimmying in response, he returned venomously, "I will not be berated!"

"And I am Oracle," the Seer hissed. "I shall speak however I choose and to whomever I choose. Especially you." Myrth clicked his beak in frustration snapping just shy of the wolf's nose, before folding his arms across his chest and withdrawing in a huff. He looked away from the Seer and concentrated on steadying the Earth Cloud around them. Oracle chuckled darkly after a moment of silence, "You really don't know where she is?" he asked.

"She's with Trillip. He keeps the Promise."

"I should hope so. The timelines are chaotic and prophesy is at hand. All these years we have kept the humans safe in the Nesting knowing that one day a Child of Man would come from there to save us. The Promise is being fulfilled."

"Trillip will keep her safe," Myrth repeated, an attempt to convince himself as much as the seer.

Trillip was gone. D'Mique launched herself at the mange in front of her not waiting for the Land-Nymph to reappear. Its beak lashed out closing on her side. The rush of adrenaline powered her sword, driving the blade deep into the mange's neck, pulling free and dropping from the creature's jaws before the pain washed over her. Trillip's blade whirled through her vision beheading the mange as she fell.

Gasping she turned to him, "We have to find the horse!"

"I think we should find safety first," he said.

"If we meet any more mange on the ground we're done," she argued, assessing his wounds. *All things considered, he's better off than me,"* she thought. Clean, deep slices traced his arms and legs, bleeding slowly. Only one wound marred his narrow face, blood flowing down his neck and chest.

"Come on," he said taking hold of her arm, "Let's get out of here."

D'Mique startled awake rocking from side to side as the black horse plodded on beneath her Trillip leading it down the road. "Stop Trillip. I have to get off," she said after a moment. Trillip looked over his shoulder at her, stopping. The gash down his cheek had scabbed over since that night in Sawelt, a dark purple crack in the chiseled alabaster; unlike the mange bite in her side that had become infected despite all her efforts. Bitterly she shook her head, *"I'm just not the surgeon my mother is,"* she chastised herself, not for the first time. Clambering from the saddle, stiff from both riding and her wounds, she stumbled away into the brush with her hand on her side.

Trillip sank to the ground in front of the horse waiting. D'Mique stared hard at the pebbles before her, her stomach roiling. This time, unlike the previous two stops, there was no vomit. She concentrated on breathing and closed her eyes. The wound in her side throbbed with each breath. The fight with the mange danced through her mind again as she listened to the sickness beat through her body, dread following in its wake. When her stomach settled she straightened and stared north along the road they were following. She could still see the traces of the Greater Daemon's passage although they faded more each day. According to Trillip a bit further north this road met a trade route that traveled east and west. To the east it traveled straight to the coast near Ebony Bay, and to the west it wended toward the Quartz Mountains and the city of Gemma, Myrth's last known destination.

Trillip stood up and smiled at her when she reached him. She returned the smile halfheartedly. "How are you?" he asked.

"I'll make it," she said noncommittally, tapping down the doubt that fluttered at her heart. His eyes narrowed straining to judge her actual state. "I will," she said, "We're nearly there, right?"

He nodded, "Yes, we are."

A few hours later they came to the crossroads. Where the road they followed met the trade route a small cluster of buildings had grown up, including an inn, stable and a handful of market stalls. Trillip looked up at D'Mique, his relieved announcement that they had made it, dwindling on his lips. "We'll find help here, Lady," he said, "Then we'll be on our way to Gemma."

D'Mique shook her head. "We should follow the daemon," she said staring eastward, trying to keep her voice steady. The fading tracks skirted around the cluster of buildings and crossed the trade route, paralleling the road as it marched toward the setting suns. Trillip followed her gaze eastward.

After a moment he nodded, "Very well, Lady. But we need to tend to your wounds first. Come on," he said starting toward the inn.

A welcoming smile greeted them as they approached the inn, the scrawny human instantly pleased to see them. "You've made it just in time," he called, hurrying to take the horse's lead. "Supper is hot and ready for serving and welcoming beds can still be found for you and your lady."

"'Still be found,'" Trillip repeated. "You have other guests?"

"Why yes, a great company of elves."

"Elves," Trillip and D'Mique repeated. "My friend," Trillip continued, "is wounded. I was going to ask after a surgeon in the area but elfin magic would be better. Where can I find them?"

"They are just sitting down to supper," the human answered.

"Help her in," Trillip instructed, hurrying away toward the inn.

He rushed through the heavy wooden door and into the common area. A dozen thick tables greeted him all of them brimming with elves. "I need a healer," he announced. My friend is gravely wounded." The elves passed nervous and curious glances from one to another and back at him.

"Define 'gravely'," a soft voice replied.

"She has been poisoned, her wound festering." His words met more silence, but this time the glance that covered the room landed on a pair of soldiers, one male, one female, sitting together near the head table. Trillip forged a path toward them pushing past the other elves. They glanced at each other before the male elf stood. "Please," Trillip said, allowing the word to hang between them.

"Do you have money, Child of the Waves?" the elf asked.

Trillip glared at him but answered, "I'm good for it."

The scrawny human appeared in the doorway D'Mique leaning heavily against him, almost limp, dark elfin eyes confronting them. The soldier studied her a moment as well before nodding. "Thank you," Trillip continued leading the way back across the common room, eyes glued on D'Mique. Together they trooped into the innkeeper's private quarters where the scrawny man laid the now unconscious D'Mique down on a padded bench. He hurried for a blanket and pillow to make it marginally more comfortable. The elf pulled D'Mique's clothing and bandages away from her wound with a grimace. "What bit her?" he asked.

"A mange," Trillip answered kneeling beside her, resting a hand on her forehead. Fever ate at his skin and he grimaced.

"What are mange doing on the Plain?" the elf asked under his breath. Trillip ignored the question intent instead on watching the elf work. The soldier laid his hands over the wound and probed it and the surrounding tissue. "The poison has spread far; this will take a bit of work," he assessed. Trillip nodded in response, resting his eyes on D'Mique's profile. He sat quiet as the soldier worked starting with the bite and its infection before moving away from the punctures as he sought the poison. An hour slowly passed and dinner in the common room ended and the dishes cleared. Elfin magic finally quelled the poison in D'Mique's system and her fever abated.

With a sigh Trillip relaxed, exploring his surroundings without leaving her side. Soft warmth filled the room from the large fireplace that drove back the gathering shadows to the hanging tapestries. It was a rugged coziness inviting to both family and friends. As the conversations in the other room dwindled the female soldier poked her head in, but did not interrupt her partner's work.

When she disappeared Trillip studied the soldier's uniform. "You're from Gemma. Are you on your way to the city or out on patrol?" he asked. The elf sighed and stopped working taking a chance to rest as he eyed Trillip.

"We're on our way to Gemma we've been recalled to the city." He paused as Trillip nodded his understanding. "You're a long way from home as well Child of the Waves. Are you escorting the lady back to the Vale?"

"'Vale?'" Trillip echoed, "Oh no, she's not a Vale Warrior." He added in a whisper, "She's from the Nesting." The soldier attempted to hide his astonishment by turning back to D'Mique and his work but Trillip took note of it. Trillip let his words settle in the room before asking, "Do you keep the Promise, Friend Elf?" he whispered.

The elf glanced at him then back to his work, "What would you ask?"

"Do you know if the Master of Earth is in Gemma?"

The soldier stopped again and gave Trillip a hard look. He nodded, "We were told the Masters were going to Gemma. I do not know if he is there at this moment."

"Will you take him a message? Will you tell him that the trail fades but Trillip and D'Mique are following it to Ebony Bay?"

"The trail fades but Trillip and D'Mique are following it toward Ebony Bay," the soldier repeated. Trillip nodded. "Yes, I will tell him this." He stared at D'Mique as he spoke. "There will be no charge Master Trillip for I keep the Promise. She is as good as I can make her. I have mended as much of the poison's damage as I can. Understand that I am a combat healer, no more. But she will recover the rest on her own. She should rest here a few more days," he trailed off and stared hard at him. Trillip returned the stare waiting on him to continue. "But if you are tracking someone for the Earth Master you cannot afford the wait." Nodding to himself he continued, "She can sit a horse when she awakens—of this I'm certain—but recovery will be hampered by the hardships of the road."

"I understand and I know you understand our position," Trillip replied. "I thank you for your service and advice. You saved her life...of this I am certain," he added. Nodding the soldier turned and left without another word. "Travel swiftly," Trillip whispered looking down at D'Mique again.

The Road to Sea Spray

The morning of their fifth day in Olimidia Sylus shook them awake. "Get up, it's time to go," he barked. Marco struggled awake, yawning. "Myrth wants us in Sea Spray."

Next to Marco Kryoso rolled out of bed, "Myrth's in Sea Spray?" he asked.

"He'll meet us in Gemma," he said, "Kryoso go down to the commissary and order some rations," he finished.

"Yes, Commander," the Mortak said, hurrying to obey.

The others packed quickly and, as the suns rose, hurried out into the courtyard where Kryoso waited bulging packs already strapped to their horses. In addition, Sylus' large black carried a roll of winter coats and fur-lined blankets. Mounting they headed north in the early morning light, the air just hinting at autumn's approach. Beyond the center palace and Academy the business district continued, the near-empty road passing a school where several dozen children played just before entering a sprawling residential district. It was the only school in Olimidia and the children there the only children. Marco pushed Mara from his mind as she entered his thoughts unbidden. Beyond the school the road snaked through a neighborhood of large estate houses. "There's my house," Clippen said pointing to a two-story manor. It sat back away from the road, the front yard planted with a colorful variety of shrubs and trees. A stone pathway led around the plants and up to the house while behind the house a stable and paddock peeked through the trees.

"You never went to see them," Kryoso observed.

"I didn't want them to be sad when I left. Besides, I stopped to visit on my way to Dragon Ridge before."

"Surely they would rather see you than not, even if it saddened them," Kryoso insisted.

"Have you returned to your family since coming south?" Clippen asked.

"No. I have no family," Kryoso said sitting up straight in the saddle. "I am orphaned."

"Then you have no authority to speak of families."

"I only know that if you were my son, I would rather see you," Kryoso answered.

"Hmph," Clippen quickened his pace, taking the lead as they left the city.

Just before the north gate another small business district huddled around the road, mostly two-story inns. Beyond the north gate they climbed a smooth incline to the lip of the basin where a broad, well-traveled road met them. For three uneventful days and nights they traveled quickly along it, and in the early morning hours of the fourth day they came to a fork in the road where a large inn sat. Beside the building several horses milled about in the paddock. To their right the road led to Gemma, their ultimate destination. But to the left, the direction they were going in, it would take them to Sea Spray, the Water Master's palace.

"Will we be returning this way?" Clippen asked. "We could leave some of our extra supplies in their storage room," he said indicating the inn.

"No, it will be faster to take the north road through the Forest of Fear," Sylus said.

"The Daemon Woods?" Marco squeaked, horror stories from his childhood drifting through his mind. The others looked at him their expressions a mixture of incredulity and sympathy.

"Yes," Sylus answered Marco, "But it will cut off almost three days' travel time."

"As long as we aren't snowed in," Clippen added under his breath.

"We'll have Nepo with us," Sylus said dismissively, as they turned left continuing on their way. The day passed quickly and near dusk they stopped in a clearing beside the road. Sylus sent Clippen and Kryoso for firewood before turning to Marco. "Marco, when they return start the fire," he instructed. "I'm going to try contacting Myrth."

"Yes Commander," he answered. Sylus sat alone near the horses and retreated into meditation. Marco felt the forcelines change as the elf wove a safety net around the encampment. Every night since leaving Olimidia he had done so and every night Marco had felt him weave the patterns. No one in Gaity had mentioned being able to feel others working the forcelines. *"Perhaps I should mention it,"* he thought looking at the elf. *"But it's probably something he can't help with, anyway,"* Marco thought with a sigh.

Kryoso was first to return laying out a neat pile of firewood near Marco. After arranging the wood Marco hunkered down over the small pile and closed his eyes, looking down at his hands in the Mage Realm where they sparkled with red fire sources. He pulled the light from them, endowing a piece of wood with the fire force. The wood burst into flames, its green life energy eaten by a hungry red cloud of Fire magic. Marco opened his eyes. He held his hands out to the flames, trying to win back some of the heat his magic had cost him.

Clippen came up beside him with a huge armful of dry brush. He piled it near Marco's fire commenting, "Nice fire. It's almost the right color." Marco studied the flames. His magical fires had been improving nightly, the color moving steadily closer to natural flames. Tonight just before they curled into the wood the fire's brilliant orange color turned to a fresh, vibrant green. He shrugged. Kryoso sat down beside him handing over a packet of dried fish. Clippen sat across from them with his own packet. They ate in a comfortable silence as the suns set and stars began sparkling in the darkness above. After he finished eating Marco lay back on his bedroll, a sense of infinite space and peace overcoming him as he closed his eyes, easily sinking into the Mage Realm.

The golden earth cloud floated about him embracing him. There were no currents here, just the gently swirling cloud of gold. Scanning the cloud, he found his vision drifting high over the land as if he were flying. A black shape caught him by surprise as it moved slowly through the cloud. It looked like a puddle of spilled ink. Marco focused on it. It was to their east flowing directly toward them. As it neared them a searing pain shot through Marco's head, and he screamed as if someone had driven a white hot poker into his temple! The pain drove him from the Mage Realm and he flew to his feet staring eastward. Panic welled up in his throat. Clippen jumped up next to him his quarterstaff at the ready. Kryoso on his other side drew a sword. "What is it?" Marco hissed as the pain slowly ebbed replaced by growing panic.

"Daemons," Clippen answered. "You felt them cross the ward too?" he asked.

"No," Sylus whispered, drawing his own sword, "It isn't daemons. It's something else."

"What else could trip the safety net?" Kryoso asked.

"Daemon-spawn," Sylus said. He held out his hand calling to the Earth Power. Marco closed his eyes looking into the Mage Realm. He watched the golden cloud solidify beneath Sylus' hand. Controlling his breath he opened his eyes, trying to stay in the Mage Realm, as if he were trying to stay asleep after awaking in the night, super-imposing his vision over the Physical Realm. Three mounds of tiny pebbles piled up before Sylus where the Earth currents were gathering and knotting together. Clippen shifted nervously and Kryoso sheathed his sword, pulling out his crossbow. Marco reached out to the earth cloud trying to duplicate Sylus' trick, pulling the Earth Cloud to heel before him. When he looked at the Physical Realm he saw that he had made a solid rock form rather than a pile of pebbles. A wave of fear engulfed them all, driving away his disappointment over the wall. Marco gasped releasing his hold on the Earth Power. As he did so his mound of rock melted back into the soil.

"I'm here Marco," Clippen said, stepping forward spinning his quarterstaff, pink eyes ablaze with confidence. "If you're going to make a wall, make it tall and round with a roof," he added with a sarcastic smile.

Marco glared at him, "I was trying for pebbles," he muttered. Out in the darkness a rustling and mewling carried toward them as the daemons-spawn approached.

"The easiest way to stop a person from using magic is to call their name," Almira said in his head. He remembered the lecture as if it had happened yesterday. *"All you have to do is distract them. Hit them, surprise them, it does not matter, just break their concentration and you will break their spell. All magic forces the powers of nature into unnatural patterns, patterns that can be maintained only in the Mage Realm. Once the will of the mage is removed the*

patterns revert to normal. The only exceptions are the Masters. Their will sets the natural patterns."

Marco turned his attention to the darkness and the daemon-spawn closing in on them. Beside him Kryoso closed his eyes joining Marco in between realms. He bent the forcelines to his will, working Fire from his hands, endowing the crossbow bolts as Marco had endowed the firewood. He aimed for the darkness far beyond their camp and pulled the trigger. The bolt burst into flame streaking through the dark. Where the bolt came to rest, about one hundred yards away, the grass burst into flame and a sudden bright red light illuminated the daemon-spawn.

Marco struggled to make sense of the creatures as they flowed through the flickering light. He picked out their huge orb-like eyes—milky white instead of infernal red—bulging above a hairless muzzle full of crooked fangs. Just above the eyes sat a cap of bone that grew into two flat horns which curled down by the eyes before turning up into sharp points. Midway down the neck a ruff of sleek white fur blossomed; the rest of the wolf-like body was covered in black curly fur.

Marco closed his eyes trying not to think about the daemon-spawn. He focused on the Earth again this time working on a single, fist-sized ball of rock at a time. When he held four of them he turned to Sylus, watching as the elf flung his first pile of pebbles into the daemon-spawn. The creatures gibbered in return. Kryoso loosed another bolt. This time he aimed for a creature just inside the firelight of his last shot. Marco watched it burst into flames and nodded. "Kryoso's bolts are endowed with Fire, bursting into flame when given life energy to feed on," he thought, a soft smile creeping across his lips. He worked quickly, pulling Fire energy from his hands, setting it around the rock balls. He spared a sliver of his attention to watch Sylus throw his pebbles again.

He'd been under the impression that Wind was used to move the earthen balls. However as he watched, he saw Sylus draw To and Fro patterns. He struggled with the concept for a split second, *Almira taught me that To and Fro was only used with life energy for healing and with Fire energy to heat or cool things. But this! I never would have thought of using it to throw things!"*

Sylus drew several "To" patterns, small triangles of Earth energy, within his pile of pebbles. With his flinging hand as a focus he drew the corresponding "Fro" patterns out in the darkness. The pebbles moved with lightning speed from "To" to "Fro." Again, the daemon-spawn gibbered and chattered.

Marco created the "To" pattern within the golden globe of rock. Flinging his will outward, he drew the "Fro" pattern about twenty yards away from them; he could feel the "To" pattern pulling on the globe of Earth as he worked. Once the last line of the "Fro" pattern had been drawn the rock leapt from his hand and flew through the air, exploding on impact, the Fire endowment flashing outward, eating life energy. The explosion and flames staggered the advancing swarm of daemon-spawn. Marco sent the other three globes into the swarm as quickly as he could draw the patterns.

When his ammunition was gone he glanced at the physical realm. The daemonic creatures had reached their campfire! Somewhere beside him Clippen kept the beasts at bay. To his left Sylus drew his blade, hacking at the creatures as they rose to meet his attacks on their hind legs. They batted his thrusts and blows away with bony forelimbs. Sylus pulled the earth out from under them, knocking them over and exposing their underbellies. He stabbed desperately at the pale flesh. Two more creatures attacked the elf and he ducked under their horns rolling away. He needed more time, a bit of space between him and his attackers in order to grab the Earth forcelines. With a deep breath Marco closed his eyes. He pulled on the Earth Cloud around Sylus and yanked it upwards forming a wall. Sylus stumbled to a halt inside his half-formed shield of Earth and formed a pile of pebbles. He then forced Marco's wall away—pain lancing through Marco's head as the elf overrode his will. Marco stumbled backward as the wall of Earth dissipated and the elf's pebbles lashed out, cutting through the trio of creatures that had surrounded the wall. Behind the pebbles came Sylus' blade.

Marco turned to his other companions glancing at Kryoso and his Fire endowed sword as he attacked another daemon-spawn, his blade taking a greater toll on them than Sylus' rocks. Wherever the blade struck the flame crawled over the black fur eating the Life energy. On his left Clippen whacked at the creatures' softer parts with his staff, keeping them away from Marco. Marco stepped back into the Mage realm and pulled the Earth Cloud into five more fist-sized balls. He endowed them with Fire and sent them out into the pack of waiting killers.

Five quick explosions decimated the daemon-spawn line, lighting up the night. Marco saw several corpses by the light of the fires. His companions each landed killing blows as their foes turned toward the explosions or flinched away from them. Marco opened his eyes reentering the Physical Realm. There were only a few creatures left! Clippen fended two off with his quarterstaff while Sylus and Kryoso had another three between them. Smiling, Marco turned back toward the night. A creature reared up before him. It roared, a fetid odor engulfing him. Marco screamed and back-pedaled. The creature's front legs slammed downward into the ground where Marco had been standing. He lost his balance and fell backward as the daemon-spawn leapt for him. "Stop!" he screamed flinging an arm outward. The earth erupted upward encasing the creature in stone, leaving only its head free.

Marco gaped at it! The golden Earth Cloud blazed around the daemon-spawn, plainly visible to Marco. Sylus appeared around the stone encasement, his bright green blade slicing easily through the daemon-spawn's neck and the strange head fell, rolling across the ground, stopping at Marco's knee. Numb Marco shakily regained his feet. He checked to make sure he was not in the Mage Realm. *I can't have just done that!* he screamed at himself. He took a deep breath and exhaled. The stone around the daemon-spawn returned to the soil, the headless corpse dropping to the ground at his feet. Marco stared at it for a full minute. When he dragged his eyes from the dead creature, his companions were staring at him.

"You were able to do that spell while under attack," Sylus said, awed.

"I was able to do that spell from the Physical Realm," he whispered, a panic rising in him as he spoke. He thought, *It really happened!* His mind reeled, *But it couldn't have! Magic can only be performed in the Mage Realm! That's why it's so easy to counter! Just distract someone and the spell is broken!* He saw his thoughts echoed in the others' eyes.

"That's impossible," Clippen whispered coming closer to him. "You're remembering it wrong. You were probably between when you cast the spell."

Marco watched as black blood seeped down the Land-Nymph's quarterstaff. *"Maybe I am remembering it wrong. Yeah that's it,"* he conceded silently, *"I was between Realms."* He nodded slowly.

"It's not impossible," Sylus said as he wiped his blade on the corpse before them, "Just unusual. Only the strongest mages can do so. And they usually keep it secret." Clippen and Kryoso stared at him then returned their gazes to Marco. "People need to believe magic can be countered easily. In all cases," Sylus continued. "It's what keeps people sane and mages free." They all nodded slowly.

"Then we will keep this secret," Kryoso said, "secret from everyone."

"Everyone except Myrth," Sylus whispered leaning in toward Marco, who met the elf's black eyes and saw a closely held secret there. Marco had an inkling of knowing, just a little tickle. Remembered conversations pushed to the fore, *"Myrth was the only one who could teach him. Myrth was the only mage in the land who was as strong as he was."* He released a breath he didn't remember holding thinking, *"Myrth...can work magic from the Physical Realm."*

Swallowing, Marco walked away, ending the conversation, and started packing his bedroll. "I don't want to stay here this campsite is spoiled," he said.

"I agree," Kryoso said after a moment starting to pack as well. Sylus and Clippen joined them without another word. Once the fire was out they started down the road again, afoot as the horses were too skittish to ride. The road lay shrouded in darkness Rysk yet to rise and the Fiery Sisters long gone. They walked slowly along it for almost an hour before Sylus called a halt in a small grove of trees. They unpacked again and started a small fire, Kryoso's flames burning a pale blue. Marco lay down as soon as his bed was unrolled and studied the encampment. Although he saw only the Physical Realm he could feel the cloud of gold around him and the sparks of Fire tickling along his skin. Strangely he had no sense of the blue and gray cloud of Air and Water that he knew was all around him. He stepped into the Mage Realm and found the miasma of Water and Air waiting for him. Slowly he opened his eyes concentrating on keeping the forcelines in sight. The Earth Cloud glowed softly around him. He could see and feel the small eddies of the power that enshrouded him. *"Why is this happening?"* He wanted to ask Sylus about it but stopped himself again. *"He won't know. Only Myrth will know."* With a sigh Marco closed his eyes and was soon asleep.

From beside the fire Kryoso studied Marco as he slept, "Poor thing," he said at last.

Clippen eyed him then glanced at Marco. "Poor us if we make him mad before we get him to Myrth," the Land-Nymph said with a wry smile.

"No," Kryoso said, studying the sleeping human. "He is not a violent creature."

"Do you pity him?" Clippen asked.

Kryoso shook his head, "No. But he will be Myrth's favorite weapon now."

"He will be Myrth's apprentice, "Sylus whispered. "Go to bed you two," he ordered. "I will take the first watch." Reluctantly they obeyed.

Kryoso's Affinity

The commander woke them before dawn and Col's fiery red light saw them back on the road. A couple hours later they passed into a dark quiet wood; the horses' steps echoing too loud in that hushed world. No birds sang and when the breeze rustled through the trees their sighing only deepened the silence. "We're almost there," Sylus said with a note of forced optimism. Despite the close silence of the forest they passed through it uneventfully and came out on the shore of an expansive lake, its inky water reflecting the sky and far island perfectly. Sylus and Clippen dismounted and started across the pebble-strewn beach the lake wore like a necklace. Marco scanned the shore for a pier or bridge. There was none. Nor did he see any other trails or roads. "How do we cross?" he asked.

"This is Water's realm," Clippen said. He waded into the dark lake until his hands trailed along the surface.

"We're going to swim?" Marco asked incredulous.

Clippen laughed and shook his head, "Just watch," he said. He stood still, the cold water lapping at his thighs for several minutes. Then the dark mirror shattered and churned, a huge black shape emerging just ahead of Clippen swimming toward the shore.

Marco gasped, "That's a korsk!" he shouted, "Clippen!" As he lunged toward the Land-Nymph, the korsk's sleek snake-like head slid free of the water, the creature hissing, sending a trill of ripples across the water as its fangs glistened in the sun.

"Calm down, Marco," Sylus chided, "Master Nepo controls the korsks here. They are tame."

Unconvinced Marco eyed the creature. It wasn't slowing. Then its eyes cleared the water. Panic welled up in Marco, "Clippen! Move! Its eyes!" he shouted. The korsk's eyes held no daemon-fire, glowing a milky white instead, like the creatures last night! Clippen turned to face the korsk and threw himself backward just as it lunged out of the water. The Land-Nymph disappeared under the waves. Marco urged his horse forward.

"Clippen!" Kryoso shouted.

"Marco!" Sylus cried.

His warning pulled Marco up short. A tremendous crash shook the beach as the korsk threw itself ashore, pulling itself from the water with the six-foot bone spikes on its front flippers. The spike nearest Marco had lodged into the sand missing him and his horse by bare inches. The horse screamed in terror throwing Marco to the rocky shore. Pain seared through his shoulders and back and for a split second, his vision flashed black and white, stars bursting across the sky. Above him the dark flipper of the korsk came into view, the spike angling for his head. Screaming Marco rolled away scurrying backward on his hands and feet. Sylus was suddenly there pulling him toward the trees. When they reached the trees Marco regained his feet and looked out at the shore. The remains of his panicked horse had distracted the korsk long enough for the rest of them to get away.

The korsk ate steadily. Clippen soaked from head to toe, panted beside them. "That could have been me!" he squeaked. Marco studied his friend as the panic ebbed within him. Kryoso approached them with his and Sylus' horses in tow. Clippen's horse was nowhere to be seen.

The korsk roared its pleasure to the forest before retreating back into the sea. "Is there a plan for getting to and from the island without the korsks?" Sylus asked turning to Clippen. The Land-Nymph shook his head. They stood contemplating the far shore for several minutes.

"I have an idea," Kryoso said with a heavy sigh. He handed the horses to Clippen and trudged out to the shoreline. Stunned, Marco watched him go before starting after him, but Sylus grabbed his arm shaking his head. Marco glared, although the effort was wasted as Sylus retreated to the Mage Realm. Curious Marco followed him while turning to watch Kryoso work. The Mortak wove a thin line of Water and sent it questing towards the black haze that marked the korsk's position. Just as the Water touched the korsk, a thread of power as black as the korsk, flew along the line of Water and snapped into the creature. Shocked, Marco fell from the Mage

Realm gaping at Kryoso. *"That black thread was Shadow Magic!"* his mind screamed. Clippen and Sylus wore identical looks of horror. The korsk surfaced slowly before the Mortak, its eyes glinting opaque silver, identical to Kryoso's, but the others paid no attention lost instead in astonishment.

Kryoso looked back at them and gestured toward the creature. Swallowing hard, Marco started for the daemon-spawn followed by Sylus and Clippen. Stopping just out of reach Sylus asked, "Do you have complete control of it?" Kryoso nodded, a dreamy look on his face as he maintained the shadow pattern that controlled the korsk. The Mortak waded into the chill waters, the others following him to the korsk leaving the horses on the shore. Kryoso pulled himself up onto the korsk's back using a water-logged knotted rope tied around the beast and a series of metal rings embedded in its slick-furred hide. More rings traced the korsk's back. Once they had all clambered aboard sitting near a ring, using it as a hand-hold, the korsk started for the island. An uncomfortable silence fell over the world, broken only by the shush of the water as the daemon-spawn moved.

Upon reaching the island's steep rocky shore they dismounted and fled up the bank to the tree line. Kryoso left the korsk last, trudging slowly up to where the others waited, stopping a few feet below them staring up at them awaiting judgment. "Kryoso," Sylus started.

The Mortak fell to his knees. "Yes," he whispered, "that was Shadow Magic."

"But how can you know Shadow Magic?" Clippen asked after a moment.

Kryoso looked up at him sunlight sparkling in his opaque eyes. "Some Mortaks have this affinity, and we keep them secret knowing how they would be treated by others, their lives forfeit. I..." he looked down, "I thought it was worth dying, sharing my secret with you." His words trailed into uncomfortably heavy silence.

"You need not fear us Kryoso," Sylus breathed, "It was indeed worth it and we will keep your secret. From everyone," he added eyeing Marco and Clippen who nodded. "Good," he said before turning and leading the way up the hill and into the forest.

"We seem to be collecting secrets," Marco muttered following him.

The Water Master

arco struggled up the hill and stood beside Sylus. Before them a deep blue crater lake parted the forest. At its center sat a white palace, its large spires glinting in the sun. Not far to their right a sandy causeway stretched from one shore to the other. "Do we have to worry about the wildlife in this lake?" Marco asked contemplating the depths.

"No," Clippen said starting across the wide sandy berm. Skeptically Marco followed him, a cautious eye on the water. At the other end of the sand, two human guards in blue and gray livery flanked the causeway. They bowed low to Clippen allowing them all to pass unquestioned. A short, steep walk beyond the shoreline brought them to the eight-foot high wall enclosing the palace, flowering vines draped across its top trailing to the ground. Within, delicately scented flowering trees shaded the ground and a winding path of mossy stones led around the corner of the nearest building. Clippen continued down the path and around to the palace's front door. Two more guards, these ones feline Semians, stood there also bowing low to Clippen as they passed. Clippen pushed open the heavy door and entered a pale blue receiving room, round with a glass dome ceiling. Opposite them sat another large door which Clippen led them through as well. Beyond, an elegant vaulted hallway stretched toward the back of the palace, the walls monochromatically blue. The size and coolness of the walls contrasted sharply with the hardwood floor that glowed cheerily in the light of a dozen stained glass panels set in the ceiling far above. Two more liveried feline Semians guarded the opposite end of the chamber and another thick door.

"Shall I announce you, Lord Clippen?" one of them asked as the party approached.

"Please do," he answered.

The Semian guard bowed and entered the room beyond. "My Master, the wayward Lord Clippen and companions are here to see you!" he shouted.

"Show them in," a honeyed voice commanded. Sylus quickly pushed ahead of Clippen entering the room first. Apprehensively Marco followed Clippen in, Kryoso trailing behind.

The Water Master's throne room matched the hall they had just left, hardwood floor, blue walls and a glass ceiling. Most of the ceiling glass was clear showing the clouds gathering above them, but here and there stained glass sparkled in the sunlight sending patches of color dancing about the throne. A large feline Semian lounged across the throne oblivious to the patches of color flitting around him. Teal pants and white boots covered his lower body while his upper body remained bare. Tawny fur, barely darker than Marco's skin, covered his muscular chest and arms, and a flowing mahogany mane surrounded his lion face, his human ears, just visible, peeked through the tangles. He had been about to speak to Sylus, but his honey-brown eyes studied Marco instead.

"Hello," he purred at last, "You must be one of Myrth's pet humans." He smiled lazily then turned his attention to Clippen, "Lord Clippen," he greeted.

"My Master Nepo. I return to your home," Clippen bowed at the waist. Nepo tilted his head acknowledging the bow.

"And the incomparable Commander Sylus," the Master greeted, a harsh tone suddenly coloring his voice. Sylus bowed at the waist as well. "Who else have you brought me?" he asked, looking beyond Marco.

Clippen introduced, "This is Kryoso and Marco—,"

"Are you ready to depart, Master Nepo?" Sylus interrupted.

"Where?" Nepo asked, making a big show of stretching and lounging back in his throne. He threw his long legs over the armrest, sitting sideways and smiling lazily at the elf.

Sylus turned icy as he spoke, "You know where Master Nepo. We are to meet Myrth in Gemma. You are to bring your honor guard."

Nepo sat up, suddenly intense, a dangerous gleam in his eyes. "I have argued this point with Myrth. My honor guard is not 'coming' because my honor guard is already there! Myrth took half of my guard away to Dragon

Ridge, the other half will remain here with Sage and continue their own training." Sylus, flustered, started to protest but the lion-man held up a hand, "This includes my apprentice, and I will accompany you alone." Sharp dislike broiled between them as the silence grew.

"And you are ready to go?" Sylus prodded, drawing himself up to his full height.

Nepo drew back, a lazy look coming over his face and he smiled, "It is nearly sunset Commander Sylus," he said, "You have traveled long and hard and there are soft feather beds here. If we left now we would be in the Wild Woods at night."

Sylus studied the Semian. Nepo returned the stare his smile frozen. "Clearly," Sylus sighed, "I am not going to win this point Master Nepo. Let us start tomorrow."

"Of course, Commander," Nepo said, triumph flowing from him along with the words. He rose from his throne as if pulled suddenly vertical by strings. Marco swallowed as he scanned Nepo's full height, easily reaching eight feet. "I will show you to your rooms," Nepo said, his voice dripping honey once again.

Long strides took him to the right-hand wall in seconds and the others had to hurry to keep up, Sylus nearly running. By pushing on a panel bathed in red light from the stained glass above, Nepo opened a hidden door and disappeared down a hallway, the others trailing behind. They traversed a downward-sloping corridor—its walls, floor and ceiling all made of stone—that passed through the earth and leveled off after a few dozen paces. A few more feet on and the ceiling above them turned from stone to glass, looking out on a watery world. *"We're under the lake!"* Marco thought in awe, stopping to stare up at the filtered sunlight that danced through the depths above them turning the hallway a murky blue-green. Doors branched off on either side and through the arched ceiling Marco could make out a glass dome beyond each one. Master Nepo stopped at a door, "Your suite, Commander," he said pushing it open. The same murky light that lit the hall bathed the room beyond, settling over a deep white bed and a handful of bookshelves.

"I will dine alone, Master," Sylus said curtly as he closed the door behind him.

With a shrug, Master Nepo continued, opening the next door on the left for Kryoso. "Will you be joining me for dinner?" Master Nepo asked as the Mortak walked past.

"I would be honored, Master of Water," Kryoso said, bowing formally.

"Good. I will see you in the throne room after sunset," the Semian replied with a small return nod. "Clippen, will you want your old quarters?" he asked.

"Of course, Nepo," Clippen replied.

"Then I will let you continue on," Nepo stopped at a door on the right. "This is your room, Marco," he said swinging the door open with a flourish. "Clippen is the next door on the right."

Marco surveyed the gloomy room which was furnished in the same style as Sylus'. "Thank you Master," he said, starting in.

"Will you dine with us?" Nepo asked.

"With pleasure, Master," Marco smiled up at the lion-man.

"Please, call me 'Nepo' friend Marco," the Master invited with a soft grin before taking his leave.

Clippen called from his door, "I'll knock for you at dusk," he said, tilting his head and smiling, making it a question.

"Please," Marco returned. With a nod Clippen disappeared into his room. Marco entered and closed the door, surveying his new surroundings and drinking in the sudden lonesomeness that fell welcome over him. Oil lamps lined the glass walls and he pulled Fire from his hands to light them, the flames burning a brilliant white chasing back the murky light that fell through the glass dome. A small metal stand sat against the wall off to one side of the bed and invisible from the door. A large basin of clear water perched over a small burner occupied the furnishing. Smiling, Marco lit the burner as well and waited impatiently for the water to heat. He toured the bookshelves, not recognizing any titles in the collection or some of the languages they were written in. Once his bath water was ready he stripped and washed out his hair using a wet towel to remove a cycle's worth of dust and grime. Satisfied with the results he opened his pack and pulled out his Potentate uniform, hesitating over the cap before leaving it aside and dressed.

Just as he finished dressing a short knock on the door announced his companion's return. When he opened the door Marco gaped. Two Clippens stood in the hallway. Marco did a quick double take. *"No. Only one Clippen,"* he corrected himself. The other Land-Nymph was slightly shorter although his chiseled features were identical to Clippen's, his eyes a clear sharp purple instead, and his long white hair, cut slightly shorter than Clippen's thick mane, lay in a wispy cloud about his shoulders. They both wore identical gray cotton outfits. "Marco," Clippen started, indicating the Land-Nymph beside him, "this is Tekalo, Chosen of Water." Marco bowed low before the Land-Nymph. The apprentice's sharp purple eyes glittered as he returned the bow.

"My cousin tells me that you may be named Chosen of Earth," he began, his voice a handful of octaves deeper than Clippen's, a refined, rich baritone.

Marco hesitated, taken aback by the words. *"Chosen of Earth?"* he repeated internally. He shrugged, "That remains to be seen," he said returning the smile to his face.

"Come on," Clippen said, "I'm starving." The three started down the corridor toward the throne room, walking in silence to the panel that hid this hall from the rest of the palace. While they had been in their rooms the throne room beyond had been outfitted with a large table. Nepo sat at the head of it pouring a deep red wine into his glass conversing quietly with Kryoso. The Mortak was dressed in black and white finery that went well with his hair and set off his eyes. He and Nepo glanced over at them and smiled as they approached.

"Good evening," Nepo said, "Please, sit." There were three unclaimed chairs and place settings near Nepo, one next to Kryoso and two on the other side; the rest of the table lay empty. Tekalo moved to sit at the single setting to Nepo's right. Clippen and Marco sat across from him and Kryoso.

As servants brought plates of food Nepo conversed with Clippen who sat beside him. Marco studied them surreptitiously, while the soup and roasted vegetables were served. They talked, heads together, smiling occasionally and laughing under their breath. Old friends reunited—their voices pitched just above a whisper but inaudible. Tekalo leaned across the table catching Marco's eye. "They've known each other for years," he supplied, "They studied at Gaity together, served in the Potentate," he added with a weighty eye to Marco's current uniform. A large platter of roasted meat drew Marco's attention away from his companions, and he fell on the first warm meal he had eaten in days. Across from him Kryoso picked through his food at a sedate pace his attention divided between it and Tekalo's conversation. "What of Marladon?" Tekalo asked.

"My master is well last I heard," Kryoso replied. "We are not in contact though. Our bond is not of that nature." Tekalo nodded his understanding as Marco frowned. "I do miss the Fortress," Kryoso added with a sigh, his high voice carrying a dusky note of sadness. An hour later unable to eat or drink anything more Marco retired to his room, full of thick gravy and half-remembered dinner conversation about Kryoso's life as the Fire Master's steward; he promptly fell asleep.

A polite knock interrupted Myrth's meditation. He slowly returned to the Physical Realm, the golden Earth cloud surrounding him visible even after stepping from the Mage Realm, providing perpetual light rendering the natural gloom of the room irrelevant. "Come," he instructed, adding as the elf entered, "Have the others arrived?"

"No Master, not the others. An elf recently returned from the field has a message for you." The world seesawed slightly around Myrth registering his surprise at the announcement. "Shall I show him in?" the assistant asked, frowning in his vain attempt to ignore the slight tremor.

"Yes, of course. Light a few lanterns first," he added. The assistant bustled around the room lighting lamps while Myrth stood and straightened the pillows he had been meditating upon. The Master collected Jerrold from his favorite nap spot at the foot of the bed and carried him to the table near the door where he deposited the dragon fairy before taking a seat. With the stage set and the lights on, the assistant darted out of the room and returned a moment later with a high-ranking soldier, a combat healer by his insignia. He was shadowed by his second in command, a stern-faced female. They knelt just inside the door, dropping to both knees and bowing their heads in unison. "Welcome," Myrth greeted.

"Master of Earth, I was asked to deliver a message to you," the first elf responded.

"Join me, please," Myrth invited. They rose but only the first approached the table, while his second took two steps back and hovered near the door feigning disinterest. The perfect choreography pulled a smile from Myrth as the healer sat, sparing a nervous glance for Jerrold. "Tell me of this message," he instructed.

"Three days past my party took shelter at the crossroads where the trade routes meet coming out of the Broodlands—"

Myrth shot out of his chair toppling it behind him, pulling up just short of leaping across the table at the elf, "Was there a human female, a lady warrior?" he asked. The walls groaned around them.

"Y-yes, Master," the elf replied, his eyes darting between the walls and the hawk-man looming over him.

"And the message?"

"The trail fades but Trillip and D'Mique are following it toward Ebony Bay," the elf repeated as he had promised. Myrth straightened and turned beginning to pace back and forth between the table and the bed. Near the door the second's sword returned to its sheath.

As Myrth paced, the groaning walls quieted. "Tell me of the message, Trillip, and D'Mique," Myrth said, his voice calm again.

"Three days past we stopped at a crossroads," the soldier began again. "As the suns set, a Land-Nymph and human arrived, the Land-Nymph asking aid for the human who had been gravely wounded. I was able to save her life," he hurriedly assured Myrth when the pacing abruptly stopped, "and instructed that they stay at the inn and rest for a few days. They refused. When the Land-Nymph heard that I was to return to Gemma he asked me to carry a message to you."

"That is the exact message?" Myrth questioned.

"Yes. 'The trail fades but Trillip and D'Mique follow it toward Ebony Bay.'" Myrth closed his eyes departing for the Mage Realm. Rising high above the land he looked toward the far off eastern shore, toward Ebony Bay, studying the Earth Cloud and the flowing forcelines that drifted toward him. Dropping back into the physical realm he opened his eyes lost in thought. The soldier continued, "Both the Land-Nymph and the lady were injured, though the lady was poorer. When I healed her, I was able to pull away mange poisoning and fill her wounds. I warned the Land-Nymph that she should not travel, but he insisted they continue on the road. They left early the next morning going, as they said, toward Ebony Bay." He paused a moment studying the Earth Master, then continued, "she was well enough for the journey."

Myrth's attention returned to the elf. "Thank you for this message. Thank you for your help."

"I serve proudly, Master," the elf replied, standing. Myrth nodded dismissing the elf and his second in command.

Once he was alone again he returned to the Mage Realm combing through the forcelines, searching for any sign of the Greater Daemon. Finding none he reached out to Sylus and found him dozing in Sea Spray. "Sylus, hurry along," he directed, smiling as the commander startled awake.

"We will be there in four days' time," Sylus replied not bothering to leave his bed.

"Hurry," Myrth restated before returning to the physical realm, his gaze resting on Jerrold where he slept on the table.

"Marco," an insistent voice called through his dream. "It's time to go, human!"

"Human?" Marco pulled himself awake opening his eyes and meeting Tekalo's sharp purple gaze.

"Everyone is ready and waiting out on the grounds. Get up. I do believe Commander Sylus would leave you behind," the apprentice informed him.

Marco stretched and sat up, struggling out of the soft bed and rummaging through his pack for his Honor Guard uniform. "You look ready," he said, taking in the Land-Nymph's clothes and travel pack as he dressed. "I thought you weren't coming."

Tekalo glowered, "We shall see. My Master is fickle and he may change his mind if I show up prepared to travel." A moment later he exclaimed, pointing at Marco's pack, "Is that a Potentate cap?" Marco nodded closing the pack. "You are a Potent?" Again, he nodded. Tekalo gave Marco an appraising look and waited for more.

Marco eyed him skeptically before relaying the short version, "I was training in Pattern Magic with an advanced class in Gaity. The day of the test for Potentate came and the teacher dismissed me. I refused to leave so I had to take the test."

"And you passed?" Tekalo asked.

"I have the hat," Marco said pointedly.

Tekalo chortled loudly, "You do indeed! How fortuitous. Reminds me of when I became Chosen. There were about a dozen candidates. Master Nepo walked through the room dismissing people. When three remained he asked us each to do a trick with Fire. I can light a candle. So I became Chosen. But it's the only thing I can do with Fire, my antithesis. My father insisted we learn to light a fire, Clippen and I, that is. Although he is attuned to Air rather than Water, we are Children of the Waves." Marco thought of the perfect fires Clippen could conjure from the heat in his hands. Shaking his head he shouldered his pack and followed Tekalo, pulling his hair back into a ponytail while they walked down the underwater hallway through the empty throne room and out into the mossy courtyard where a party had gathered.

Sylus, Kryoso and Clippen stood together in a tight knot. Opposite them stood a second group consisting of a lean female elf, a green-haired goblin with pale yellow skin, and a large fairy, perhaps two feet high, who fluttered between the others. Although he had no visible ears his remaining features were the same sharp chin and high cheek bones as the Land-Nymphs, his pale lavender skin only a shade darker than his wispy hair, set off piercing teal blue eyes. Huge butterfly-like wings, shades of gray shimmering across the scaled surfaces, kept him aloft. All three wore the blue and gray livery of the Water Master matching the guards who surrounded them all.

Nepo and a Gray Daemon stood equidistance between the two groups. Taken aback by its appearance Marco reminded himself that the gray were civilized, *"Unlike black ones. It's a shame they are the rarer of the two species."* The daemon was elderly and bent, a long white beard stretching from his horse-face chin to the ground. Long ears trailed down to his stooped shoulders and his skin, wrinkled and weathered, was a uniform gray, the color of deep winter skies. He leaned on an oaken staff, his gnarled clawed hands idly petting the wood. Nepo loomed over him. "You are not going, Sage!" the Water Master boomed.

"Now, now, child," the Gray Daemon returned, "We most certainly are going."

"Myrth's orders were for you to bring your honor guard," Sylus added from where he stood.

"Myrth has my honor guard."

"Myrth has summoned us, Nepo," the Gray Daemon replied, "We are half your guard. Joined with Sylus and his mages you are practically at full strength."

Master Nepo scanned the courtyard. His furious glare landed on Tekalo and Marco, and he hissed. "Regardless of any other decision, you are not going!" he said, pointing at Tekalo.

Tekalo bowed his head. "I am a member of your honor guard," he said.

"You are my apprentice. If something happens to me you will be Water Master. If something happens to both of us, there will be no Water Master."

"That doesn't sound good," Marco whispered.

"You shouldn't be going either," Nepo continued with a glare at Marco.

"What? Why not?" he asked.

"You will be Myrth's apprentice. If something happens to Myrth you could take Earth untrained. Earth unchained," he emphasized the word, "would be unacceptable."

"Then a deal Nepo," Sage, the Gray Daemon, said. "Leave the apprentices behind and take us." At his words Nepo folded his arms and closed his eyes.

"Master Nepo," Sylus snapped, "Leave your apprentice behind if you wish, but Marco must be taken to Myrth! He is untrained!"

Nepo remained still for a full minute. "Marco and Tekalo will stay here. The rest of us will go," he decided at last.

"Master Nepo—" Sylus started.

"I have decided!" Nepo shouted, anger boiling along the edges of the words. Marco's breath caught in his throat. He could feel the pull of the Master's power causing the hair on his arms to prickle. A cloud of Air and Water gathered at Nepo's will, manifesting in the physical realm as dark clouds roiling in a silent storm above them. Huge stinging raindrops suddenly pounded the courtyard, a cacophony of sound to accompany the raging wind that descended. Marco glanced into the Mage Realm at the electric blue currents encircling the Master but turned away from them as movement in the courtyard drew his attention.

People threw themselves to the ground around him. The short-haired elf and goblin knelt as the fairy lay prone between them, his gossamer wings a bedraggled wash of color in the rain. The Land-Nymphs too fell prone to the mossy ground and Kryoso knelt with his head bent. Sylus, taken aback by Nepo's sudden rage bowed low, waiting for the downpour to pass. Through it all the Gray Daemon remained standing, a calm grandfatherly peace emanating from him. He smiled at Marco as their eyes met. As suddenly as the storm of anger had begun it ended. Nepo, closing his eyes for a moment, heaved a sigh and released the forcelines, the downpour slowing to a drizzle. "I bow to your will, Master," Sylus said into the soft rain. Nepo's gaze fell on Marco who had remained standing through the storm. Shocked at the realization Marco started to kneel.

"Don't bother Marco," Nepo said stopping him with a slight gesture. Embarrassed, Marco straightened. "Guards!" Nepo shouted causing his Honor Guard to flinch. A moment later a pair of humans appeared. "See that my apprentice and his guest remain under house arrest," Nepo instructed.

"Yes, Master," the guards replied in unison.

"He is not to leave for any reason." Nepo continued, hard brown eyes glued to Tekalo, where he still lay on the stones.

"By your command," the second guard intoned.

"Do we understand each other, apprentice?" Nepo hissed.

"Yes, Master," Tekalo answered, his words clear despite the stones he spoke into. Nepo waited a moment a pessimistic scowl furrowing his brow. Tekalo stood slowly and turned away. "Come Marco," he said trudging back toward the front door. With a sigh Marco followed him.

The guards followed a few feet behind, tailing them until they reached the throne room's secret passage where they halted, allowing their charges to enter the passage alone the panel sliding closed between them. Once they were away from the guards Tekalo's attitude returned to its former self-importance. "Hurry, Marco," he instructed. With a smile Marco followed him to the end of the underwater hallway and into his quarters.

Though decorated the same, Tekalo's room seemed more lived in. The shelves were full, clothing burst out of the wardrobe and tumbled into a heap at the foot of the bed where it was joined by blankets, papers and an assortment of books and scrolls.

"Here's the plan," he said, pulling a large scroll from the shelf and unrolling it across the table, grabbing an assortment of treasures to weight the corners. It was a map of the Fanterra plain and surrounding environs, large blue arrows criss-crossing its surface. "Here is Sea Spray, where we are. Here is Gemma, where we need to be," he pointed to the two locations as he spoke. "Nepo and the rest will reach Gemma by traveling along this road, here." He traced a road south and east. "Through the Wild Woods, south of the Forest of Fear then up through the Gemm Hills to Gemma."

"If we take this route," he placed his finger on a northern road, "through the Wild Woods, skirt the western edge of the Forest of Fear then up over the Quartz Mountains and down into Gemma, we'll get to Myrth at least a day before them."

"Wait!" Marco said studying the Land-Nymph. "You're not serious are you?"

"Well, it is slightly more adventurous than the southern route. But still—"

"No. We have to stay here!" Marco replied.

Tekalo studied him. "Now Marco. I didn't take you for a coward," he said.

"Coward? We were ordered to stay here by the Water Master. Your master."

"And we were ordered to Gemma by the Earth Master," Tekalo returned. "Myrth has seniority. His word is the final law," the apprentice reasoned.

"But...the guards," Marco tried. "How are we supposed to get out?"

"Well that's easy enough," the Land-Nymph said pointing up to his glass ceiling.

Marco looked up, "What? Go through the ceiling?"

"Yes. You're an Earth Mage."

"Yes, but it's a glass dome on the bottom of a lake!" Marco shook his head, confounded. Tekalo laughed.

"Glass? It isn't glass, Marco. Your eyes have deceived you. That is stone," he said to the transparent ceiling.

"Stone?"

"It was a present from a long forgotten Earth Master."

Marco studied the dome from the Mage realm. The golden Earth Cloud clung to it. "It is stone!" he opened his eyes and looked at the Land-Nymph whose smile, half-innocent, half-mischievous, seemed to reassure him. "But there's still a flaw in your plan, Chosen One," Marco continued. "Sylus is taking the northern route over the mountains."

"He is?" Tekalo was taken aback for a moment. He studied the map before them.

"Yes," Marco said into his silence.

After a moment Tekalo smiled up at him. "Then we will go straight through the Forest of Fear and into Gemma from the west," he said with a triumphant laugh.

"Straight through the Forest of Fear?" Marco squeaked. "I have nothing to barter with. The Mud Trolls aren't going to let us pass unmolested!"

"Marco," he replied, "You're an Earth Mage. They're Mud Trolls! You own them."

Marco's heart fluttered at the thought of leaving and of the adventure Tekalo had laid before him. But it wasn't the Mud Trolls that made him hesitate. "I can't," he whispered, remembering the Water Master's anger. "Nepo—" He shivered at the sudden thought of the fierce rainstorm that had pelted them not so long ago.

Tekalo smirked and waved a dismissive hand at the thought. "So long as we reach Myrth first my Master will be unable to do anything."

"It's still no," Marco sighed. Tekalo looked away, silent for a minute before spindling the map and returning it to the shelf. Marco watched the landscape disappear and stared at the roll of possibilities where it sat.

"I can't go," he whispered, shaking his head. "I won't go."

Tekalo sighed. "I understand, I do," he commiserated. "I'll just go alone," he continued with a nod, as if facing a final dread. Marco gaped at him as he placed the map in his travel pack, shouldered it and headed out the door, slamming it closed behind him. For a full minute Marco stared at the closed door, shocked. *"Water's Apprentice is going to cross the Fanterra Plain alone,"* he thought, *"alone through the Forest of Fear."* Sighing he picked up his own travel pack. "I can't let him go alone," he said to himself as he left the room.

"Tekalo!" he shouted down the hall. There was no answer and no Land-Nymph in sight. Marco started running.

"I knew you'd change your mind," Tekalo called from behind him. Stopping Marco spun around.

"I haven't changed my mind. But Nepo's right, you're his apprentice and someone has to protect you."

"Is that what you are? My protector?" Tekalo said smiling coyly, a laugh in his voice. Marco shook his head in exasperation, lost for words. "Come on then," said the Land-Nymph, striding past. Marco followed him to an unused room. "Okay," he said setting his pack down on a table near the door. He stared up at the ceiling, lost in thought for a moment.

Marco waited patiently. *I should be running for the guards,* he thought suddenly. Instead he waited, travel-pack weighing him down.

"I'll move the water, you move the stone," Tekalo instructed at last, "You first, just a small hole."

"Wait, you should move the water first so that it doesn't fall through my hole," Marco corrected. Tekalo studied him for a moment, sizing him up.

"All right, I'll move the water first," he said with a shrug. Closing his eyes he stepped into the Mage Realm. The thick blue-green cloud of water parted above them, letting in a sudden beam of sunlight, the clear stone magnifying it, bathing the room in intense white. Marco squinted in the sudden brightness before closing his eyes and reaching out to the Earth Cloud. Using his will, he drilled a hole in the dome above them, expanding it slowly as he opened his eyes until it reached two feet across. Tekalo pulled water down through the hole willing it to fall in an unnatural diagonal, and as it touched the polished floor it froze. Startled, Marco looked into the Mage Realm, studying the patterns as Tekalo formed the ice into a tight spiral that soon reached Marco's head in height. He worked directly with the Water miasma, foregoing any patterns and, from what Marco could see, there was no variability between the miasma above the hole, that falling through the hole, and the icy ramp Tekalo coaxed into being. When the ice reached the hole the apprentice picked up his pack and started climbing, leading them to freedom.

Stepping out of the Mage Realm Marco studied the ice. The ramp, far from smooth, offered a strong, sure surface and he found easy footing as he followed the apprentice to the top of the dome. Although it looked like real ice there was something amiss, as if the ice were not quite natural. At the top Marco peered out at the blue-green well that formed around him, looking up at the laughing circle of sky and glancing nervously at the smooth wall of water. Dark shapes flitted beyond the water-walls. "Close the hole," Tekalo urged after a moment. Blushing, Marco released the Earth Cloud and the dome reformed beneath the icy floor they now stood on. Water sloshed around them as Tekalo worked, turning the well sideways to form a tunnel and extending the ice along the bottom of the tunnel, drilling toward the distant, unseen shore.

With a sigh Marco followed Tekalo along the hole he had bored through the water. If he didn't know otherwise he would have thought the walls made of smooth jade stone, translucent enough to see fish-shaped shadows on the other side. He glanced down at the icy walkway that still offered decent footing. *"If I fall from the ramp,"* he thought, *"I'll find myself about twenty feet below the water's surface and another ten feet from the lake's bottom."* A sudden crash echoed through the tunnel and air rushed by rippling his hair. Marco spun around. Tekalo was allowing the ice to melt and the tunnel to collapse behind them. His heart leaping to his throat, Marco hurried to stay close behind the apprentice, afraid of being caught in the collapsing tunnel.

The Land-Nymph brought them steadily higher in the water, the ice walkway angling upward seeking the surface. Once their heads broke the surface Tekalo adjusted the tunnel, pushing water away from them so they wouldn't get wet; the tunnel's walls shrinking beside them until they were completely free of lake water. Once they were within swimming distance of the shore Marco felt certain that Tekalo would let the tunnel and walkway collapse around them and they would simply swim the rest of the way. However Tekalo continued to push the water away from them and walk the ice bridge all the way to shore. Not even the last few inches of water touched them.

When they stood on the sandy beach Tekalo turned around and laughed at the palace, a great giddy bellow echoing across the waves. Marco turned, certain he was laughing at someone, but the far shore was empty. "That was amazing, if you want my opinion," the apprentice added, bowing slightly to Marco. Marco smiled haltingly in reply. "We make a beautiful team, Marco. I'm looking forward to your Choosing."

"My Choosing," Marco echoed as Tekalo turned away and started through the woods toward the next body of water. There was no reply. *"I'm to be Myrth's apprentice...."* Marco followed in the Land-Nymph's wake thinking, *"How am I supposed to react to that? I don't know enough about Myrth. In fact I only know rumors and stories and probably less than half of them are true."* A quick downhill jaunt brought them to the shore of the inland sea. "Wait!" Marco called, suddenly pulling the apprentice away from the water, remembering, "The korsk!" He hesitated, thinking while Tekalo stared, *"Sylus didn't mention the attack, did he? Will Kryoso's secret get out if I say anything?"*

Tekalo pulled his arm from Marco's grip with a disdainful look on his face, "Korsks are for non-Water mages," he chided. Spreading his hands before him the ice walkway reformed, wider than before and Tekalo started across his bridge.

"Oh," Marco muttered, following him. Halfway across he looked down in time to see a large dark shape pass below them. "How thick is this ice," he asked, thinking back to his ferry ride from Gaity and remembering the strength of the korsk that had nudged his boat. "If one decides to investigate the ice it will dump us in the water," he finished.

Before him Tekalo shrugged. "Strong enough to hold us," he assured.

Swallowing, Marco picked up his pace, willing Tekalo to hurry. The Land-Nymph seemed oblivious to the danger beneath them and a small eternity passed before they stepped off the ice and onto the pebbled beach where Marco had watched the korsk slaughter his horse the day before. There was no sign of trouble, not even the horse's body remained. Free of the water, Tekalo took a shuffling dance step across the beach laughing under his breath. He smiled at Marco, coming to a stop. "Are you ready?" he asked.

"I'd better be. I don't think you'll make a bridge for me to go back."

Tekalo shook his head, chuckling as he skipped off through the trees, leaving Marco to trudge quietly behind. Tekalo stopped every few minutes to wait unperturbed for his companion. Some way into the forest, Tekalo stopped beside a rotting hollow tree and reached inside a dank hole about halfway along its length. Marco blinked in surprise as he pulled out a travel pack and two hastily folded pieces of paper. "Hmm," he said reading the outside of each paper. "This one is for you," he said handing one to Marco.

"Me?" Marco took a step back before reaching for the paper, eyeing the travel pack as well. "Who's it from?" he asked.

"Clippen," Tekalo said bending to read his note. Marco watched him read. Then, chuckling, the Land-Nymph deposited the note in the new travel pack and rummaged through its contents. "A few rations and an extra blanket," he announced looking up at Marco. "What does your note say? Clippen says that Sylus is going to travel the North Road, and that if you aren't with me I had better go to Dragon Ridge and try to follow Mistress Jay." He paused, "which doesn't make much sense. I think his mind is a bit scrambled."

Marco gaped at him and then at the note. "But how did he know to leave these here?" he asked.

Tekalo smiled at him. "We're cousins. We grew up together," he said with a shrug. "This is our tree," he added patting it lovingly.

With a frown Marco unfolded the note and read:

Marco,

If you have followed my cousin, I apologize. I think Nepo knows he will not stay behind, and told Sylus as much. "Since Clippen is not with him, someone has to keep Tekalo alive."

I snatched as much as I could from the packs but I dared not take more so soon. There is one more drop-tree at the fork in the road just outside the Forest of Fear. Tekalo knows it. I will try to leave more food for you both.

Clippen

Marco looked up at Tekalo. "He says that he will try to leave more food at a drop-tree just before the Forest of Fear. He also says that Nepo didn't expect you to stay at Sea Spray."

Tekalo nodded shouldering the second pack, "Very good. I think we're in for a lovely journey, don't you?" With a growing sense of unease, Marco followed the apprentice down the trail.

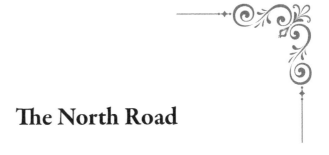

The North Road

Pallan fluttered above the plain, his gray wings catching the noonday sunlight, shimmering. Below him stretched the Fanterra Plain, a patchwork of greens, grays, and golds, crisscrossed with roads of varying sizes and stages of disuse. The troll forest began just half a mile ahead, a blighted landscape where the air stagnated and dark heavy clouds seeped upward from poisoned ground to obscure the rotting trees. Legends told of days when it was a beautiful glen, a deep restful place to linger before climbing the Quartz Mountains to the north, before a Greater Daemon died there, its carcass poisoning the area, driving life away, replacing water with black tar and teeming underbrush with matted thorns. Only trolls lived there now, an uneasy neighbor to the root elves in the east and the mountain bastion, Hawkethorne Valley, in the Quartz Mountains. Pallan's eyes traced the southern road as it traveled east, swinging wide of the forest before turning toward the Gemm Hills and Gemma. The road below him, the northern route, traveled along the forest's western edge before joining Hibend Trail at the base of the Quartz Mountains. He fancied he could see the trailhead in the hazy distance although that may have simply been wishful thinking.

The fairy spun slowly in mid-air searching for the party. Back the way he had come six horses trudged along the road. The two Palace Blacks, bearing Sylus and Leona as if they led a parade, set the pace for the group. A number of paces behind them Master Nepo's large gray warhorse brought up the rear. Movement further south drew Pallan's eye and he squinted, trying to make out the two figures traveling on foot several hours behind the horses. Frowning, Pallan drifted down to where Sage sat meditating. "High Mage," Pallan began alighting next to him. "Yes, Pallan?"

"I think Tekalo and the human are following us."

"Of course they are," Sage answered.

"You know this?" he asked, a weighty emphasis on the middle word.

Sage shook his horse-like head, "No, but it is Tekalo's nature," he said before drifting back into meditation.

Pallan sat beside him. "Do you suppose Nepo tries to leave Tekalo behind just to vex him?" the fairy asked after a moment, a smile crossing his sharp features.

Sage chuckled, opening his eyes. "Perhaps you should signal Tekalo so that he doesn't overtake us."

For a moment Pallan contemplated his words then he stood and bowed low before launching himself skyward. Spotting Tekalo again he tipped his wings in the sun, caught the light upon them and reflected it back toward the wayward apprentice. Pallan fluttered a moment waiting for acknowledgement. Two flashes answered him, one from Tekalo and one from Nepo. His heart sank. "Not what I had in mind," he thought as he dropped back to earth and sat beside Sage. "Nepo thinks I signaled him," he said. Sage opened his eyes again and studied the road they had traveled. Nodding he ran his clawed fingers through his white beard.

Nepo's war horse soon thundered through the trees, closing on them, the other five horses ranging behind. Sage hefted his oaken staff and thumped Pallan's head as they pulled to a sudden stop, the horses sending up a wave of gravel and dirt that pelted the pair on the ground. "What is it?" Nepo asked leaping from the saddle.

Pallan rubbed his head as he answered, "A mistake Master Nepo," he said. "I was surveying the land and signaled you by mistake."

Nepo took a step back, a sudden glare covering his features. "A mistake?" he asked.

Sage thumped Pallan again. "Ow! Sage! You already hit me for it!" Pallan shrieked, ducking away from the Gray Daemon as he hefted the staff a third time.

"It's the least you deserve," Sage mumbled.

Nepo glared at them. "A mistake?" he asked again. He turned slowly, his honey-eyes growing fierce as he found Clippen. Clippen looked away, his face blank. Nepo turned back to Pallan and stalked toward him. The delicate fairy knelt, bowing low as the Master advanced. "That signal was for Tekalo, wasn't it?" he asked, stopping a few inches shy of Pallan. Swallowing hard, Pallan closed his eyes and bowed lower, head to the ground. Nepo hunkered over him, leaning close, speaking softly, "I will compel you to answer me, child of the waves," he said, his voice boiling with contained anger.

"Yes, Great Master," Pallan breathed at last, "Tekalo follows us."

Nepo stood, "Alone?"

"No. The human is with him."

"Nepo glared at Sylus, "It seems your wish to unite Myrth and Marco will come true."

Sylus bowed in the saddle. "I will not deny my relief, Master. But I do wish they had obeyed you."

"Well, of course they wouldn't," Sage added.

"This trip is forfeit Sylus," Nepo continued. "The bargain has been undone."

Sylus gaped at the Water Master for a moment then his surprise turned to anger. "You will turn back?" he asked.

Nepo stood a long moment in thought before shaking his head and sighing, his anger a momentary flash flood that left as quickly as it arose. Pallan breathed a sigh of relief. Nepo looked over at Clippen. "What did you leave him?" he asked, "When your pack mysteriously disappeared."

Clippen smiled, "Rations, an extra blanket, nothing much."

"And I assume there is another package for him?" Nepo continued. "Let's see it." Clippen pulled a bulging burlap sack from his saddlebag and handed it over. "More rations," Nepo recited, sorting through its contents, "Another blanket and two daggers."

"My daggers?" Leona, the short-haired elf, exclaimed. Her dark eyes narrowed menacingly. Clippen smiled at her. "You thief!" she spat. Clippen ducked his head, an acknowledgement and smiled.

"Fine," Nepo said handing the sack back to Clippen. Remounting he continued, "I suppose there's a drop-off somewhere?" Clippen nodded. "We'll leave you to drop the supplies and then catch up to us at Hibend Trail."

"Yes Master," Clippen said. Nepo started down the road urging his gray to a gallop. The elves flanked him followed by Kryoso and the goblin. As the horses disappeared Sage smiled at Clippen then retreated into the Mage realm. Pallan scrambled up onto his slumped shoulder, grabbing hold of Sage's staff. Calling Air to his will, the Gray Daemon formed it into a disc beneath him, using it to levitate off the ground and fly forward. As they picked up speed, they flew past the horses scouting the road ahead. Alone, Clippen pulled out a piece of paper and a pencil, scribbling a hasty note for Tekalo and Marco instructing them to catch up as quickly as possible. He detoured from the main road swinging wide to the drop-tree and hiding the sack in it before hurrying after the group.

"That's Pallan," Tekalo said squinting into the sky. Stopping, he rummaged in his travel pack pulling out a silver mirror. Marco watched as he flashed sunlight back up into the sky.

"Tekalo," he began, watching for an answering flash, "Who's Pallan?"

"The fairy that's with Nepo," he answered.

"From Nepo's honor guard?" Marco asked. Tekalo nodded. "Why did you return the signal then?"

"Well, he obviously saw us." The apprentice shrugged as he replaced the mirror.

"But won't he tell Nepo?" Marco asked. Tekalo studied the sky for a moment.

"Maybe," he said with another shrug before starting down the road again.

"Why would he signal us?" Marco asked following him. Tekalo was quiet so long Marco thought he wouldn't answer.

"They are only about an hour ahead of us," he said at last. "Maybe they were stopping and Pallan was worried we'd stumble upon them."

"Or maybe Clippen was caught leaving us something," Marco suggested. Tekalo nodded but said no more.

Two hours passed before they reached a fork in the road guarded by an old hollow tree. Tekalo hurried over to it and retrieved a burlap sack from its rotting trunk. He rummaged through it and pulled out a pair of matching daggers. "Oh no," he breathed, "These are Leona's. She's going to kill Clippen."

"Is that another note?" Marco asked pointing to the paper sticking out of one dagger's sheath. Tekalo pulled it free and unrolled it. He read it quickly, his face falling as he read.

"Clippen says Nepo knows we're following. He, Clippen, hopes we catch up to them on Hibend Trail."

Marco surveyed the land. To the west the grass of the Fanterra Plain receded quickly to gray empty soil. East of the road dead trees grew marking the Forest of Fear, their pale gray branches meshing together, blocking the ground from the sunlight. Close to the forest, the air stagnated, turning dusty and dark as the black clouds hanging over the dead trees consumed the sunlight. Marco stared along the road following it eastward with his eyes as it traveled toward Gemma. If they turned east now, the road would take them far from this blighted place, looping southward as it traveled parallel to the Forest of Fear. While the road they intended to take, the north road, hugged the western edge of the forest overhung by dead branches in places. Ahead of them, in the distance, the lofty monolith of Imperial, the tallest of the Quartz Mountains, dominated the horizon along with two smaller peaks sitting in attendance. The five quartz monoliths thrust from the center of the Southern Peninsula as if a giant child had arranged them in play. West of the Quartz Mountains ran The Crest, an unbroken cliff and to the east sat the Black Mountains, effectively cutting the Southern Peninsula in half—the Fanterra Plain dominating this side of the mountains while the Blasted Lands and Mount Myrs overran the northern half.

"Let's catch up with the others," Marco suggested, an involuntary shudder whipping through him as he eyed the darkened dead forest.

"It looks so much safer on a map, doesn't it," Tekalo concurred, staring at the forest as well, tucking the daggers and note back into the sack. "I think I agree with you, Marco." With his own last look at the dark shadows filling the dead forest Marco followed Tekalo north.

They walked quickly along the road, occasionally watching the dead forest for signs of movement. Stories claimed that only trolls and their pet mange lived within the forest, burrowing beneath the surface, raiding the roads that bordered it. As the Fiery Sisters set, Tekalo came to a stop, eyes closed, facing north. Marco waited patiently surveying the forest beside them. With the light fading the shadows deepened beneath the dead trees, reaching out toward the living world around the forest. "We need to stop and set camp," Tekalo sighed. Marco surveyed the sky. Although Col and Nix were setting, Rysk's wan light blanketed the road. "I can feel Nepo ahead of us but we shouldn't travel beside the forest much longer," Tekalo added.

"You want to camp here?" Marco asked eyeing the forest.

Tekalo followed his gaze before answering, "We don't have a choice. The forest stretches all the way to the Quartz Mountains. Traveling beside it in the dark will be more dangerous than sitting beside it with a fire." He turned and left the road, walking west, putting some distance between them and the dead trees. Soon they huddled around a fire started by Tekalo, which burned a cheery orange-yellow. From time to time they glanced back at the Forest of Fear, but each time there was nothing to see.

"Stories tell of a tar lake in the middle of the forest," Tekalo whispered, tired of the silence eating away at them. "In Mistress Jay's collection there's a map of this area that labels this forest as Dremain Woods. What is it called where you are from?"

"Our maps call it the Forest of Fear," Marco replied. A blood-chilling howl punctuated his comment. Startled, Marco and Tekalo looked again to the looming forest across the road. Marco stood slowly, retreating into the Mage Realm. Before him the Forest of Fear burned, a tangled mass of Life, Earth, and Shadow, the blackness of Shadow outweighing the gold Earth and green Life. It was impossible to see if anything approached through the tangled forcelines.

Tekalo scrambled for a dagger, "Do you see anything?" he asked.

"No," Marco said, "all of it is Shadow. If any daemon-spawn is coming I can't see them." As he spoke a large Shadow form parted from the forest. Marco stepped from the Mage Realm Tekalo gasping beside him. The horse-sized creature seemed part dragon. Its sharp-beaked head swiveling toward them as Marco gaped, "It's a mange, he breathed. *"But they're myth!"* his mind screamed as the large red eyes, aflame with daemon-fire, focused on them. Its hiss sliced through the night, cutting into them, its spiked tail glinting in Rysk's blue light as it stalked toward them. Marco started pulling Earth into fist-sized balls. The mange mewled, an oddly excited sound from high in its throat. As he threw the first ball at the mange's chest, pain exploded through his head and the world went black.

The Fiery Sisters climbed above the horizon dragging dawn across the trailhead where Nepo and his party had set up camp. Nepo greeted the suns where he sat near the guttering fire with a knot of worry in his stomach. Last night Pallan had reported that Tekalo and Marco were two hours behind them a fire set for the night. Before crawling into bed Nepo had drifted along the forcelines searching for Tekalo. Although his apprentice was near, Tekalo wasn't due south of them where the fire had been. He was in the Forest of Fear. Nepo woke the camp instructing them to pack quickly. He stormed about, a bubbling sea of worry and anger ready to break at the first provocation, while the others scrambled to comply.

With the camp cleared, they started up Hibend Trail without breakfast. Two huge statues flanked the trailhead, burly human soldiers that held up a stone banner marking the end of the Fanterra Plain and the beginning of Hawkethorne Valley; the Masters held no political power within the Quartz Mountains. Passing beneath the sign Nepo's party traveled swiftly through a maze of large gray boulders, the trail a well-traveled pebble-strewn path. The boulders grew larger as they closed on the Quartz Mountains flanks, changing from dull gray rocks to shiny quartz. Clearing the boulder maze the trail angled upward, a pile of rocks that moved to hug the first quartz monolith, Sakwa. Above them white and pink quartz shimmered in the morning sunlight, rainbows dancing along the surface, falling around them through the air. This close Imperial's weight was lost, occluded by Sakwa and Owin, the two peaks flanking it. When the trail touched the mountainside it narrowed to allow only one horse at a time, the pebble-and-earth slope giving way to a rough-hewn path carved into the side of the mountain. Nepo's party stretched out behind him, the horses' hooves clanging dully on the rock.

Sage and Pallan floated beside Nepo hanging in mid-air. "Do you want us to go look for him?" Sage asked quietly. Nepo didn't reply. "He should have caught up to us by now." Nepo looked away from the trail searching the sky; Sage waited.

Nodding he agreed, "Go look for them," he said quietly. "We'll wait for you at Summit Meadow."

"By your leave," Sage bowed his head then sped away retracing their steps as fast as he could fly.

The horses climbed higher clinging to the side of the monolith. Once there might have been a guardrail, but people rarely used the trail and its upkeep had tumbled from the Warlord's priorities. Near noon they reached Sakwa's summit. The trail flowed into a wide set of stairs that climbed up through a gap in the quartz and spilled them into a sparse meadow where soil and water had gathered on the top of the stony mountain. Nepo dismounted and turned his horse free to graze on what grass it could find. The others followed his lead, joining him where he sat, all of them looking toward the trail head waiting. "They should have been here by now," Sylus muttered.

"I know," Nepo mused.

"What should we do?" he asked, giving the Master an anxious look.

"There isn't anything to do," Nepo shrugged, "We'll wait for Sage and Pallan. Maybe they found something."

"Maybe Tekalo decided to take the southern road after all," Sylus offered.

Nepo studied him for a minute before nodding, as unconvinced as Sylus was by his own words.

The Fiery Sisters continued their relentless trek across the sky, and an hour passed before Sage and Pallan topped the peak alone. Pallan parted from the high mage before he landed next to Nepo, joining Clippen, the goblin Jenna, and Leona a safe distance from the Water Master. Sage came to rest before Nepo and Sylus. "I'm sorry," he said, "We couldn't find them." Nepo studied the Gray Daemon a moment before closing his eyes and bowing his head. "We found the camp they made last night," Sage continued, "It wasn't cleared."

Sylus gasped, "What? He was taken?"

Sage shrugged, "There was no sign of a struggle. But it isn't like Tekalo to leave a campsite uncleared."

"I can't feel him," Nepo whispered opening his eyes. They sat silent for a handful of minutes.

Leona approached, kneeling beside Nepo. "Master, do you mean to make camp here?" she asked. "If we do not leave soon, we will be climbing

Imperial in the dark." Sylus sighed at her words. "Pallan told us what they found," she continued. "I'm sure he is well regardless of his circumstances."

"Leona's right Nepo," Sylus said, "We can't stay here and we can't afford to go back and look for Tekalo. Marco is with him; they'll be fine." Nepo turned away from Sakwa's trail and looked behind them at the lofty crown of Imperial where sheer gray quartz lined with snow and ice greeted him. The largest of the Quartz Mountains loomed above Sakwa's summit meadow, casting a haughty shadow over the other peaks. Like Sakwa little vegetation grew on its slopes. Cracks crisscrossed its surface instead, some of them offering enough purchase for a lone scraggly tree or clump of weeds as gray as the surrounding rock. One crack stood out from the others, carved deeper into the mountainside by generations of climbers—the trail to Hawkethorne Valley.

Nodding Nepo stood and whistled for his horse. "Let's go," he said voice low and gruff, "We're wasting time."

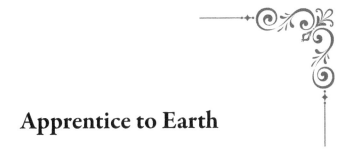

Apprentice to Earth

The soft darkness slid away as Marco awoke. "Some High Mage you are," Almira said, "Knocked out from behind I assume." Fuzzy memories returned with his surroundings—the mange in the firelight then glimpses of dead trees and stone passages as he was dragged along the ground. Marco opened his eyes wishing Almira really was with him. He was in a close dark space, warm and dusty. His ribs protested against the metal bars beneath him that dug into his back. To his left torchlight flickered on the stone ceiling above him illuminating more black metal bars surrounding him.

"I don't think he's awake yet," Tekalo said, distant and soft.

"If I could I'd throw something at him," Almira returned. Startled, Marco turned toward her voice, ignoring the pain that barreled through his head and the flash of white light that exploded behind his eyes. As his vision cleared he focused on her, noting her own metal cage, which was not quite large enough to stand up in, separated from him by a narrow hallway. She had lost her veil, exposing her softly tanned face to the chamber's weak torchlight. He smiled when their eyes met, joy stampeding through him in the wake of his pounding heart. She returned the smile and her face softened, the mockery dissipating.

"Well, he is awake," Tekalo said from a cage to the left of Almira's. Marco glanced at him. A bright bruising marred his marble-white profile but beyond that he looked unharmed.

"Almira," Marco croaked, struggling to sit up, "How?"

She didn't wait for him to ask further questions, "We were captured a couple days ago," she grimaced as she added, "Mud Trolls. We were on our way home, to Hawkethorne."

"We?" Marco asked. Almira nodded toward the cage to Marco's right. A tall human slumped against the back wall, his arms outstretched, his wrists bound to the metal bars. He appeared unconscious, chin touching his chest and his blond hair caked in dried blood, forming a limp curtain that shielded his face from view.

"The Mud Trolls do not like Temeres much, he tends to try and kill them," Almira added. Their dislike had translated into a maze of overlapping wounds and bruises in varying states of healing; some of the deepest cuts looked infected, the largest bruises blossoming across his pale bare mid-section. He wore only mud-crusted black trousers and scuffed black boots. Fresh blood covered the bindings at his wrists where they cut into his thin limbs.

"Who is he?" Marco asked softly.

"Temeres is my bodyguard and escort," Almira supplied. The blond stirred lifting his head slightly, his narrow chest pulling in a deep steady breath. He found Almira as he awoke then turned bright hate-filled eyes on Marco. Marco flinched from the strength of the gaze but did not look away. "I was called back to Hawkethorne not long after you left Gaity," Almira supplied.

"I am uninjured," Tekalo added a sting lilting through his voice. Marco ignored him, studying Temeres instead. "Now that you're awake, we can get out of here," he added. A questioning glance at Tekalo brought further information, "There isn't enough water here for me to work against the bars and Almira can't harm them directly, although she can harm trolls directly," he added with a chuckle. "And he's only a human," the Land-Nymph finished with a dismissive nod toward the other man.

With a second studious glance at Temeres, Marco closed his eyes and retreated to the Mage Realm. Pain pounded through his head pulling him toward the Physical Realm with each beat. He studied the forcelines, concentrating on the earth cloud that billowed around him mixing oddly with the miasma of Air and Water. Each metal prison cube formed of crisscrossing bars, sat dark and formidable against the clouds of power. Marco returned to the Physical Realm and struggled to his feet, hunched over at the waist from the small size of the cube. He studied the welds that held the bars together. "Strong enough to keep us in," he thought, "If we were only human." He pulled the Earth Cloud to his will, calling it through the bars to coalesce at his feet making a head-sized ball of rock.

"It's a start," Almira muttered. He ignored her letting the ball fall back to sand and hiss into the floor, returning to its original form. He spared her a half-hearted glare before closing his eyes again and pulling the Earth Cloud up from the floor and into his cell. He willed it into a stalagmite and as it came to heel, metal squealed—amazingly loud as it jangled through the prison cave—and groaned as it gave way around the stone intruder. He directed the growing spike of stone toward the front wall of his prison forcing its tip between the bars, pushing outward. The welds snapped, the bars falling away before the intruding spike. Marco reformed the stalagmite flattening it into a disc, forcing the bars to spread wider allowing him passage. He opened his eyes to judge the size of the hole before nodding and releasing the Earth Cloud. The stone disc dropped to the floor as sand that hissed through the remaining bars before reforming the stone floor.

Marco clambered through the hole he'd made scanning the hall in either direction. To the right it traveled another twenty feet before ending, to the left it traveled around a bend disappearing in shadow. Only now did it occur to him that his escape had been too loud for a prison break. He strained to hear anything but no shuffling footsteps echoed along the stone. Almira cleared her throat bringing his attention back to her. Smiling he leapt across the hall, grabbing the bars of her prison. "You'll need the key," she said joining him at the bars, clasping his hands in hers. Warmth shot through Marco at her touch. He looked along the edges of the cube until he found the lock on top of the cell.

"Are you hurt?" he asked studying her, trying to focus on her words and not the weight of her hands on his.

"No, Temeres is very good at his job. Go find a guard and get the key," she ordered.

"Try to manipulate him," Tekalo offered. Marco and Almira eyed him skeptically, drawing a nonchalant shrug from the Apprentice. "Or not, what do I care?" Marco studied the far end of the hall wondering why no guard had come at the sound of the cage falling apart.

"Just knock him out or kill him," Almira said, "Then drag the body in here and get the key. You're not the Earth Master yet, don't try to manipulate him." With a nod Marco turned and crept down the hall, his heart pounding in his ears, deafening. He crept around the bend into another cage-lined corridor and paused, inventorying the prison and finding that all were empty. No dishes, no straw, nothing littered the interiors of the cubes to show they had ever been occupied. The air remained heavy, abandoned and disheartened. "Still no guard," he noted as well, "Was the breaking metal not as loud as I thought?"

Beyond the prisons the corridor ended in a stout door, its iron hinges bolted to the rough stone wall on one side, but no lock or knob adorned the other. He paused, Almira's words sidling through his mind, *Just knock him out or kill him,"* and he looked down at his empty hands before glancing around the hallway. With no weapons presenting themselves, he pulled the Earth Cloud to his hand and formed a hefty club. Stepping from the Mage Realm he concentrated on the club, feeling its weight as he hefted it to his shoulder experimentally swinging it, willing it to stay solid in his hand and not turn to sand and return to the floor. Satisfied that it would obey he crept forward. He nudged the door open slightly with his hip, pushing it outward on silent hinges, just in front of the door stood a great shaggy form, a Mud Troll Marco assumed. Marco squeezed through the opening club first, pushing on the door as little as possible so as not to knock it against the creature.

Free of the door Marco brought the stone club down on the troll's head. A sickening crunch echoed along the corridor and the creature slumped to the floor—no other sounds, no more movement. Heart fluttering in his throat Marco rid himself of the club by releasing the Earth Cloud before nudging the troll with his toe. Still nothing. He bent over and grabbed the creature by one of its broad arms and struggled to pull it into the dungeon corridor. As he lifted the dead weight, his heart stopped; he feared his club had been very effective. Once inside the dungeon, Marco laid the troll to the side and studied it. It was covered in greasy matted hair, its body broader than Marco though not as tall. Beyond that it seemed quite human. No claws, no fangs. Its only clothing a leather loincloth, barely covered anything. With a sigh Marco collected the keys from the belt that held the loincloth in place. He looked into the troll's face as he retrieved the keys. Short horns sprouted from its temples. Above its broad nose its beady eyes were glazed over, making them appear black. There was no life within.

With a last look at the troll Marco straightened then hurried back to the others. He worked his way through the keys first at Tekalo's cell, then Almira's—sparing a moment for a quick embrace, then Temeres'. When he had Temeres' cube opened he crossed to the back wall to release him. Temeres watched Marco with startling blue eyes, a feral smile lighting his face. The leather cords holding Temeres in place bit into his skin, bleeding his wrists with even the slightest movement. His leather boots had saved his ankles from the same fate. "Are you well?" Marco whispered blocking Temeres from Almira's view.

"Well enough to escape," Temeres croaked in a low voice.

"We need a blade to cut these," Marco observed studying the bindings at Temeres' ankles. Tekalo appeared beside him studying the bonds as well. "Did you see where our weapons went?" Marco asked them looking around the hallway.

Tekalo shook his head, "I was knocked out," he said.

"As was I," Temeres added, each word full of pain and bitterness.

Almira joined them laying a hand on Temeres' cheek. "Hush my Guard. You did all you could and continue to do so. Marco will take on your burden while you recover." Surprised by her words Marco and Temeres looked at each other. Temeres weighed him with a steel-coated gaze, but said nothing. "We lost our weapons in the tunnels long before they threw us in here," Almira supplied. I expect we will never see them again.

Marco turned to her, "You weren't knocked out?" he asked.

"I fear that many of my opponents underestimate me once they find out I'm a woman." She sighed, "It doesn't last long though. One crispy-fried troll later and I was knocked out as well," she finished smiling viciously. "The sharpest knives are made of stone, Marco," she added nonchalantly, brushing Temeres' matted hair from his forehead.

"Ah," Marco thought bending down and cupping the Earth Cloud in his hands. He formed it into a sharp stone knife, complete with a rough handle for gripping. He studied the blade, sharpening it, hardening it, for a handful of minutes before standing and holding out his handiwork for the others to see. Almira and Tekalo looked at him instead of the knife, the same choking thought painted across their faces. "What?" Marco asked.

"Did you make that HERE?" Tekalo asked, the emphasis on his final word carrying more than any single word should. The apprentice's surprise brought back Marco's conversation with Sylus. He concentrated on the knife, forcing it to remain whole, forcing his mind to calm. He asked himself the same question...but didn't dare answer it.

"Of course not," Almira said her voice only slightly hesitant. "Like you, Marco is just really good at stepping between. I taught him after all."

Swallowing hard Marco left them to it and moved to Temeres' left wrist. The leather bit deep leaving no space for the stone blade to slip in between it and the man's flesh. Marco followed the strap to where it looped around the metal bars. Working carefully, he slid the blade between Temeres' wrist and the bar, sawing through the leather strip, the pressure drawing a soft hiss of pain from the other man. "Sorry," Marco muttered, hurrying, hoping to lessen the pain. Without warning the cord snapped and Temeres slumped forward, crying out as his full weight landed on his still-bound right wrist. Almira and Tekalo helped him, pulling him up, bearing his weight. Marco crossed to Temeres' right hand as Tekalo braced the man against the back wall. "One more," he warned working the stone knife behind Temeres' wrist. Bright red fresh blood welled from the bruised skin. Temeres breathed quick and shallow, pain shivering along his limbs and across his chest. "I'll hurry," Marco said, sawing quickly through the strip. As the leather snapped Temeres fell forward again, landing on Almira and driving her to her knees beneath his weight. Tekalo helped him up again. Marco moved to the man's ankles, slipping the knife quickly between the bars and Temeres' boots. With his ankles free Tekalo helped lower him to the floor where he lay on his back panting and shivering, eyes closed.

"He's lost a lot of blood," the apprentice noted.

"He'll make it?" Marco asked, his voice low.

"Yes," Temeres rasped, "he will." He rolled to his side and painfully struggled to regain his feet, standing upright only with Almira's help. He rested, head heavy against her shoulder eyes closed again. "I will," he repeated.

"I'm glad that's settled," Tekalo added, "Come on." He turned and started down the corridor.

Marco motioned toward Temeres, "I can help," he said. Nodding consent Temeres draped an arm across Marco's shoulders. With Almira bracing her guard's waist the three started after Tekalo, catching up to him at the dead troll where he was searching the body.

"Nothing," he concluded, straightening. "He's not even armed really. How was he supposed to stop us from escaping?" Tekalo surveyed the walls near the door with his hands on his hips, chewing his lower lip, tiny fangs glinting in the dim torchlight.

"What are you looking for?" Marco asked.

"Weapons," he replied pushing the door open and disappearing through it. Almira opened the door and held it for Marco and Temeres. In the corridor beyond Tekalo stood near a weapon rack surveying an assortment of blades and bows. He hefted first one then another, testing their weight and balance before discarding them on the floor. Almira surveyed the rejects, a delicate frown tracing her mouth and brow. "Here," Tekalo handed a blade to Marco, "This isn't too bad." Marco pushed the sword away, "No," he said. "I already have my weapon."

Tekalo eyed him for a moment, "Do you?" he asked.

"Yes, the Earth Cloud."

Almira chuckled darkly at his answer.

Tekalo smiled at him. "Alright," he said. He returned the saber to the rack and chose a different one for himself. "Come on," he said starting down the corridor to their right.

Temeres nodded toward the blade Tekalo had replaced, "I'll take it." As Almira collected it Marco studied the man leaning heavily against him. Although his breathing was steady it came in short pain-filled pulls and, as they had walked he had barely kept his feet steady beneath him, Marco practically carrying him instead. "And that crossbow," he continued feebly raising his free hand to point to the far end. Almira grabbed it as directed then shouldered it and a small case of bolts before rummaging through the pile of weapons Tekalo had created, collecting more bolts for the weapon. Satisfied she had everything she followed Tekalo with the weapons Temeres had requested still in her possession. Before following them, Marco and

Temeres both glanced back the way they had not chosen seeing only an empty corridor, its rough torch-lit walls the only witness to their escape.

Tekalo led them through a maze of tunnels. At every crossing or fork he paused closing his eyes. For a moment they stood in silence, and then Tekalo would choose a path and continue. After the third pause Marco asked, "What are you doing?"

"I'm following the freshest air, the deepest miasma," he answered, his tone hinting at annoyance. Marco left it at that. They met no trolls or mange as they wended their way through the underground settlement, each turn the apprentice took leaving Marco feeling more lost than before. Then, slowly, it seemed that the corridors they followed began sloping upward more often than not. Marco's mood lightened and Tekalo made his decisions faster as they progressed. Then a mange emerged from a side passage ahead of them, its bulk filling the corridor before them. Instinctively they all flattened themselves against the stone, trying to blend into the shadows. The mange turned away from them, hunkering down close to the floor, snuffling at the dirt. An eternity full of racing hearts and shallow breaths passed before it started forward searching slowly as it moved, disappearing around a bend in the tunnel.

When it had disappeared Tekalo inched forward, stopping to survey the Mage Realm when he reached the side passage. With a glance in the direction the mange had gone Tekalo retraced its path, the floor of the new tunnel growing rocky and wet as they traveled. Now Marco could feel the fresh air; they were nearing the surface. Ahead of them the tunnel leveled off and widened into a decent-sized cavern. But they stopped and pulled back into the shadows upon entering it. Before them a pair of Mud Trolls and a mange stood guard. Tekalo closed his eyes and took a deep breath hefting the sword. "I can take them," Marco said placing a hand on Tekalo's arm. He stepped away from the safety of the shadows. Entering the Mage Realm he drew a quake sphere around the guards. Then he opened his eyes. "Hey!" he called. The guards turned toward him their movement setting off the quake. He felt the forcelines snap together vibrating around him. The cavern rumbled and pebbles danced across the dirt floor. With a hiss, the mange leapt at them just as the roof near the mouth of the cavern collapsed, burying the trolls under a pile of boulders.

Tekalo rushed forward to meet the mange, sword-first. It snapped at him, sharp beak clicking harmlessly inches from his arm. Tekalo ducked around the creature and aimed a blow at its serpentine neck but it dodged. Marco pulled the Earth into a large ball and threw it at the mange as it circled around toward Tekalo. The ball hit with a satisfying thump, startling the mange, which turned and flung itself at Marco. Tekalo lunged driving his blade into the retreating creature. A crossbow bolt thunked into its side as it spun between its attackers screeching defiantly. Tekalo's sword suddenly plunged between its ribs and it mewled as it crumpled to the floor. Almira waited with another bolt ready but the daemon-fire in its eyes faded away. Marco sighed and walked over to the cave-in as Tekalo surveyed the mange. From the Mage Realm the boulders formed fluffy clumps of Earth. He pushed them aside with his mind, reforming the cave's entrance. Then he walked out into the cool night air followed by the others.

"Very nice," Almira whispered in his ear as she walked beside him, Temeres nodding in agreement still relying heavily on her for support. Marco smiled at the compliment straightening further as he walked.

Free of the troll tunnels they found themselves at the foot of a hill. All around them dead gray trees stood vigil, their branches clawing the dark sky. Any leaves had moldered away long ago and the dusty soil would not support new growth. Almira studied the black clouds above them. "Dawn is still some time off," she whispered, a hesitant note coloring her voice. "We should find shelter and make camp. Allow Temeres to rest."

"Follow me," Tekalo instructed striking off into the night. He led them first one way then another through the dead trees. As they walked roots reached up to trip them and branches snagged on their clothes and hair. Then the trees were gone. Before them a glistening blackness spread out across the ground. "Misery Lake," he breathed, stepping forward and kneeling down on the dark shore.

"We've reached the center of the Forest," Temeres announced. "We're safe now. The trolls don't come here. Superstitions keep them away." They walked along the lake's shore until they came across a hollow in the thick brambles that grew along it where they stopped and gathered enough wood for a fire. Almira started a small, sickly gray-yellow fire that gave off very little light but plenty of warmth. The slight light dancing from it lit up the encircling trees and thorn bushes casting soft, half-shadows around them.

Marco sat down beside her as she rubbed her hands together to reclaim the warmth she'd spent on the fire. "That's a strange color," he began, eyeing the fire with a smile.

Almira smirked. "I was trying for black so it wouldn't attract any attention."

Marco nodded as a new thought occurred to him, *"Here I am thinking that my fires have to be as natural as possible. And apparently, there are reasons not to make them orange."*

"Where are you and the Chosen One going?" she asked leaning her head against his shoulder. For the briefest moment he felt the strain of the last few hours leave him and thrilled at the feel of her next to him again.

"Gemma," he answered.

"We can travel with you until we reach the Gemm Hills. Our roads diverge there. Temeres and I must head north into the Quartz Mountains and you will continue east into the Hills.

"You said you were on your way to Hawkethorne," Marco probed.

"Yes."

"Every now and then," Temeres supplied from Almira's other side, "the Warlord asks his Mage Princess to return home."

"'Mage Princess,'" Marco repeated. "You're a princess?" the world shifted under him at the revelation.

She waved it away, "A minor title at best, made even more minor by my position in the Potentate. Warlord Herdan is just lucky Palo plays along and allows me to return."

Marco sat in silence for a while feeling Almira's warmth against him. "And what about tonight?" he asked leaning into her, his lips pressed against her soft hair. She moved, sitting up and looking into his eyes before smiling and kissing him. For a moment he hung suspended in fire, warmth spreading through him.

"Tonight, I will keep watch while you sleep, my love," she whispered across his lips, forcing him back, "Now lie down."

He did as he was told resting his head beside her thigh.

The following day Temeres managed to keep his feet on his own. He collected the weaponry from Almira before striking camp. Then, walking stiffly but with a steady determination, he led the way through the dead forest toward the Gemm Hills. As the day passed his wounds knitted and it seemed that most of the bleeding stopped, but the deeper ones festered. Marco followed close behind keeping a wary eye on the other man, glancing down at the occasional drop of blood he left to mark their trail. Near dusk he pulled up short and motioned Almira to stay behind him. She closed the distance between them and hid her face between his shoulders, a makeshift substitute for her missing veil. Tekalo and Marco stopped as well, flanking him. "I know you stand before me," Temeres said to the trees in front of them. "Come forth!" A moment later a trio of heavily armed elfin warriors stepped from behind the trees, their long white hair and pale skin matching the dead forest, their dark eyes mirroring the blackened soil.

"Name yourselves," the middle warrior commanded hefting a crossbow.

"I am Temeres, Protector of her highness Princess Almira of Hawkethorne Valley."

"I see the Princess; she wears a Potent's uniform," the warrior to the left said.

"And you?" the middle warrior asked pointing his crossbow at Tekalo and Marco.

"I am Tekalo, Chosen of Water. This is Marco, Chosen of Earth," Tekalo replied haughtily. A worried look passed around the elves.

"What brings you this way?" a voice said behind them. Marco spun around grabbing for the Earth Cloud. Four more elves had appeared behind them wearing the same gray uniform as the three in front.

Temeres answered ignorant of the startled tension that exploded behind him as a large rock appeared in the air near Marco. "I am escorting the Princess to Hawkethorne Valley. We were ambushed. Two days later the Chosen Ones arrived. With their aid we escaped the Mud Trolls. We wish only to reach safety."

"Drop your weapons Chosen of Water, Protector, and we will escort you to Gemma," the first elf said. With a shrug Tekalo let the troll blade fall to the ground. One of the new elves bent to retrieve it.

"Don't bother," he said. "It was a weapon of necessity not choice." The elf straightened, leaving the blade where it lay. Temeres' weapons joined it unceremoniously. The elf didn't bother stooping for them either as they started off through the trees.

As the darkness of night blanketed the land the forest dwindled—dead twisted trees giving way to gray bushes and rolling grassy plains that steadily grew into green-frocked foothills. The elves led them around a hill and onto a large road that ran straight toward the upper lip of a deep-cut ravine. As it plunged over the edge, stairs took the place of the well-traveled hard packed dirt. On the first few steps Temeres hissed and paused, breathing deep and steady before attempting the next. As they descended they collected a gaggle of curious children who followed along just out of reach of the guards. Up against the far wall a wide doorway flanked by more guards led underground. Beyond, the passage glowed with a cheery orange light. As they passed through more elves came to greet them. They exchanged hushed words and sideways glances before the newcomers spoke.

"Come. We will take you to our healer," one offered, his face schooled to a neutral blandness as he studied them. Now, bolstered by these new elves, their original escort continued along the wide road walking past a series of smaller caves that were set off from the main road by lattice doors, some of these stood open inviting them into the warmly lit shops beyond while others were closed and dark—*"Closed for the night,"* Marco thought. Leaving the storefronts behind, the corridor opened up into a large cavern dominated by an open-air pavilion. They passed under the white canvas eaves and stopped beside a pool of water where an elderly female elf sat. "Merry," the lead guard greeted. "We found these four on the outskirts of the Forest of Fear. They escaped from the Mud Trolls."

"Come, show me your wounds," the elder said in a sing-song voice, motioning for them to sit beside the pool. With Almira's help, Temeres sat gingerly before the elf. Small cuts closed and the bruising faded as she ran her hands over his face and head, then down along his shoulders and arms, passing over his torso and legs last. The largest gashes remained and she studied them closely. "There is mange poison here," she said motioning to several deep slices over his ribs. She closed her eyes and laid her hands over them. Marco felt the magic gather to her will. Glancing at the Mage Realm he watched the green swirling maelstrom of Life pierce Temeres' wounds, dancing beneath the surface of his skin. After a few moments the healer opened her eyes. She moved on to a deep puncture near Temeres' heart that was ringed with greenish bruises. Again the healing magic concentrated over the wound and worked within it. When she removed her hands the wound was closed but the bruising remained. "These last wounds," she said, sounding tired, "I have removed the poison and infection but," she shook her head, "If I heal them now, tired as I am, there will be scar tissue. Given a few days' rest I can heal them with no scarring."

"I care not for scars," Temeres said, "Heal them now if you are able." With a nod she returned to her work.

Afterward she turned to Almira. "I am well, healer. I wish only a plate of food and a soft bed," she said. The elf smiled.

Marco nodded. "That's all I want too," he said echoing her.

"And you?" the Healer asked turning to Tekalo.

Tekalo knelt before the healer. "A mange took a bite from my shoulder," he said. He pulled his shirt gingerly over his head. The wound glistened wetly, bruising around the fist-sized hole spilled across the apprentice's shoulder and onto his back. Marco gaped, then glared at Tekalo, waiting for the Land-Nymph to acknowledge him. The healer passed her hand over the hole and magic blanketed the wound boring into the hole. Soon the bruising faded and the hole narrowed but did not close.

"Again," the healer said, pausing, "I can close it now and leave a scar, or I can rest and there will be no scarring."

"Close it now," Tekalo said, "We need to hurry on our way." With a slight nod the healer continued her work. When she finished and her hands fell away a large patch of shiny white flesh remained.

"Thank you," Almira said bowing to the healer. She turned to the closest guard, "My protector and I must hurry to Hawkethorne."

"Of course. We will see you to the river passage," he said with a nod, "and we can provide you with new weapons, Protector," he added, gesturing toward a weapon rack. As Temeres followed him across the cavern, Marco reached for Almira's hand. She took his, squeezing.

"When I finish in Hawkethorne I will follow you," she said. He pulled her close, kissing her, willing her softness into him. For a moment she pulled back, startled, and the brief thought of being engulfed in flames darted across his mind but then she kissed back. Temeres clearing his throat brought their moment to an end, and she pulled away reluctantly, glancing toward her glaring protector who suddenly seemed very dangerous, bristling with blades and bows. "I will not be far behind," Almira added grabbing him by the chin and pulling his face back to hers for another short peck.

"I know," Marco answered, "I'll wait for you."

"I appreciate that, Marco, but don't. If you have the chance to complete your mission do so." He nodded and waved as she trailed after the three elves and Temeres traveling back the way they had come. When they were gone the other elves led the two Chosen deeper into the underground city.

For nearly a mile they followed a series of alcove-lined passages, each hollow an elfin home. Then they entered a large gloomy room. Across the room an intimidating iron door sat guarded by two burly elves. "These two are expected," their lead escort began, "The Master of Earth will wish to see them."

"And they are?" the taller door guard asked.

"I am Tekalo, Chosen of Water. My companion is Marco, Chosen of Earth," Tekalo answered.

"I will take them to the Earth Master," the guard said, unlocking the door and gesturing for them to enter. A short dark tunnel spilled away from the door, angling downward. For ten feet, they felt their way forward, their eyes slowly adjusting to the darkness. Then the walls fell away and they found themselves in a giant underground dome, a black glass lake filling the bottom, and all of it dominated by a giant stalagmite in the center. Lights twinkled across the lake's surface, pinpricks of orange dancing like tiny stars. The guard led them toward a short pier that jutted from the slick rock shore where several small skiffs waited. Taking one of the larger boats the three took turns paddling toward the spire. At its base another dock greeted them where more elves helped them disembark.

"The Earth Master is expecting us," Tekalo told one of the new elves who then hurriedly disappeared into the spire palace. They followed after the elf, wending their way up several flights of smooth, carved stairs until they reached a slick black door.

The guard knocked and Myrth's familiar rumbling bass greeted them. The elf ushered them into a somber, well-lit room. Myrth sat on his black cushion, back to the door. "Your apprentice has arrived Master Myrth," the elf introduced, bowing as Marco and Tekalo entered.

Marco's heart skipped a beat. *"Myrth's apprentice,"* his mind screamed.

"My what?" Myrth asked, his deep bass voice echoing in the room.

"Your apprentice and Water's as well," the elf repeated as Myrth looked over his bony shoulder at them.

"Leave us," he commanded, his voice delving lower. With a deep bow, the elf disappeared. Marco swallowed hard meeting Myrth's eyes as the Master studied them from where he sat. An intense anger burned through them. Once the elf's booted footsteps faded away Myrth sprung, stepping lightly toward them, a rumble filling the room as the doorway disappeared sealed by the Earth.

"Master Myrth," Tekalo began, "We have come as you requested." The Land-Nymph bowed low grandly flourishing his hand. Myrth ignored him, his pearl-gray eyes boring into Marco instead, pulling a wave of panic from the man. Marco dropped to his knees, remembering Nepo's anger in the courtyard the other morning. He closed his eyes and bowed his head.

"I don't recall having an Apprentice," Myrth whispered, the room around them slowly shimmering in response to his agitation.

"No Master," Marco said. His voice shook and he took a deep breath to steady himself. "You don't. But —"

"Hush, Marco," Myrth cut him off running a clawed hand through his black hair. Marco fell silent. "You are here Tekalo," Myrth continued, "Where are Nepo and the others?" he asked.

"They should be here soon," Tekalo assured him.

"Really?" Marco could feel Myrth's disbelief trickle off the word as he turned his fierce gray eyes on Tekalo.

Belatedly Tekalo knelt beside Marco, "Nepo wished for us to stay in Sea Spray," he stammered. "But you ordered all of us here. So we came. They shouldn't be more than a day behind us." Myrth took his hand from Marco's head and closed his eyes retreating into the Mage Realm. He stood over them in silence for some time, the swaying room settling as his anger dissipated. When Myrth at last opened his eyes they flashed dangerously. Marco swallowed hard and looked back at the floor.

"Commander Sylus has just told me a very interesting tale," he said. "Nepo requests that I keep you both locked safely away until his arrival tonight or early tomorrow. Sylus too would like to speak to you," he said to Marco. "Tekalo, if you would be so kind?" Myrth continued, indicating a far corner of the room. Tekalo rose dejectedly and went to sit in the corner. Walls grew from the ceiling and floor trapping the Land-Nymph.

Sighing, Myrth knelt before Marco. "Sylus also told me much about you, Marco." Marco kept his gaze on the floor, waiting. "He says you can see the Earth Cloud and work it from this realm," the hawk-man breathed.

"Yes Master," Marco answered, his words barely audible.

"That is rare strength even among the Soil Children. For a Man to wield such power..." Myrth trailed off. He contemplated Marco for a silent minute. "I cannot let you run around untrained."

"I would like training," Marco said looking up at Myrth, "and answers to my questions." An eager smile crossed his face.

"Yes, but first you must be made my Apprentice."

"Yes Master," Marco said, heart leaping at his decision.

"And I think I will wait for Nepo and Sylus to finish with you first," Myrth finished with a barely concealed sneer, his eyes flashing angrily. "Otherwise I would have to defend you from Nepo and you may have noticed, he's a bit taller and stronger than me." Myrth indicated the corner opposite Tekalo. Marco's smile faded. He stood and went where he was told sinking to the floor, back against the far wall. The floor and ceiling erupted into walls, sealing him in a three foot square box identical to Tekalo's. With a soft chuckle Marco pushed the Earth Cloud away drilling a hole in the wall, widening it until it framed his and Myrth's faces perfectly. Myrth glared at him through the newly made window. "I trust you to stay there Marco," he said, voice hard. "I can incapacitate you if I need to." Laughter dying in his throat, Marco frowned. "Close it," Myrth ordered.

"Yes Master," Marco said as he let the hole close. Around him silence grew thick and with nothing else to do he curled up on the stone floor and slept.

Long after nightfall an elf returned to Myrth's chamber, waking Marco as he knocked and entered. "Master, the Water Master and his party have arrived. They are ferrying across the lake now." Marco sat up slowly, stretching as much as the small room would allow.

"Bring Nepo and Sylus to me and settle the others with my people," Myrth instructed beyond the wall. Silence descended again punctuated with the occasional rustling of cloth, presumably as Myrth dressed.

Marco chewed over the thought of Nepo and Sylus being angry. Disappointment welled up in his heart. *"Was following Tekalo a good idea? I couldn't have let him go alone."* Shortly three sets of footsteps marched up the stairs and into Myrth's room past his walled-in corner. There was more silence then Myrth rumbled, "Now tell me how your apprentice beat you here by half a day."

"Master," Sylus began, "Nepo ordered Marco and Tekalo to stay in Sea Spray."

"Which they did not! Now they are both in harm's way," Nepo shouted.

"I need them here, Nepo," Myrth said.

"Aren't you just being overly cautious?" the Water Master asked. "You have my guard and yours. You have Jay and Marladon. What good are two apprentices?"

"Oracle has seen this battle. I need both humans," Myrth answered quietly.

"Marco and D'Mique," Sylus added a tired note in his voice.

"You should know that I have not yet apprenticed Marco. I thought you would like to talk to him first," Myrth continued ignoring Sylus.

Another minute of silence engulfed the room beyond the wall then Nepo hissed, "So, where is my apprentice and his wayward friend?" A window drilled through the stone revealing the lion-man to Marco.

Sylus, staring at the corner where Tekalo waited, smiled, "Ahh," he said, "So peaceful, so unaware."

"So dead," Nepo growled. He stalked toward Tekalo leaving Marco's field of vision as Sylus turned his glare on the man.

"Marco," Sylus began closing the distance between them, throwing open the confining walls.

"Sorry, Commander," Marco said hurrying to stand. Sylus backhanded him before he could straighten sending his head rocking backward, stars bursting across his vision as the stone greeted him. He stepped away from the elf, sidling along the wall until he'd reached the corner eyes warily fixed on the commander.

Sylus heaved a sigh and closed his eyes. "We made a deal," he said. "I made a deal! You and Tekalo for the rest of Nepo's honor guard. You had no right to void that deal! Nepo can take his honor guard home because of you!"

"I—"

"No! I don't want any words from you. I just wanted your pain," he hissed raising his fist. Marco flinched as he continued, "A little pain as a warning not to cross me again." Marco looked down at his feet and then turned away. Sylus glared at him a moment more and then turned and left. Standing in silence Marco looked out at Myrth. The Earth Master was sitting on his black cushion watching Marco, face studiously blank. Sylus knelt beside Myrth his back to Marco. After almost a minute the doorway filled with Nepo, blocking Marco's view.

Marco's breath caught in his throat and his heart skipped a beat as the Semian entered. The Water Master loomed over him, "So, what makes you think you don't have to follow your commander's direct orders?" he asked. Marco pressed against the wall willing it to make room for him as Nepo closed the distance. Looking askance he noticed that the stone had obeyed him and molded around his body. Then Nepo's large claws clicked against the dark stone inches from his face.

Marco swallowed, "I didn't want Tekalo to go alone. He was planning to go through the Forest of Fear. I only wanted to keep him safe," he stammered.

"So now disobedience is noble?" Nepo leaned close, his soft breath tickling against Marco's skin.

"No, Master Nepo."

"You have broken Commander Sylus' word. My honor guard and I need not stay."

"I know." Nepo hissed loudly, fangs bared just above Marco's neck. Marco pulled away burrowing deeper into the stone.

Nepo pulled back and a half second later continued, "You are not mine to discipline Marco, so I will leave it to Sylus' discretion. But know this, Myrth is not a kind Master. You would be best off not trying him as you have tried me."

"Yes, Master Nepo," Marco said, letting out the breath he'd been holding. He kept his eyes averted. After staring down at him for a full minute Nepo left. Marco watched him take a seat next to Myrth opposite Sylus.

Nepo sighed and shrugged. "As we are already here," he said to Myrth, "We shall stay."

"Well that's very kind of you," Myrth said. "Marco!" he called, "Join us!" Marco pushed away from the wall and turned to stare at the mold his body had made. Reaching out to the Earth Cloud he smoothed the wall, filling the void, before entering the main room and glancing at his fellow prisoner. Tekalo sat in his corner, sniffling. He pulled himself straighter and surreptitiously wiped his face when Marco looked at him, though his sniffle and the bright red swelling across his cheek ruined the effect. Marco hurriedly looked away, trying to lessen the apprentice's embarrassment, and sat between Nepo and Sylus directly across from Myrth. Myrth smiled at him, but there was no joy in it, "I am the Master of Earth," he said quietly. "I offer you the opportunity to be my Chosen Apprentice, Marco of the Nesting, Mage of Man."

"Before you accept or decline," Nepo added, "Let me explain. The Master is responsible for setting the natural pattern of the forcelines. The Natural Pattern," he repeated deliberately emphasizing each word, "Deviating from the set patterns could destroy our world."

Sylus interrupted him, "When a mage alters the pattern, it returns to the set pattern once the mage has removed his will. When a Master alters the pattern it stays altered."

"What you do will not be undone. Masters do not err," Nepo continued. The words sent a thrill along Marco's arms.

"I am one with the Earth forcelines," Myrth said, and Marco looked back at him. "They are tied to my life. If ever something should happen to me the forcelines would drift, the Pattern lost. If anything ever happened to the forcelines it would affect my life." Myrth took a deep breath and closed his eyes. "When I bind you as my apprentice, I will tie the forcelines to your life as well. In this way when I die, the patterns will not drift but will then be yours alone to maintain."

"There is no way to undo this." Nepo added, pulling Marco's face up with a strong hand under his chin. His intense honey eyes bored into Marco's own. "Now is the time to decline. There is no shame in doing so." Marco met Nepo's glare for a long minute. He felt the Semian willing him to back out, to drop his eyes and retreat to the corner, to stop being foolish. He gently pulled away from Nepo not looking away until the Water Master's gaze softened. Then he sat in silence, staring at his hands where they rested on his knees.

"This is what I need to do," he whispered. He met Myrth's eyes. "This is what I need to do," he repeated, finding strength as he spoke. "I need training. Only you can train me. Would you train me if I were not your apprentice?"

"No," Myrth replied.

"People have told me that I am a strong Earth Mage. Not only that but I'm human. I can do nothing greater than become a Master." A fierce light ignited within Myrth's pearl eyes.

"I don't think you'll have to worry about that anytime soon," he snapped.

"Could anyone else train me? Commander Sylus leaves me doubtful," Marco added, glancing at the elf.

"You could find strong Earth Mages in the Potentate, but none as strong as you," Myrth answered. "In time, you would best them and be left to train yourself."

"That is unwise," Sylus added, head bowed.

"Then the choice is made for us Master Nepo," Marco said with a nod, looking up at the lion-man.

"Perhaps we will not regret it," Nepo replied, baring his fangs.

"Lie down with your head here," Myrth instructed, indicating the black pillow in front of him. Marco did as he was told. "Close your eyes and join me in the Mage Realm." Marco did so, constructing bodies for himself and the Master within his mind. They stood together surrounded by the golden Earth Cloud. "Look at me," Myrth directed, "Really look, and tell me what you see." Marco studied Myrth for a moment before he realized that the cloud passed through the Semian not just around him.

"The Earth Cloud drifts through you," he said.

Nodding Myrth reached out and laid a hand on Marco's head in both realms. "Don't fight it," he said, his voice issuing straight into Marco's head. Marco took a deep breath and tried to relax. A wave of cold pushed over him, working from his head down. He gasped and opened his eyes. Sylus and Nepo had shifted position taking hold of his arms. Tekalo was at his feet, an unreadable grimace on his face. The soft gold light of the Earth Cloud tinted his vision as tendrils of Earth undulated above him. Watching from both realms, the tendrils settled on his skin before sinking into it.

He screamed, surprise, fear and pain balled into sound. As the Earth sank, icy darkness pierced him, thousands of pin pricks like grains of sand burrowing through flesh and bone. Buried deep, it quested through him, following his limbs to his stomach, up his spine. He screamed again, struggling against Sylus and Nepo, trying to run from the power as it settled in his head. Then, with a tick, the world went dark and his struggle ended. Warm blackness covered him, buoyed him, and caressed him. He took an experimental breath and found that he was still alive. He contemplated moving, but a too-heavy weightiness fell upon him and all he could do was spin. A slow, lazy spinning. He tried again to lift his head or an arm and when that proved futile he struggled to wiggle his toes. Only then did he realize he had no body to move. He was only the cold darkness spinning lazily. There was no body spinning, no heart beating no lungs breathing. Just Marco the Dark, spinning. The thought of his name slowed the spin, lightened the darkness and the heavy weight of his mind. *"Marco,"* he thought to himself. *"I am Marco."*

With that the spin ended and falling replaced it. But like the spin, it was a lazy, slow fall. Downward Marco traveled and as he did the world grew warmer, brighter, the blackness replaced by a redness. *"Fire,"* Marco thought, *"My friend."*

"Two coherent thoughts and still falling? I'm impressed." Myrth's deep voice rippled the red-dark around Marco. *"You've lain long enough in the power, Marco. Time to come up. Up and out of the Womb."*

"Myrth," Marco thought and the world snapped back into the solid light of the physical realm. With a shriek, Marco flung himself forward pulling away from Sylus. He fought against Nepo, his skin burning where the Water Master touched him. Nepo released him with a sigh.

"Easy, Marco," Tekalo offered. "Calm yourself. The pain of the first binding will soon fade." Marco focused on the world around him and concentrated on slowing his breathing. His body was back, the light was back, but the dark spinning blackness remained just behind his eyes. He closed his eyes and started to lay back smiling at the thought of returning to the Dark. "No, no, no," Tekalo chided, grabbing him by the upper arm. "Don't go back. Not yet." Marco glared at the Land-Nymph.

"You will learn to travel to and from the Womb in time Marco," Myrth rumbled behind him. "For now I need you to remain in the physical realm."

Marco closed his eyes and sighed but said nothing.

"Now," Myrth said, "if you concentrate you can feel my presence. Reach inside you, not out to the Mage Realm."

Marco concentrated, delving into his bones where the sand grains of power had come to rest. Once there he felt a strong pull toward Myrth. "Yes," he said. "I can feel you." There seemed to be an echoing pull. "There's an echo," he said.

"That is Sylus," Myrth supplied. Marco concentrated on the echo and he could feel the elf at the other end. Faintly, just at the edge of his senses, there was a second echo similar to Sylus but different. Marco opened his eyes. "There is no hurry to become accustomed to the power," Myrth continued, "But I ask that you not enter the Mage Realm for now. This is a condition all Chosen abide by for the first few weeks." Marco closed his eyes and took a cleansing breath before nodding. He could feel the Earth in his bones, the deep patience hiding Fire and rage, and the Earth all around him, the ponderous dance of the planet.

Myrth sighed. "We are joined, Marco. We are one. Rest until you can stand again."

"It takes a while to get your bearings," Tekalo offered.

Marco nodded, "Thank you, Myrth," he said.

"Master," Myrth corrected. "And you had better not be thinking Tekalo and Nepo are the typical Master-Apprentice relationship. If Tekalo was my

Apprentice, he wouldn't have strayed more than once I assure you." Myrth glared at Tekalo as he spoke. The apprentice Land-Nymph looked away.

"Now," Nepo began, changing the subject, "when you called to Sylus earlier, you said Jay had arrived and that there are only three of us missing."

"Yes," Myrth reached behind him and pulled out his Fire Jar setting it in front of Nepo. I have received word that D'Mique and Trillip are headed toward Ebony Bay."

"The Black Lands," Nepo said.

"Yes, but I get no reply from Marladon." His words dropped the temperature in the room and both Nepo and Sylus stared at the enclosed Fire in the jar.

"He probably left his jar behind on purpose and is hunting the daemon by himself," Nepo supplied.

Myrth nodded. "Maybe. Fire doesn't appear to be drifting so at least he's alive. Oracle says that we will all gather here. I have no reason to doubt him. It is simply a matter of time."

"Master," Sylus sighed, "How long do we wait before traveling to Nightmare? Oracle is a very good seer I know. But it is Time's nature to shift." Myrth stared at the Fire and didn't reply.

"If we know the daemon is there," Nepo added, "We should go there."

Fallen into Shadow

The next day saw them on the road again, their Palace Black traded for two farm-quality mares, nine days' worth of travel rations divvied up between the saddle packs. As they rode, one eye on the ever-fainter trail to their left, D'Mique struggled to piece together her memories from the day before. As they were leaving she had been treated to a brief glimpse of the elf who had saved her. But nothing more. "I just can't remember anything after..." she trailed off. She remembered the mange fight, and she remembered replaying it in her head as she rocked back and forth on the Black's back. "I must have faded out as I rode," she thought, "I don't remember the inn or the elf." So Trillip had filled in the gaps relaying her struggle with the poison, the decision to go east in pursuit of the daemon, and the message the elf carried to Myrth.

Three days' travel along the trade route brought them to the edge of a dark wood. Ahead of her Trillip slowed, stopping at the verge. As D'Mique approached a thick silence fell over the forest suppressing even birdsong and dimming the afternoon sunlight. Gray moss covered the tree limbs, hanging down in dusty lace curtains, a stray breeze swinging the strands back and forth, providing the only movement beneath the heavy canopy. D'Mique felt a sudden pang of homesickness, "It feels the same as the Dark Forest," she said, stopping beside Trillip. "I've been away so long," she added silently.

"Yes," he said, "This is Bantu, a daemon stronghold."

Swallowing, she squinted northward, searching the far distance. A day after they left the trade route inn she had lost the Greater Daemon's trail. Despite continued searching, no sign remained. "Should we go around?" she asked at last. "Maybe we could find the trail."

Trillip shrugged. "Bantu runs along the coast between Ebony Bay and the Black Lands. It's longer than it is wide. If the daemon didn't cross back to the south that means it's gone to one of those places instead. We should rule out Ebony Bay first then find the Fire Master." He continued, "He rules the Black Lands," when he noticed her confusion.

"I wish we could know that the daemon didn't go south," she said.

He smiled, "I think you would have seen a sign of it crossing the road again if it had."

"It could be hiding in there," she said, nodding at the forest.

Trillip studied the sky for a moment in response then smiled at her. "I think we can make the fort before nightfall, but if not the trade route is patrolled by goblins."

"Trillip," she said before repeating her observation, "We can't ignore that possibility."

"No, but for now we should go to Ebony Bay and then, if the daemon isn't there, find Marladon. By meeting up with him we can contact Myrth again and let him know we lost the trail just west of Bantu." Nodding, chewing on his words, D'Mique pulled her sword and started forward. Drawing his sword as well Trillip followed.

The darkness soon closed in around them enshrouding them in a soft, familiar silence. When the last of the sunlight danced far behind them D'Mique stopped, closed her eyes and took a deep cleansing breath, a familiar ritual from home. She opened her eyes and smiled. "I never realized how much I loved the quiet of the Dark Forest."

"I suppose, growing up in a stronghold it makes sense to enjoy the daemon's quiet," Trillip replied.

"I never understood why my ancestors settled there," she continued, "The villagers cower behind their walls and fear the forest in daylight and at night, but we stay anyway."

"Perhaps others like the quiet as well," he opined.

"Do you?" she asked, a teasing smile crossing her lips.

"No," he said curtly pushing past her. Frowning, she followed.

The hours crept past as they traveled, the gloom deepening. D'Mique scanned the ground for signs of both the Greater Daemon and the Black Daemons that lived here. She found neither on the hard dry earth, although she took comfort from the occasional deer track or bird feather that caught her eye. The trade route narrowed as they traveled as if the stronghold forest intended to suffocate it. Tendrils of moss draped low, curtaining the underbrush. *"I think the Suns have set,"* D'Mique thought looking around and up at the canopy covering the road. The sky patches above were a deep indigo blue. "Trillip," she started. Then suddenly they broke from the trees and entered a large clearing, a stone fort squatting before them. Trillip paused a moment to survey the area. The Fiery Sisters had disappeared below the horizon and the last of their red light trailed away across the sky. Rysk sat just shy of the zenith struggling vainly against the darkness. The fort's gate had been shut for the night, bolted against the daemons that lurked in the shadows.

"We'll have to knock," Trillip murmured continuing toward the structure, his shoulders visibly relaxing.

D'Mique swallowed, relaxing as well, and hurried after him. At the gate he rapped on the thick planks with the pommel of his sword. They waited. Trillip knocked again, three harsh explosions that shattered the quiet of the clearing.

"Who knocks?" a gruff voice asked at last, a small window opening near the top of the wall. The cat Semian glared at them, his pale amber eyes aglow in the gloom.

"I am Trillip, Land-Nymph, in service to the Earth Master. This is my companion D'Mique, Child of Man," he introduced.

"You come late to the fort," the Semian replied.

"Yes." Trillip offered nothing more.

"Do you mean to leave the gate barred?" D'Mique asked incredulous.

"Daemon you are not, so enter," the guard answered formally, sparing her a glare before slamming the window closed. A series of clanking locks and thudding bars followed his disappearance and soon the gate swung open, closing quickly behind them after they entered, locks and bars hastily replaced.

Beyond the wall, wagons and horses jumbled together in the yard, a tumultuous blend of scents and colors. Across from the gate a large inn-like building offered shelter, warmth and a bed. "No food though," D'Mique thought, "if they do things the same here as at home." Trillip dismounted and led his horse through the throng, D'Mique trailing him. After tying their horses to an empty post and grabbing their saddle packs, they pushed past a number of armored goblins and into the building. Inside, the fort's inn was divided into a dozen three-walled semi-private rooms, each with a small fire-pit, two cots and a small table. Extra bedding lay stacked in the center, along with firewood. Trillip chose an empty area setting down his packs as D'Mique sank onto one of the cots and lay down.

She lay still for a moment surveying the other guests. A handful of human and Semian merchants milled together around two different fires. They laughed jovially and grinned mightily as they talked, shaking hands as deals formed. Apart from them sat their guards, the majority of them goblins in the plain functional armor of the wandering soldier-for-hire. A tight group of Semian guards all wearing the same muted green livery controlled the room opposite them. Like the goblins the Semians watched more than they talked, painfully aware of every move made within the fort. "Here," Trillip said, setting a pile of dried fruit in front of her. "Eat." When it was gone she drifted toward sleep.

From the soft sweet darkness a jumble of shouts and screams awakened her. D'Mique bolted from the bed reaching for her sword before her eyes focused on the room around her. Trillip stood near sword poised across his shoulder. Beyond him, she saw goblins clambering for the door, donning helmets and jerkins as they ran. Glowing liquid color marked the passage of the Semians as they joined the fray. "We're under attack!" she screamed starting forward as well. Trillip grabbed her, using her momentum to swing her around, hugging her close.

"Wait, Lady. You're still weak, let the goblins take the first rush," he ordered, sharp and sweet in her ear. Head against his chest she waited, listening to the clanging rage of battle beyond the inn, drowning all but the desperate, high-pitched equine screams. Beneath it all, against her skin, she felt the soft steady beat of Trillip's heart. "Now," he hissed, releasing her as he launched himself toward the door. She followed him, his candy pink hair a beacon in the hazy gloom.

Outside, screaming horses swam around gutted overturned wagons, the scattered belongings strewn across the yard in ruins. Huge black shapes fought in the middle of it all, swords flashing as goblins and Semians dove around the shadowy mass. Beaks and claws flashed in the sudden glare of torchlight as the bravest merchants forged after their guards daggers drawn. "Mange!" Someone shouted as the light danced off writhing scales bringing definition to the daemon-spawn horde. D'Mique charged forward joining with a pair of dark-skinned goblins as they strove to kill one. Her blade landed squarely on its flank pulling its head around to face her. Outflanked, the mange toppled to the ground a goblin blade sunk deep into its throat, black blood pooling at her feet.

"Lady!" Trillip shouted, his blade flashing beside her as another fierce beak snapped closed just shy of her face. He parried its attack and the goblin raced forward driving his blade into its chest. The mange's knees buckled and glass broke beneath it as it toppled forward. The goblins worked to retrieve their blades as Trillip struck its head, silencing it and adding another body to the growing pile of corpses. D'Mique took a step back sword ready as she surveyed the scene. Two huge mange broke from the main force and ran toward the main gate, ramming it with heavy shoulders in an attempt to break it down. She watched amazed as they charged again. "What are they doing?" she asked. "They climbed the walls to get in," she thought, "Why bother breaking the door down?"

The second charge knocked the gate outward, splintering it as it fell from its hinges. D'Mique, startled by their success, hesitated only a moment before starting toward it. "Trillip!" she shouted. Deep black shapes scuttled through the broken door—four sharp spikes for legs, a human torso with massive arms, and a goat's head. The daemon's eyes were glowing milky white instead of burning with fire but there was no mistaking them. "Daemons!" she shrieked increasing her speed and raising her sword. The daemons turned toward her bleating in answer to her scream. The closest one swung its sword high overhead bringing it down in a sharp arch toward her head. Her own blade caught it just short of her face, deflecting it as the force jolted through her arm. She ducked away and sliced at the daemon's torso, licking along it, just deep enough to draw blood. Chattering, the daemon swung again and she dodged away drawing her sword back, ready for another large swing. A second daemon joined them, a heavy mace descending as it charged forward. D'Mique rolled away kicking out at the spindle blade-legs. She connected knocking the mace-wielding daemon to the ground. As it struggled to regain its feet silver light sliced through the gloom and Trillip's sword severed its head. D'Mique scrambled to her feet as its head hit the ground, her eyes following the Land-Nymph into battle. She charged after him toward the broken door, joining a trio of goblins as they pushed forward in the Land-Nymph's wake.

Daemons closed around them but fell back as goblin blades cut deep. D'Mique dodged a high swing dropping to one knee. Pain shot through her as she landed, another daemon tripping over her, the sharp hoof that formed the tip of its blade-like leg driving into her calf. She bit back a scream and struggled to clear herself from the beast as her sword sliced easily into its side. It threw itself away from her, white goat-eyes swimming to red flame before it screamed in rage and fear. Blades dug into it as she pulled herself up struggling to balance. Two gray-furred Semians appeared beside her as she surveyed the courtyard. They too watched as goblin blades turned the daemons back. Near the front of the group she found Trillip, also falling back as the goblins pushed forward, driving the daemon-spawn away from the fort. No one followed them into the surrounding trees choosing instead to hold the gate and wall, satisfied when the last of the beasts had retreated into the darkness.

Relieved, D'Mique limped forward, pushing past Semians and goblins to stand beside Trillip. He surveyed her, his smile turning to a concerned grimace when his eyes landed on her leg. Taking her by the hand he pulled her to a nearby wagon box and sat down. "Let me see," he instructed, lifting her leg and setting her foot gingerly between his thighs. Only when she saw the blood-soaked cloth below her knee did pain course through her, tickling along her leg and up her spine. She gasped as he explored the wound, long fingers gently moving along the tear in her pant leg where the daemon's blade-foot had stabbed. "It's not deep," he said after pulling the thick wool away from the wound and studying it. She met his gaze catching a flash of fear in his emerald eyes before he looked away, studiously contemplating her calf. For the first time she saw the blood matting his curls. Concerned she combed through his hair searching for a wound. Trillip hissed, suddenly grabbing her hands squeezing hard. D'Mique froze, her heart leaping as his bared fangs glittered. "Don't," he warned, releasing her. The warmth of his hands sat heavy on her skin.

"But you're bleeding," she protested.

"It's nothing," he said, "I'll take care of it."

Swallowing she stared hard at him. "I'm not willing to leave it at that," she said a moment later. Trillip met her glare, brow furrowed in concentration.

"Fine," he said, "You can help." He stood and took her by the hand leading her across the yard at a steady, limping pace. Around them goblins boasted of their kills while the Semians went to work moving bodies—horses, mange and Black Daemons - into a pile. Scattered amongst the broken wagons, merchants surveyed their losses—some of them weeping openly. Inside they returned to their cots and Trillip pulled a wad of cloth from his saddle bag and tossed it to her. D'Mique wet the cloth with water from her canteen and nodded toward Trillip's cot. With a frozen grimace painted across his alabaster face he obeyed, sinking gently to the bed.

D'Mique ran her fingers through his soft curls, gently pulling the bloody mats apart. Near the crown of his head just short of his right ear, a shard of glass fell away, revealing a shallow gash. She dabbed at it, gentle but persistent. Trillip grabbed her wrist, sucking air sharply through his teeth. She stopped, waiting for him to release her. When he didn't let go she returned to work anyway, cleaning the wound and moving down away from it. Using more water from the canteen, she started washing the blood from his hair. He tossed his head back as the cold water hit his forehead. Stopping, she looked down waiting for him to settle.

Red rivulets coursed across his marble skin as if his candy pink hair had lost some of its color in the wash. Their eyes met and he blinked slowly as calm certainty filled them. *"He's...beautiful,"* she thought, goose bumps rising along her arms as she became very aware of how close she stood to him, how warm his hand on hers. *"Stop,"* she chided, forcing herself to break eye contact and stare at the top of his head, *"Focus,"* she added, looking at the bloody rag in her hand. He stood, pulling her hand away from his head and down to his chest. She looked at his face again, watched the sadness grow around the corners of his eyes and tug at the edges of his mouth. *"He has a wife,"* she thought, *"sort of."* Trillip leaned forward cautiously invading her space. Swallowing D'Mique closed her eyes. She felt him hovering above her a moment before his lips brushed hers and fire spilled through her. Gasping, eyes open, she watched him pull back and straighten. A sudden hunger had joined the sadness in his eyes. He took a deep breath and looked away.

"My apologies, Lady," he whispered. "I had no right."

She shook her head, "Please Trillip, don't apologize."

He looked at her hard for a long moment then smiled. "I rescind my apology. But it was inappropriate." He returned to his cot. "In all the fighting," he said changing the subject, "did you notice the daemon's eyes?"

D'Mique thought a moment then nodded, "Milky white, like the scalawags. But I saw one revert to daemon-fire after it was wounded."

"And the mange as well," Trillip added. He sat chewing his lower lip in thought.

She caught herself staring at his sharp fangs as she nodded. With a shake of her head she added, "The mange tonight scaled the wall when they attacked the fort. Then they broke down the door and let the daemon's in." Trillip took a long slow breath and stared at the ceiling, his narrow chest rising and falling slowly. "Are coordinated attacks normal?" she asked quietly. He shook his head but didn't elaborate. With a sigh of her own she lay back staring at the ceiling as well. "Has the plan changed?" She glanced across at him when he didn't answer and found him staring at her, the weight of his gaze speeding her heart. "Trillip," she added, tasting his name, remembering the heat that had poured through her, the feel of his lips pressed against hers. He focused, visibly pulling his attention to her words. "Are we still going to Ebony?"

"Yes," he whispered. "I see no reason not to. We should travel with one of the merchants just in case the daemons attack again. Then on to Fortress Nightmare." He rolled over facing away from her as he spoke, "Get some sleep, Lady," he added. "We have a busy day tomorrow."

Another day's travel through the close darkness of Bantu Forest saw Trillip and D'Mique reach the other side. Although they had failed to formally travel with a merchant, enough of them streamed along the track that it didn't matter. Guards bristling with weapons kept pace with them along the route. With the forest dwindling away behind them the land fell away in a series of cliffs and spread out to greet a dark steel-colored sea. The port town of Ebony Bay twinkled between the cliffs and the waves many of the buildings stilted against tides and storm surges. Trillip stopped to survey the city and D'Mique pulled up beside him. She sighed shallowly, accustomed to the ache in her side, aware of the tension too deep a breath would place on her ribs. She gave the road a cursory glance but the only signs she could find were those of passing carts and horses, merchants on their way to the sea. "Are we going there?" she asked nodding toward Ebony Bay.

"Do we need to?" Trillip asked.

With a shrug she said, "I only see merchants Trillip. There's still no sign of the daemon. Maybe if we head north we can find his path crossing the road."

"If it isn't in Ebony it went to Nightmare," Trillip said—a matter of fact and not for the first time. D'Mique swung her horse north along the road staying close to the edge of the forest, eyes on the track as the animal plodded along. Trillip followed her without a word and they traveled northward for the remainder of the day. As they walked they were passed by the occasional merchant party trudging southward to Ebony Bay, the guards—Semian and goblin alike—paying them little mind. As the Fiery Sisters sank they pulled aside, trading the road for a copse of trees where they made camp. D'Mique clambered gingerly from the horse and sank to the ground. "We will be in the Black Lands in three more days," Trillip said closely watching her movements.

D'Mique nodded. "Still no signs Trillip," she added, staring out at the field to the west, the tall waving grass lost to the descending soft gray twilight. "What happens if there are no more signs...at all," she murmured.

Trillip closed his eyes in thought answering without opening them, "Then we will know there is no more sign of him beyond the Crossroads. That knowledge will also help Myrth."

For three days they traveled the north road as it followed the coastline; the land around them growing sparse and rocky as they walked. Each day passed the same as that first with no sign of the daemon. Each day ended the same as well, a hasty camp created as Nix and Col dropped below the horizon and D'Mique grew more troubled. "Where did it go?" she asked the second night, not expecting an answer and receiving only a desolate silence from Trillip, punctuated by his glass-green contemplative stare. Not for the first time their eyes lingered on each other longer than necessary and they looked away from each other awkwardly. The next morning the road led them into a series of foothills dotted with a series of black rock outcroppings. Beyond the foothills the land gently fell away, rolling out into a large bowl. Here the black outcroppings dominated and soil gave way to igneous rock for large stretches of earth. The grass of the plain was gone replaced by waxy, olive-green bushes and thick-skinned trees. D'Mique shook her head, "I doubt I'll find anything out there," she muttered.

Trillip nodded. "Let's go find Marladon and contact Myrth. We can let him know what we haven't found." He started down the road into the valley adding, "The fortress is at the center of the bowl. We will be there soon enough and you can rest." They descended to the valley floor and wended through a series of small copses and outcroppings. Here and there the lava-scarred land burst forth in color—tiny white and purple flowers belying the harsh landscape. As the afternoon wore on Trillip and D'Mique found the road heading toward a thick blanket of fog. "Usually," Trillip said noting the bank ahead, "the fog stays in the fortress' moat. Strange," he added.

"Nightmare is in there?" D'Mique asked warily staring at the fog bank.

Trillip nodded watching the fog as well, not breathing for a moment. "There may be beasts in there," he said, oddly emphasizing the word 'beasts.'

"Beasts?" D'Mique repeated. "More myths proving to be real?" she asked.

Trillip eyed her skeptically before continuing, ignoring her question, "We should reach Nightmare in an hour."

D'Mique sat for another minute, then dismounting, she drew her sword and started into the fog, Trillip following suit with a grimace.

Myrth followed the Earth Currents, searching, as he had done every day. Nepo's glares had grown deeper as they waited and as the days passed. "Why wait Myrth," the Water Master had asked. "Everyone is here except your second human. We shouldn't be waiting. We know the daemon must be in the Black Lands—" Myrth waved away the remembered argument and studied the Black Lands again. From where he floated in the Earth current it looked the same as before. Fire and Life and Earth, Air and Water, all in their rightful place.

"The daemon must be there but it's still hidden," he acknowledged silently. Heaving a sigh he opened his eyes returning to the Physical Realm. A half-seen shimmer sat in his head, a brief remembered detail from the realm he had just stepped from. "Wait," he said aloud. He stood, spinning to face the Black Lands. Closing his eyes again he returned to the Mage Realm and the forcelines. The Black Lands loomed before him in another instance. Myrth gasped. They were suddenly covered in Shadow. In a split second, black roiling clouds of power had pulsed outward from the central valley engulfing the low volcanic plains. Myrth watched as they traveled away from the plains, lapping at the mountains and forests.

"Myrth!" Oracle's call shattered the Mage Realm.

"I saw!" Myrth shouted back aloud. He stepped back into the Mage Realm studying the Black Lands once again. "Marladon, where are you?" he whispered. He looked to Fire where it pulsed and danced beneath the planet; it remained chained to the Fire Master; Marladon still lived.

"Myrth?" Myrth opened his eyes slowly turning to focus on Nepo who stood in the doorway. Myrth sighed.

"The Black Lands are closed to us," he said. "They lay blanketed by Shadow."

Nodding, Nepo studied him for a moment. "Marladon?" he asked at last.

Myrth shook his head in reply. "The future has shifted. We can wait no more," he said instead. "We will leave for Nightmare in the morning."

Without a word Nepo turned and left.

D'Mique moved silently through the fuzzy gray world, listening intently to the muffled sounds around her. The thick fog parted only grudgingly, cutting visibility down to a few feet in any direction. Half-remembered stories of the monsters that lived in the fog flitted at the edges of her consciousness, but she tamped them down before the fear that accompanied them could trickle through her. As they approached the fortress the fog thinned slightly, though it was still a thick veil around them. Deserted houses loomed out of gray curtains suddenly reminding D'Mique of Sawelt. *"The farmers,"* she thought, *"They probably fled."* She wondered aloud, "Did they go to the fortress or into the hills?"

"Probably the latter," Trillip answered. After a mile the farms disappeared from the roadside, returning Trillip and D'Mique to their featureless world.

D'Mique felt herself pass into an open space though she still couldn't see more than a few yards in any direction. She counted off two hundred yards. "A defensible clearing," she thought. Trillip grabbed her arm and pulled her to a stop beside him. "Wait. We're here."

She studied the fog before them and as she stared the vague outlines of a large stone wall loomed before them. At the base of the wall the ground fell away into a deep chasm where the fog coursed in slow eddies, lapping against the crust of black rock D'Mique stood on. Instinctively, she took a step back. Just to their left a thick wooden drawbridge stretched across the fog moat leading to an open unguarded gate.

Hefting her sword D'Mique followed Trillip across the bridge and into the fortress. Passing through the wall she noted the two portcullises that had been lifted to allow entrance. Beyond the gatehouse a cobblestone courtyard opened up around them. "It's like Dragon Ridge but without the roses," she thought. Where the Tower of Elements rose in Dragon Ridge a stout black stone fortress squatted. Four humans stood guard before the closed double doors crossbows leveled at Trillip and D'Mique.

Trillip stopped, holding up his hands, "We have come from the Earth Master, seeking an audience with the Fire Master," he said. Two guards exchanged glances then stepped forward. A third knocked sharply on the door which opened almost immediately as another human, this one wearing black and red livery, appeared. The guard and servant exchanged a few whispered words before the servant stepped forward holding his own hands out, mirroring Trillip.

"Your horses," he said gesturing toward them. D'Mique and Trillip handed them over, watching as they disappeared through the fog. Trillip started forward but the first two guards stopped him, aiming their crossbows at his chest again.

"No weapons within," one of the guards said motioning to their swords.

Trillip gaped. "Since when?" he asked.

"Since the Master decreed it," the guard sneered. Trillip stood in thought for a moment before dropping his sword to the stones. Reluctantly, D'Mique stooped and set hers down, swallowing back a sudden wave of panic.

"This way," the fourth guard said opening the door. They followed him into a vaulted main hall, the ceiling stretching upward into shadows. The fortress walls were polished obsidian, an unrelieved black. Only smoked-glass lanterns adorned the walls, there were no tapestries to keep the cold stone at bay, no show of golden wealth, not even a potted plant. They followed the main hallway as it sloped downward into the earth, passing by several branching corridors on either side. As they walked the barren hall warmed and at the end another set of large double doors sat closed.

The guard knocked on the door. "Go away!" a voice growled from the other side.

"Master, two visitors have come through the fog. They are sent by Master Myrth," the guard answered. Silence answered him.

"Send them away!" the Fire Master growled. The guard looked over his shoulder at Trillip and D'Mique. He shrugged.

Trillip glowered at the door and the guard in turn. "Master Marladon?" Trillip tried, "We must contact Myrth first."

Once again there was only silence for a long time, "Very well, enter if you must!" he answered at last. The guard opened the door for them, allowing them into the room and closing the door behind them with a solid echoing thunk.

The throne room beyond the door was a touchable inky black, reminding D'Mique of Myrth's own throne room. Here and there along the walls muted fires burned, not bright enough to alleviate the darkness for more than a few feet in any direction. "Master Marladon?" Trillip called.

"Here," the Fire Master replied from the far end of the room. A black flame came alive, its edges wavering, lined with white sparks. An enormous space separated them.

"This room," D'Mique whispered. *"It has to be the size of a small village,"* she thought. Slowly Trillip led them toward the strange flame, their footsteps loud in the palpable silence. When they reached the black flame a golden light clicked on. D'Mique blinked in the sudden brightness illuminating the throne of the Fire Master. It stood on a dais before them carved from black stone, matching the rest of the fortress. Trillip took a step back, gasping and reaching for a sword that was no longer there. D'Mique glanced from him to the figure on the throne. A memory nagged at the edge of her brain, *"Well, Master Marladon is a Mortak. But the Promise holds all species,"* Sylus' words from long ago echoed in her head. The figure on the throne was not a Mortak.

An ape Semian occupied the throne, a scepter lying across his lap, his deep red cloak spread out behind him. Black fur covered the Semian's body leaving only his face bare. He smiled at them revealing thick fangs. "Where's Master Marladon?" Trillip demanded.

"I'm afraid he had to step out for a time," the ape said. "He left me in charge," he flourished the scepter to draw their attention to it.

"Where is your Master?" Trillip asked, slowly, quietly, anger heating his words.

"I am here."

D'Mique spun around as the words slithered from the darkness. Behind them the shadows billowed upward, double blazing globes appearing in the deepest recess of the room as the Greater Daemon rose from the floor where it had been laying. It filled the room, the weak torchlight scintillating along its scales as it moved. D'Mique reached for her sword. *"Gone!"* she screamed in her head, "Gods above," she hissed. The daemon took a shuffling step toward them its mismatched legs carrying the sectional body smoothly over the glossy marble floor. Four blade-like legs and two massive forelimbs, ending in clawed, hand-like paws, clicked across the marble as it drew near, its horned head traveling down to greet them.

D'Mique retreated until she bumped into Trillip, her stomach falling away leaving her cold and shivering as it approached. The daemon dropped its large wedge-shape head to look at them. Its mouth split the narrow point of the wedge, its white globe eyes riding high in either corner. It smiled, its thin-lipped mouth pulling back over sword-sized teeth. "Take them to the dungeon," the daemon hissed. D'Mique pulled her eyes away from it as movement engulfed the throne room. All around them dragons melted from the shadows. Their narrow eyes glowed milky white against black metallic scales.

"Come," the ape said rising from the throne behind them. D'Mique threw a sharp look toward it and gasped. What she'd taken for a cloak unfurled into a great pair of red wings.

"Definitely not a Semian," she thought.

The creature smiled again and signaled behind her with a nod.

"No!" Trillip screamed as a bone-crushing pain overwhelmed her and the ground fell away. Darkness closed in.

D'Mique opened her eyes to a soft red glow. She held still waiting for the throbbing in her head and the nausea to subside. But the more aware she became the thicker the pain grew until a slight whimper escaped. A moment later opaque silver eyes swam into her field of view. The Mortak sighed, smiling. "Oh good, you're awake," he said. "We were worried about you."

"Kryoso?" D'Mique whispered. *"That can't be right,"* she thought, *"His voice is too deep."*

The Mortak laughed, "Now, we don't really all look alike, do we?" he said. "I'm Marladon," he introduced. "Kryoso is my, was my, lieutenant."

"The Fire Master?" D'Mique thought, "We've found him!" she said aloud.

"D'Mique?" Trillip asked bending over her, "How are you?"

"I feel sick," she whispered.

"One of the dragons batted you across the room. You're lucky you're not dead," he replied.

"How long was I out?" she asked.

"A few hours," the two men replied in unison.

Master Marladon disappeared for a moment. She tried to sit up but could not. Gasping, she stopped moving. When the Master returned he held out a tin cup of water, "Drink this, Lady," he said helping her prop her head up. She took a slow shallow sip. Ignoring the metallic wash she closed her eyes and focused on the pain.

"I wonder if anything's broken," she thought. After a moment she opened her eyes and asked, "Where are we?"

"We are in my dungeon," Marladon answered spreading his arms grandly.

"Why?" D'Mique asked.

Master Marladon squinted at her, "'Why?'" he echoed.

"Well you are a Master. The Fire Master. Why are we still in here?"

Marladon laughed, his voice dropping to a velvety baritone, "And how would you use the power of heat and fire to escape, Lady? Unlike many mages I am crippled and cannot touch any other power." He turned away from them a moment before sighing and continuing, "My dragon army is enslaved, even Gideon, Dragon King. I could call magma to tear the fortress to the ground, killing us as well," he added the last with a dismissive wave of his hand. "If Krindin came close enough I could pull the heat from his body or fry him!" he said, mimicking the action, his words intensely angry. "Satisfying, but we'd still be in here," he finished with a dark bitter chuckle.

D'Mique studied him as he sat staring at her. He was slightly shorter than Kryoso she estimated. His black hair brushed his shoulders in what was once an elegant cut. Though the dungeon grime marred his fine white shirt and tight black pants, he was still regal in stance. A perfect beauty radiated from him, not dampened by a thin scar that crossed his left cheek from temple to mouth.

"But that was alone," Trillip said.

Master Marladon tilted his head at the Land-Nymph. "True. I was alone," he said.

"And, if we could get out of here you know a way out of the fortress," Trillip continued.

"Of course. But what are you thinking?" Marladon asked.

Trillip cleared his throat while looking forlornly at D'Mique. Then he continued, "We're both warm-blooded."

"Hmm. Yes but Myrth might be upset if I fry his pet human," Marladon said with another dark smirk. Trillip stopped, his mouth open, trying to decide if the Master was joking. D'Mique glared at the Master until he laughed, "Go on," he said, "What is your plan, Trillip."

"You can take heat from us, perhaps enough to heat the metal?" Trillip finished. "I know your limits, Master. But I also know your specialty."

"Specialty?" D'Mique echoed.

"I can increase and decrease heat to an extent," Marladon explained.

"To such an extent that the metal would become pliable?" D'Mique asked, the implications sinking in as she spoke. The Fire Master nodded once eyeing her, judging her reaction. D'Mique met his silvery gaze, "We could bend it enough to get out," she concluded. Marladon nodded again, shifting to sit flat on the ground legs crossed. Using his finger he scratched in the dirt, mathematics from what D'Mique could tell.

After a few lines he closed his eyes for a long minute. "The problem is twofold," he said, opening his eyes and studying them as he spoke. "If I increase the heat too much I will fry you and if I take too much from you I will send you into hypothermia."

"Oh," D'Mique said.

"How much is too much?" Trillip asked.

"Two or three degrees."

"That's all?" D'Mique and Trillip gasped together.

"That's not all," Marladon said with a sigh. "These bars are iron. Iron doesn't become workable until its red-hot and last I checked humans were not quite that hot; not even angry ones." He smiled at D'Mique as he said it. "The solution I have considered is extremely dangerous to you both. I can take heat from you, Lady, raising it as I do and I can deposit it within you Trillip. Because you are a creature of Water, my elemental opposite, you should be somewhat protected from my power. I can then draw the high heat from you, dropping you to freezing, raise it again and put it into the metal."

"Why not deposit our heat straight into the metal?" D'Mique asked.

He held up two fingers as he replied, "First, it will dissipate without a Fire Source or Life to hold it; second, I can't reach red-hot by taking direct heat from both of you." He closed his opaque eyes again.

"What about when a guard comes to feed us?" she asked. "He could be another source of heat."

Marladon smiled at her, shook his head and opened his eyes. "Well. Aren't you nicely naive? They didn't put us here as prisoners or hostages. They mean for us to die here. I haven't eaten in five days. And, I suspect, when my water pail is empty they won't be refilling it."

"We are here until we die D'Mique," Trillip added.

"So there are no other choices," she said quietly.

Marladon sighed again. "No. There are no other choices. I will freeze you, Lady, hoping human flesh regains heat quick enough to save you, and I will cook Trillip from the inside, hoping his affinity to Water saves him. Only then will I be able to melt the bars and free us."

"Us?" D'Mique thought. "Or at least you," she added aloud. "We could just as easily die."

"You're not afraid of death," Trillip stated. She looked at him a long time before nodding in agreement.

Marladon met her gaze. "You're right and the whole plan could fail. Then I would die here with you," he added under his breath, "alone, except for your corpses." He studied his equations again, frowning. "Are you ready?" he asked looking up.

"Yes," D'Mique said as Trillip nodded. Marladon stood and made his way over to the cell bars kneeling arm's length from them. Trillip moved to his side and sat. With a glance Marladon took the Land-Nymph's offered hand. They both looked to D'Mique. Frowning she imitated them.

"Take my hand," the Fire Master instructed. They weighed each other, eyes locked as she held out her hand. His soft touch sent a shiver through her.

D'Mique breathed deep trying to slow her racing heart. *"It'll be okay,"* she told herself. Then the Fire Master struck. Instead of a gradual cooling, a sudden freeze knifed its way through her body, bathing her in glacial ice, tearing a gasp from her throat. Her teeth started chattering as pain and numbness coursed through her. Beside her Trillip screamed and thrashed, his skin reddening. Another wave of cold passed through D'Mique and her body buckled, the world dimmed. She fought for consciousness, her eyes sliding to where Trillip now slumped, unmoving. His skin suddenly paled, his body convulsing. Around Marladon the air shimmered and a blast of super-heated wind covered the three of them. Pain seared through her again and, screaming past chattering teeth, every muscle shivering, she instinctively moved away from the Master, a deep fear of the creature settling over her. The temperature continued to climb as she dragged herself away and reached for a still shivering Trillip, who was also struggling away from the Master, helping him. Marladon, eyes closed, sat with his hands outstretched just shy of the metal bars. Before him the metal began to glow, first a dull red then slowly, increasing in intensity, turning a red-orange. He suddenly threw himself backward and lashed out with his foot, kicking the iron bar, which gave under the sudden pressure and bent. Standing he kicked at the bar repeatedly, bending it further as the color faded, the heat dissipating into the metal and air around them.

Marladon turned to face them, studying them. "Are you well?" he asked. D'Mique fought against her chattering teeth and convulsing muscles. Beside her Trillip seemed to be suffering equally. The Fire Master closed the distance between them, "How do you feel?" he asked, laying a hand on Trillip who flinched away from the touch.

"I'll live, I think," he chattered, "considering I was just flash-fried and then frozen that is," he added.

Marladon asked, "Do you want my help?" When Trillip nodded, he closed his eyes and moved his hand from Trillip's arm to his chest. After a moment Trillip breathed out with a sigh. His shivering lessened and soon he was sitting, wincing as he moved.

"Now I need an elf," he said lightly. Marladon clapped him gently on the shoulder and smiled at D'Mique who still stared at him warily, shivering violently.

"I have frightened you," he said, "I don't blame you, really. I was very frightened of my Master when he showed me the power of Fire." He stood and helped Trillip to his feet as well before continuing, "The Masters are dedicated to the sanctity of life, Lady. I would never harm you on purpose, not without dire circumstances and your permission. I keep the Promise." He offered his hand, bowing slightly at the waist.

"Let's get out of here," she whispered standing on her own. Marladon's smile turned downward at the corners and he straightened. Dismissing her refusal, he turned and headed for the newly made door without another word. Squeezing through the close gap the Fire Master motioned for them to wait before disappearing soundlessly down the dim corridor. A moment later he reappeared with the key releasing them. Six cells made up the remainder of the dungeon all carved from stone and fitted with iron cage fronts. The doors to all but one cell hung open. Marladon peered through the bars of the other locked cell and stopped as a whimper, almost part hiss, issued from the dark at the back of the small room.

"Gods and daemons," the Master breathed, leaping for the door, slamming the key home as he landed. Flinging it open he disappeared into the darkness. A moment later he cooed, "Dear friend," from the gloom. D'Mique grabbed a nearby torch and entered the cell, bringing light to the back of the space. Before her a pony-size dragon curled around the Fire Master, its horned head hidden in the Mortak's protective embrace. The dragon, its body covered in dried blood, its scales marred by half-healed wounds whimpered again. Marladon hugged it closer in response. "Oh, Mort, what have they done to you," he whispered, a sob marring the low whisper. The dragon pulled away and turned its face toward the torch. Ugly red sockets greeted D'Mique where once there had been eyes.

"He tried to stop the usurpers from throwing me in here when I was unconscious and they blinded him when they couldn't enslave him," Marladon hissed. He and the dragon looked at each other a moment before he continued, "Of course, Mort," he said, rising, "Come." He took hold of a small horn in the center of the dragon's bony lower jaw as it rose to its feet.

"You can talk to them?" D'Mique asked.

"They are my creatures," the Fire Master said in answer.

D'Mique looked to Trillip for greater explanation. "Just as I belong to the Water Master or the goblins belong to the Earth Master," Trillip offered, "dragons belong to the Fire Master. He can communicate with them on several levels. All anyone else can hope for is an almost-heard voice."

Marladon led the dragon past, dried blood flaking off as its muscles worked beneath its green scales. They started for a spiral staircase at the end of the hall—the only visible exit—the dragon, almost a yard wide, barely fit. *"This dungeon wasn't meant for dragons,"* D'Mique thought as she and Trillip trailed behind them. *"But the rest of the castle was,"* she added remembering the vast hallways and rooms from before. Halfway up the stairs they turned off into a slightly wider hall; the door swinging quietly shut behind them. "This is a servant hall," Marladon explained. "It leads to the kitchens. From the kitchens we can take a passage out through the midden then we just scale the moat and sneak away out of the valley."

"Do you know that the fog has spread from the moat and has engulfed the valley?" Trillip asked as they walked.

"No," Marladon answered after a moment. "But that doesn't change our plans. It only changes how much caution we must use." They continued down the dark narrow hallway. At the end Marladon opened a door onto a huge kitchen. No fires glowed in the line of ovens along the wall, nobody bustled about the tables and sideboards, not a single pan or knife was out of place—the kitchen was abandoned. "I fear all my servants are gone," Marladon lamented as they entered and crossed the stone floor to a second set of large doors. "As well as my loyal guards," he added, unbarring them and swinging one side open.

Milk white eyes blinked in the gloom beyond the door and Mort hissed as a black dragon thrust its head into the kitchen, alabaster horns and ebony scales melting from the dark beyond, barring their path. "Gideon," Marladon breathed giving way for the dragon, "Dragon King, why do you bar my way?" A soft hiss answered the Fire Master.

"But surely, the Dragon King has no Master save himself?" Marladon continued. "Isn't that how it was before? You remember before?" Marladon stared intently at the dragon as he spoke. A purple ink, so dark it was almost black, swirled briefly in the milky whiteness of the dragon's eyes then disappeared. Marladon sighed hanging his head. The black dragon continued out of the hallway and into the kitchen, bodily forcing the escapees to back away from the door. It hissed again snapping its jaws at Trillip. "I can't break the spell!" Marladon admitted as he turned away from the dragon bringing Mort around with him. "I almost have him back!"

They made their way across the kitchen, the blind, green dragon mewling and cringing with fright as the great Dragon King hissed behind them, herding them with well-aimed snaps of its jaws. "Come Mort, all is not lost," Marladon comforted. "I will try again to reach our King." Leaving the kitchen, they turned toward the front of the castle.

"Gideon!" Marladon snapped. White and deep purple swirled in the depths of its eyes as it stared down at the Fire Master. Marladon reached out to the dragon king, a pained stubborn mask settling over his face. The Mortak closed the distance, drawing a hesitant hiss from the black maw and a warning snap of the dragon's jaws. Undaunted, silver eyes locked on the milk-white pools, Marladon reached out and rested a hand on the deep black scales. At his touch, purple spread outward from the center of the dragon's eyes and covered the white. As the color deepened the dragon screamed, its voice shaking the room around them. Marladon leapt for its jaws, clamping its mouth shut, hushing it. "Gideon King, we are trying to sneak out," he admonished. Mort mewled softly bowing his horned head low to the floor. Gideon softly pulled his snout from Marladon's hands and turned back around, back toward the midden exit. Confidently Marladon grabbed Mort's horn and followed the dragon king.

Beyond the kitchen doors mounds of refuse gave way to a narrow path. A few short steps brought them to the bottom of a crevasse that ran perpendicular to the midden. Dark jagged walls rose up on either side allowing just enough room for Gideon to pass between them. They were at the bottom of the moat and above them the weight of the Fire Master's fortress glowered. "Come," Marladon whispered leading the way, "We can climb out along the back ridge." Trillip and D'Mique followed him and the dragons into the fog-laden chasm, sparing a quick glance back the way they had come.

Daemon Hunters

Nix and Col kissed the sky, their light slowly warming the party—horses, griffins, elves, Semians, humans and a dragon fairy—that milled about before the main entry to Gemma. Nepo made his way through the group, Myrth a pace behind him, as he checked on supplies and mounts. Bags were tightened and retightened, saddles inspected. Weapons clanged as beasts shifted. The two honor guards formed a decent party when combined. Every few moments the Water Master turned to glare at his shorter companion as he worked until he reached his own mount. Settling smoothly in the saddle, Myrth stopped him with a clawed hand to his lower leg, saying, "Be careful." Nepo smiled down at him but said nothing, nudging his horse to a walk. Half the party, his honor guard, broke from the group to trail after him, followed by Jay and her elite soldiers on their griffins.

Myrth watched until the last of them had melted into the golden plain, heading west toward the Black Lands. He then turned to stare at Marco and the remaining guards. With a sigh he chided, "Check it again, Marco." In response Marco frowned, but obeyed, surveying the Earth Cloud and noting the jagged peaks that had formed in the segment Myrth had "given" him.

"Start small," Myrth remembered his Master saying, *"Work the soil until you know it will always remain steady."* Just as he had learned, Myrth taught Marco. *"This small thread, tied to your center, this is the Soil. Keep it steady, so the crops can grow."* Marco's agitation this morning roiled all the lines, of course, requiring a portion of Myrth's own will to steady them. However, he left the Soil line entirely in Marco's control. His apprentice moved quickly to smooth the ripples, calming it, keeping the soil balanced. "Soon," his master's remembered voice continued, *"Soon."*

315

Satisfied, Myrth made his way to Jerrold and mounted the horse-sized dragon. Judging Nepo's head start sufficient he motioned for the others to follow, Sylus and Marco flanking him.

Nepo's gray warhorse led the way across the plain while Sage, Pallan, and Jay scouted ahead and Myrth and his guards trailed behind. That day and the next, as they traveled, the Black Mountains sliced sharply across the horizon as they grew from the plain. From the Mage Realm, the land ahead of them wallowed in Shadow, waves of it lapping outward, engulfing the other elements. On the second day the three Masters halted just shy of the Shadow Magic's darkness and surveyed it. "It carries on the wind," Jay whispered, "Eating the Miasma."

Myrth studied the Earth Cloud as she spoke, watching as the gold light shrank beneath the black eddies, "The forcelines still exist beneath it," he observed, "It hasn't overpowered them." He quested along a larger stability line, the weight of the Shadow dragging behind him as his conscience moved. "I can still work with the forcelines," he informed the others. "We should be able to continue." For a moment he hesitated his mind seeking Marco, passing along his impression of the Shadow-covered land before them.

Marco pulled his eyes from Pallan where the fairy danced on the wind above them, and glanced at Myrth as the shadow-covered thoughts reached him. A shiver of fear tripped through him but he stilled it quickly, checking the Soil line out of habit now, watching the ripple of his emotion travel away from him in all directions affecting the entire Earth Cloud. As his Soil line calmed so did the rest of the Cloud, his will acting on his line while the weight of Myrth's will forced the eddies back to form throughout the rest. He surveyed the Shadow-filled lands as well and turned to Kryoso next to him.

For a moment words hung between them before Kryoso shook his head slightly, "I can do nothing against this, Marco," he breathed.

Before Marco could respond a flash from Pallan's wings caught his eye, "They've found something!" he shouted. The Masters glanced at Pallan then Nepo kicked his horse to a run, forging into the knee-deep Shadow Magic, leading the rest.

They followed Pallan to the foot of a large knoll and shuddered to a halt as the fairy landed. "What have you found?" Tekalo asked pulling even with Nepo.

"Death," the scout whispered.

"Come," Nepo ordered, dismounting and leading his horse up the slope. Sage stood at the top, motionless, a stray breeze playing with his beard as it carried the scent of death to them. At the top the Masters and their honor guards stood still, surveying the small bowl before them, the copse of trees at its center and the unmarred golden grass covering it all. "In the trees," Nepo whispered, breaking the spell and starting forward.

Pallan fluttered at eye-level, "Nepo—" he started, eyes ashen, but the words died as the Master descended.

Sage sighed, "The trees were the perfect place to camp," he said. Myrth nodded at his words and then followed Nepo, signaling for Marco to follow him. They caught up to Nepo at the verge - a sickly rot hanging in the air, warning them of what awaited beneath the trees hidden from the harsh sunlight of the open plains. With an assessing glance toward Marco, Nepo continued past the first line gliding easily between the rough trunks, ignoring the bramble underbrush. The others fell in line behind him, drawing even once again when he stopped and covered his muzzle with a furry hand. Drowning in death, they surveyed the grove's treasure.

They had been a group of refugees. The charred remains of their wagons held barrels, kitchen tools and crates. Precious belongings that had been spirited away from their abandoned homes lay crushed, scattered in the dirt. Their standard hung limp in the center of the encampment, a winding black dragon on a field of gray stating their allegiance to Marladon and their Fog Valley home. What remained of the refugees, their bodies, lay scattered about, butchered. Marco's stomach turned at the sight and he spun away, his agitation shattering the Earth Cloud around them, sending jagged waves pulsing along it.

The ground shifted slightly beneath them and a tremor rippled outward from Marco, before Myrth's will engulfed the area, smoothing the Cloud and forcelines. "Peace, Marco," he chided. "Look to the Soil." Marco took a deep breath - realizing too late what he had done—the scent of death engulfing him. He faltered, falling to his knees. Myrth laid a hand on his shoulder and cold iron flowed from it, chasing away the faintness, sharpening Marco's mind again. The copse of trees and its horrifying contents melted away replaced by the golden cloud of Earth. As Marco stilled, the Soil forceline did as well, the undulations of his agitation smoothing until the power flowed sedately along the line, an ever-dependable stream. Swallowing, he sought Myrth's gaze, expecting a chastising glare. But the hawk-man's pearl eyes were serene. "You will learn Marco," he whispered, his voice thrumming from the golden cloud around them, "it will take practice."

"Come on," Nepo whispered, starting toward the closest pile of debris, dismissing Marco's reaction. Kneeling, he inspected a disemboweled torso. "Daemons," he hissed, "but we're so far from a stronghold." He paused a bit before continuing, "They were simple farmers, not a blade between them." He surveyed the clearing, piecing together the story from tracks and scuff marks, looking for patterns. He stood suddenly and pointed to a gouge in the ground, "Dragon," he said.

"A dragon? Working with the daemons?" Myrth asked, momentarily contemplating the gouge himself before glancing around the clearing, "We don't have time to bury them. A pyre will be best."

"I'll collect the others," Marco offered, hastily turning and retreating toward Sage and the others and the relative safety beyond the trees. With a sigh Nepo knelt over the nearest corpse, trying to study it without seeing it.

"Daemons," a strange voice hissed from the other side of the clearing. Myrth spun toward the newcomer as Nepo stood. A Potent was standing at the edge of the clearing; a veiled Semian with two red feathers in his cap. He bowed low, "I was looking for Marco but thought you might have more need of me, Masters."

"Princess Almira of Herdan's Court?" Nepo asked. She nodded confirmation.

"Almira," Myrth repeated, "It has been many long months since I saw you last." She nodded. "Looking for Marco?" She nodded again. "We need to make a pyre for these bodies and then get on with our hunt," he said.

Almira surveyed the remains before stepping over to the nearest corpse and hauling it toward the wagon. "I will help and then set the fire."

As she worked, the rest of the party, led by Marco, arrived. Marco's heart leapt to his throat when he saw her. "Almira," he called rushing forward, elation bubbling through the Earth Cloud as he ran. Almira had just enough time to empty her hands before he reached her scooping her into his arms as she lifted her veil. They fell into each other drowning in the heat of their kiss. The earth rumbled again, and Marco was only tangentially aware of Myrth's will descending over the clearing once again.

Myrth stalked over to them and pulled them apart. "Love, good," he said, "But you still must remain centered, Marco, always and in all things."

"My apologies, Master," Marco said bowing his head, searching through the cloud for Soil and smoothing it.

Almira backed away a step as he did so, her gaze weighty as she stared at him through the veil. "You—you're..."

"Yes, Marco is my apprentice," Myrth responded before Marco could do so.

"But he's with the Potentate," Almira said.

"I will inform Palo in good time," Myrth offered, his will retreating from the clearing once again leaving Marco cold and the Earth Cloud unperturbed. Almira shook her head but said no more. Myrth left the pair and returned to Nepo's side while the Honor Guard swept through the clearing, piling bodies near the wagon and sifting through the remains for anything that could be salvaged.

"Where is Temeres?" Marco asked.

"He follows the tracks of these butchers in the other direction. He will run them to ground then we will catch up to him," she hissed.

When the last body joined the pyre Almira lit it, "My final gift to you, innocent travelers," she breathed as the flames leapt for the sky. For a moment the group stood in silence and stared at the lost lives as flames consumed flesh.

"Come on," Nepo said. "We need to end this. Sage, Tekalo, stay here and tend the fire." He waited for Tekalo to nod before turning away. The lion-man's gaze rested on Myrth for a moment before he left and gathered his mount. Nepo's honor guard followed without question while Jay and Sylus looked at Myrth for confirmation. Myrth nodded and his group collected their mounts. Marco held tight to Almira as the others returned to their saddles.

"You must go with Myrth, my love," she whispered. "And I must catch up to Temeres quickly. When I find him we will swing east and start for the Fortress. With luck we will meet again."

"I want you to come with me," he replied, pouting.

"Our duty does not allow it," she whispered, closing the distance between them and breathing into his ear. "But one day our paths will intertwine again and until that day I will love you." He hugged her close, willing her to stay with him, but he knew she was right. He let her go and watched as she turned away, hurrying off along the daemon's trail, hunting the creatures that had slaughtered the refugees. Marco mounted and turned to follow the others.

D'Mique scratched the blind dragon's head between his ruined eyes, pulling a smile from the creature. In front of her Marladon and Trillip stood shoulder to shoulder surveying the fog. The dragon king stood behind them all, his narrow head scanning the fog to the left and right. A pained bellow shattered the silence around them and swords flashed to the ready. Gideon hissed as he stalked toward the shadowy forest on their left. "Black Daemon," Marladon whispered. D'Mique left the blind dragon and joined the others. As she did so, another bellow echoed through the fog. She strained to detect movement in the forest. "There," Marladon pointed.

Ghostly, pale white eyes gleamed in the darkness beneath the trees as a pack of Black Daemons emerged. They bristled with weapons that clanked as they marched through the underbrush on their spindle-legs, goat-like heads swiveling to face the group. Surprised, they paused for a beat before the lead one cried out, its bellowed challenge drawing a hiss from Gideon. D'Mique took a deep breath and readied for the charge. As the daemons lunged forward fire erupted, engulfing the front line. Writhing and screaming, the daemons fell or tumbled over each other in their attempt to escape the sudden onslaught. Startled, D'Mique backed away, fear blooming in her chest. She glanced at the Fire Master who stood unmoving beside Trillip.

More fire erupted in the back lines of the daemon horde scattering them. As the flames spread panic and the daemons fell back, the milky white of their eyes faded, replaced by the normal burning red. A short minute after the horde had emerged from the forest their onslaught had collapsed into a fiery chaotic swarm. None of them came any closer than the first line of flames Marladon had called forth. Gideon remained guarded, close behind them, head swiveling, looking for others. But none came. As the remaining Black Daemons fled back to the forest Trillip relaxed and Marladon sighed, "Come on. The Greater Daemon's influence has spread through the valley. We have to get to Myrth."

They continued through the fog along the edge of the forest eventually climbing out of the valley and leaving it behind. As they topped a ridge, Marladon pulled up short and chuckled while Gideon beside him squawked. Brow furrowed, D'Mique hurriedly finished the climb. At the top she looked down at a small, motley army led by a lion-man Semian atop a large gray horse. "You're late," Marladon scolded.

"And you've lost your fortress," Myrth added, moving out from behind the gray horse, his own dragon mewling at the dragon king. Gideon hissed in reply. Marladon started down the hill, waving away the Earth Master's comment. "I'm glad we found you," Myrth continued.

"I'm glad we found you," Marladon repeated, emphasizing the last word. He stopped just out of reach of the gray mount and studied the other Masters. "Your guards rescued me, Myrth. I thank you for sending them," he said indicating Trillip and D'Mique with a slight nod of his head. "Of course, I would have preferred Kryoso's return."

"So the daemon is—" a flurry of white interrupted him as Clippen rushed forward tackling Trillip to the ground, both of them joined a split second later by Tekalo. Nepo chuckled as Myrth glared at the wrestling figures. D'Mique took a cautious step away from the three as they clambered to their feet. Clippen and Tekalo stood at last with their heads together, embracing Trillip.

"So, the daemon is at Nightmare?" Myrth asked again.

Marladon nodded, "Flights of dragons patrol the Black Lands, enslaved by the daemon. I was able to free Gideon, Mort we found in the dungeons. I do not know how the daemon is able to steal my dragons."

"It is more than dragons it enslaves," Sylus added, "We have met many milk-eyed daemon-kin in our journey here."

"Dragons are not daemon-kin," Marladon added his voice dropping slightly as he eyed the elf. Sylus held up his hands in a gesture of surrender.

"Of course not," Jay interjected. She looked up at the sky, "We will find a campsite," she said to Myrth, indicating her own elite soldiers before urging her griffin into the air.

Marladon watched her go before turning back to Myrth, who had retreated to the Mage Realm, and Nepo.

Silence stretched between them for a moment then Marladon turned to Marco, "I can feel you," he said. "Who are you?"

"I am Marco, Chosen of Earth," Marco introduced.

"Chosen?" Trillip echoed.

"You took an apprentice?" Marladon asked.

With a small sigh, Myrth opened his eyes and nodded.

"I would like to apologize for him," Marladon smirked as he spoke to Marco. Marco returned the smile although it withered under Myrth's glare.

Nepo urged his mount forward turning the horse in the direction Jay had disappeared. "We can save this all for later," he said, "Come on." The company fell in behind him and followed after Jay. Clippen and Tekalo joined Trillip on the ground, walking and leading their horses, holding each other close as they walked. D'Mique returned to the top of the hill for her blind charge before joining the goblins near the rear of the group.

"Lady Warrior," Rogan greeted, nodding, a thin-lipped smile flashing across his face.

"Rogan," she returned with an equally formal nod.

"Welcome back," Tierren added with a warm smile. He held out a scabbard and sword. "You'll need this."

"Oh, Lady," Genow cried, sliding from his horse as it walked and pulling her close before she could respond to Tierren's gift. "I'm so glad you are well. He studied her. You are well? We heard you were injured....I... I didn't want to leave you."

"You look road-weary," Tierren added.

"Trillip and I have traveled a long road," she admitted finally releasing Genow, "He kept me safe just as he promised," she added, reassuring the elf.

Genow frowned, "I was so worried about you," he said. "I kept telling myself I never should have left you."

D'Mique shook her head, "If you hadn't left, Myrth might have died."

"We would have died without question," Rogan added from his horse. "When we make camp you will have to tell us your tale, Lady" he added. A tremor ran through her as the night-black throne room and white-eyed dragons melted from the shadows of her mind, the Greater Daemon's orb eyes blazing as they found her.

Genow caught her as she started to fall. "D'Mique!" he cried, steadying her, helping her keep her feet.

"What is it?" someone asked. Through the cotton haze that had descended she caught sight of Trillip, his candy pink hair pulling her back to reality. The Land-Nymph took her from Genow, holding her close. He briefly relayed their travels and their meeting with the daemon in Nightmare, their harrowing journey reduced to simple sentences. "She's been through a lot," he finished, his voice a soft purr against the side of her face.

"It sounds like the daemon's a mage" Kryoso added when the tale finished, "A Shadow Mage." Marco passed a brief look to the Mortak but Kryoso pointedly looked away from him.

"How many dragons were enslaved there?" Tierren asked.

"I don't know," Trillip answered, "At least six, probably more."

"Did you see any weaknesses?" Tierren asked.

Trillip shook his head, "No. No weaknesses." His words hung heavy as they walked on in silence their footsteps suddenly heavy, D'Mique holding him.

Marladon watched the fire dance before him. The small army sat arrayed in concentric circles around the central fire pit where the Masters gathered close. "It was Krindin," Marladon said into the silence. Jay nodded absently beside him as Myrth's gray eyes slid open.

"Krindin?" he repeated. Marladon nodded. "That was your guest from the North wasn't it?" Again Marladon answered with a nod.

"That —" Nepo started but he clamped his jaws shut and glared upward, mastering the sudden burst of emotion. "We should send someone north," he said after a moment. The anger coloring his voice suggested someone with weapons.

"We will," Myrth assured him, "once we have dealt with the daemon."

"Dealt with the daemon," Sylus repeated from where he sat just behind Myrth, beside Marco and the trio of Land-Nymphs, "Easier said than done, Master."

Myrth turned and glared at him, "Oracle has seen —" Myrth began.

"Oracle would have us knock on the front door and show the daemon our pair of humans. Then graciously accept its surrender." Jay interjected.

"Between here and the fortress there are dragons, mange, and Black Daemons, all controlled by the usurper," Marladon added, "We'd never survive a frontal assault."

"Trillip and D'Mique already entered through the front once," Myrth reminded him.

"As two wanderers, not as an army, Myrth," Marladon replied. "Gods and Demons." He paused a long moment holding everyone's attention before finishing, "I do not wish to go back," he breathed, his words heavy as the silence grew.

"I will take my elite guards into the vale tomorrow and harry the daemon's forces," Jay lilted after a moment, "Cause a distraction. Nepo should take his guard to the north and do likewise."

"My whole guard?" Nepo interjected, his smile dripping sardonic glee. Myrth spared him a minimalist glare.

"Your current force," Jay clarified. "That should leave a path for you, Myrth and Marladon, to return to the fortress."

Nepo sighed, "Very well. I'll take my remaining guard into the mountains as Jay suggests."

"If you meet a flight of dragons," Marladon said, "Your best strategy will be to hide from them."

Nepo shook his head, "No, Gideon King should come with me. He might be able to turn them back to us."

"No," Marladon said, rising, certainty hardening his voice, "Gideon King will come with me. The dragon king must return to his throne."

"Do you think the enslavement spell can be broken by Gideon?" Myrth asked.

"Yes," Nepo answered.

Marladon looked from Nepo to Myrth, "Perhaps," he admitted after a moment.

"Gideon King should come into the mountains with us," Nepo said again. "We will find dragons with the daemon forces. We can save them. Without Gideon we will have no choice but to kill them."

Marladon glowered at the lion-man before studying the flames. "The Fortress is also full of dragons," he said. "How will we get to the daemon when he is surrounded by my army?"

"You know all the servant passages," Myrth said, "We can sneak in. You were able to save Gideon you should be able to break others free if we meet them." He paused, looking past the group to Mort, the blind dragon. "What to do with Mort," he wondered aloud.

Marladon followed his gaze. "We take him with us and leave him near the moat. He'll be alright there." After a moment he continued, "Nepo can take Gideon King north and hope he will be able to break the spell as well as I could. If we can reach the throne room undetected we should have a chance."

"But at what cost?" D'Mique asked under her breath. "How many of us will die for this chance?" Eyes turned toward her in the darkness reflecting the fire's glow.

"Would your life be such a high price to pay in order to save our world?" Myrth asked. D'Mique looked away leaving the question unanswered.

"Nepo and Jay will leave first," Marladon said returning to planning. "That should clear us a path." Nepo nodded in response as the Fire Master continued, "We will give you a day's head start."

"One last day," D'Mique added silently.

The next morning Nepo and Jay took their guards and left, traveling in opposite directions, Gideon reluctantly leaving Marladon behind and trailing after Nepo's war horse. All the rest of the day Myrth, Marco, Kryoso and Marladon sat in quiet study surveying the Mage Realm while the others remained on guard in the physical one. At first light the following day they started east, retracing Marladon's route. Taking to a dusty track that wound between the hills and rocky outcrops the party made good time. Mid-morning, upon rounding a bend in the road, the party pulled up short. A group of Black Daemons blocked the path ahead, busily scavenging a meal from a corpse in the center of the road. At the sound of the horses some of them looked up, their eyes gleaming milky-white. One screamed defiantly and launched itself toward them raising a thick sword overhead. The others followed, screaming as they launched themselves at the party, eager for fresh meat.

Marco reached for the Earth Cloud, forming his ammo as Myrth and Marladon retreated. "No Marco!" Myrth called grabbing him by the arm and shaking him. "Wait! Let the others take care of it. It's only six daemons!" Marco looked between the retreating Masters and the advancing wave of bladed legs before releasing the stones and backing away regretfully. "You were told not to touch the forcelines!" Myrth hissed in his ear.

Clippen retreated to the Mage Realm while Commander Sylus took up a position in front of him. Standing beside Genow, D'Mique drew her sword as well, falling back to her original charge of protecting the healer. Trillip, armed with a second spare blade, joined Tierren and Rogan, rushing forward crying out. But as suddenly as the attack had begun, the daemons came to a stop frozen in mid-lunge. Startled by the stop D'Mique gasped. "Clippen has caught them all in a web of Air," Genow provided. The daemons stood defenseless, struggling against the unyielding bonds, as the three swordsmen plowed into them. Three swords gleamed in the setting suns' light and three heads hit the ground. The three remaining daemon-spawn screamed their dismay. Once more the blades swung and Clippen released the corpses.

"Well done," Sylus commended. "Burn them all quickly before we lose all light."

As the others worked to clear the mess from the road Marco glared at Myrth, silently demanding an answer as to why they'd retreated.

"Our powers must be used with caution," Myrth responded with a sigh. "We will only use them as a last resort against otherwise insurmountable odds. Look now to your Soil Line." Myrth instructed. "Can you see how to fix it?" For a moment Marco stared at him unsure he'd heard him correctly. Then he retreated into the Mage Realm and concentrated on the tendrils drifting through him, sorting through them looking for his soil pattern. When he found it, it was jagged and broken!

Shocked, he opened his eyes, "What happened to it?" he asked, glaring suspiciously at Myrth and Marladon as they smiled sympathetically in response. He sifted out the Soil pattern again and smoothed it, allowing it to drift lazily through him and westward across the plain.

Myrth nodded his approval and finally answered the question. "You were instructed to stay away from the forcelines Marco. I expect you to obey. If you cannot heed this warning because I have asked then look to your Soil line. Look what has happened to it." He paused a moment, letting the words seep in. "When Masters do any work, with any power, we must always stop and check the forcelines, repair any damage we find. This holds true for any stressful situation, any strong emotion. As the forcelines are tied to us, when we are agitated they become agitated. Even if we do not remember being upset we must check them."

"Sometimes there will be no damage," Marladon added as an aside, "But you should build the habit of checking."

"When we work, we must always return the forcelines to their natural state, to the state they were in when we were first tied to them." Myrth stared at Marco a moment before adding, "You should know too that when a powerful mage like Clippen works magic near a Master it is possible for him to disturb the forcelines. When you travel with strong mages you should check that they have not altered your patterns."

Marco nodded his understanding but a tickle of dread flitted through his head. Something about their words troubled him. "Every time I touch the forcelines I disturb the patterns," he said. Marladon and Myrth nodded in unison. "I am reined in," he said. "Before I was apprenticed I could do anything without consequence. Now everything has a consequence."

"No, Marco," Myrth said with a sigh. "Even before being apprenticed you were disturbing the forcelines when you worked. You simply did not know of the consequences. By apprenticing you I can train you to use your powers wisely and mind how your powers affect others."

"Should I feel betrayed?" Marco asked after letting his words sink in.

"Marladon does," Myrth said.

Marco looked over at the Fire Master who simply turned away without speaking.

As the twin suns set, they reached the top of the final ridge overlooking the Black Lands. Myrth motioned for a halt and surveyed the valley below and its thick, dark blanket of fog. "We're stopping, right?" Trillip whispered. He looked pointedly up at the sky, "Rysk hasn't risen yet."

With a sigh Myrth started forward down the ridge. "Is there a point in waiting?" he asked, "We won't be able to see down there regardless."

"Stay on the road," Marladon advised as they followed Myrth.

At the base of the hills Myrth's black horse melted away eaten by the thick fog. With a sigh, remembering the previous journey through it, D'Mique followed reluctantly. Sylus caught Kryoso's eye and they stopped beside Marco. Kryoso shook his head. "My Lord Marladon said it was Krindin. If it was, he hid his affinity as I hide mine. I never would have guessed he had power enough to call forth a Great Beast. This magic is beyond my skill."

Sylus shook his head and urged his horse forward leaving Marco behind with Kryoso. "Maybe we pin our hopes on Oracle's miracle humans after all," he muttered under his breath.

The horses picked their way slowly forward through the soft inky darkness, following a road no one could see. A shrill screech to the right brought everyone to a halt until the sound's muffled echoes rippled away through the darkness. D'Mique strained against the night trying to see or hear the beast. Nothing. But Marladon signaled them to remain still. A moment later a rustle to their left caught her attention. Something large was moving in the dark. Behind her a horse moved slightly, the soft jangle of its tack ringing loudly through the fog. The fog-hidden creature stopped mid-rustle and for a long minute there was nothing more. D'Mique moved closer to Genow, waiting. Then the earth shuddered underneath them and the fog swirled outward away from them as the creature leapt in their direction. Marco's horse reared suddenly, dumping him to the ground and racing away. The unseen creature screamed and chased after the horse. A bone-shattering roar sounded behind them and the muffled darkness birthed a cacophony of screams, thundering footsteps, and bodily thuds followed by a horse's scream. Silent darkness returned.

"Let's go," Marladon whispered starting forward again.

They crept through the darkness, mindful of every muffled hoof beat and jangle of harness buckles from the remaining horses. Marco followed close behind Marladon as he stopped every few yards to stand and listen, waiting for the next threat but none came. Then two yellow pinpoints melted from the fog. "What's that?" Marco whispered.

"The Gateway," Marladon replied. "Leave the horses here," he instructed the others. They worked quickly and quietly to turn the mounts loose in the fog. As the horses drifted away the honor guard crowded close together around Myrth and Marladon.

"We need to use the same route to get in that you used to get out," Myrth said.

"We left through the kitchen into the moat and climbed up near the back of the fortress," Marladon relayed.

"Then that's how we'll get in," Myrth said starting to his left.

"Myrth, we should wait until daylight," Marladon interrupted, "Rest a moment." Myrth surveyed the others then nodded before closing his eyes and stepping into the Mage Realm. A huge stone dome formed over them growing silently from the black soil beneath their feet.

After it formed Myrth sighed, "Marco," he said, "Check your pattern." Marco hesitated but then closed his eyes and looked at the soil pattern. It eddied slightly in the wake of Myrth's working. Marco smoothed it and opened his eyes, looking up, surveying the Mage Realm. The whole world was dark here, shadow magic filling the valley around them, muting the other forcelines even the Earth Cloud. Marladon started a small fire at the center of the dome, its smoke drifting through the hole Myrth had left at the top of their shelter.

"This is the safest we'll be for the rest of this mission," Marco thought, dropping to the dirt beside Rogan and Tierren.

With the guards asleep around them Marladon sat staring across the small fire at the pearl-eyed hawk-man. "Myrth," he started, "you do have a plan for once we get into the fortress, right?"

Myrth contemplated the low flames before him for a long time and no answer came. A bitter chuckle escaped the Fire Master. Myrth met his opaque eyes with a glare and asked, "It's in the throne room?" Marladon nodded slowly. "We'll sneak through the servant passages and surprise it."

"And then?" Marladon pressed.

"We attack," Myrth said.

Marladon nodded and turned to survey the handful of guards around him. "And if that doesn't work? Despite what Oracle has seen," he added with a sharp bite.

"Then we'll die and it will fall to Nepo and Jay to continue the fight." The Masters sat in silence, their thoughts running separate races. "What do you think?" Myrth asked leaving the Mage Realm completely, his forceline maintenance finished for the evening.

"I think we don't stand a chance against my enslaved dragons and that daemon."

"What would you have us do Marladon?" Myrth whispered. Marladon turned back to the fire. He watched it dance for a long time before laying down turning over and falling asleep. Myrth closed his eyes and watched the shadowed Mage Realm around him. The island of color that had accompanied him into the dark valley offering little comfort against the visions that played through his head.

Lady Warrior, Mage of Man

The party crept forward on their hands and knees toward the lanterns that marked the Gateway, a guardhouse west of the main entrance to the fortress. After passing through the unguarded arch they turned northwest and crossed quickly to the edge of the moat. Here the cliff face was shattered into jagged ridges, perfect toe and finger holds. Myrth crawled backwards over the edge descending slowly. The goblins followed him, then the Land-Nymphs. Genow and Marladon climbed down together, then D'Mique, Marco, and Kryoso. At the bottom they spread out, keeping watch while the others descended, Sylus bringing up the rear.

At the bottom of the moat there was no fog. Springy black lichen covered the ground. Here and there, neon purple plants sprouted, growing without sunshine. Engulfing it all, the swampy stench of the place forced them to breathe shallowly as they followed the Fire Master toward the front of the fortress. Marladon picked his way around the plants and strewn rocks until he reached the midden heap D'Mique remembered from their previous journey. Above them, cut into the cliff wall, sat a pair of closed metal doors. Marladon propped one door open and surveyed the kitchen beyond, which was deserted.

He motioned for the others to follow and scrambled around the garbage pile and into his kitchen. D'Mique and Trillip followed close on his heels followed by the others. When they were all standing inside Marladon led them into the huge, empty kitchen, running quietly across the stone floor and through a single wooden door and into the maze of hidden servant corridors that ran through the fortress. Marladon led them quickly down first one then another.

After a few minutes Marladon slowed, D'Mique, Marco and Myrth crowding close behind him. He waved them to silence, motioning for them to stay behind as he continued forward slowly and pushed open an unassuming door on their right. Beyond the door the darkness lay in a suffocating blanket over the throne room, its oppression broken only by a sickly green light that emanated from a cloak of green flames covering the Greater Daemon's body. Heart pounding, D'Mique took a moment to study the creature in detail. It lay curled up, apparently asleep in the center of the great room, with its huge triangular head resting on its massive front feet. Both feet and head were easily five feet across at their widest point. A black sickle-shaped claw tipped each front toe, mirroring the black wedge-shaped horns sprouting above the daemon's eyes which were closed hiding the white orbs that glowed within them.

The entire length of the daemon was covered in patches of bristly black fur and loose, wrinkled folds of skin. Its body was sectional, like an insect's, and two more pairs of legs sprouted from its mid-section. These legs ended in sharp, almost blade-like points, similar to the legs of a Black Daemon. D'Mique swallowed hard as she gazed at the daemon. *"It's abdomen is its only weak spot,"* she thought. Movement across the room caught her eye. Dragons milled about in the darkness. Their white eyes gleaming pale green, reflecting the daemon's fiery cloak. There were at least a dozen of them hidden in the darkness, as they had been when she first came here.

"I can feel them," Marladon breathed, barely audible. "I can save them," he motioned toward the dragons. Myrth motioned for them to retreat back to the passage.

Away from the door he whispered, "You would have to break the spell on the dragons one at a time Marladon."

Marladon nodded. "I might get one before the alarm was raised, but it is more likely that the alarm will sound when I begin breaking the spell not during or after." Myrth bowed his head in thought. "I don't want my dragons killed, Myrth," Marladon warned, his whisper acrid.

"If we attack the daemon, the dragons will come to his rescue," Sylus interjected.

"Then we would have to fight them," Tierren said. Marladon shook his head, frowning at them.

"We could lure the dragons to one side of the chamber and then I'll wall them off," Myrth suggested. "That would leave the daemon unguarded."

"We need live bait for that plan," Rogan added.

For a long minute they sat in silence. "Okay," Myrth said at last, "Tierren, Rogan, Trillip and Clippen, you'll come with me," he said. "We'll sneak along the wall away from the daemon. When we're far enough along we'll show ourselves. The dragons should move toward us and I'll wall them off. The rest of you will leave right after us and attack the daemon as I throw up my wall." A small squeak escaped D'Mique.

Myrth's hand flashed out and he grabbed her by the face covering her mouth. "Oracle says you will win D'Mique," he reminded her, staring into her eyes until she nodded slightly. Releasing her he continued, "And you, Marco, pattern magic only." He waited for him to nod in agreement before starting down the servant's hall, "Okay, let's go."

"Don't kill my dragons, Myrth," Marladon warned again as the hawk-man returned to the door slipping through it, followed by the goblins and Land-Nymphs. After a ten-count Marladon led the rest of them out the door, creeping along the wall in the opposite direction.

D'Mique's heart beat too loudly as they glided along the wall. Smooth stone behind her cold to the touch, offered no comfort as the Greater Daemon came back into view. Skin crawling, she chided herself, *"Think less. Myrth is so sure we'll win. But..."* she trailed off staring again at the monstrous daemon before them. She inched along the wall Marladon and Marco ahead of her, Genow behind, followed by Kryoso and Sylus. When they'd worked their way a quarter of the way around the room a high-pitched chittering suddenly shattered the tense silence. The group froze. D'Mique's breath caught in her throat, threatening to turn into a scream. The Greater Daemon's eyes slid open, white globes piercing the thick blackness. The chittering grew louder, pressing on D'Mique's temples, filling the room in a wash of sound, a physical assault.

The daemon chuckled, "What's this?" it hissed. Torches flared to life throwing light across the huge throne room, blinding them as the daemon gained its feet. D'Mique blinked, holding her sword before her, and focused on the daemon's wedge-shaped head nearly thirty feet above the ground. Black dragons writhed in and out of the shadows thrown by the torches. Their white eyes swung toward Myrth's party. "Little rats?" the daemon asked as it surveyed both parties, "And," its horned head tilted in

Marladon's direction. "And a ghost?" it hissed, slicing the air above it with a foreleg. A weak wail of pain reverberated through the room. "Krindin, your master lives," the daemon growled.

D'Mique's eyes followed the movement. A figure writhed on the ceiling, pinned by his wings, arms and legs, his abdomen a ruined mess. Parts that should never have seen the light of day dangled from the winged ape Krindin. Gasping, she looked away focusing on the daemon, trying to master her breathing. "Easy D'Mique," Genow said, placing a hand on her shoulder, "don't look."

"Yes, look away," the daemon taunted focusing on D'Mique. It added, "Kill the rats," nonchalantly throwing the command over its shoulder. Dragons uncoiled from the ebony fringes of the room and stalked toward Myrth and his party, their heads down, hissing as they moved.

"Don't hurt them!" Marladon screamed, forgetting the daemon for a split second as the goblins drew their swords and rushed forward into the room following Myrth as he ran to meet the dragons. Trillip stood beside Clippen near the wall. As Clippen threw out his hands the front line of dragons crashed into a solid barrier of Air. "Don't hurt them!" Marladon shouted again. More dragons, not caught in Clippen's barrier descended on Myrth. Dropping to his knees, Myrth threw up a stone dome around himself. The dragons fell on it, clawing at it, desperate for the prize within.

"Marladon! Look out!" Kryoso screamed suddenly, moving away from the wall. Marladon looked up, realizing for the first time that he stood beside the daemon, and slid to a stop, dodging backward as the daemon's jaws snapped closed a hands' span in front of him. D'Mique moved forward startled into action by Kryoso's movement. The daemon's head pivoted, jaws opening again, arm-length fangs seeking the Fire Master. Marladon threw himself backward onto the floor as the jaws closed again. With a shout Kryoso leapt for the Master and the daemon snapped again. "No!" Genow screamed as the daemon's jaws closed on Kryoso. With a gasp D'Mique stopped near Marladon's head, droplets of blood suddenly flung outward as the daemon violently shook the captured Mortak. It flicked its head and threw Kryoso into the wall near where they had come in. Genow spun on his toes and rushed back across the floor to the broken Mortak's side throwing himself down and sliding on the smooth stones. Marladon regained his feet in one movement and ran after Genow, leaving D'Mique alone, staring up at the Greater Daemon.

With a shout she raised her sword, shifting her weight to face the creature. A sharp hiss answered her shout and the daemon cocked its head to one side eyeing her closely, "You again. What are you supposed to be?" it asked over the continuing roar of the dragon battle behind it. Before she could answer Marco stepped up beside her a scowl of determination on his face, surrounded by a dozen fist-sized stones that floated through the air. Throaty, mirthless laughter bubbled from the daemon. "Two Man-children?" it asked. In reply Marco endowed his stones with Fire and flung them unceremoniously at the daemon's face. Startled, the daemon reared back, catching the brunt of the explosions on its chest.

Fur singed, the daemon shrieked in response and lashed out at the pair of them. Marco ducked the huge hand but it crashed squarely into D'Mique, sending her into the wall near Genow and Kryoso where she crumpled unmoving. Marco rushed backward, pulling the Earth Cloud toward him, but unsure how to attack the creature next. Then the daemon's hand surrounded him pinning him to the floor. Stars burst across his vision and the air escaped his lungs. The daemon grabbed him from the floor lifting him, hissing, "What now, boy?" it asked. Marco willed the Earth into stone spears and burrowed them deep into the daemon's hand. With a scream it dropped him. Marco hit the floor hard and rolled away from the creature. Forming the Earth Cloud around him like a shield he regained his feet and spun to target the daemon once more.

Sylus stood near the daemon's further front leg. As Marco watched the elf brought his sword solidly down on the daemon's finger forming a deep gash. Blood welled up in the blade's wake and the daemon screamed. It reared up on its bladed back legs, pulling away from the battle before glaring down at the elf. Filling the marble hall with a scream of rage the daemon lunged for Sylus. As it did so Marco formed the Earth Cloud into a large stalagmite. It grew longer, thicker, taller as Sylus dodged away from the daemon. Within seconds it was taller than the daemon and nearly as long. Waving his hand Marco turned the fluid Earth Cloud snake toward the daemon, lashing out at the creature, aiming for its wedge-head, catching it unaware and landing a blow squarely between the daemon's eyes.

The daemon screamed in pain shaking the throne room again. Marco's snake lashed around beside the daemon and looped around its throat. Stone coils squeezed, picking the daemon up off the ground and tossing it across the room. A deep pain flashed through Marco, starting in his gut and flaring outward, traveling through his arms and legs. The stone snake reached for the daemon again and picked it up before slamming it into the floor. It lay still. Across the throne room the enslaved dragons halted their attack on the stone dome and suddenly looked around dazed, their eyes swirling from white to gold and purple. Marladon ran toward them, "Come, Dragons!" he shouted. They focused on him and followed as he turned and raced for the throne room's entrance. "Find your king!"

With a thud Myrth's dome fell, broken into a pile of rubble around him, ruining the sudden silence left in the wake of the dragons. The Earth Master was doubled over coughing up blood. "Tierren!" Rogan screamed, running forward, catching Myrth as he crumpled to the floor. "I'm here, Myrth!" he said, holding the bleeding Master.

"Marco," Myrth gasped, "Stop him..." Tierren reached them and looked across at Marco as the giant stone snake reached for the daemon a third time.

"Marco! Stop!" Tierren shouted. Startled Marco released the Earth Cloud and looked over at the goblins, gaping when he saw Myrth cradled between them and surrounded by rubble.

Horrified, Marco realized what he had been doing. *"The Earth Cloud!"* he screamed at himself, *"I wasn't supposed to touch it!"* Marco hurried to Myrth as the stone pillar dissolved into sand and melted back into the floor.

Behind him the daemon shakily regained its feet. With a hiss it focused on the group gathering around Myrth, and moving toward them put out the lights, engulfing the room in blackness once again. For a moment the only light in the room were the daemon's globe eyes then a series of fireballs lit the room as Marladon advanced on the creature. The daemon chuckled, the fire doing little visible damage. Marladon's orange fire flaring across the green flame shield the daemon donned. "Did you think to harm me with fire?" it asked, charging to meet the advancing Master, ignoring the gathering around Myrth.

"Help us, Marco," Rogan growled, drawing his attention back to Myrth. In the leaping light of Marladon's fireballs he could make out the two goblins and Sylus cradling the master.

"Mind how much power you draw from me," Myrth hissed, pain and anger lacing each word. Suddenly fearful, Marco studied the force lines and the Earth Cloud. Gasping, he knelt before his master, watching as Earth drifted, its once strong golden currents eddied and muddied pooled around the throne room, mingling with the deep Shadow magic that added to the darkness of the room. "Make them whole, Marco," Myrth finished, "I will help as best I can."

Marco glanced toward the daemon before joining Myrth kneeling between the boulders. "We'll watch over you," Tierren said standing, moving to join the Land-Nymphs beside the daemon. Trillip and Clippen occupied its attention, darting between its legs, swiping at its underside while it chased Marladon between the pillars along the edge of the room. With a dangerous glare on his face Rogan followed Tierren, blade drawn.

For a moment the world remained fuzzy and dark. D'Mique wasn't sure if she was awake or asleep. Above her, behind her, she could hear the clangs and thuds of swords, running feet on stone and the occasional crackle and spit of fire. Beneath her lay a cold stone floor that trembled with the sounds as well, amplifying them. Reality crept back over her and she startled fully awake focusing on the sounds, blinking in the darkness. She turned over, wincing as pain shot through her head, and focused on Marladon's fireballs as he harried the daemon. By their light she saw the Land-Nymphs and goblins attacking, dodging amongst the daemon's legs, avoiding its snapping jaws and unsteady swats. She tried to stand but fell back to the floor as nausea rolled over her. *"Oh gods,"* she thought, assessing herself. *"Nothing feels broken."* She took a shallow breath and focused on not vomiting. Once she thought her stomach would obey she tried again, standing slowly, leaning against the wall until her stomach and head settled. The daemon and Land-Nymph battle had drifted closer while she struggled to stand.

Testing her sword arm, feeling for sprains and breaks, she looked around for her sword and found it near where she had awakened. Stooping to retrieve it set her head spinning again and she paused, finding comfort in the weight of the sword in her hand as she stood with her eyes closed. A sudden scream near her brought her back to the throne room. The daemon faltered before crashing to the floor, the Land-Nymphs finally successfully wounding one of its legs. With a second scream it struggled to stand.

"Now!" she urged silently, forcing herself away from the wall and rushing forward, lifting her sword. The daemon noticed her sudden movement and focused on her, hissing. The over-powering chittering filled the darkness again, beating into her head, trying to stop her advance. Grimacing, she pressed forward through the wall of noise raising her sword. With a scream of her own, she dove for the daemon her blade leading the way. Answering her, the daemon tried to stand just as D'Mique's sword sank deep into its globe eye, her weight following it and driving the blade deeper. For a moment, pain, anger and surprise flared, filling the white globe eye and the daemon groaned. Then it slumped back to the ground and the light faded from its eyes, leaving the room suddenly, eerily, dark and silent.

Marladon lit the lamps a moment later bathing them all in a soft orange glow. D'Mique sank to the floor near the corpse numb. Trillip was there beside her speaking, but she couldn't focus on his words. Through the fog she was half aware of the others, Myrth, Sylus and Marco to her right, the goblins close to her. Genow appeared in front of her talking too. She smiled softly at him as his cool, healing magic poured through her, chasing away some of the fluff that filled her head. "Are you well, Lady?" Genow asked. Trillip took her hand and concern colored his face and brightened his eyes. His touch solidified the world around her and she nodded slowly.

Seeing this Trillip returned the nod. "Good," he said. Then, standing, he pulled her sword from the daemon's eye and with a great swing he sent the blade through the daemon's neck, severing its head. He turned to Marladon, "I present to you Master Marladon, D'Mique, Lady Warrior."

Returning Home

S lowly life will return to normal," Marladon thought as he watched the approaching army from his highest turret. Kryoso sat upon the low wall beside him, playing with a dark ball of Shadow. "Stop," Marladon ordered at last. "I will have no Shadow magic here."

The ball winked out in a puff of light, "Yes, Master," Kryoso said sighing. He sat quietly for a moment listening to the pennants above them whip in the wind, watching the army as well. A flight of dragons suddenly passed overhead painting the turret in shade before landing in the courtyard below. "Myrth will be leaving today," Kryoso lilted, "Will I go with him?"

Marladon scoffed and turned to him. "Do you want to go?" he asked, a flash of concern drawing his face downward, his scar deepening as the muscles beneath it worked.

Kryoso smiled. "Of course not," he said.

"Then you shall not. You were only a loan," the Fire Master replied with a warmth in his voice. They smiled at each other and Kryoso dropped gingerly from the wall, wincing over his wounds. Genow's healing had continued from the moment he had reached Kryoso's side in the throne room battle until this morning. Every hour he had seen to the Mortak, every hour accompanied by Marladon's worried glare, until this morning when the elf had deemed the steward recovered. Marladon took his companion around the waist and helped him down the steps through the castle and out into the courtyard.

They arrived in time to watch Clippen and Trillip greet Tekalo as he dismounted, plowing into him, their weight and momentum carrying all three to the ground where they rolled around in a tangle of alabaster arms and legs. As they disengaged a veiled Potent appeared, melting from the ranks of Nepo's entourage, accompanied by one of Herdan's elite soldiers. "Almira!" Marco called, running for her and taking her in his arms. He tore her veil away and kissed her, laughing. Myrth followed his apprentice sedately, nodding at Nepo. Outwardly there was no sign of the havoc that Marco's stone snake had caused Myrth as the forcelines were torn from the Earth Master, ripping muscle and tissue as the ethereal chains were pulled from the Semian's soul.

"Where did you find these?" the Earth Master asked, indicating the assortment of soldiers behind the Water Master.

"We collected them as we went," Nepo said. "Most are refugees from the valley. We did find the Potent and her guard as we swung back south." He sat a moment in silence before smiling, "You did it! I admit I had my doubts."

Myrth shook his head, "D'Mique did it," he corrected quietly, nodding as she and Genow joined the gathering. "Now that you're here, I will make preparations to return to Dragon Ridge. We will depart tomorrow."

"Wait," Nepo stopped him with an upraised hand. "Who is 'we'?"

"Yes, Myrth," Marladon said coming up behind them as well. "Exactly who is leaving?"

"Not I," Kryoso retorted. "I was only a loan."

Myrth studied them for a moment before turning back to Nepo. "I suppose you want the Land-Nymphs back," he said. Nepo nodded.

"Master," Trillip called, disentangling himself from his comrades. Nepo and Myrth both looked at him. "I..I wish to stay with D'Mique. I would like to go where she chooses."

"What?" Clippen asked as Tekalo gaped at him. "But, Trillip..." he trailed off.

Trillip shook his head. "I am the Water Master's creature, it is true, and I am always your cousin, your friend. But..."

"Trillip," D'Mique said, "What are you thinking? You should —"

"What? Be with my people? Why?" The emerald shards of his eyes sharpened. "I can choose any new assignment now that the Honor Guard will disband. I will go with you."

"I ... I don't have to go back to Dragon Ridge?" she asked.

"No," Sylus answered. "You don't have to. I can transfer you anywhere you'd like. Trillip is correct that this honor guard will be disbanded." She stood silently thinking, weighing not only his words but the sentiment Trillip had voiced.

"I will return with you, Master Nepo," Clippen said into the ensuing silence.

"I doubt I have a choice," Marco added under his breath.

"But Marco," Almira said, "Always remember that you are a Potent. You may return to Gaity at any time."

"I will visit you there as often as I can," he said, kissing her head, wrapping an arm around her.

"I would like to return with you, Myrth," Genow said after a weighty silence, "and continue my training." Nepo glared at him but kept quiet.

Tierren and Rogan exchanged glances then nodded in unison. "Master, you may always call on us. But I ask that you send Samsha back to Herdan. We will return to the Warlord," Tierren relayed. Myrth nodded in understanding. Then they all looked at D'Mique waiting.

"I want to go home Myrth," she said, the words bringing tears behind them. "I want to see my mother again."

"If that's your wish, then it will be done," Myrth said.

In her mind, she saw the red and gold leaves of the Dark Forest falling softly around her as she approached Dornak. The flabbergasted guards would gape at her and her companion when they reached the North Gate because no one there had ever seen a Land-Nymph. For the briefest moment her revelry shattered at the thought, her heart trilling, *"Trillip will be there!"* Then the vision returned. The crowd would gather outside her mother's house after they were inside, she lived so close to the main gate that news of their arrival would reach the far end of the village only after they were safe inside. Her mother would welcome them with tearful hugs and a shower of kisses. Then she would make them a meal full of Last Seed's harvest. And only once they were full and the wine had been poured would they, she and Trillip, tell her mother stories of their summer.

"Afterwards," she continued, chasing away the warmth of her mother's hearth, "I will return to Dragon Ridge."

Myrth smiled. "As you wish, Daemon Slayer."

The End

About Sherrie A Bakelar

O nce there was a little girl who loved stories. She loved to listen to them and she loved to tell them. She loved stories in all forms: art, games, written words, movies, television shows, music, and theater. Imagine her joy when she found out that it was possible for a person to grow up and spend their whole lives sharing stories! Sherrie lives in the Intermountain West with her family and friends, and a small menagerie of furry and scaly children.

Connect with Sherrie A Bakelar

Follow Sherrie A Bakelar on Twitter[1]
Find Sherrie A Bakelar on Facebook[2]
Your next read is waiting at Books2Read[3]!
A World Bible can be found on World Anvil[4]!

If you've enjoyed this book, or even if you haven't, please consider returning to the site where you purchased it and leaving a review. Reviews are the lifeblood of independent authors!

---

1. https://twitter.com/SBakelar

2. https://www.facebook.com/SherrieABakelar

3. https://books2read.com/ap/nOOKkO/Sherrie-Bakelar

4. https://www.worldanvil.com/w/the-lady-warrior-saga-sbakelar

Other Titles By Sherrie A Bakelar

Great Danes Don't Hunt Werewolves
Life is confusing enough when you're a teen in a new town and a new school. A person can find themselves lost and alone, navigating an alien world full of unusual customs and strange rituals, even when they're human. Being a werewolf? That makes everything so much harder. Now, finding yourself in love with a human? Well, that just takes the cake! Yet, life has a way of tripping you up. Sometimes love is the start of an unexpected adventure and you just know it will last forever and change your life for the better...and sometimes it's the beginning of the end and you'll never be the same again.

In My Time of Dying
When you're Called to help another, death can't stand in the way. Eloise Fontaine was always running off to save someone or something, and, with her death, Eloise' twin sister, Ebony Fontaine, inherited more than a pile of belongings, she inherited her sister's final mission. Reluctantly, Ebony agrees to see it through, before she too passes away.

The Land-Nymph Child, The Lady Warrior Saga, Book 2
With the Greater Daemon dead and the Fire Master restored to his throne, D'Mique spent the winter adjusting to life in Dragon Ridge. Yet, as spring nears, she finds herself hunting vicious killers in the city of the

Land-Nymphs accompanied by her star-crossed love, Trillip. Meanwhile, with the fragile, post-daemon peace shattered, the seer Oracle is haunted by visions of blood and war and he finds himself wondering why D'Mique always seems to be at the center of things when trouble begins to brew.

The Land-Nymph Child

The Lady Warrior Saga, Book 2

Oracle stepped from the shadows beneath the pines. Before him, a cobblestone plaza bathed in the blue light of Rysk. "I know this place," he thought just before realizing he had returned to the dream. A fountain gurgled softly before him. Five soft-white flowers were growing out of it, shining at the stone feet of the first masters, the Hero Masters who had battled the first Greater Daemon to come to their world; fighting through the untamed-forcelines that ravaged the land. The planet's spasms had been as great an enemy as the daemon, greater, some argued. Oracle looked around and scented the breeze. It blew down from the north, carrying a hint of blood. He followed the scent cautiously, creeping forward on all fours, as if he were a giant wolf rather than a Semian.

He took the road north from the plaza, up the hill to the center of the crater city. A ghostly figure stood in the middle of the road. It sat upon wolf-like hindquarters, its cane planted firmly on the ground before it. Scraggly, claw-like hands held the cane. Oracle stopped and stood, "Sage?" he asked.

The goat-like head looked up. "They won't be in time, Oracle," the Gray Daemon said. "They can't save her."

"Save who?"

"They can't even save themselves." Sage sighed and shook his head sadly, his incredibly long white beard dragging across the ground at his feet, tracing waves with each shake of his head.

Oracle opened his eyes. Sunlight filtered down through the trees above him. He blinked and replayed the dream, repeating aloud to himself what

349

Sage had told him, forcing sleep to swaddle him while he worked to commit the words to memory. "Save who?" he asked himself, adding, "This is bad. Blood on the wind in Olimidia and a warning from Sage," he sighed. Crawling from his bedroll, he quickly packed his equipment, cleared the campsite, and then mounted his horse. "I'm half a day from Sea Spray; perhaps a quick detour to see what the real Sage has to say," he thought, sending the horse trotting down the little-used track.

All around him, the Wild Woods grew close and dark, the sunlight barely reaching the lower levels of the forest. He remembered calling the darkness home. The Wild Woods sheltered many who would rather hide from society. Once it had even sheltered him, but that had been long ago, when he'd been nothing more than a howling child, driven mad by visions that haunted him. Day and night ghostly messengers followed him through the woods, taunting him, startling him, and berating him for deeds he did not do and demanding things he didn't understand. That had been long before his move to the palace of the Warlord Herdan where the soothing seer had taught him to tame the Time Magic that flowed around him.

The morning passed uneventfully and he soon found himself on the banks of the Sea of Scorn where the pebble-strewn beach reached out to caress the cool dark water. Across the waves, a rocky island, the Island of Hope, rose from the center, housing the Water Master's palace Sea Spray. Oracle dismounted, turning the horse loose on the shore before wading out into the lake. He stood motionless, waiting. Soon, a wagon-size creature surfaced, its round, thick-furred back lined with metal rings breaching the surface some yards from the shore. The creature's snakelike head appeared a moment later, its daemon-fire eyes marking it daemon-kin. The korsk hissed a greeting to Oracle, the nest of dagger-sharp fangs that lined its mouth glinting in the mid-day light of the twin red suns, the Fiery Sisters. Unlike the wild korsks of the Eternal Sea, the Water Master had tamed those who lived here in the Sea of Scorn, putting them to good use.

Oracle growled at the beast, holding his ground as the daemon-spawn used its front flippers to pull itself ashore, coming to rest with a final splash in the shallows beside Oracle. He used the ladder of metal rings to clamber up onto its back. Up here, more rings acted as handholds for anyone willing to ride the korsk across the inland sea. The riders had to get a bit wet, but it was the fastest way across. In fact, if the Water Master was in no mood for company, it was often the only way across. With Oracle perched on its back, holding on to a pair of rings, the daemon-spawn shoved itself back into the water with help from the six-foot long, bone spikes protruding from the leading edge of its flippers. It sank below the waves until Oracle was thigh-deep in water before swiftly delivering him to the steep, rocky shore of Hope Island. The Water Master's visitors found no gentle beach, inviting landing, or welcoming pier on this side of the sea and the only way guests could finish their journey was to jump into the water and flounder ashore. Not for the first time, Oracle found himself thinking that the Water Master enjoyed the sight of disheveled guests, soaked through to the bone.

Oracle splashed ashore as the ferry beast disappeared once more into the murky depths. He climbed slowly up over the white boulders, leaving paw prints and puddles behind him, until he reached the shoreline path. He took a moment to wring water from his cloak as he surveyed the well-traveled path that ran around the entire island, parallel to the rocky coast. At unevenly spaced intervals, branching paths led into the narrow band of forest that had managed to sprout between this rocky shore and the interior caldera lake. Oracle started right, looking for the first branch inland and it was not long before he had traded one shoreline for another. While the outer shore was steep and rocky, strewn with boulders, this inner shore sloped smoothly, though still at a steep angle, into the inner lake. The differences did not stop there. While the first lake was cold, dark, and murky, the inner one seemed light and refreshing. It sparkled clear blue before him, its limpid surface clothed in perfect reflections of the scuttling clouds above. Oracle turned right again and walked along the pebbled shore. He came to a sandy causeway that stretched across the perfect blue water, joining with yet another rocky shore. Here, at last, ringed in lakes and shores, sat the palace of the Water Master, Sea Spray. The walled grounds took up the entire island. Huge stone domes dominated the palace's architecture.

As he approached the first of many entrances, two elfin guards hailed Oracle. "Seer Oracle," one said, head ducked low so that he was talking to his own chest for a moment before his black orb eyes met Oracle's amber ones. "We weren't told of your arrival."

"No," Oracle said, stopping before the guards. "This is not an official visit. I wish only to speak to my friend; where can I find Sage?" he asked.

The first guard stared at him, unsure of how to answer.

"He is in the training yard, seer," the second elf said, bowing.

"Thank you." Oracle stepped past them and into a lush garden. Here inside the palace walls, the ground beneath his feet lay covered in moss and water-dark stones, while thick ferns and vine-laden fruit trees lined the path he followed toward the back of the compound. The squat, domed palace of the Water Master sat surrounded by a tropical forest rampant with color. Water flowed everywhere: between the mossy stones, trickling down from the palace walls, gurgling from springs cut into the granite island. Out behind the palace, the trees gave way to an open dirt area edged by a thick, shaded carpet of grass.

Pairs of soldiers were scattered across the dirt training area, sparring with a variety of weapons. The wolf-Semian stopped a moment to survey them. This was Nepo's honor guard, painstakingly rebuilt after Oracle had forced Nepo to send the last group to Myrth. Oracle's friend Sage was nominally in charge of the armed forces within Nepo's palace but it was a charity position. Despite the official title of Commander of Arms, Sage did not do anything more strenuous than whacking the occasional lazy soldier on the head with his cane. The real commander of Nepo's forces was currently sparring in the center of the training yard with her best friend. The short-haired elf, Leona, swung her halberd expertly in a wide, defensive arch, blocking the sword-swing of her partner. The clang of metal on metal cracked the air. Oracle scanned the grassy verge halfheartedly and was surprised to see Sage seated under a shade tree at the very back of the palace grounds. Oracle hadn't expected to find Sage here with the soldiers. He made his way around to the Gray Daemon. "Sage?" he asked as he sat down beside him, positioned in order to see both Sage and the elf as she sparred. The Gray Daemon showed no sign of hearing him. Oracle took a long, deep breath, resigned to waiting. His friend sat deep in meditation.

Oracle could feel the air around him tensing, ebbing and flowing in response to the high mage's will. The seer drifted into the Mage Realm, pulled along by the current of Sage's power. Oracle's vision of the Mage Realm did not include the elemental clouds and currents that usually greeted mages upon entering the Realm. Rather, the world around him grew dark, his vision full of pinpricks of light. He knew Sage was here somewhere, perhaps right beside him, but he could not see the way an Elemental mage saw. By tarrying here, in the darkness and concentrating on a single point of light, he moved toward it. The pinprick grew as he approached, resolving into a cloudy white ball. The clouds swirled, coalesced, and a face formed. The Lady Warrior D'Mique stared blankly back at him from the swirling mist within the ball. He dipped into the ball, pressing through its skin, scattering D'Mique's image.

Within the ball, the scenery changed. Here gray strands twisted, braiding and unbraiding, as they flowed past him in all directions. The strands ranged in thickness from fine silken threads to huge cables. Here, the silence of the Mage Realm had been replaced by the soft hissing of the strands as they rubbed across each other and their echoing hiss reverberated through the air. Not knowing what they had stumbled upon, the first seers, had called this place the *Hisseth*, naming the gray strands Braiding Snakes. That was ages ago. Now they knew the Braiding was made of timelines—Time Magic forcelines; one for each soul on the planet, clumping together as each life touched another. The *Hisseth* held its secrets close but over time the seers had realized that it was a separate plain, a construct distinct from the Mage Realm, physical realm and Void. Many seers reached the *Hisseth* by following a timeline from a single person, or their own, down through the Mage Realm and into the bubble as Oracle had just done with D'Mique. However, Oracle knew many ways to enter the Time Realm and had spent many mad hours here as a child.

Within the construct of the *Hisseth*, Oracle's mind created a surrogate body for him to reside in. One that was quite a bit younger than his real body. He knelt amongst the Braiding and reached for one of the thicker strands before him. Voices engulfed him, roaring in his ears, ebbing as he separated the strands. He spotted the one strand he was looking for, pulling it out of the Braid. It made a wet, sucking sound as he separated it from its parent. Next, he let the small strand run through his hands. He could hear D'Mique. The words were disjointed, unattached. He closed his eyes and images flickered before him, painted in his mind: D'Mique with her sword, D'Mique bathing in a stream, D'Mique huddling in the dark.

"What do you want?" Sage asked, shattering Oracle's concentration. Oracle opened his eyes, snapping back to his true body. Sage's dark, beady eyes closed again as Oracle's deep amber ones opened.

"I've been having dreams of late," he said. Sage remained motionless before him. "You were in the last one," he continued.

"Was I?" Sage slid back into the physical realm, eyes opening again, studying Oracle. "And was I a victim or the hero?"

Oracle caught the edge of the daemon's smile before Sage smothered it. "Neither," Oracle said, "you stood before me as I roamed Olimidia. You warned me that it was too late to save her."

"Hmph," Sage shifted into a more comfortable position, "I wonder what I was talking about."

AVAILABLE JULY 2020

Don't miss out!

Visit the website below and you can sign up to receive emails whenever Sherrie A Bakelar publishes a new book. There's no charge and no obligation.

https://books2read.com/r/B-A-WJFX-IRUMC

BOOKS 2 READ

Connecting independent readers to independent writers.

Did you love *Lady Warrior, Mage of Man*? Then you should read *In My Time of Dying*[1] by Sherrie A Bakelar!

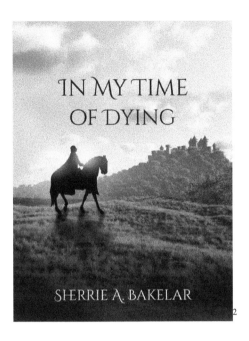
[2]

When Eloise Fontaine passed away from a heart attack, she left behind a pile of her belongings, a horse and her unfinished business. It now falls to her twin sister, Ebony, to fulfill Eloise' final Calling, Find the Farm Boy and save the kingdom, before Ebony passes away herself. Goaded on by her sister's ghost, Ebony sets out from her humble cottage to find the Farm Boy and help in his quest to regain his kingdom, usurped decades before by the Wizard King.

Read more at https://artist.sbakelar.com/.

1. https://books2read.com/u/3LV5B1

2. https://books2read.com/u/3LV5B1

Milton Keynes UK
Ingram Content Group UK Ltd.
UKHW010930280823
427620UK00001B/184